Hot Sir
Blinded by
the Boss

ANNIE CLAYDON

LOUISA GEORGE

AMY ANDREWS

MILLS & BOON

Published in Great Britain 2019
by Mills & Boon, an imprint of HarperCollins*Publishers*
1 London Bridge Street, London, SE1 9GF

HOT SINGLE DOCS: BLINDED BY THE BOSS © 2019 Harlequin Books S.A.

200 Harley Street: The Enigmatic Surgeon © 2014 Harlequin Books S.A
Special thanks and acknowledgement are given to Annie Claydon for her contribution to the *200 Harley Street* series.

200 Harley Street: The Shameless Maverick © 2014 Harlequin Books S.A
Special thanks and acknowledgement are given to Louisa George for her contribution to the *200 Harley Street* series.

200 Harley Street: The Tortured Hero © 2014 Harlequin Books S.A.
Special thanks and acknowledgement are given to Amy Andrews for her contribution to the *200 Harley Street* series.

ISBN: 978-0-263-26834-8

09-0219

MIX
Paper from
responsible sources
FSC
www.fsc.org
FSC™ C007454

This book is produced from independently certified FSC™ paper to ensure responsible forest management.

For more information visit: www.harpercollins.co.uk/green

Printed and bound in Spain by CPI, Barcelona

200 HARLEY STREET: THE ENIGMATIC SURGEON

ANNIE CLAYDON

To the ladies who lunch, Yve, Nicky and Vicki.

CHAPTER ONE

'So which is it, then?'

'Eh?' Charlotte King was busy trying not to notice that Edward North was currently going through his pockets to find the key to his office, and she had lost the thread of the conversation that was going on around the nurses' station.

'Which do you think? Secret love-life, or no love-life?' Paula craned across the desk to get a better view. 'Wonder if he needs a hand with that?'

Charlotte swallowed a laugh. 'What? You know where he's left his keys?'

'No. But I'm really good at finding things.' Paula's smile left no doubt that she was contemplating a thorough investigation and possibly a body search.

'Too late. He's got them.' Allie grinned at Paula. 'And I reckon he's got a secret mistress somewhere.'

'When does he get to see her? In between here and the hospital, I'd be surprised if he has much time for anything else.'

'He has time to swim.' Allie's blue eyes flashed mischievously.

'Yeah?' Paula's attention was on Allie now.

'Mmm-hmm. I left my trainers downstairs in the gym the other day and went to fetch them after work. He was in the pool, doing laps.'

'Hmm. Perhaps I'll go buy myself a swimming costume. Common interests can be very important in a relationship.'

'So you've thought this through, then?' Charlotte wished that Paula and Allie would keep their voices down. Not that the nurses were in any danger of being heard. It was difficult enough to get Edward's attention even when he was supposed to be listening to you. It just seemed somehow wrong to be talking like this.

'Who hasn't? I reckon he just needs a good woman. And I'll apply for the position if no one else is interested.'

Allie laughed. 'Steady, Paula. Remember there's a queue and I'm in it. Charlotte, too, eh?'

Charlotte considered the prospect. She couldn't get away with a lie that big. 'Yeah, okay. Just to keep you two company, though. I don't have time for dating.'

Or the money. Or the inclination, most of the time. Apart from when Edward… Her gaze wandered over to the glazed wall of his office. He was behind his desk now, deep in thought, a stack of papers and books in front of him.

'Yeah, right.' Paula was laughing now. 'Guess we could share him around.'

Oh, no. Edward wasn't for sharing. He was for being loved, nurtured by one woman, not passed around like a beautifully wrapped, enormously sexy parcel. He looked up, as if somehow the thought had penetrated the walls of his office, his eyes suddenly focussing in Charlotte's direction.

She could feel the flush spreading up from the back of her neck to her cheeks. Edward might be for one woman, but that woman definitely wasn't her.

Charlotte turned, trying to pretend that he hadn't just caught her staring at him. 'I'll leave you to do that. I've got to do my last ward round and my friend is bringing Isaac here soon.'

'Really?' Paula always made a particular fuss of Isaac. 'What do we owe that pleasure to?'

'There's no school today and my friend's been looking after him. Lucy's got a date tonight so she's dropping him off here before she goes on to hit the town. If you see them, will you get them to wait here?'

Paula nodded. 'Sure thing. Take your time.'

Edward North had just got to the complex part. Not that tomorrow's microsurgery wasn't all complex, but this particular section was intricate in the extreme. Running through it in his head was his preferred method of preparation, and the swimming pool in the basement of the Hunter Clinic his preferred place. Working his body seemed to free his mind, but he couldn't be assured of solitude until the clinic was closed for the day, so his office was going to have to do.

'No. Not like that...' He shook his head, muttering in disgust at his own ineptitude. He'd have to start over now. Or at least from the last set of microscopic sutures. Edward took a breath, cleared his mind, and...

The image that floated into his mind was nothing like the one he was concentrating on building. Pale chestnut hair, bound in a tight knot at the back of her head. Light brown eyes. He couldn't see the flecks of gold from this distance, but he knew that they were there. Somehow Charlotte's eyes had impressed themselves on his consciousness when he had difficulty in recalling the names, let alone the eye colour, of most of the rest of the nursing staff.

She'd looked away, then. Blushing.

The exact mechanics of that particular form of vasodilation was child's play alongside the complexities of its causes. Most things were. Edward closed his eyes, cleared his mind, and went back to the matter in hand.

Lucy was already standing at the nurses' station when Charlotte returned from her ward round.

'Hey, Lucy, you look nice. I won't be a minute. I've just got to pick up my coat.' Charlotte looked around. Just one glimpse of her son after a long day was always enough to lift her spirits.

'Sure. Why don't you leave Isaac here with me?'

'Isn't he with you?'

'No. He ran ahead up the stairs. I called after him to wait for you here…'

For one split second the two women stared at each other. Charlotte almost choked as something squeezed tight around her heart, and then instinct and the sure knowledge that she needed to move *now* took over.

'Go downstairs, Lucy. Make sure he's not slipped out of the building. I'll look for him here.'

She glanced over in the direction of Edward's office. The view inside was partially obscured by a long, low cabinet, running the length of the glass wall and designed to keep the mess of books and other artefacts under some semblance of control, but she could see that he was no longer sitting at his desk. Not that he'd probably notice if a whole horde of five-year-olds started roaming the corridors, but he'd been the only one there and beggars couldn't be choosers.

Isaac shouldn't have gone into any of the treatment rooms. He knew not to do that. All the same she looked, trying not to panic, trying not to cry. Allie hadn't seen him and neither had Paula. She opened every cupboard, every locked door, just in case. And each time her baby wasn't there the agitation in the pit of her stomach grew.

'The receptionist says that he can't have got out of the building. He would have had to have either opened one of the back doors, and they're all alarmed, or gone straight past her.' Lucy arrived back upstairs, red and breathless.

That was something, at least. Mind you, there was plenty of trouble right here that a five-year-old could get into. The swimming pool… Charlotte remembered the swimming pool in the basement and felt suddenly sick.

'I'll call Security…' She grabbed for the phone and then dropped it. Either she was hearing things, or…

Isaac laughed again. That was definitely not a hallucination.

Lucy had heard it, too. 'Where is he?' Lucy looked around wildly.

Another laugh. This time deep, round and rich. The kind of laugh that Edward might have, only Charlotte didn't think she'd ever heard him laugh. Wordlessly she swung round and marched towards the door of Edward's office, opening it without bothering to knock.

For a moment, in the relief of seeing that Isaac was safe, she didn't register the scene in front of her. Somehow she noticed that Isaac's favourite toy, the blue bunny that he carried with him everywhere, was sitting in Edward's black leather chair, and that Edward was on the floor.

'Isaac!' Charlotte gulped out his name. 'What are you doing?'

Her son looked up at her. Innocent blue eyes and dark blond hair framed the sweet smile which never failed to dissolve her anger and dispel her fears.

'Hi, Mum. I'm making water.' He picked up a small red ball from the box in front of him. 'Look, you take one red one. That's…'

'Um…oxygen.' Edward got to his feet quickly, facing Charlotte with a slightly abashed air. 'So you're Isaac's mother?'

'Yes.' She ducked around Edward. She could deal with him later. 'Isaac, come here, please.'

'But, Mum, I haven't shown you. Look…'

'We mustn't bother Mr North any more, sweetie. Where did you get that from?' She looked at the molecule model kit in front of him on the floor. It looked like a great toy and she wished she could afford something like it for Isaac, even if he was a bit young for it at the moment.

'It's Edward's.' Isaac shot a pleading look up at his new friend, who ignored him completely and sat down in his chair, remembering just in time to pull the blue bunny out from under him before it got squashed. He proffered it to Isaac and when he didn't show any inclination to take it propped it up against the phone.

It had been a long week, and Charlotte had just about had enough. You could only take so many small crises, each one popping up hard on the heels of the last, before life became one big crisis.

'Then put everything back in the box and say thank you to Edward. We've got to get home.' Hopefully she could get out of here before the temptation to tear Edward off a strip became too great. Didn't he realise that someone would be looking for the stray five-year-old who had wandered into his office?

Isaac shot her a look which left her in no doubt that he wasn't in agreement with that decision, but complied anyway. One down, one to go. Charlotte turned to Edward, who was arranging the blue bunny into a crossed-legs, hands-behind-the-head posture which gave the impression that he was leaning back against the phone, sunbathing.

'I'm sorry he…interrupted you. We'll be going home…'

The sheer force of his gaze stopped her. Thoughtful. Intensely blue. And at this moment tainted with an uncertainty that was unlike Edward.

'Were you looking for him?'

'Yes. But it's all right, he's here…' Charlotte just wanted to hug Isaac. As soon as she got out of Edward's office that was the first thing she planned to do.

'I should have let you know he was here.'

He'd recovered himself now. Whatever emotion he did or didn't feel was locked away somewhere, no one's business but his own.

'That's okay. I've found him now…' She was shaking. So tired that she was almost in tears. All she wanted to do was get home. 'Isaac, will you give Edward the box back, please?'

Isaac seemed to have got over his disappointment and carefully collected up the box and laid it on Edward's desk. 'Thank you.'

'You're welcome.' Edward gave Isaac a guarded half-smile and a little formal nod and her son copied the expression in return. 'Don't forget… What's his name?'

'Stinky.'

Edward raised one eyebrow. 'Well, don't forget Stinky, then.'

He looked up at Charlotte and she tried for a smile.

'Will you stay a moment, please, Charlotte?'

This was the last thing she needed right now. She knew that Isaac shouldn't have been running around the clinic on his own. Edward didn't need to tell her that, and it went without saying that it wouldn't happen again. 'Isaac, will you go and sit with Lucy, please? Just for a minute.' She pointed to the patients' seating area outside.

'Here.' Edward leaned forward, towards the boy, proffering a handful of change. 'Get something for yourself and Lucy from the vending machine. D'you think Stinky wants anything?'

'No, he doesn't. He's not a real rabbit, you know.'

'Of course not. Well, something for you and Lucy then…'

Charlotte was about to stop Isaac from taking the money, but Edward had already put a selection of coins into his hand and Isaac was halfway towards the door. At least he remembered to thank Edward. She straightened herself and prepared for the dressing down that was coming.

'I'm sorry, Charlotte.'

'Eh…?'

'You must have been worried when you couldn't find Isaac.'

Worried? Frantic, more like. 'I…I'm sorry he bothered you.'

'He was no trouble. He seems to like molecules…' Edward almost smiled and then thought better of it. Too bad. In that brief moment his eyes had seemed bluer, and his dark good looks less brooding.

'He's only five. He likes putting things together and taking them apart again…' The rush of relief at finding Isaac had left her feeling like a limp dishcloth. And now this. Instinctively Charlotte put one hand to her brow, as if to shade herself from the intensity of those blue eyes which seemed to hold so much that was unsaid.

'Hey. What's this?'

He was on his feet, his hands on her shoulders. Edward had the worst timing of any man she'd ever known, bar none. Of all the times to choose to be kind, this was the one most likely to reduce her to tears.

'Nothing. It's nothing. I'm okay.' She tried to avoid his gaze.

'Clearly you're not.'

There was a note of tenderness in his voice that she hadn't heard before. Something warm about the arm which wound around her shoulder. Something about his scent that made her instinctively sink into him, even though she knew that this was probably one of the worst ideas she'd ever had in her life.

Under the crisp white shirt there was some serious musculature. Strong arms, and a flat, hard stomach. For the second time in the last few minutes the swimming pool flashed into Charlotte's head, but this time the image was considerably more inviting.

'I'm okay…' Charlotte thought about pushing him away and then decided that putting her hands anywhere near him would be far too much of a temptation. 'Really. I'm fine.'

He seemed to feel it, too. He stepped back quickly, almost as if she'd burnt him, and turned towards his desk. 'If there's anything that's bothering you, you should let someone know.' He thought for a moment, obviously considering himself an unlikely candidate for any kind of emotional disclosure. 'Lizzie, perhaps…I'm sure she'd be able to do… whatever's needed.'

Edward had switched back into professional mode and the relief was almost palpable. 'No. There's nothing. I just had a bit of a scare when I couldn't find Isaac…' She bit her words back. Nothing like blaming the very person who had just tried to help her.

'I'm sorry. It won't happen again.'

That was supposed to be *her* line. She smiled up at him, wishing that she could smooth some of the creases on his brow. 'It's okay. He's safe, and that's all that matters. I'm sorry he disturbed you. He knows he mustn't wander around here.'

'That's all right. It was nice to talk to him.' He gestured stiffly towards the molecule model kit. 'His approach is refreshingly creative, compared with most.'

Was that a joke? It was difficult to tell with Edward, but the possibility intrigued Charlotte. She could see Lucy and Isaac out of the corner of her eye, settling themselves down on the sofa with their drinks. They'd be at least another five minutes, and hadn't Paula always said that Charlotte only needed five minutes to get anyone to open up?

'What's it for? If you don't mind my asking?'

'You can use it for anything. I'm thinking of DNA sequencing.' The way he brushed off the question almost made her believe that everyone had a model of a DNA sequence somewhere in their office.

'Ah. Right. Anyone in particular?'

'Mine, actually. Just a snippet of it, of course. But don't you think there's something rather interesting about actually being able to look at something that's the very basis of your own make-up?'

'I'd never really thought about it.' Now he mentioned it, there was. There was an obscure symmetry about the concept that made her smile, even if she didn't properly understand it.

'You should. It would be interesting for Isaac…' He narrowed his eyes. 'Perhaps when he's a bit older.'

'Yes, I think so. Is that all?' She should go now. She'd managed to stem her tears for the moment, but who knew how long that particular dam was going to hold? Hopefully until after Isaac was safely tucked up in bed.

'Are you going home? I'm going your way. I'll give you a

lift. The buses are horrible at this time of day—' He broke off, as if he'd let something slip that he shouldn't.

How did he know she took the bus home? And how did he know which way she went? Charlotte stared at him.

'I've seen you waiting at the two-three-nine bus stop. And the two-three-nine goes almost directly along my route home. Of course you could be catching the number thirteen, but most people who do that walk down to the Oxford Circus stop, so they can get a seat—' He broke off again, obviously wondering whether that was too much information.

'Right. Next time I want to know which bus to take, I'll know who to ask.' She grinned at him. 'But it's okay, really. You must still have work to do and we'll be going in a minute.'

He shrugged. 'I was operating at six this morning, I should have been gone hours ago. And... You look tired.'

Perhaps Edward noticed more than everyone thought.

There was no perhaps about it. He clearly did. Somewhere inside a smile formed at the thought that some of those things were connected with her.

'We...we can't. Isaac needs a proper car seat...' It was a pity. The buses were always packed on a Friday evening and she could have done with a ride home.

'No problem. I have one fitted in my car.'

Something told Charlotte that Edward had worked all of this through before he'd even made the offer. The complex equation balanced two shopping bags, one child and an indeterminate number of full buses, crawling through the traffic, against one child seat, a comfortable car and a lift home. He probably already knew what she was about to say.

She smiled, wondering whether he'd factored that in or not. 'Okay. If it's no trouble. Thanks.'

CHAPTER TWO

EDWARD GAVE NO explanation for the brand-new child's car seat when he opened the back door of his sleek dark blue car and waved Isaac inside. Perhaps the girls at work were right. Perhaps he *did* have a woman somewhere. A woman with a child. So much for Paula's assertions that it couldn't hurt to try to breach Edward's reserve.

All the same, there was nothing wrong with taking a lift from him, and Charlotte couldn't deny that this was a great deal nicer than the bus. Not having to continually grab at her bags to get them out of the way of someone else's feet. Isaac safely strapped in behind her, with Stinky on his lap. Leather seats. The quiet strains of music floating at her from four different directions. She began to relax.

'It would be more convenient for you to drive to work.'

As they passed Regent's Park Edward's customary forthrightness broke the silence.

'Yeah. More expensive, too.' She grinned at him. 'Congestion charge, parking costs.'

He nodded. 'I thought you were going to say you liked the bus.'

'It's not so bad. You meet a lot of interesting people on buses.'

'So it's a social experiment, then?'

Maybe for Edward. It was a matter of necessity for Charlotte. 'You could call it that. We like it on the top deck, don't we, Isaac?'

'Yeah. You can see into people's windows,' Isaac piped up from the back seat.

'Can you?' Edward paused for thought. 'What do you see?'

'Christmas trees.'

'In July?'

'No, at Christmas.' Isaac's voice took on the tone of patient explanation that he sometimes used with adults. 'We counted how many Christmas trees we could see on the way home.'

'So you're a mathematician. Is that why you're called Isaac? After Isaac Newton?'

Isaac seemed to have succeeded where the combined talents of the Hunter Clinic had failed. That was definitely a joke, even if Isaac didn't appear to understand it.

'Who?'

Charlotte rolled her eyes. 'He's five, Edward.'

He nodded. 'So you're keeping Newton for later.' He made it sound like leaving the best chocolate in the box until last. He raised his voice, speaking to Isaac again. 'So how many Christmas trees did you count?'

'A million.'

'Really? You live on the moon?' Edward's lips twitched and Isaac cackled with laughter. Although neither seemed to be quite on the same intellectual wavelength, they clearly shared the same sense of humour.

'Noooo. Kentish Town.'

'That explains it, then. Are you sure you didn't count any of them twice?'

Isaac shrugged. 'Maybe. It might have been a hundred.'

It seemed so natural to laugh with them. The obvious thing to do. 'It was three hundred and forty-nine, wasn't it, Isaac?'

'That's right. Three hundred and forty-nine.'

Edward nodded. 'Impressive. That's a prime number, you know.'

'What's a prime number?'

Edward shot a helpless glance at Charlotte and she shrugged. All of a sudden this quiet, reserved man had become almost talkative, and against her better judgement she actually wanted to hear what he had to say for himself.

'It's…um…it's a very special number. There are lots of them. I dare say they'll teach you about that at school.'

'When?'

'Er… Pretty soon, I imagine. Ask your teacher.'

'Okay.'

Lucky escape. Charlotte mouthed the words at him and he raised one eyebrow, as if he'd been in complete control all along.

'How many are there?'

She saw the line of Edward's jaw stiffen as it became apparent that she had spoken too soon.

'More than you can count. Even if you ride on the bus all day. The first prime number is two. Then five…'

By the time he'd worked his way up to twenty-nine and shown no signs of flagging Charlotte decided to step in. At this rate they could be driving to Birmingham and back before either Isaac went to sleep or Edward got to the point where he could no longer work out the next prime number in his head.

She turned in her seat to face Isaac. 'Edward's got to stop counting now, sweetie, because he's driving and has to keep his eye on the road. I'll explain all about prime numbers when we get home.'

'Okay.'

It was nice having her in the car. She smelled good—like soap and roses. Rose soap, maybe. Edward ran through all the possibilities in his head and surprised himself with how delicious each of them was.

She didn't just smell nice; she *was* nice. Whenever he saw her with the clinic's clients she was always the same. Gentle, reassuring, and yet with a hint of fun about her. She made people smile. But Edward couldn't help but think there was more. When he'd seen her at the bus stop the other day, huddled under her umbrella in the pouring rain, there had been a defeated slant to her shoulders that had made him want to stop, but his nerve had failed him. Getting involved with people wasn't what Edward did.

'You must like jazz?' She was stretching her legs out in front of her. Smiling.

'Very much,' he said. 'You?'

'I don't really know. I've not listened to much. I like this.'

'Good.' He could have left it at that. Would normally have left it at that. But against his better judgement he wanted to prolong the conversation. 'Most people just automatically say they love jazz, irrespective of whether they've listened to any.'

She gave a little laughing nod, as if she knew just what he meant. 'It's one of those things that you're meant to like, isn't it? I mean if you admit to not knowing much about jazz, then it's like owning up to being some kind of barbarian.'

'I don't think you're a barbarian.' He thought she was a damn sight more honest that most people.

He was rewarded with one of the smiles that she was so free with. This one seemed just for him. 'That's all right, then.'

Charlotte asked him to drop them in the High Street, but when Edward insisted on taking her all the way home she directed him to a quiet backstreet. Small houses—many of them shabby and unkempt. He parked outside a house with a neat front garden. The front door badly needed a paint job. Charlotte jumped out of the car, unbuckling Isaac's seat belt while Edward took her shopping bags out of the boot.

'Can I carry these in for you?'

'No. No, that's okay, thank you. Thanks for the lift.' She picked the bags up with one hand and took Isaac's hand with the other. 'I'll see you on Monday.'

'Bye, Edward. Thank you…'

She shot a glance of approbation in her son's direction

and then turned away. Suddenly it seemed that she couldn't get rid of him fast enough and a vague feeling of disappointment nudged at him.

'Bye, Isaac. Nice to meet you…'

The boy twisted his head around as his mother marched him away, and gave him a grin, but Charlotte seemed caught up with her shopping bags. There was nothing to keep him so Edward got back into his car. As he turned in the road he noticed in his rearview mirror that the front gate was sticking and that she was struggling with it. He almost stopped the car and got out again, but then she kicked it and it snapped open, and she walked up the front path without looking back.

Charlotte slammed the front door closed behind her and dropped her shopping, leaning back against the door. Home. Half of her wished she was still in Edward's car and that they really had been driving to Birmingham and back. Newcastle, even. The other half was glad that he was gone before he'd had a chance to see the threadbare carpet in the hall and the second-hand furniture in her sitting room.

'Is Edward your boss, Mum?'

'He's a surgeon. At the clinic.'

'So he makes people well? Like you do?'

'Yes, darling.'

Isaac nodded. 'He's nice'

Charlotte found herself smiling again. 'Yes, he is, isn't he?' She picked up her shopping bags. 'Now, let's see what we've got for supper, shall we?'

It was only a short drive from Edward's house back to Charlotte's, but it was like travelling from one world to another. The trendy shops and cafés gave way to houses which seemed even more run-down than they had yesterday evening, and when he drove slowly along Charlotte's road it didn't seem any more salubrious than the last time he'd been here.

Perhaps he shouldn't have come. At ten o'clock on a Saturday morning she could be out, or having a lie-in…anything. But he was here now, with Stinky sitting next to him on the front passenger seat. If she wasn't there, then maybe Stinky would fit through the letterbox.

Cars lined the pavement, and he had to drive past her house to find a parking spot. As he did so he caught a glimpse of her on the doorstep, between the broad backs of two men who seemed to be crowding close in on her. What he could see of her stiff, upright frame, screamed that there was something wrong.

Edward accelerated into a free space. 'Don't move, Stinky. I'll be back in a minute.' He lunged out of the car, and down the road, to where her front gate stood open.

'Charlotte!' Now that he was closer he was sure that he was right. She was dressed in sweat pants and a tee shirt, bare feet on the doorstep, but she stood as tall as she could, the door almost closed behind her, her face fierce and determined. 'What's going on?'

She stared at him as if he'd just landed from another planet. One of the men swung round to face Edward, his pudgy face harsh. 'Nothing to concern you, sir. Just a bit of business with the lady.'

Her face had flushed bright red. Tears rimmed her eyes, before she quickly brushed them away. These guys were bad news. They stank of the kind of aggression which dressed itself up in cheap suits and a nasty attitude.

'Then you have business with me.' Edward pushed in between them and stood next to her on the step. He wanted to put his arm around her, ask her if she was all right, but this wasn't the time. 'Step back. Now.'

They stepped back. The anger that was raging in his chest must have been showing in his face, because the expression on the face of the larger of the two became slightly less belligerent. Edward pressed his advantage. 'Now, what's all this about?'

'Are you this lady's husband, sir?'

'I'm her legal advisor.' Suddenly Edward was mightily glad that he'd left Stinky in the car. This was rapidly beginning to look like a confrontation of some sort, and holding a battered blue rabbit in his hand wouldn't have helped.

He felt Charlotte's fingers on his arm. 'No, Edward. Please.' Her voice was almost a whisper.

If she wanted him to go, she had another think coming. Edward didn't shift his gaze from the two men. 'Who are you? Do you have some identification?'

One of the men reached slowly into the inside pocket of his jacket and drew out a wallet. Opening it, he held it out for Edward to see.

Debt collectors. What had Charlotte got herself into? No time for that now. A child's whimper sounded from the other side of the door and he felt Charlotte's small, convulsive movement against his arm. 'Go inside, please, Charlotte. Close the door.'

She looked up at him. Cheeks pink, her lovely eyes still brimming with tears. She hesitated, obviously torn between going to comfort her son and dealing with the men on her doorstep.

'Go and make sure Isaac's okay.' He spoke gently to her and she nodded quickly, disappearing inside the house.

One down, two to go.

He turned to the two men. 'I assume you're not in possession of a court order with regards to this property?'

'No, sir.' Somehow the man made that sound like a threat.

'In that case I'm asking you to leave now. I'll speak to you when you're standing on the pavement.'

The men exchanged a look. Obviously they considered that browbeating him was a different matter from a lone woman and a child, and Edward didn't bother to conceal his disgust as they turned and took their time in walking down the path.

'There is the matter of an unpaid debt, ma'am.'

Edward looked round and saw Charlotte back in the doorway, pulling a pair of sneakers on. She must have settled Isaac and come back out again.

'You don't speak to her. If you've something to say, then say it to me.' Edward had just appointed himself, unasked, into the role of protector, but he didn't care. No one else was around to do it.

'I need to speak to the lady.' The man's voice suddenly became gentle. He'd seen a way in and was trying for it. Be nice to her, then divide and conquer.

Edward looked round at Charlotte. It was one thing to expect her to go along with his instructions at the clinic, but here… Here she had Isaac to think of, and she wasn't going to give that responsibility away too easily.

'You can speak to my…' She walked down the path and stood next to him. 'My legal advisor.'

The man pressed his lips together. 'In that case…' He turned to Edward. 'We're looking for this lady's husband. We have reason to believe he's here—'

'He isn't,' Charlotte broke in vehemently. 'I haven't seen him for over a year.'

'We'd like to check, madam.' Deftly the man had turned back on Charlotte.

'You have no right of entry to this property. The lady's already told you that the person you're looking for isn't here, and that she doesn't want you in her home.' Edward folded his arms to indicate that this was now an end to the matter.

'Fair enough. But do you know where he is?' The question was aimed at Charlotte again.

This time she gave her answer to Edward. 'I don't…'

He nodded, laying his hand on her arm with as much tenderness as he could muster. 'They're allowed to ask you whether you know where the person they're looking for is. It's entirely up to you whether you answer or not.'

'We haven't lived together for eighteen months. I have the name of his solicitor.' Her voice was almost a whisper, her eyes pleading. Not just for him to help her get rid of these men. For him to understand.

'Can we have that at least…please?' The word *please* seemed to stick in the man's throat and he took another step forward, as if this was an invitation into the house.

'Wait there.' Edward turned to Charlotte and she nodded. She knew as well as he did that if she could give these men something it might get them off her back. 'Go and get it, then.'

She hurried inside and Edward indulged in a staring contest with the men, open hostility buzzing between them. She returned, clutching a piece of paper with a hastily scribbled address on it, and gave it to Edward. 'Here it is.'

Edward turned back to the men on the pavement. 'Right. The lady hasn't seen her husband in months, and she doesn't know where he is. She's given you every assistance she can in locating him, and this ends her involvement in the matter.'

'All right.' The man snatched the paper that Edward proffered. 'And you're sure you don't know where he is?'

'Doesn't sound very likely to me,' his companion sneered, forcing home the point. 'Doesn't he want to see his own kid?'

Edward heard Charlotte's sudden intake of breath and fought to stay in control of the fury that swept over him in a red-and-black wave. Much as he'd like to, getting into a fight with these guys wasn't going to help. 'You've asked your question and you've got your answer. You know full well that the law prevents you from harassing this lady any further or from speaking to a minor.' He pulled his phone out of his pocket. 'You've got ten seconds to get going before I call the police.'

The two looked at each other, grins on their faces. Edward wondered how many people actually followed through with that threat. He started to thumb the numbers on the screen.

'All right, mate.' The larger of the two, who was obviously the lead man, held up his hands in surrender. 'We're going.'

'Tell your head office to expect a letter, confirming the information that this lady's given you. She knows nothing more which will assist you, and she wants no further contact with you.' Edward pressed his advantage home.

The two turned without a word and Edward watched them lumber off down the road and climb into a shiny SUV. Business was clearly booming for them.

'Go and see to Isaac. I'll just keep an eye out here for a couple of minutes.' The SUV roared past them down the road, with the engine being gunned so that it made as much noise as possible.

He looked around. Charlotte was still there, her face burning so red that he probably could have warmed his hands on it if he'd needed to.

'Thanks, Edward. I'm sorry you had to see that.'

'It's not your fault. Those guys had no right to act the way they did.'

Her gaze dropped to the cracked paving stones at their feet. 'Yeah, I know. It was such a shock to see them on the doorstep, and they were so intimidating...' She looked as if she was about to burst into tears and then visibly pulled herself together.

Turning, she hurried back up the path and opened the front door. 'I'm really grateful to you, Edward. I'll...' She had the grace to flush an even deeper red before she gave him his marching orders. 'I'm sorry, but I need to go and see how Isaac is. Will you excuse me? I'll see you on Monday.'

The door closed, and Edward found himself standing alone. What was he supposed to do now? Charlotte had made her intentions more than clear, and he supposed he should leave. But he was damned if he was going to leave a woman and child alone in this situation.

Edward strode to his car, snatched Stinky up from the front seat, and walked back to her front door.

CHAPTER THREE

ISAAC WAS WHIMPERING in her arms. He was trying to be brave, but his little body was shaking as he clung to Charlotte. She wanted to go and find those men and punch them. More than once.

There was a noise at the letterbox and she tried not to jump. Isaac fell silent, staring at the door.

'Charlotte? Charlotte, I have Stinky here. That's what I came for this morning. He's too big to put through the letterbox.'

She thought about telling Edward to leave him on the doorstep. She might possibly have been able to, whatever the consequences later on, if she hadn't seen the look on Isaac's face. It was as if he'd just seen the cavalry, riding hell for leather over the horizon.

Perhaps he was right. Maybe his five-year-old mind was able to see a little more clearly than hers. She wouldn't be all that surprised. Edward engendered such a plethora of different emotions in her that her judgement wasn't to be trusted where he was concerned.

'I'm coming…' she called out to him, and took Isaac's hand, leading him to the door. She took a deep breath and opened it.

She had hardly registered it before, through her tears and her panic, but Edward's eyes looked a brighter blue than usual. His hair darker. There was less of the suit and tie about him and a great deal more of the enigma, with his dark shirt and jacket giving him an almost dangerous look. Even the blue stuffed toy, grasped lightly in his long fingers, couldn't dispel the feeling that here was a hero, come somehow to save her.

'Hey, Isaac.'

He might only have been able to spare her son a half-smile, but it would have melted an ice hotel, launched a battleship, and cracked a grin on the face of a statue.

'I brought Stinky for you.'

Isaac looked up at him and wiped his nose on his sleeve. Charlotte resisted the impulse to tell him to use a tissue on the grounds that she'd been doing the same herself just a moment ago. This morning Isaac could do anything he liked, as long as she could see just a glimpse of his smile.

'Thank you.' Isaac's voice was small, quavering, and it tugged at Charlotte's heart.

'Bit of a morning, eh, little man?' Edward suddenly seemed to realise that getting down onto Isaac's level would be a good idea and dropped to one knee, proffering the boy's toy.

Isaac nodded, reaching for Stinky. Charlotte felt his hand slip out of hers and he walked uncertainly towards Edward, then seemed to throw all caution to the winds and flung his arms around Edward's neck.

'Hey… Hey, there.' For a moment Edward's hands fluttered awkwardly. Then he wrapped his arms around Isaac, hugging him as if he could hold him tightly enough to make everything all right.

For a moment all Charlotte wanted was to be in on that hug.

'You know what?' Edward had got to his feet, taking Isaac with him. Safe and sound in his arms. 'You and I have a job to do. We're going to tell your mum that everything's going to be okay. That we'll look after her.'

Isaac nodded sagely.

'I think we could all do with a cup of tea. What do you say?'

'I want milk.'

'Good idea. I'll have some milk, too. And we'll make your mum a cup of tea.'

'She likes coffee. The kind with the froth on top.'

Isaac had a tight hold of Edward's jacket collar, his other arm wrapped around Stinky. Charlotte knew that his tears weren't too far below the surface, but Edward seemed to be reassuring him with his sheer bulk and unflappability.

'Okay. Tell you what—we could go out for coffee, if you'd like.' His gaze moved from Isaac to Charlotte. 'What do you think?'

'I…' She wanted his arms around her so much. His comfort. Charlotte pulled herself upright, squaring her shoulders. 'We're all right. Really.'

'Yeah. I can see that.' He reached forward, touching her cheek so lightly that she shivered. As his hand dropped to his side his fingers skimmed his thumb, as if he wanted to test the exact nature and volume of the tears he'd brushed away.

'We can manage, Edward. I don't know what I would have done if you hadn't turned up just then, and I can't tell you how much I appreciate it…' Good start. That was really going to make him feel that it was okay for him to go away now, wasn't it?

'But…?'

'But I can't keep you. You must have things to do.'

Edward always had something to do. His head was always buried in a book, or some papers. Even when she'd chanced to see him in the street he was always deep in thought, and half the time he didn't even acknowledge her, either because he hadn't seen or didn't want to see.

'I don't think so. In fact I've nothing to do today. It's only fifteen minutes over to my place.' He pursed his lips, as if he'd surprised himself by the invitation as much as he'd just surprised Charlotte. 'We'll get coffee on the way, and we can talk…privately. Perhaps I can help.'

She could have turned his help down for herself, but she had Isaac to think about, and Charlotte had no choice but to grab at any and every offer that came her way. And there was the matter of that nagging need at the back of her head, which wanted her to explain to Edward, tell him that she wasn't the person that all of this made her seem. She was going to have to swallow her pride and go for coffee.

Edward had waited in the hallway while she dragged on a pair of jeans, shoved her feet into her sandals and splashed her face with water. Her eyes had looked puffy in the mirror, but she hadn't wanted to keep him waiting for too long, so she'd dropped her make-up bag into a canvas holdall along with a few of Isaac's favourite toys to keep him occupied.

They'd stopped at a coffee shop and Edward had ushered them in. Isaac had slipped his hand into Edward's, tugging at his jacket until he'd lifted him up to see over the counter. He seemed to trust that if he stuck with his new friend no harm would come to them, and Charlotte hoped that her son was right.

Now they turned into a wide street, dappled by sunlight shining through the branches of the trees. Turned again into a short drive, behind a high wall hung with greenery, and came to a halt outside a double-fronted Georgian house, white-painted with slim, elegant lines.

It was quiet here. Far enough from the main road for them to be able to hear birdsong. Charlotte handed Edward the cardboard coffee holder and busied herself with getting Isaac out of the car.

The silence between them was oppressive. Edward seemed awkward as he opened the front door, walking inside without even asking them in, and Charlotte began to wish that she was anywhere but here. Apart from being at home, that was, waiting for the phone to ring again.

'Well…' He clapped his hands together awkwardly, like a man who was unused to guests. 'Here we are.'

'Yes.' Charlotte stepped tentatively over the threshold, holding tightly onto Isaac's hand. Inside the house it was tranquil—a cream-painted hallway, pictures on the walls, green plants everywhere.

'Let's go into the sitting room.' Edward seemed to galvanise himself into action and opened a wide panelled door, ushering them through it.

Sunlight streamed through the front windows onto pale oatmeal-coloured sofas at the front. A TV, nestling unobtrusively in one corner, conceded pride of place to a state-of-the-art sound system. The room ran the full depth of the house, and next to the French windows at the back stood a grand piano.

'What a lovely room.' She gave her son's hand a squeeze, although whether it was to give or receive confidence she wasn't quite sure. 'Isn't it, Isaac?'

Isaac was too busy looking around to reply. At the lines of glass-fronted cabinets, heavy with books. The green plants, arching gracefully around the windows.

'Come and meet Archie.' Edward beckoned Isaac over towards the French windows, where a ginger cat lay stretched out on the carpet, basking in the warm sunlight.

'Is he a lion?' Isaac looked up at him gravely.

Edward laughed. 'Well, he's not very fierce. You won't need that.' He gestured towards Isaac's plastic ray gun, which he'd insisted on bringing along with him.

Isaac stowed the ray gun in his pocket, just in case he'd need it later, and followed Edward over to where the cat lay. He watched solemnly as Edward tickled its ears and then its tummy as it rolled over, luxuriating in his touch.

'Do you want to stroke him?'

Edward was letting Isaac approach the creature in his own time, and Charlotte smiled as Isaac slowly reached out.

'He's growling.' Isaac snatched his hand away.

'No, that's purring. It means he likes you.' Edward drew back a little, letting Isaac stroke Archie.

'Be gentle with him, sweetie. Remember that he's much smaller than you are.' Charlotte stayed at her post by the door, still not sure whether to accept the quiet welcome of this place.

'Would Isaac like to watch some TV? While we talk?'

'Oh. Yes, he might do. Thank you.' Charlotte took the remote that Edward proffered and found a channel that Isaac liked, turning the sound down to a quiet murmur.

Edward set a low coffee table in front of the screen, put Isaac's frothed milk onto it and opened a cupboard, drawing out the molecule modelling kit.

Charlotte grinned. 'You're going to let him play with your toys?'

'If I share, then maybe he'll let me have a go with his ray gun. Will he be all right here?'

'He'll be fine. Look, he's already made a new friend.' Charlotte nodded towards Isaac, who was talking confidingly to Archie, stroking him carefully.

'Good. Well, we can talk through here.'

There was a door at the far end of the room, by the piano, and Edward disappeared through it, leaving Charlotte to get Isaac out of his jacket and settle him in front of the television.

She took one last look at Isaac, and then took a deep breath. Time to face Edward now. Now that keeping up appearances was no longer an option it was going to have to be the truth. She just hoped that he would understand.

He was sitting at a table in the large kitchen, studying the coffee in front of him as if there was some solution in there. She could tell him the answer to that. She'd tried it enough times herself. She mustered a smile, and sat down opposite him.

'So who's Archie named after? Archimedes?' She pulled her own coffee towards her and peeled off the plastic lid. It was smooth and strong and the caffeine hit her straight between the eyes.

He looked up, suddenly aware of her presence. 'Yes, actually. Although it's a mispronunciation, of course. Am I that predictable?'

'No. I thought of the most unlikely thing I could and suggested that—' She broke off as he smiled at her. That smile did all kinds of things to her, none of which were going to be of much help at the moment.

'So.' His gaze dropped to his cup again. 'You're in trouble, aren't you?'

'Yes. I am.' She should have realised that Edward would cut straight to the point. He wasn't much for small talk. Charlotte hadn't anticipated how much of a relief it would be. 'It isn't what you think.'

He looked up at her. Those deep blue eyes were almost irresistible. 'I'm not thinking anything.'

'You're always thinking something, aren't you?'

A trace of a grin tugged at his lips. 'Yes, I suppose I am.'

Suddenly she wanted to defend herself from all the implications of what Edward had seen and from whatever conclusions that agile, razor-sharp mind of his was working its way towards. 'The debts aren't mine, Edward.'

'I know. It was your husband they were looking for…'

'He'll be my ex-husband soon. Very soon, if everything goes as planned.'

Maybe she should have been a little less vehement about that. Said it a little more as if it was a matter of fact rather than an avowal of innocence. Edward seemed far more at home with facts than emotions.

'Have you asserted your separation financially?'

'Yes. There are no more joint accounts and credit cards. The house and the mortgage are in my name.'

'Then you have nothing to worry about. As long as you've applied for a Deed of Separation, and you're not jointly liable for any of his debts…'

'How do you know all this?' The question had occurred to Charlotte on her doorstep, but she'd pushed it to the back of her mind.

'I have a degree in Law.'

'As well as being a surgeon?'

'I…um…I was advised to wait until I was eighteen to go to medical school. I was at a loose end.'

'So…' The gossip was correct, then. 'You *are* a genius?'

'They called it "gifted" when I was a kid. Now it's called High Learning Potential.'

The twitch of his lips told Charlotte that they were just labels, which Edward didn't set much store by.

'I don't need to be a genius to know that there's more to your situation than what you've told me.'

There was a lot more. Charlotte grinned at him almost automatically, the way she did whenever anyone offered anything that sounded a bit too much like sympathy. 'Really?'

'Yeah, really. And you're not going to convince me otherwise with that smile, either. Even if it is a very nice one.'

Stop now. One thing at a time. Having Edward as a concerned friend was already turning her universe upside down. It was a bit too soon for compliments.

'You're right, that's not all. My husband had…I think it's probably fair to say *has*…a gambling addiction.'

'And that's why you left him?'

'I wasn't that smart. I didn't know about it until the bailiffs started calling. The first one was the day after Isaac's second birthday.' She sighed. She didn't need to go into details; he was getting the gist. 'I started out by paying his debts. He promised me that he'd stopped, and I believed him.'

'But he lied?' He was blunt, but there was no brutality there. Just the truth.

'Yes, he just kept on racking up the debts. Internet gaming sites, card games… He maxed out our credit cards and I dipped into the money I'd inherited from my parents just to keep a roof over our heads.' Charlotte gulped in a breath of air. This time she was going to do things better. She had to for Isaac's sake.

'But you couldn't hold it together.' Another flat, emotionless statement of the inevitable facts.

'I did for a while. Then he left. That was eighteen months ago. I sold the house, paid off all the debts, and managed to scrape enough together for a deposit on a smaller house. Made a new start for Isaac and me.'

Edward just nodded.

Caught in the force of his concentration, Charlotte realised that Edward was not an absent-minded, other-worldly creature. He was thinking things through, his ruthless single-mindedness not allowing a single detail to escape.

'Does your husband know where you are?'

'Yes, he knows. I was hoping that he'd come and see Isaac but he never has.'

Charlotte heaved a sigh. She didn't need to tell him about the thing that had damned her the most—it didn't affect the problem at hand. Anyway, it was humiliating. Even more so than having to admit she was being chased by her husband's debtors.

She met those blue eyes again. Ever questioning, but not as judgemental as she'd feared.

'And you said your divorce is in the pipeline?'

'Yes. I have the Decree Nisi and I'm waiting for the Decree Absolute. I'm hoping that he won't throw any spanners into the works and put in a last-minute objection.'

'Do you have any reason to think he will?'

'No... Maybe... I don't know. Peter's not exactly the most predictable of people.' Charlotte sighed. 'He's not strong. He'll do whatever gets him through the day and forget all about the consequences for tomorrow.'

'You don't trust him.'

Damn right she didn't. She had very little reason to. 'No, I don't. The men who called this morning aren't the only people looking to get paid. I had a telephone call last night from someone who said I owed money for a mobile phone bill.'

'Do you?'

'No!' She was protesting too much again. 'My phone's a pay-as-you-go…'

Charlotte reached for her handbag to show him the phone and Edward stopped her, laying his hand on her wrist.

'It's okay.'

'It isn't. The divorce won't protect me if he's managed to raise a line of credit in my name, and I've no money to pay off any more of his debts.'

It was as if she and Isaac were being dragged back into the nightmare that she'd worked so hard to get out of, and there was nothing she could do about it. Charlotte gulped back the tears, pulling her hand away from his grasp.

'What did you tell them?' He was still calm, almost icy cool. Still focussed on the facts.

Charlotte took a deep breath. She should try to sound a little more grateful, Edward had already helped her more than he had any reason to. 'I said that I had no knowledge of the account in question and asked them to put everything in writing and send it to me.'

'Good. We can start making enquiries on Monday. In the meantime, is there anyone that you and Isaac can stay with?'

'Not really. My parents are dead and I don't have any brothers or sisters…' She tried to smile, make light of it, but Charlotte had never felt so alone. 'We'll be okay. I'll take the phone off the hook and lock the door…'

'You'll stay here.' Even Edward seemed surprised at his uncompromising words.

'No! I mean…Edward, it's kind of you to offer, but I couldn't think of it.'

'What about Isaac? I gather that Sunday mornings are a favourite time for debt collectors to make their calls. He's old enough to know what's going on now.'

Low blow. He'd found the spot where her guilt was almost unbearable. 'I thought he was too young to remember. But when those men called this morning…'

Isaac had understood exactly who they were and had

launched himself at them, trying to drive them away, trying to protect her. Charlotte had managed to keep hold of him, and the men had smirked at each other as she bundled him back into the house.

She heard Edward sigh.

'Look, you need to get yourself and Isaac out of the firing line for a few days, until you have a chance to sort this out. I've plenty of room here—there are two spare bedrooms upstairs—and you'll both be safe.'

He didn't mince his words, or dress it up to make it sound as if she had a choice, but he was right. She *did* need to get her son away from this nightmare, and she had nowhere to take him.

'Charlotte.'

He reached out to her, his finger tipping her chin upwards. His shrewd blue eyes saw straight through her. There were no excuses, no way that she could just fob him off with something.

'Where else are you going to go?'

CHAPTER FOUR

HE HADN'T MEANT to be cruel, just to look at the situation rationally. But when she finally gave way to her tears, her forehead sinking until it almost touched the surface of his kitchen table, her body trembling with the effort that it seemed to take her to cry, Edward realised that she wasn't the only one who was in over her head. He didn't feel equal to this—not the crying woman at his kitchen table, or the vulnerable child on his sofa—and the knowledge that he was way past the point of dispensing some good advice and leaving them to it wasn't helping much.

'Hey.' He reached out, touching her arm tentatively with the tips of his fingers. 'Charlotte, please don't.'

She ignored him, and it had been a stupid thing to say anyway. Charlotte was at perfect liberty to do whatever she wanted. It was him who didn't want her to cry, because it wrenched his heart so much to see it.

'Okay. Well, you can cry as much as you like. But I'd appreciate it if you'd keep it down a bit or Isaac will be in here, blasting me with his ray gun for upsetting you. Which I didn't mean to do, by the way.'

Her shoulders stopped shaking. Slowly she raised her head. For a moment Edward was unsure about whether she was going to burst into laughter or start crying again. He decided to wait. He'd probably said more than enough already.

'I'll pay you rent.' Her voice was low, a little unsteady, but there was no doubt that she was back in control of herself.

'No. I won't accept it.' She opened her mouth to protest and he silenced her with a look. 'That's not negotiable.'

'I could clean for you.'

'That's not going to work either. I have a cleaning lady and there will be hell to pay if you put her out of a job.'

Somehow, from somewhere, she managed to find a smile. It was like basking in a ray of sunshine on a rainy day. 'I wondered whether it was you who kept all these plants watered.'

'We have an…understanding. She looks after Archie and the plants, doesn't move anything that I'm working on, and I keep out of her way and don't forget to pay her. Works like a dream.'

'I'm sure it does. Does she cook?'

'I imagine so. Not while she's here, though.'

'I'll cook for you, then.'

She narrowed her eyes obstinately and a sudden flood of longing gripped him. He hadn't counted on these sorts of complications, and wondered whether what he was about to do was wise.

'Okay. Deal.'

She bit her lip. 'Isaac won't be any trouble. He won't touch any of your things. I'll make sure of it…'

That sounded a bit dull. 'I can put anything that I don't want touched away out of his reach. And he can be as much trouble as he likes.'

She gave a tremulous laugh. Charlotte wasn't just a pretty face; she was tough, too. And brave. And about a million other things, all of which he felt inexplicably driven to find out more about.

'You have no idea how much trouble a determined five-year-old can be and, trust me, you don't want to find out.'

'Well…I'll leave that to you. What I mean is that you should make yourselves at home.' His mother was always telling him that this house was far too big for one. Granted this was not what she'd had in mind, but the principle was a good one. There was more than enough room for him to carry on with his life, undisturbed by two house guests.

'Thank you. I really appreciate this, Edward. And it'll only be for a few days, while I get everything sorted out.'

'You can stay as long as you like.'

He knew that it would take longer than a few days to work this out, and he didn't want her or Isaac going back home until it was. They'd both been through too much already.

After he'd taken them back to Charlotte's house, to pack what they needed, Edward had left them to their own devices. They had their own routine, which clearly involved eating and sleeping at regular intervals, and he had his, which disregarded any such practical activities in favour of whatever he happened to be doing at the time.

When he parked outside his house on Sunday evening his mind was still racing from the concepts that had been explored in the afternoon seminar he'd attended, and then endlessly again afterwards over sandwiches. The house was dark, and as he slipped his key into the lock on the front door it occurred to him that Charlotte might have taken her son and left, leaving a note on the hall table for him to find when he got back.

'Oh, no, you don't...' He muttered the words to himself, since she wasn't around to hear them.

He slid the key into the lock and the door gave by six inches, then caught. The chain, which usually hung unused from the frame, barred his entry. At least he wasn't going to have to get back into his car and drive over to Charlotte's house, to make sure that she and Isaac were all right.

All the same, there was the small matter of being locked out of his own home. Ringing the bell would probably wake Isaac up, as would bellowing through the letterbox, so Edward pulled the door to, twisting the key to relock it.

He seldom took the path around the side of the house, and

he jumped as a pair of iridescent orbs appeared from the bushes. 'Locked out as well, eh?' Archie swished his tail. 'Yeah, I know. It's a bit much.'

Discomfiture that his arrival home hadn't provided the usual well-ordered release from the complications of the world began to swell into anger.

He didn't need to find the key for the French windows; they were standing open. She was there, in the failing light, curled up in a chair on the stone-flagged patio.

'Charlotte!'

She jumped, throwing off the woollen jacket that was wrapped around her shoulders and twisting around. When she saw him she smiled, and Edward felt the hard edges of his anger melt.

'It's you…' She rubbed her eyes with her hand, as if she had been dozing.

It occurred to Edward to make the point that there wasn't much to gain by locking the front door if she was going to fall asleep with the doors to the patio wide open. But that sounded rather too much like criticism, and he'd already seen her flinch enough times when she or Isaac did something that she thought he might disapprove of.

'Did I wake you?'

'I must have just dropped off…' Her gaze swung from him to the house and then back again. 'Ohhh. I locked you out…'

That didn't seem so much of an issue as it had a moment ago. 'Putting the chain on the front door's a sensible precaution at night.'

'And falling asleep with the patio doors open isn't.' She gave a little self-deprecatory smile.

He shrugged, as if he'd not thought about that. 'Why don't you give yourself a break? You're safe here. No one can find you.' No one apart from him. He liked that thought so much that he dumped his briefcase on the stone flags and pulled up a chair, sitting down next to her.

She nodded. 'Thank you. Having a safe place to stay has meant a great deal to me and Isaac.'

'So you've had a good day?'

'Yes, thank you. We had lunch and then went to the park. They've got a great playground there, and a lovely cafeteria. We played football, as well.'

She made it sound like a real treat, and Edward found himself smiling, wondering whether football wouldn't have been preferable to a dark, humid lecture theatre. She and Isaac were a small, self-sufficient unit, though. They probably wouldn't have wanted him along.

'Sounds nice. Have you thought about what you're going to do yet? With regard to your situation?' He tried to put it delicately.

'I called Paula and she's going to lend me her laptop tomorrow. I've drawn up a list of things I need to find out about, and then I can start in on sorting everything out.'

Edward had left his own laptop on the coffee table, specifically so she could use it if she wanted to go on the internet. He should have thought that she wouldn't touch it, or allow Isaac to either, without asking. 'No need for that. Mine's right there.'

'Oh. Thank you.' There was a hint of awkwardness in her manner as she slid to the edge of her seat. 'Would you like something to drink? There's some hot chocolate…'

Her determination to pay her own way seemed to know no bounds. Everything he did for her—things that he gave without expecting anything in return—was entered on a balance sheet in her head to be repaid at a later date. Edward was debating whether he should tell her that she really didn't need to wait on him like this, but she was on her feet already.

'Hot chocolate would be great. Thank you.'

Since she so much wanted to do something for him, he supposed he should let her, and Charlotte's bright smile as she disappeared into the house tentatively proved his theory.

She brought him a mug of creamy hot chocolate, along with a plate of home-made biscuits.

'Thank you.' He took a sip and nodded his approval. Archie materialised from his nightly tour of the garden and curled up under her chair. If she'd been feeding him as well as she seemed intent on feeding Edward he couldn't fault the animal's change of allegiance. 'There's something I want you to do for me.'

She brightened noticeably. 'Yes, of course. What is it?'

Too late, Edward realised that he should have chosen his words more carefully. The impression that she was about to do him a favour was accurate enough, in the context of the amount of thinking time he'd already given to her plight, but Charlotte probably wouldn't see it that way.

'My father has his own practice at law, and I want you to consider making an appointment to go and see him. He can advise you and get his investigative team to find out exactly what's going on. With my dad on your side, you can get things sorted out quicker and more efficiently.'

'But I can't afford to pay a lawyer, Edward.'

'You won't need to. If I ask him, he'll do it for free.'

She hesitated. For a moment Edward thought that her pride was going to let her see sense and give in to expediency. Then she shook her head.

'No, I can't do that. It wouldn't be fair. Please don't mention it to him.'

He sighed. 'What isn't fair is that you're spending time on researching and fighting your own battles when there are people who will happily help you out. It's not just you that it makes an impact on—it's your work at the clinic.'

That particular argument didn't stand up to much scrutiny. Charlotte must have been worried sick over the last couple of weeks, but she'd never shown any evidence of it on the job.

She frowned at him. 'I wouldn't let anything get in the way of my work.'

'I know you wouldn't mean to, but none of us can be expected to give a hundred per cent when we're under the kind of pressure that you're facing at the moment.' He was pressing hard, exploiting every chink in her armour.

She hesitated. 'Edward, I… You're confusing me.'

Well, now she knew how *he* felt. 'It's very simple, Charlotte. Trust me.'

Two little words, spoken almost as a throwaway to emphasise his point. He should have known better. If he'd thought about it for two seconds he would have realised that trust was something she had a lot of difficulty with.

'I'm sorry.' Without another word, she got to her feet and disappeared into the house.

Edward leaned back in his chair and stared out into the evening shadows. Archie slid past his legs, waiting to be stroked, and he ran his fingers thoughtfully along the cat's back. Adjusting to the complex myriad of emotions that Charlotte and Isaac had brought to the quiet peace of his home was proving more difficult than he'd imagined.

The green reflective eyes seemed for a moment to understand his frustration, and then Archie was off again, his instinctive urge to chase shadows getting the better of him. Edward silently wished him better luck than *he'd* had tonight.

Edward had left the house before she was up the following morning. Charlotte went through the routine of getting herself up and ready for work, and Isaac ready for school, almost on autopilot. She was well aware that she'd walked out on Edward in the middle of a conversation last night, and common courtesy demanded that if he decided to broach the subject again she should have some kind of reasoned answer for him.

'Mum…?'

'Yes, Isaac.'

'Is everything going to be all right?'

She sat down opposite him at the kitchen table. 'Of course it is. What makes you ask that, sweetie?'

Some kind of understanding of the situation they were in, perhaps?

Isaac shrugged. 'I don't know.'

His brow was still furrowed, perhaps as a result of the unerring radar that seemed to alert him whenever something was wrong, even though he didn't grasp quite what it was.

'Look, sweetie. Those men came to our house by mistake on Saturday—they weren't looking for us. We're staying here with Edward for a few days, while I get everything sorted out, but that's going to happen very soon. Everything's going to be okay.'

'Do you promise?'

He still lived in a world where she could make everything right. Those trusting eyes would give Charlotte the courage to face anything that the world could throw at her. They'd even give her the courage to ask just one more favour from Edward.

'Yes. I promise. Cross my heart.'

She'd gone straight to Edward's office when she'd arrived at work and left a note for him on his desk. As luck would have it, he returned from his morning's surgery just as Allie and Paula were both within range of the nurses' station, beckoning Charlotte into his office in full view of both of them.

She was aware that two pairs of eyes were following her every move, so knew she'd better make this quick. 'I wanted to apologise. For last night…'

'You have nothing to apologise for. Why don't you sit down?' He threw himself into his leather chair.

'Because…' Charlotte shifted uncomfortably from one foot to another. 'We said we'd be discreet about our current living arrangements. And we're being watched.'

'Really? By whom?' He glanced around his office, perfectly oblivious of the stares that were homing in on them through the glass.

'Don't look…'

His attention swung back to her, and Charlotte began to wonder whether it wouldn't have been better to leave well alone. Edward's gaze made her feel as if he were undressing her. Taking his time and getting it absolutely right.

'There—will that do?'

As long as he didn't keep it up too long. 'That's fine. Allie and Paula are at the nurses' station. Watching us.'

'Ah. Well, in that case, I'll just pretend to show you this…' He flipped through the pile of journals on his desk, pulling one out and opening it. 'Then you can sit down and pretend to read it.'

His lips twitched slightly as she took the journal from his hand, and Charlotte suppressed a grin. His sense of humour might be an acquired taste, but it was well worth the journey.

'You wrote this?' She read the title of the paper slowly, just about getting the gist of it.

'Yeah.' He leaned forward across his desk. 'What do you think?'

'I don't know. Give me a couple of months to work my way through it…'

'Then you'll need to sit down.'

Charlotte gave up the unequal struggle and plumped herself down on one of the deep-cushioned leather easy chairs which were reserved for guests. Edward swung around in his own office chair, making sure that his back was to the glass wall, and shot her a conspiratorial look.

'So what do you want to speak to me about?' His finger nudged at the note on his desk.

Charlotte took a deep breath. 'I was being pig-headed last night. I'm sorry.'

'You have nothing to be sorry for. I'm not…' His intent blue gaze found hers and held it fast. 'I'm not great with certain kinds of solutions.'

What did he mean by that? Edward's usual forthright way of expressing himself seemed to have deserted him for the moment. 'I don't understand what you're saying…'

He sighed. 'I'm saying that I'm not as good with people as you are. I can be insensitive at times.'

'No, Edward…' She wanted to take him by the shoulders and shake this nonsense out of him, but she was being watched. She had to stay still and pretend this was just a conversation between two work colleagues. 'You've shown me and Isaac nothing but kindness.'

His eyes betrayed his confusion. 'Is this your way of letting me off the hook?'

'No. I'm paying you the respect of being honest with you. The way you've done with me.'

His slow smile penetrated every dark corner of her being. Filled her mind with the kind of ideas that she'd been trying not to think about for the past three days.

'Thank you,' he said.

'You're welcome.' Charlotte was sure that there was a more appropriate response than that, but she couldn't fathom what it might be at the moment. Not without the kind of body language that would get her into deep trouble. 'Look, what I wanted to say was that I'm over trying to make out that I can do everything by myself. If the offer's still open, I'd be really grateful if your father could spare a little of his time—perhaps just to talk to me and give me some general advice.'

He nodded. 'The offer's still open; there was no time limit on it. I'll give him a call.'

'Thanks, Edward. I really appreciate it. You'll tell him that, won't you?'

'I will.' He pointed to the journal in her lap. 'You know, if you're going to do this properly you should at least look as if you're reading.'

She picked up the journal and looked at it. 'Better?'

'Much. If anyone asks, what's our excuse for talking to each other?'

'I've probably been disputing some of the conclusions you came to in this article.' Charlotte jabbed her finger at the page in front of her and threw the journal down onto his desk.

'Very theatrical.' His eyes flashed as he leaned forward, picking up the journal and clipping something to the pages before he passed it back. 'Here's my father's card. I'll give him a call right now and tell him to expect your call this afternoon.'

'You're enjoying this, aren't you?'

'I wouldn't say *enjoying*. I think you've made the right decision....'

'I meant the secret rendezvous stuff.'

'Oh. Well, that adds a certain frisson. D'you think it's working?'

'Probably not. But at least I've got a measure of deniability.' Charlotte slipped the business card into her pocket and closed the journal, passing it back to him. 'Will you be working tonight?'

'No. Do you want a lift home?' He grinned. 'You could wait for me by the park gates if you like. With a wig and a pair of sunglasses, no one will think it's you...'

'I'll wear a pink carnation in my buttonhole.'

'Yeah. That would be a nice touch. Match your ears.'

Her ears weren't the only things which felt as if they were burning up when Charlotte walked back past the nurses' station.

'Not so fast.'

Paula's murmured words stopped her in her tracks.

'Sorry?' She was going to have to brazen it out.

'So what's the story, then? You and Edward North?'

'He was just showing me a paper he'd written. In one of the journals. Something that came up.'

Charlotte pushed her hands into her pockets and curled her fingers around the business card, just to check that it wasn't about to leap out of her pocket and embarrass her even further.

'Well, make sure that something comes up more often.

After all...' Allie shrugged '...one thing might lead to another.'

'I don't have time for anything like that. Isaac's the only man in my life at the moment.' It would be as well if *she* remembered that, too.

'Spoilsport. Surely you get time for a night off once in a while?'

Paula's tone was edged with concern. She might tease, but underneath it all she had a good heart.

'Edward North...he needs someone like you. And he *is* gorgeous.'

'And headed this way...'

Charlotte had been deliberately not looking in the direction of Edward's office and it was Allie who raised the alarm. Edward was striding towards them, and Charlotte caught the quick exchanged glance between Paula and Allie as he passed behind her. A little too close.

'Charlotte.'

There was something intimate about the way he said her name. Or maybe it was just her imagination. Charlotte didn't dare to look in Paula's direction.

'Mrs Ashe is here a little early with April. If you're free, then I'll see them now.'

'Yes, of course.' Charlotte reached over for the notes and followed Edward into the plush, comfortable consulting room.

The seventeen-year-old took a nervous breath as Edward began the careful, precise work of taking the dressings from the side of her face. The previous week he had used skin flaps to revise the scars that a road accident had left, and today April was to see the result. His small nod, and a fleeting glance in Charlotte's direction, revealed that he was pleased with his work.

'Does it look horrible?' April was chewing her lip.

'No. Mr North's got to take a careful look, but so far everything's fine.'

The other nurses sometimes complained that it was pretty much impossible to gauge Edward's reactions to anything, but today he seemed more transparent than usual.

She ventured a little more reassurance for April. 'It's a little raised at the moment, but that's normal. It'll settle over time.'

'Yes.' Edward was taking her lead. 'I'm very pleased with the way it's healing.'

Charlotte laid her hand over April's, feeling the tremor of her fingers. 'When you look at yourself in the mirror, remember that we're at the very early stages of healing right now. Your procedure went well, and everything's going just as it should. You'll see a lot of improvement in the coming months.'

'That's okay.' April managed a smile. 'I know.'

She might be young, but April was much more pragmatic than some of the clinic's clients, who seemed to expect that the miracles Edward performed should take effect immediately. Charlotte reached for the mirror, but Edward already had it, and was handing it to April.

'Everything's looking good, April. There's very little swelling, and I can see you've been doing all the things that Charlotte told you to do when we saw you last. Keep up the good work.'

'Thanks.' April took the mirror and looked at her reflection. 'That's not so bad.'

Charlotte grinned at her. 'No. Not so bad at all. Now, I'll show you how to massage it gently. With just a little more work, we can make it even better.'

CHAPTER FIVE

THE SMELL COMING from the kitchen was gorgeous. Mouthwatering. Edward wondered how he could possibly be so hungry when normally he ate far later than this, and sometimes not at all if he got involved with what he was doing.

'Do you know what's for dinner, Isaac?' He sat down on the sofa next to the boy, who was fidgeting restlessly.

'Yes. Mum made it yesterday.'

'Would you like to share?'

Isaac thought for a minute, and Edward wondered if he ought to rephrase.

'Lasagne.'

'Sounds great. I like lasagne.'

'Me, too. I like it here, too.' Isaac thought for a moment. 'When are we going home?'

Edward glanced towards the open door of the kitchen. No Charlotte. She must be able to hear their conversation, but it didn't appear that she was going to help him out.

'Whenever you and your mum want to.'

'Can we stay until next weekend?'

'Yes, if you'd like to. What's happening next weekend?'

'The men are coming again.'

'No, Isaac...' Where was Charlotte when he needed her? She didn't seem to have any difficulty in turning up almost like magic whenever she was needed at a patient's bedside.

'Your mother's done nothing wrong. Those men aren't allowed to come back, and I'm going to make sure they don't.'

'How?' Isaac slipped off the sofa and approached Edward, laying both hands on one of his knees, clearly intent on a man-to-man talk.

Edward took a deep breath and leaned forward. 'That's a secret. But I promise you that we'll stop them from coming back.' He held out his right hand. 'You want to shake on it?'

Isaac gave him a puzzled look.

'Here.' Edward picked up his right hand and gave it a gentle shake. 'That means that I've made a promise to you and I can't break it.'

'Like that?' Isaac proffered his right hand and shook Edward's again.

'That's right. Just like that.' This was going better than he'd thought it might.

Isaac proffered his hand again. 'I promise I won't touch your piano any more.'

A noise from the kitchen door made Edward look up and he wondered how long Charlotte had been standing there.

'I'm sorry. He only played a couple of notes and I wiped the fingermarks off…'

'Don't worry about it.' He turned back to Isaac. 'How does not touching my piano unless you ask your mum or me first sound?'

'I won't touch your piano unless I ask Mum or you.' Isaac sealed the bargain with a handshake and then ran over to the piano stool. 'Can I touch it now?'

'No, Isaac, it's time for dinner. Go and wash your hands.'

Isaac pulled a face, but ran out of the room. Charlotte's eye was on him all the way.

'How do you do that?'

She'd picked up the lasagne, newly out of the oven, and was carrying it through into the dining room. Edward followed with the salad.

'Answer all the questions? I just tell him the truth.' She laid the dish down onto a padded table mat, her shoulders drooping suddenly, as if someone had loaded some extra weight onto them. 'Well, most of the time. I still want to shield him, but he's getting to an age when that's not so easy.'

Edward wondered whether he should mention the fact that Isaac plainly wanted to do the same—to shield his mother. Probably not. He shouldn't interfere.

She'd put a small glass vase of flowers on the over-large oval table, which Edward had never managed to fill but had bought because it balanced out the proportions of the room. He liked balance. Order and proportion helped him to think. Charlotte had laid a place for him at the head of the table, and he sat down.

It was the strangest feeling. Charlotte on one side of him, helping him to a generous portion from the dish and pushing the salad bowl towards him. Isaac on the other side, sitting on a cushion so that he could reach the table. It was almost as though they'd taken him in, rather than the other way round.

'Would you like some water?' Charlotte was still on her feet, leaning across the table to place a beaker of water in front of Isaac.

'No, thank you. Why don't you sit down? I'll get some wine.'

She hesitated. Clearly debating whether or not she was going to allow him to contribute to the meal even in this way. 'Um…yes. Thank you. That would be nice.'

Edward got to his feet and went to the kitchen, fetching a couple of glasses and a bottle from the chiller. When he returned he was gratified to find that she'd done as he'd asked, and was sitting, her hands in her lap.

He placed a glass in front of her, uncorked the bottle and poured.

'Thanks. That's enough.'

She'd only let him half fill the glass but that was okay. It was the principle of it. Something had been accepted into the routine that they were building.

Isaac was watching his every move, eyes wide as saucers. 'Can I have some?'

'No, sweetie, this is for grown-ups.' Charlotte quietened him with a quick look.

'Pleeeease.' Isaac was obviously unused to not sharing everything with his mother.

'I've got something better for you.'

Edward gave him a conspiratorial grin and the boy quietened. He went to fetch a sturdier glass from the kitchen cupboard—not the fine crystal that he'd given to Charlotte, but a nice-looking faceted tumbler—and grabbed a bottle of sparkling raspberry cordial from the fridge.

'Here you are.' He set the glass in front of Isaac and filled it. 'Try this.'

He sat down, aware that Charlotte's smile was on him. It seemed to slide into his senses, warm and tingling, like fine brandy. Isaac took a sip from his glass and gave the same nod of approval that his mother had given when she'd tasted her wine. He was a part of this little treat.

Funnily enough, Edward felt a part of it, too. Eating together…praising Charlotte on the meal. Hearing the silly jokes passing between Isaac and Charlotte, which both of them expected him to laugh at, too. He was probably expected to tell a few, as well, but he couldn't think of any that they might like at the moment. But even that didn't seem to matter.

The doorbell rang.

Isaac jumped and would have spilled his drink if Edward hadn't put out a hand to steady it. Instead his fork slithered to the floor, bouncing across the rug and clattering noisily on the wooden parquet.

'Let's not answer that.' Edward shot a grin at the boy. Doorbells didn't appear to be his favourite thing at the moment, and who could blame him?

'It's okay.' Charlotte passed her own fork over to Isaac and bent to retrieve his. 'It might be something important.'

Isaac's gaze pleaded silently with him.

'So what if it is? We're eating.' A feeling of bravado, quite out of proportion with the deed, sparked in Edward's chest.

'But it could be a friend. Someone you know.'

Unlikely. And if it were they'd know him well enough not to give up after the first ring. Opening the door when the bell rang was one of those things that Edward classed as optional.

'If it is they'll ring again. Or phone me.' Edward generally picked up the phone. Unless he was in the middle of something really interesting.

She laughed. 'Aren't you even curious?'

Edward shrugged. 'It's probably someone wanting to sell me something.' And, anyway, he was making a point.

'And a man's home is his castle, eh?'

'Er...possibly. In a manner of speaking.' It was certainly somewhere that his mind could wander freely. Explore the nuances that everyday life seemed to ignore so heedlessly. He hadn't thought about the aspect of fortification, though...

Charlotte leaned towards him. 'It's just an expression. One size fits all.'

She was smiling at him, and that smile seemed to banish all thoughts of whether, either in truth or in paradigm, his home really was a castle. All he could do in the face of such unarguable persuasion was smile back.

'Yeah. Well, then, whatever size my home is...' he flipped a glance towards Isaac, hoping he'd get the point '...or I am, it's definitely a castle. Which means I don't have to answer the doorbell if I don't want to.'

Isaac seemed to understand and turned his attention back to his meal. Charlotte was more difficult to satisfy.

'So... Don't you think you're missing out on something?'

'Like what?' Like the world that she seemed to inhabit? The one where she seemed to navigate chance meetings and random conversations so easily.

'I don't know. That's the thing, isn't it?'

He shook his head. 'It's no one. And, anyway, we're eating.' He turned back to the plate in front of him. 'And this is very good.'

CHAPTER SIX

CHARLOTTE HAD STACKED the dishwasher, sat with Isaac until he started to yawn, and then taken him up to bed. She tucked him in, along with Stinky, in the small second guest room which adjoined her own, and closed the connecting door between the two. Isaac had slept soundly for the last two nights, and showed no signs of doing anything else tonight.

Edward had seen to it that Isaac should feel at home here. When he'd taken them both back to the house on Saturday afternoon he'd filled the boot of his car with Isaac's things—toys, games, clothes—so that he shouldn't wake in the night and find himself in a completely strange place. Somehow the molecule modelling kit had found its way up here, too, and Charlotte wondered whether Edward had put it there. The thought made her smile.

When she got back downstairs the room was silent. Edward was in an easy chair with his nose in a book. Not wanting to disturb him, Charlotte retreated to the kitchen and set about cutting sandwiches for Isaac's lunch tomorrow.

It was awkward being alone with him. At work, and when Isaac was around, she had a reason to ignore the desire to touch him. Now it was just him and her, and the empty space between them seemed almost to be daring her to breach it.

She'd finished the sandwiches, and was sitting at the kitchen table wondering what to do next, when the door opened quietly.

'Hey.'

'Oh…' She jumped, almost spilling the cup of coffee in front of her. Suddenly she noticed that the deep blue open-necked shirt he'd pulled on when he got home emphasised the colour of his eyes. 'You're busy. I didn't mean to disturb you.'

He shook his head, as if the concept were new to him. It probably was. Short of a nuclear explosion, it was practically impossible to divert his attention away from what he was doing at work. 'You don't need to sit in here, you know.'

'Yes… I mean, no. I mean… I don't want to get in the way.'

'You aren't. I'd appreciate the company.'

He meant it. Edward who had always seemed so aloof at work, so self-sufficient. And yet he'd surprised her by seeming to understand just how she and Isaac felt. There was a great deal more to Edward than met the eye.

'Me, too. I'll…make some coffee, shall I?' She looked at the mug of instant in front of her. 'Some fresh coffee.'

'That's okay. I'll do it.' His mouth quirked. 'Refreshments and snacks don't count as cooking.'

His quiet, dry humour curled around her like a delicious full-bodied chuckle. 'Oh. So you're beginning to chip away at our bargain, are you?'

'I don't think so. I don't remember any mention of brewing, looking in the fridge, or pouring.' He measured the coffee into the machine and switched it on. 'And I certainly don't recall having covered electrical appliances.'

She smiled at him. 'I'm going to have to watch myself, aren't I? Next time I make a bargain with you, I'll make sure I read the small print.'

Did that sound a bit too forward? Hopefully everything would be settled in a few days' time and she would be on her way back home. Edward would forget her as he moved on to his next project of interest.

'Yeah. Always read the small print.'

He flipped open the cupboard doors and pulled out two cups, his long fingers placing them precisely on the counter.

He had a delicate touch. He had to have. Microsurgery was one of the most challenging disciplines in a challenging world. And Edward was the best at what he did—just like everyone else at 200 Harley Street.

He made the coffee and picked up her cup with his own, taking it into the sitting room, as if unsure whether she might follow otherwise. Charlotte perched herself on the sofa, casting around for something that she could make conversation about.

'This is a lovely room.'

He nodded. 'Thank you.'

'Do you play the piano much?' From the wide-ranging collection of CDs on his shelves, and the grand piano, Edward was obviously passionate about music. In the three days that she and Isaac had been here, though, he'd never once opened the piano. Never once switched on the high-end audio equipment.

'Most days. Do you play?'

'No. I love listening, though.'

He must have changed his routine because of her presence. Maybe she could encourage him to change it back again.

Edward didn't move. 'I wouldn't want to wake Isaac.'

'You won't. He's upstairs and he's fast asleep.'

Maybe she shouldn't have asked. Maybe this was something private, that Edward didn't like to share.

It *was* something private—she could see it in the way he hesitated. But then he made his decision, jumping up and striding across the room. Charlotte tried not to notice the ease with which he lifted the heavy lid, or the way that his shoulder flexed as he propped it open. Suddenly his mastery over the large, shining instrument was physical, as well as just a matter of the mind.

Sitting down, he raised the lid from the keyboard and lowered his fingers onto the keys. 'Any requests?'

For a moment she couldn't think. Then Charlotte knew what she really wanted to hear. 'Something *you* like.'

He nodded. Charlotte was expecting something classical, but the soft strains of *Ain't Misbehavin'* started to float across the room. Mesmerised, she moved closer and he beckoned her over, shifting up on the long piano seat to make room for her.

She swallowed hard. The music invited her. The way he made the song sound as if it had been written just for her. His sensitive fingers stroked the keys. Charlotte wanted nothing more at that moment than to sit next to him, be a part of this world. *His* world.

He raised one eyebrow at her hesitation, and the music swelled in reproach. She gave in and slid onto the edge of the stool, angling her body away from his.

'You'll fall off…'

The music dropped to a few notes, played with his left hand, while his right arm curled around her waist, pulling her further onto the stool. She was not quite touching him, and the seat was plenty long enough for two, but that didn't seem to make any difference. She could practically feel his body moving against hers.

There were a few chords that seemed to be his own addition to the mix, and then he segued into *As Time Goes By.*

'Mmm. Love this one.' She closed her eyes and let the music wash over her.

'Yeah. Kind of sad… Haunting.' He added an extra verse and chorus onto the end and then smoothly moved on into another melody that she couldn't name, but which she recognised from an old film.

'You like this?'

'I feel I should be in a cocktail dress and expensive jewellery. Leaning against the piano and sipping… I wonder what they were drinking in *Casablanca*?'

He chuckled. 'Champagne?'

'You remember?'

'No. Just a guess. I've got a bottle somewhere, if you'd like some.'

Charlotte laughed. 'No. I don't have the cocktail dress.' Or the jewellery. Her mother's ruby necklace, the one that she thought she'd never part with, had been sold and the money spent on the bricks and mortar of her house. The one that she'd been driven out of just a few days ago.

He seemed about to say something, then stopped himself. Moved on to play another song. The soft, melancholy chords filled the air around them.

Suddenly the music stopped. 'Hey…. Hey, what's the matter?'

She felt him turn, but didn't raise her head. She didn't want Edward to see the tears.

Too late.

His fingers touched her arm, hesitantly at first, and then more resolute. She felt his arm around her and, try as she might, couldn't bring herself to break away from him.

'It's nothing. Just the music.'

'Much as I'd like to think that it was my playing that moved you to tears, I doubt it.'

She wanted to hold on to him. It felt so natural to do so. But she shouldn't. She'd always been a sucker for the quiet type, and the last one she'd got involved with had almost destroyed her life.

'I…I'm just afraid that I'm going to lose everything. And you've been so kind…'

'You're not going to lose anything.'

He hugged her tight and she gave in and buried her face against the protective arc of his chest.

'Did you ring my father this afternoon?'

'Yeah. I've arranged to leave work early tomorrow and go and see him.'

'Good. You can stop worrying, then. He'll sort this out for you.'

'I know. Thank you. I'm just being silly.'

She felt his fingers stroking her hair. Just for a moment, before he snatched his hand away again. This must be torture for someone like Edward. So self-contained, so controlled.

He didn't really *do* tears. She tried to move away from him, but his arm kept her firmly in place.

'You're not being silly. You lost everything once. It's natural to fear that it'll happen again.' He drew back, holding her shoulders tightly. Bending to capture her gaze in his. 'It's not going to. You're going to fight it.'

'I haven't got anything to fight with. All my savings are gone, and…' She couldn't even say it. The money was just a number. It was the loss of little things that she'd hoped she'd always keep that hurt the most. Memories…presents that people had given her over the years. The cot which, at one time, she'd hoped might see some more use. All Isaac's baby stuff. It hadn't fetched much, but every penny had counted when she'd been trying to put the deposit on the house together.

He shook his head. 'I wish you'd told someone. The clinic might have arranged an employee loan, or if not…' He pressed his lips together, apparently not wanting to finish the 'or if not'.

'I'd only been there for a couple of months. I was just glad to have the job. The extra income meant I could make the mortgage. Anyway…it would just have been another debt that I couldn't pay back.'

'So you sold everything you had?' His grip on her shoulders relaxed and his hands slid down to her elbows.

'Pretty much.' Charlotte put it to the back of her mind. 'But that's okay. Things are easier now. I've had a pay rise, and the first year's always the worst with a mortgage.'

'And I guess the extra shifts come in handy?'

He'd noticed, then. The way that she grabbed every bit of overtime that came her way, even though it meant that she had less time to spend with Isaac. 'Yes, they do.'

'You've worked hard. No one's going to take that from you. Just explain everything to my father and let him sort it out. And in the meantime you can stay here. Isaac seems… well, he doesn't seem to mind the arrangement.'

'You've made us both very welcome. Being here has been

so good for Isaac.' It was Edward who had been good for Isaac, not the house. Providing a broad pair of shoulders that her son felt he could rely on. For that matter, he'd been good for Charlotte, as well.

'You can stay as long as you like.'

'Thank you. But we won't outstay our welcome.'

Like always, his smile was reticent, hard won, but all the better for it.

'Then I think we'll be okay. I can outlast you.'

No doubt he could. At the moment Charlotte reckoned that she had about ten minutes before she made a fool of herself and threw herself into his arms if she didn't find something to distract him.

'Will you play something else?'

Edward couldn't get the image out of his head. Charlotte in a dark figure-hugging dress. Something sparkly at her wrist and around her neck and a glass of champagne in her hand. Leaning against the piano, the gold flecks in her eyes reflecting the light better than any jewel could.

He played for a while on autopilot, while he added the fine detail to his vision. Then the real Charlotte broke in, her body warm and moving to the rhythm next to his.

'You'll have plenty of offers if you ever decide to give up the day job.'

Her smile made him stop thinking and start feeling as he ran his hands across the keyboard in a short, improvised cascade of notes.

'I used to play in a bar. When I was at medical school.'

'Yeah?'

'It paid better than stacking shelves. And I got to keep the tips as well.'

'Tips are always good.'

'Yeah. Made a big difference.'

'I bet you spent them on books.'

'Um… Yeah. Okay, you're making me feel predictable again.'

With Charlotte he could begin to fathom what people saw in small talk. It was easy. Delightful. Maybe they were getting a little too close to flirting, but that would be okay as long as he kept playing. Somehow the music made pretty much anything permissible.

She laughed. 'I think you're one of the most unpredictable people I've ever met.'

'Dancing to the beat of a different drum, you mean?' People had said that to him, and *about* him, all his life. That he was gifted. Different. That he didn't need the company of his peers as much as he needed to fulfil his potential.

'*Is* it a different drum? I rather thought that it was the same drum, but you just hear it a little more clearly.'

Edward let the thought percolate. 'That might be one of the nicest things anyone's ever said to me.'

The unexpected idea that words might not be enough to express his feelings on the matter occurred to him. He wanted to hold her again.

She smiled and his theory morphed into a tried and tested fact. Charlotte's smile held so much more meaning than words, and he allowed himself to bathe in it, feeling its warmth lap against his skin.

He didn't know how long he played for, and didn't much care. However long she sat here next to him, her body melting into the rhythm of the music, it wouldn't be enough.

When finally she drew away, another of those gorgeous smiles on her lips, the world felt suddenly cold.

'You play wonderfully.'

He nodded in acknowledgement. 'You listen wonderfully.' It was more as if she'd been a part of the music, shaping the emotion and cadence with him, although her fingers had never touched the keys.

She laughed, getting to her feet. 'I should go and get some sleep, though. Thank you for a lovely evening.'

'My pleasure. We should do this again.' The words escaped his heart before his head could issue the caution against asking for trouble.

She flushed a little and nodded quickly. 'Goodnight, Edward.'

He played a short, quiet goodnight, listening to the sound of her footsteps on the stairs. Then he closed the lid over the keys.

Charlotte was everything that he held himself aloof from. The instinct and emotion that he saved only for his music seemed to bleed into her whole life. It was captivating—tantalising, even—but it was a language that he didn't know how to speak. However much she tried not to disrupt his life, however well-behaved Isaac was, the two of them had the power to turn his well-ordered existence upside down.

Archie roused himself, stretched, and joined him on a restless errand to the kitchen, which had no particular purpose other than his need to go somewhere. Edward poured himself a glass of wine from the bottle they'd opened at dinner, leaving Archie to pounce on his food bowl as if he hadn't eaten in years, and wandered back into the sitting room. The book that he'd abandoned in favour of going to talk to Charlotte still lay on the sofa, and he picked it up, flipping it open. This, at least, he knew how to handle.

CHAPTER SEVEN

CHARLOTTE KNEW THAT Edward would be here somewhere. She hated that she needed to see him so badly, but she had nowhere else to go. She slipped through the reception area, avoiding the last stragglers on their way out of the clinic at 200 Harley Street, and ran up the stairs.

Edward's office door was closed and locked, but she could see his jacket, slung over the back of his chair. There was only one other place that he could be.

She left her coat and bag on one of the chairs in the closed-up nurses' station and took the stairs down to the basement. The gym was in darkness, but she could see lights shining through the glass doors which led to the pool.

Suddenly her courage failed her. She'd already accepted too much from Edward. Already allowed herself to get too involved with his life. He was quiet and kind, creative and a little quirky. But then her husband had been quiet and kind, too. She'd thought that she could see hidden depths in him, where actually there had just been an angry void that he'd sought to fill with the thrill he got from risking everything on the cards.

Charlotte turned. She knew that Edward was here, and that at this time in the evening he was probably alone. Walking away was the best thing to do. The only thing to do.

She'd go upstairs to fetch her coat. Then come back down again, using the back stairs, so that no one would see her.

'What are you doing here?'

She'd been so lost in her own emotions she hadn't even seen that there was anyone on the stairs below her. Instinctively she turned to run upstairs, but it was too late. Edward had seen her.

It *had* been him in the swimming pool. His dark hair was still wet, slicked back from his face, and his white shirt was open at the neck. Not sure what to say or do, Charlotte focussed on the logo splashed across the gym bag that was slung over his shoulder.

'Charlotte...?' He was standing two steps below her now, and they were face to face. 'What's the matter?'

'Nothing.' *Everything.* 'I just forgot something and popped back...'

The whole difficulty of dealing with Edward was that excuses were practically impossible to get away with—unless, of course, you had the time to construct a well-thought-out, fully featured alibi.

He raised one eyebrow in disbelief and shooed her up the stairs.

'Come to my office.' His keys were in his hand already, and he strode past the deserted nurses' station and unlocked the door, motioning her in. He slung his bag on the floor, in the corner, and sat down in his high-backed leather chair.

'I feel as if I'm being hauled up in front of the beak.' Small talk was the one thing that she was better at than Edward. Her only chance.

His brow clouded, but then he refused to take the bait. 'Why don't you sit down, then?'

'Do I need to?'

'You don't need to do anything. It's an invitation.'

He leaned back in his chair, propping one foot on the desk, and Charlotte slumped down into one of the visitors' chairs.

'So...what is it, then?' One last try at putting the ball in his court. Making Edward talk first.

'I...um...'

He seemed suddenly hesitant. Maybe she was going to get her way after all. They could go home, she'd make dinner, and then on the excuse of an early night she could go and cry into her pillow. That was the thing she should have done in the first place—not come running to Edward every time something went wrong.

He tried again. 'There seems to be something wrong. I was wondering how the meeting with my father went...' He backtracked slightly. 'Not in detail. I wouldn't presume to interfere with a confidential exchange between lawyer and client...'

There was no such thing as a simple question in Edward's vocabulary; there was always some accompanying detail. The way his mind worked made Charlotte smile, however bad things were. 'No. I'm sure you wouldn't.'

'It's just a broad brush enquiry. About whether you're happy as a result of...whatever it was that was said.'

'Your father was very kind.'

Straight spikes of hair had begun to fall across his forehead, and when he smiled it looked almost rakish.

'Good. And apart from being kind...?'

'He's offered to represent me, and I've accepted. I gave him some details on the phone yesterday, and he's already got an investigator to follow up on them. He's thought of everything.'

Edward nodded. 'I imagine he has. There's no need to worry.'

Her heart was almost tearing itself apart with panic. 'No. I'm sure there isn't.'

He got to his feet, unhooking his jacket from the back of his chair. 'I guess I should call your bluff and just take you home, then.'

'Peter applied for a loan in Isaac's name. One of those quickie ones you can get on the internet.' Charlotte couldn't help it. She'd blurted out what she'd come to say—what she knew that Edward couldn't mend, but somehow wanted him to know.

He slumped back down into his chair, shock on his face. 'Did he get it?'

'No, thank goodness. And your father's going to do all he can to protect Isaac from that happening again.' Charlotte could feel her shoulders beginning to droop, but the effort of keeping her spine straight was finally too much to do anything about it.

'And what about the phone bill that you were being chased for?'

'He's putting pressure on the phone company to leave me alone. It seems that there's a bit of a mix-up with names and I might be facing a few more where that one came from.'

His eyes narrowed. 'A mix-up? How could that have involved *you*?'

She'd faced a pair of blue eyes and a sharp legal mind once already this afternoon. Edward's were as kind as his father's, but somehow much more challenging. The truth had been easier the first time around.

'When Peter and I were living together...'

Tears again. What must Edward think of her?

'Hey...' He rounded his desk, dragged one of the heavy armchairs over towards hers and sat down opposite her, leaning forward until his hands almost touched hers. 'It's okay, Charlotte. I just want to help.'

All she wanted right now was to feel his arms around her. If Edward was on her side she could do anything, be all kinds of strong. She met those blue eyes again. They gave her courage for the thing that damned her the most.

'The phone bill dates back to when Peter and I were living together. He must have taken the contract out in my name and...' She shrugged. 'I didn't know about that phone—it was his second one. He had someone else.'

His face became cold, as if she'd just slapped him. 'You mean he's expecting you to pay for the calls he made to his mistress? While you were living with him?' Edward shook his head angrily. 'Oh, no...you're not doing that.'

She reached for him, but he wasn't there. He was too angry now even to see her, and he sprang to his feet and started to pace the office like a caged tiger.

'Edward. Please, don't... Peter probably didn't think of it like that. He doesn't think anything through. The phone was registered at my old address and it's up to me to prove it isn't mine...'

'Don't make excuses for him, Charlotte.'

Her own anger flared in response to his. 'I'm not. I'm just trying to work out what happened...'

'And if you keep on taking his side you'll always be a victim.'

'Oh, so *that's* what you think, is it?' She was on her feet, catching his arm, forcing him to face her. 'I am *not* a victim. I've stood on my own two feet since Peter left me, provided for Isaac...' She took a deep breath. Shouting wasn't going to do any good, and if there was anyone still in the building they'd be sure to hear them.

'I know.' Edward's rage turned abruptly cold. 'But this is not your responsibility.'

'No, it isn't. But there's another child, too—a little girl. She's not my responsibility either, but I still can't help thinking that somewhere out there that child's mother is going to be facing the same thing that I did. I might not like her very much, but I can feel for her.'

'There's a baby?'

'Not a baby—a child. She'll be three years old now.'

He didn't need to be a genius to be able to do that particular calculation. Peter hadn't just had someone else while he was living with her, he'd had a child as well.

'You've told my father this?'

'Yes. I said that he could do whatever it took as far as Peter was concerned, but that I wouldn't go out of my way to implicate his partner if there's been any fraud. That's my decision, Edward, whether you like it or not.'

Warmth bloomed in his face. 'Most people wouldn't be so forgiving.'

'I'm not either. I don't forgive her, but I won't hurt her daughter. She's no more responsible for any of this than Isaac is.'

'Maybe the best thing you can do for this woman is to show her exactly what she's got herself into...'

'That's what your father said.'

'Must be right, then.' A ghost of a grin shimmered on his mouth.

'I suppose so. But all I really want to do is to be free of Peter. Your father's agreed to review my divorce papers, to see if there's anything I've missed, and to do all he can to push it through without any hitches. That's a big weight off my mind.'

He nodded. 'My dad's not going to let you down. Once he gets his teeth into something he's like a dog with a bone, and he won't let up until he's got everything sorted out.'

She could smile now. His impassioned rage had shown that Edward didn't just pity her. He hadn't shrunk from demanding answers from her, asking the really hard questions.

'That's something you both have in common. I appreciate it more than I can say.'

He gave the customary small nod, which said he'd heard. A smile which said he'd understood.

'I should go now. I need to pick Isaac up soon.'

He shook his head. 'One more minute.' His back was against the door and he was leaning on it, his arms folded. 'I'm afraid it's no more Mr Nice Guy, Charlotte.'

She swallowed. Edward was getting darker and more dangerous again. She had to admit that she rather liked it.

'Really?' She took a step forward, tilting her head up to meet his gaze. If he wanted another confrontation he could have it.

'Yeah. You can put up a fight if you like, but you and Isaac are staying on with me until this is all sorted out. However long it takes.'

'We've had this conversation before…'

'And we can have it again if you want. You'll tell me that you don't want to impose, I'll say that you and Isaac are no trouble and that I like having you both around, and then you'll give me that look…' He grinned. 'The one that you're giving me right now…'

'And…?'

'And you'll say that you and Isaac have managed on your own up till now, that you don't need anyone.'

'That's not quite true…'

'No, it's not. You'll say it anyway, though, just to put me in my place.'

That smile of his didn't have a place. Neither did Edward.

'You're reading my mind now, are you?' Just as long as he couldn't access the part of her imagination that was engaged in stripping his shirt from his shoulders. Running its hungry fingers over his skin and allowing him to back her against the desk…

He narrowed his eyes and she shivered. There was something tender about the curve of his lips, something raw about the look in his eyes. 'I should warn you that I have a Joker up my sleeve.'

She nodded. 'Isaac. You'll say he's happy where he is and it would be wrong to put him through any more upset. That I might be able to see the debt collectors off, but I can't protect him from the stress.'

John North had said as much, advising her that if she had somewhere else to stay she should do so.

Edward nodded. His gaze flipped quickly to the sofa, which was relegated to the one corner of his office that wasn't lined with bookshelves, and then back again to her face. Maybe he really was reading her mind. The sofa would be admittedly more comfortable than the desk.

'And I'd be right?'

'Yes. You'd be right.'

The smile that made his eyes seem impossibly blue, the one that he had no trouble in sharing with Isaac, was all for her this time. 'Are we done, then?'

Not by any stretch of the imagination. 'I suppose so.'

'And your answer...?'

'Thank you. Isaac and I would like to stay.'

At least he had the grace to nod, as if the outcome of this particular skirmish hadn't been a foregone conclusion.

He stepped away from the door, hooking up his jacket and slinging his sports bag over his shoulder. 'Let's get out of here. What's for dinner?'

She'd tried to palm him off with peppered steak, but Edward had rather liked the idea of eating early and sharing pizza with Charlotte and Isaac. He liked the execution even better.

Isaac stood on a chair, a folded-down apron tied around him, dipping into bowls of sliced tomatoes and mushrooms to decorate his pizza. This was the kind of fun he hadn't had in a long time, and the feeling that the woman and child he so wanted to protect were here, safe with him...

Edward paused for a moment to consider whether *safe* and *with him* weren't in fact a contradiction of terms and then gave up the unequal struggle. For tonight it was more than enough to know that they were having fun, and that he was there to turn back anyone who came knocking on the door.

'So who's this meant to be, then?'

A grave face stared out at him from Isaac's pizza.

'It's...' Isaac had a showman's mastery of the expectant pause '...*you*!'

'Me?' Edward ignored the stifled giggle behind him. 'I don't look very happy.'

'That's your thinking face.'

'Ah. Well, I suppose that's all right, then.'

'What's yours?' Isaac peered across at Edward's pizza,

and would have toppled off the chair if Edward hadn't shot a hand out to steady him.

'It's…just a pattern.' He was beginning to learn that details could get him into trouble.

Isaac twisted his head from one side to the other. Edward wondered whether the complex symmetry was really so beyond him, and came to the conclusion that somewhere, on a chiefly instinctive level, he understood.

'It's different from Mum's.'

Charlotte had decorated her pizza with swirls and curlicues of tomato, mushrooms and olives.

'Well, your mum and I are different. We like different things.'

'Hmm…'

Isaac returned to his pizza, adding another mushroom to Edward's brow to indicate a stray lock of hair, leaving Edward to contemplate the essential differences between himself and Charlotte and thank his lucky stars that Isaac hadn't asked him to enumerate them.

The evening was warm, and while the pizzas baked in the oven Edward opened the French doors onto the patio, spreading a cloth on the table and unstacking the chairs. They ate together in the evening sunshine, and as the shadows lengthened Isaac was allowed to get down from the table. Edward fetched a ball for him to play football in the garden.

'Mind the flowers, sweetie.'

Charlotte was down on her knees, her arms around her son, talking quietly to him the way she did when she had anything serious to say.

'You can play there, on the lawn, but don't kick the ball too hard.'

It didn't matter. Isaac could have flattened every last one of the flowers in his garden and Edward wouldn't have cared. But Charlotte was his mother, and she wanted to teach him respect for the things around him, so Edward said nothing.

'How are you doing?' As the daylight failed the light in

her eyes seemed to fail as well. The effort of getting through today was beginning to tell on her.

She smiled at him. 'I'm fine, thank you.' Her gaze shot back towards Isaac as the ball veered close to the flowerbeds and he ran to pick it up. 'You've been such a star, Edward.'

Warmth suffused the whole of his body. Edward made a difference every day. The complex surgery he performed had the power to change people's lives, and it would be false modesty to claim that he didn't do it well. He wouldn't do it if he didn't believe that he excelled at it. But that was different. Somehow making just the slightest difference in Charlotte's life had the power to move him more than the considerable satisfaction he got from his job.

'I might see if Isaac wants a hand with the football in a moment.'

Her laugh was sweet and clear. Closer to the laugh that had filtered into his consciousness more than once at work, jolting him suddenly out of whatever he was doing.

'If he thinks he's got someone to play football with he won't give you a moment's peace. I don't want to keep you from anything else...'

The books would still be there tomorrow. So would the paper he was writing. This moment would be gone.

Edward stood, rolled up his shirtsleeves and prepared to take on the simple intricacies of the Beautiful Game.

She had put Isaac to bed and only returned downstairs for long enough to bid him goodnight. Edward knew why, and he hated it. She'd faced the day, but now she needed to fall apart—and she was determined to do that alone.

He spent a miserable hour trying to review the notes of a young surgeon he was mentoring, and then climbed the stairs. He could hear a quiet, muffled sound coming from Charlotte's room. She was crying.

Should he tap on her door?

No. Late in the evening, her bedroom, offering solace...

Things didn't get much more hazardous than that. He'd have to comfort her, take her into his arms, perhaps. Feel the softness of her body against his own taut, screaming frame. It wasn't a good idea. On the other hand just carrying on along the hallway and going to bed was impossible.

Edward sank to the floor at the top of the stairs. Waited. If he couldn't console her, the least he could do was watch over her—even if she'd never know he'd been there.

CHAPTER EIGHT

CHARLOTTE GREETED HIM the next morning with hot coffee, toast and a smile. Her capacity to smile never ceased to impress Edward, as did her ability to bounce back from whatever life threw at her.

'So it's the Lighthouse this morning.' She seemed to be looking forward to it.

'Yes. Sure you're up to it?'

She'd already had a hell of a week, and it was only Wednesday.

'Of course.' She settled into the front seat of his car. 'Why? Do you have any concerns?'

'No. I think it's a great idea for you to come and talk to Mercy before she's transferred over into the clinic's care. I wish I'd thought of it myself.'

He had, actually. He just hadn't been quite sure how to broach the subject. When Leo Hunter had suggested it, Edward's concerns that he might be seen to be favouring Charlotte above any of the other nurses had been put to rest.

'Lizzie didn't tell me much about Mercy. Just that she was very frightened about being in the hospital, and it took the nurses there a long time to calm her.'

'Yes, it did. That's why you'll be with her for all the procedures that we're going to do at the clinic. So that she's always got a familiar face to reassure her.'

She smiled. Mercy was going to love that smile.

'I'll do my best for her.'

Charlotte snapped into work mode as soon as they entered the doors of the hospital, following quietly behind him, listening carefully to everything that was said. Edward stopped at the nurses' station and caught the attention of a trainee nurse who seemed to have nothing to do.

'Will you get me Mercy's notes, please?'

The nurse jumped to attention, handing him the file. 'She had a good night last night. Woke up a few times, but she wasn't crying the way she did before.'

'Good. This is Charlotte King. She's going to be looking after Mercy when she comes to the Hunter Clinic.' He squinted at the nurse's name badge, because he couldn't for the life of him remember her name. 'Charlotte, this is Kendra.'

Charlotte ignored Kendra's dismissive look and stepped forward. 'Hi, Kendra. It's good to hear that Mercy's been so well looked after here.'

Kendra sniffed, obviously feeling that her role as a very junior nurse at one of the best children's hospitals in the country made her in some way superior to Charlotte. She had a lot to learn.

'You're a qualified nurse?'

'Yes, I'm an RN. Working towards being a Nurse Practitioner,' Charlotte replied quietly. She didn't seem to mind Kendra's attitude, however much it rankled with Edward.

'Charlotte!' A voice behind them made her turn. 'How good to see you—how are you?'

The senior nurse who greeted Charlotte obviously knew her well. Kendra realised her mistake and disappeared out of range as quickly as she could, followed by a small smirk of satisfaction from Edward.

'So how's Isaac?' Sandra Morton gave Edward a brief nod and then turned back to Charlotte.

'Oh, growing up. He's going to school now.'

'Really? Yes, I suppose he must be. He was such a cute baby. And how's Peter?'

A small pause.

Edward wasn't sure whether he should intervene or not, and decided that Charlotte was perfectly capable of handling the situation herself. Much better than he could, probably. He started to leaf through Mercy's notes.

'Actually, I haven't seen him for a while. He left.'

'No! But he was such a nice guy—' Sandra stopped herself. 'Obviously not.'

'It just didn't work out. But everything's good now.'

'Great. I hear you're working at the Hunter Clinic?'

'That's right. I'm here with Mr North to see one of your patients.'

'Ah, Mercy. Well, I'm glad to see that you'll be looking after her. The kid's had a bad time, and she deserves the best.'

Charlotte grinned. 'She'll get it. Just as she has here.'

Sandra nodded. There was clearly a great deal of mutual esteem between the two women and it warmed Edward to see Charlotte being treated with the respect she deserved.

'Well, I'd better get going. Call me some time—or I'll call you. Maybe we can go out one evening?'

'Yes. It's good to see you, Sandra.'

Charlotte turned back to Edward, and he flipped a page in the notes in front of him.

'You can stop pretending to read now…' She leaned towards him, whispering.

'What makes you say that?'

'Your eyes aren't moving.'

Fair enough. Edward hadn't thought that anyone would notice that he was staring at the same word on the page in front of him, listening to what the women were saying.

'I know what it says, anyway.' He snapped the notes shut.

'Can you fill me in on Mercy's history? Before we go to see her?'

'Yes, sure.' Edward looked at the sign above the door of the conference room and saw that it was empty. 'Let's go in here.'

He sat down, and Charlotte took a seat opposite him. He'd seen her at the clinic, and he knew that she was great at her job, but she always made it seem so natural. This change in context let him see just how professional she was.

'We don't know much about Mercy's background. She's thirteen years old, an orphan, and was clearly fending for herself for a while before being picked up by one of the charities working in the area. They've found a new adoptive family for her, back in Africa, and by all accounts she's very happy with them. She's been going to school and doing well.'

'Sounds good so far. Have they accompanied her to the UK?'

'No, she's staying with a foster family. I've spoken with the mother and she seems to be doing an excellent job. The problem is that Mercy doesn't want to talk about what happened to her before she was taken in by the charity.'

'So you've not been able to take a detailed medical history?'

'Yes and no. We know what's the matter with her, but I'd like to know what caused some of her problems as well. For instance, she has a perforated eardrum.'

'Hmm… Not usually a result of trauma. Although it sounds like a good probability in this case.'

Charlotte pressed her lips together in thought, and Edward ignored the little thrill of pleasure that seemed to accompany all his dealings with her.

'Your first objective is just to let her get to know you, though. See if you can reassure her so that she feels she's got a friend at the Hunter Clinic. Any information you can get is a bonus.'

'Okay. What else do I need to know?'

'She's here for surgery on a healed Buruli Ulcer.'

'That's a bacterial infection, isn't it?'

Edward nodded, pleased that Charlotte wasn't slow in asking for more information when she needed it. 'Yes, that's right. A Buruli Ulcer is relatively easy to treat when it's caught early, but if it's not—as was the case here—patients can develop large ulcers which result in disabilities and restricted joint movement as the scars heal. In Mercy's case there was a contracture which had multiple joint involvements—hand, wrist and elbow.'

He scrunched his own arm up to demonstrate the way that Mercy's arm and hand had been folded tightly in on themselves and Charlotte winced.

'Poor kid. It must have hurt like nothing I can imagine.'

'She's been through a lot. But the operation to straighten the limb, grafting in new material where necessary, was a success.'

'You did it?'

'Yes.'

That warmth again, as if her smile were caressing him. Pride because she cared that it had been Edward who had carried out the precise skin and muscle grafts which would restore some of the movement in Mercy's arm and hand.

'How much mobility will she recover?'

He shook his head. 'Difficult to say at this stage. But the prognosis is good, and if she keeps her physiotherapy up she should do well. That's another thing I want you to look at. She needs to be committed to this, and to understand how important it is for her to continue the things that she's being taught when she goes home.'

'Right. Okay, then. So I'm working on her heart, not her medical condition.'

'Primarily. Although she's going to need nurse-led care at the Hunter Clinic and you'll be providing that.'

If anyone could do it, Charlotte could.

When Edward ushered Charlotte into Mercy's room she wasn't quite sure what to expect. She found that Edward hadn't been quite honest with her.

The girl's face lit up when Edward smiled at her. 'Hello, Mercy. How are you today?'

'I am well, Dr Edward.'

'I'm pleased to hear that. I've brought someone to see you.'

Mercy's dark eyes never left Edward's face. If he reckoned that his quiet kindness hadn't got through to her, then he was fooling himself. Charlotte began to wonder what she was doing here. Edward had clearly underestimated his own capacity to reassure the girl.

There was tenderness in his eyes as he spoke again. 'Nurse Charlotte is going to look after you when you come to see me at the clinic. She's come to meet you.'

Mercy gave Charlotte a small nod.

'I'll…um…leave you, then.' Edward seemed suddenly at a loss as to what to do next.

'No. Please stay. Just for a few minutes.'

Charlotte didn't share Edward's conviction that she could gain Mercy's confidence instantly, through some magical process that he knew nothing about.

She pulled up a chair and sat down next to Mercy's bed. 'It's nice to meet you, Mercy. I hope that I can be your friend.'

Mercy nodded again, clearly deciding to adopt a wait-and-see policy. Charlotte was going to have to prove herself, but that was okay.

'I've brought you some pictures of my family.' She had photographs in her bag—of herself with Isaac when he was a baby, together with some more recent ones, and some precious images of her parents. 'Would you like to see them?'

'Yes.'

That was a start. Charlotte began with the picture of Isaac. 'This is my son. His name is Isaac, and he was born on a Saturday.'

Mercy studied the picture carefully. 'Then in my country he would be called Kwame.'

Edward's curiosity got the better of him and he leaned forward. 'For Saturday?'

'Yes.'

'I was born on a Friday.'

Mercy smiled. 'Nurse Efie.'

Charlotte grinned. 'That's a lovely name. Thank you for telling me. What's yours?'

'Abena. My English name is Mercy.'

'You have a lovely smile, Mercy Abena.'

Charlotte had been alone with Mercy for almost an hour when Edward's phone beeped. He checked the text which had just arrived and made for Mercy's room. Charlotte was waiting for him outside the door.

'Thanks for coming so quickly.' She looked nervous, moving her weight slightly from one foot to the other.

'You said "asap".'

Charlotte wasn't one of those people who peppered all of her communications with either 'asap' or 'urgent'. When she said it, she meant it.

'I've noticed something…about Mercy.' She seemed almost reticent to tell him.

'Right. What have you seen?'

'It may be nothing…'

'What have you seen, Charlotte?'

She took a breath and seemed to loosen up slightly. 'We were talking together, getting on fine, and then all of a sudden she seemed to zone out. It only lasted for a little over ten seconds.'

He nodded, turning the various possibilities over in his mind. 'The nurses have said that she seems very withdrawn sometimes. Do you think it could just be her mental state?'

'Maybe.' She clasped her hands together—a small, nervous gesture. 'It doesn't feel like that to me.'

'Okay. What *does* it feel like?' This wasn't his normal method of diagnosis, but he was willing to give Charlotte the space to prove him wrong.

'I think she may be having Absence Seizures.'

'Epilepsy?'

Charlotte nodded. 'Her eyes rolled back, very briefly, and her eyelids fluttered a little. I leant forward and put my hand on her arm and she didn't react. Afterwards she didn't seem to have any recollection of what had happened.'

'That was quick thinking. Well done.' Most people would have attributed a short period of absence to being the day-dream of a teenager, far from home and trying to block out what was happening around her.

'I could be wrong. I looked on her notes and no one else has reported anything like this.'

Edward shrugged. 'Which just means you're a bit more observant than the rest of us.'

It wasn't only that. Charlotte had a habit of looking at people when she talked to them, giving them her full atten-tion. Until he'd met her he hadn't realised just how few peo-ple really did that.

She flushed pink with pleasure. 'So you'll take a look at her? Ask her about it?'

'Nope.' He turned towards Mercy's door, twisting the han-dle. 'You're going to do that. I'll watch and learn.'

She was cheerful and relaxed with Mercy, as if nothing had happened, sitting down by her bed and motioning Ed-ward to do the same. Charlotte worked her way round to the subject of the seizure quickly, but deftly, as if it was just an-other routine set of questions which had to be asked.

'When we were talking together just now you seemed to lose me for a moment. Dr Edward and I would like to ask you about that, if it's all right with you?'

'There is…nothing.' The sudden look of hostility in Mercy's eyes spoke far louder than her words.

'I'm sure there isn't. But can we ask, all the same?'

Charlotte leaned towards Mercy, a look of gentle encour-agement on her face, and Mercy shrugged.

'Okay, then. Well, you seemed not to hear or see me for a little while. Has that happened to you before?'

Mercy's gaze flipped sullenly from Charlotte to Edward, then back again.

'It doesn't make you a bad person, Mercy. A little boy in my son's class at school has the same thing.'

'He does?'

'Mmm-hmm. The doctors can stop it, though. Dr Edward could stop it.'

'Can you?' Mercy's gaze fixed on Edward.

'Yes.' He wondered whether he should say more and decided not to. Charlotte would fill in any of the details that she thought were necessary.

'We'll have to do some tests.'

Apparently a quick wrinkle of the nose was enough to help describe a blood test to rule anything else out, and an EEG which would pick up any unusual electrical activity in Mercy's brain.

'They're okay. They don't hurt.'

'And you can cure it?'

'Of course. If it's what we think it might be, then it might well just stop all of its own accord when you get a bit older. In the meantime we can stop it.' Charlotte reached forward, taking Mercy's hand. 'But Dr Edward needs to know all about this first, so he can do the right thing.'

Mercy hesitated. 'Some people say that this is a bad spirit…'

'No. It's nothing like that, Mercy. Trust me. Sometimes we just…skip a beat for a few moments.' Mercy looked unconvinced, and Charlotte tried again. 'Dr Edward told you that he could make your arm better, didn't he?'

'Yes.'

'And he did, right?' She waited for Mercy's nod. 'Then ask *him* if this has anything to do with bad spirits.'

Mercy seemed disinclined to ask a second time, but Edward answered anyway. 'It's nothing to do with anything like that, I promise you. It's an illness, and we can make you well with medicine.'

Mercy nodded. 'I do skip a beat sometimes.'

'How often? How many times every day?' Edward leaned forward.

'Three or four. Sometimes more.'

Charlotte nodded, as if that was just the right number of times to 'skip a beat' every day. 'And how long has this been happening?'

Mercy shrugged. 'Always.'

'Mmm…' Charlotte seemed to approve of that, too, although Edward couldn't see its significance. 'So is it all right if we do the tests, then? Like I said, they won't hurt.'

'Yes, Nurse Efie.'

A quick nod of her head and she turned to Edward. 'Blood test?'

'It's what I'd do.' He couldn't resist teasing her, just a little. 'Want me to go and fetch a kit for you?'

She rolled her eyes at him to conceal her smile. 'No. I'll go.'

'Nurse Efie, eh?' Edward leaned against the railings of the hospital's roof garden, the breeze rearranging his hair into the maverick version of his usual clean-cut style. 'So come on, then. What's mine?'

'I didn't ask. You can find out for yourself. Mercy will tell you.' Charlotte took a sip of her coffee. 'She really likes you. Says that you're kind.'

'Does she?' The idea seemed to surprise him.

'So what's wrong with being kind?' She grinned up at him.

'Nothing. I try to be kind. I'm not as good with people as you are, though.'

'I think you underestimate yourself. Didn't you see her face when you walked into her room this morning?'

Either Edward didn't have an answer to that, or he wasn't sharing. 'So what made you cotton on to the name thing?'

'The mother of one of my patients told me, years ago. Apparently it's quite important which day you were born on in some parts of Africa. I just gave her the information about when Isaac was born to see if she'd pick up on it.'

Edward nodded. 'I'll have to find out a bit more about that...'

'Poor old Archie. He's not going to have his name changed, is he?'

'I don't think so. It would probably confuse him. Cats are all instinct and not much brain.' He took another sip of coffee. 'So I've put a call in to the Head of Neurology. Is there anything else I should know? I'm wondering whether there's any connection between the seizures that Mercy's been having and the burst eardrum?'

'I don't think so. We mainly just talked, but Mercy said that after her parents died she lived with an uncle. I think that was when she was beaten, because she said that her aunt made her deaf.'

Edward shook his head, staring at his coffee. 'Someone would have had to hit her pretty hard.'

'Yes. But she was having the seizures before then. So hopefully the two things are unconnected and the seizures aren't a result of brain damage.'

She looked up at Edward and he blinked quickly. Took a swig of his coffee, and then wiped his eye.

'Something in your eye?'

'No. Yes, probably.' Whatever it was it seemed to be a source of embarrassment.

'Want me to take a look?'

'I think I'll manage.' He took another mouthful of coffee. 'These kids... We have to do something...'

Charlotte laid her hand on his arm. Tried not to think about the way the hard muscle flexed at her touch and to convince herself that this was simple reassurance. 'You *are* doing something. You've given her back the use of her arm. She knows that, and she says that she's going to exercise every day.'

'It's not enough.'

'It's what we can do.'

If the other nurses at the clinic could see them now. Edward, impassioned and almost weeping over a patient. Charlotte, resorting to reason and logic. It was so unexpected as to be almost bizarre.

'I know.' He drained his cup and dropped it into hers, scrunching the two together to make a ball, which he lobbed into the nearest recycling bin. 'I want you there when Mercy has the EEG, to reassure her that no bad spirits are out to get her. I'll clear it with Leo.'

'Thanks. And thanks for listening.'

'You were right. You've done a really good job here today.'

His praise meant a lot. More than a lot. Everyone at the clinic knew that Edward's praise had to be earned. Charlotte felt her cheeks flush with pleasure. 'Thanks. I'd like to just pop in and say goodbye to her before we go. Tell her that I'll be back soon.'

He grinned. 'Do that. Then I'd better be getting you back to the clinic, or Lizzie will have my hide for kidnapping you.'

CHAPTER NINE

IT WAS CLEAR when Leo Hunter telephoned to check whether Edward had anything he'd like to raise at this afternoon's review meeting that he was not expecting him to attend. Leo knew him well enough to understand that Edward's pledge to support the new charity arm of the Hunter Clinic was on the level of research, operating procedures and maintaining clinical excellence. It didn't involve attending meetings which didn't deal with those goals.

The usual procedure was that Leo informed him that a meeting was taking place, more as a gesture of courtesy than anything else, and Edward tendered his apologies and read the minutes when they were circulated. That had always worked perfectly.

'You mean you're considering some research?' Leo's voice sounded perplexed.

'No, not really. Well, maybe if something presents itself. I'm just interested in how we can help these kids outside of simply giving them the medical treatment they need.'

There was a pause and Edward shook the handset of his phone, wondering if the line had suddenly gone dead, before realising that Leo was just taking his time in getting his head around the proposition. Edward's forte had always been in the operating theatre, making clinical decisions and implementing them. That was his skillset. He usually left community issues to someone else.

'I'll see you later, then.' Leo still sounded a bit suspicious. *'We've had to move the time from four o'clock to six, in order to fit in with the operating schedules.'*

Edward's heart sank. Six o'clock. He'd been to his share of these meetings, and they were renowned for going on until late into the night. Usually he'd be the last to object, but tonight… Actually, he wasn't doing anything tonight. But he'd been rather looking forward to doing nothing with Charlotte and Isaac.

All the same, he'd just asked for this and it seemed grudging to turn it down now. 'I'm free at six. I'll see you then.'

Edward got home at ten o' clock. Isaac was already in bed, and he hadn't expected to have a meal waiting for him, but within moments of him depositing the armful of papers that he'd brought home onto the hall table Charlotte was calling him into the kitchen

'Is that enough?' She surveyed the full plate, with three different kinds of salad and a large slice of home-made quiche.

'Are you mad? You obviously don't have any idea what I usually manage to feed myself when I get home late.'

His diet was relatively balanced, and usually healthy, but when Edward was busy cooking didn't figure much in the equation.

She dismissed his customary eating habits with a small sniff and walked over to the fridge. 'Would you like some juice? Or there's some of that sparkling fruit cordial left over.'

'I'll have a glass of wine, if you'll join me.' Edward put his knife and fork down and got to his feet.

'Stay there. I'll get it.' She walked to the wine cooler and opened the glass door, her hand hovering over the rows of bottles.

'That one…' Edward indicated a light, fruity white, and nodded when she pulled it out, holding it up so he could see the label.

He was beginning to see what his father saw in marriage. Not the meal on the table, or the fact that the lights were on in the house, but just that there was someone *there*. Someone to share the little things with—eating and drinking. Someone to talk to. Somehow the fact that Isaac was asleep upstairs and Charlotte was relaxing here downstairs gave Edward an immense feeling of well-being.

'I've got some treacle tart for afters.' She took a dish out of the fridge and put it into the oven to warm, then carried the bottle over to the table.

'Mmm. I love treacle tart. I haven't had it in years. And this quiche is really good, thank you.'

Edward opened the wine, and poured a glass for her. She took a sip and smiled.

'This is nice.'

The bottle probably cost more than the whole of the rest of the meal, but Edward wasn't about to tell her that. You couldn't buy what made the food so special and the wine so incidental. It was all about the cooking and the care that had gone into the preparation. About the knife and fork set precisely on the table, with a napkin and a glass. The flowers from the garden—just a couple of blooms—in a jug that usually lived under the sink.

'I've been stuck in a meeting for hours. It's good to get home.'

She raised one eyebrow. 'Which meeting was that?'

'Oh, one of Leo's. Reviewing the progress of the charity arm of the clinic.' Edward wondered whether she'd pick up on the unlikeliness of the whole thing.

'Really?'

If she had, it looked as if she'd decided not to ask.

'Yes. Leo seemed really pleased. There's a lot of progress being made.'

She nodded. 'So Leo and Ethan are getting on a little better?' It was an open secret that while the brothers remained professional in their dealings with the staff, they had what was euphemistically termed 'issues' with each other.

'Looks like it. Leo was praising Ethan's work, and Ethan looked genuinely pleased. A little bit surprised, as well.'

'I imagine Ethan felt he had to prove himself when he came back.' Charlotte was staring speculatively at her wine glass.

'I don't see why. Ethan's a superb surgeon.'

'Oh, Edward!' She narrowed her eyes at him. 'It's not all about how good you are at something. Ethan could be the best surgeon in the world, but he's still recovering from his injuries. He had to feel that there was an element of pity involved when Leo brought him back into the practice.'

'Yeah, I suppose anyone would. I think Ethan's realised that was never the case, though, and that Leo wanted him back for his medical skills. He was talking about the work that Leo had put into regaining the Hunter Clinic's reputation as well.'

'Really? That's good. Sounds as if they've got a bit more respect for each other now. So how's everything else going?'

'There are a lot of possibilities for expanding the charity side of the operation. Community issues to be taken into consideration—' He broke off as Charlotte hid a smile behind her hand. 'What?'

'*You've* been engaging in chit-chat about community issues, have you?'

He didn't blame her for her amused disbelief—he'd been both disbelieving and slightly amused himself. 'Well, someone's got to think about it.'

'And that's you, all of a sudden?' She couldn't disguise the warmth in her eyes.

'Maybe. We'll see. Anyway, I have some really interesting opportunities in the pipeline, both at the clinic and at the Lighthouse Hospital. And there's an opportunity for me to join one of the teams visiting Africa for a few weeks. I'd like to hear what you think.'

He paused, aware that he didn't usually do this either. Edward made his own decisions about the way his career was going to go, without any reference to anyone else. But suddenly he not only wanted to tell Charlotte, he wanted to hear what she had to say.

'That sounds fantastic. I want to hear everything.'

She pointed at the food in front of him, which had all but completely slipped his mind in his enthusiasm.

'Finish your meal first, though…'

'Yeah. Then I'll tell you all about it.'

They talked for an hour, and then Charlotte's rapt attention was overtaken by fatigue. Edward turned to a book, and when he lifted his eyes after only a page she was asleep. He lifted her feet gently up onto the sofa, put a cushion beneath her head, and went back to his reading.

Calmed by the low sound of her breathing, he let the words on the page fly through his mind, forming pictures and patterns as they went. It was as if her very presence made him more receptive—somehow more creative. The raw excitement of new thoughts, new challenges, reared up and dragged him headlong into the heady world of new possibilities that he so loved.

A sound penetrated his consciousness. Something outside in the hallway. The kind of thing that he would normally never heed, but which now somehow managed to jar all his instincts and set his nerves onto red alert.

He rose quietly and went to investigate.

'Hey, buddy. What's the matter?'

Isaac was at the front door, clutching Stinky with one hand and trying to pull the door open with the other. He ignored Edward, redoubling his efforts.

He should probably go and wake Charlotte. But she was

sleeping so soundly, so peacefully. He could at least give this a go before he did so. Walking over to Isaac, he went down on one knee beside him.

'You want to go out?'

Isaac shook his head, giving the door one last tug.

'Ah, I see. You're just checking that we're locked up safely for the night. That no one can get in.'

Isaac nodded, staring at the floor as if he was being hauled up in front of the headmaster in disgrace.

'Right, then. That's a good idea. Let's do it together.' Edward imagined that Isaac probably wanted Charlotte to accompany him, and when the boy curled his arms around his neck he almost jumped back in surprise.

'Okay.'

'Well, let's fetch your dressing gown, then, so you don't get cold. And we can have a story afterwards if you'd like.'

Isaac nodded, and Edward hoisted him up in his arms. Lifting that small weight made him feel stronger than normal. As if he was some kind of superhero who could make things right and conquer all manner of monsters—even the ones in Isaac's head.

Surgeon and Dragon-Slayer General. Edward quite liked the sound of that. And if one involved precision instruments, the other involved a large sword which could be brandished flamboyantly when the opportunity arose. There was even a fair maiden, who was currently fast asleep on the sofa, and an apprentice who was also asleep, worn out by a brief but thorough inspection of the locks on all the doors and windows and the first few pages of his favourite bedtime story.

The last half-hour hadn't involved scaling any high walls, or actually rescuing anyone, but that was okay. Another time, perhaps, when the fair maiden wasn't in such immediate need of her beauty sleep.

Isaac stirred against him, snuggling up tight.

'Let's get you back to bed, little man.' Edward whispered

the words so as not to disturb the sleeping child, and rose, carrying the boy up to his bed.

And then, before he had the chance to think about any such thing with Charlotte, he gently shook her awake, turning back to his book as soon as she had bidden him a sleepy goodnight.

CHAPTER TEN

IT HAD BEEN one hell of a tough week. The meeting with Edward's father, when the past had reached out, snatching her back into the nightmare that she thought she'd survived. Being afraid all the time, and trying not to show it to anyone.

One glass of wine with Edward on Friday, after Isaac had gone to bed, and she had fallen asleep on the sofa, waking with a start when she felt his hand on her shoulder, gently shaking her.

Today she woke to silence. A slow, sleepy climb into wakefulness, cocooned in comfortable forgetfulness. Something was missing, and she groped around in her mind for what it might be. No alarm. No… She sat up straight, propelled by panic. No Isaac, bouncing on her bed, telling her to wake up and get on with the day.

Hitting the floor at a run, Charlotte sped into his bedroom. The curtains were drawn back, the room was bathed in sunshine, and the bed was neatly made. Then she heard a noise from downstairs: Isaac's laughter, threaded through with Edward's quiet, rich chuckle.

Stupid. There was nothing wrong, no need to be this jumpy. All the same, she crept downstairs, just to check on them.

They were so involved with what they were doing that they didn't see her. Isaac was sitting on the edge of the sofa, next to Edward, with the coffee table pulled up in front of him so he could reach the keyboard of Edward's laptop. Edward, leaning back on the sofa, was concentrating hard on the screen.

'Way to go, partner!' Edward's face lit up and Isaac threw his arms up above his head, bouncing up and down on the cushions. Edward leaned forward, hitting a key. 'Do you want to try the next one?'

'That's all my teacher told me to do...' Isaac turned to him.

'Well, we don't need to do exactly what she says.' Edward shot him a look that mirrored the mischief on Isaac's face. 'You don't have to stop unless you want to. You're pretty good at this.'

'Okay...' Isaac giggled '...partner.'

Edward chuckled and pressed another key. It looked as if the two of them were fine without her for a while, and Charlotte could take her time in the shower.

When she got back downstairs, showered, dressed and feeling better than she had for weeks after a good night's sleep, she smelled coffee. The patio doors were open, and Isaac's voice drifted in from the garden.

'Is that a fresh pot of coffee I smell...?' She followed the aroma into the kitchen and found Edward there.

'Yep. Want some toast?'

'You are a wonderful man.'

He looked over his shoulder, shooting her a rakish half-smile. 'If I'd known that it just took a pot of coffee and some toast...'

'And a good night's sleep. Where's my alarm clock?'

He nodded at the clock, sitting innocently on the kitchen table. 'I happened to wake up early. I heard Isaac rambling around, and I sent him into your room to get it. I reckoned you could do with a bit of a lie-in.'

'Oh, so you've been enlisting my son in your machinations, have you?'

'Yep. He seemed to think it was a good idea, too. And I reckoned that if you did wake up, then you'd probably be a little happier to find Isaac creeping into your room.'

A good deal more relaxed, maybe. Happier…? That would depend on what Edward was there for. Charlotte dismissed the thought, and with it her fantasies of waking up to find Edward there.

'Has he had breakfast?'

'Yep. I told him that I'd be in trouble with you if we didn't keep to the straight and narrow, and he took me through the procedure step by step. Cleaned his teeth, had a wash, showed me where his clean clothes were. Do you *always* let him have chocolate biscuits for breakfast?'

'No!' Charlotte supposed it couldn't hurt just for today.

Edward chuckled. 'Gotcha. We had toast with peanut butter, and banana smoothies. Then we did some number games on the internet.'

So that's what they'd been up to. 'Isaac's homework?'

'Yes. He showed me the sheet that his teacher had given him. I found a game on the internet that made it a little bit more fun.'

'Thanks.' That feeling of dread she had when Edward did anything either for her or Isaac had almost completely disappeared now. Maybe because Edward so clearly enjoyed playing with Isaac.

'No trouble.' He buttered the toast and set it down in front of her, adding a jar of marmalade and one of apricot jam. Then coffee, hot and aromatic, with a dash of milk. Just one cup.

'I've got to go out…'

He was searching for his car keys and Charlotte pointed to the hook under the kitchen cabinet, where they were supposed to be.

'Right. Thanks. I'll be back shortly.'

'Shortly' could mean practically anything with Edward, and generally did. Charlotte opened her mouth to ask whether he'd be home for lunch, but he was already gone.

He returned an hour later, and appeared in the doorway between the hall and the living room carrying a long, thin parcel. He dumped it on the coffee table and sat down next to Charlotte on the sofa with an air of anticipation.

'What's that you're reading?' He craned over her shoulder, and Charlotte hugged the library book to her chest.

'Nothing… What's that you've got there?'

'Hmm…nothing.'

Another moment of quiet, and Charlotte returned to her book.

'Looks interesting. I haven't been there for ages.'

He was reading over her shoulder again, and Charlotte snapped the book shut.

'It's the summer holidays soon, and I thought I'd take Isaac out on a few daytrips. This book's got some really great ideas.' It seemed that—for the moment anyway—the plan that they should just get on with their lives without disturbing each other too much had gone by the board.

He grinned. 'The Natural History Museum's great for kids.'

'And for adults.' Charlotte had been looking for places which would interest her and Isaac—something that they could share—as well as a few fun places where he could work off his energy.

'And the Science Museum's just down the road, of course. There are some wonderful things there.'

'Yes.' He was going to be volunteering to come along any minute now, and the thought of Edward and Isaac together in the Science Museum sounded far too much like hard work. 'So what's in the parcel, then?'

'Ah! Thought you'd never ask.'

'So did I. Looks as if you've worn me down.' She grinned at him and he was suddenly seized with motion, grasping the parcel and tearing the wrappings from it.

'What do you think?'

'It's a…' Isaac had run in from the garden and nosed his way in between them. 'What is it?'

'Here—see?' Edward pointed to the picture on the label. 'It's a kite.'

It wasn't just any old kite, but then Charlotte doubted that Edward would be much interested in anything that didn't have a complex structure of cords and an unlikely shape. He began to unwrap the collection of disassembled struts and sails, fishing out a small booklet.

Isaac watched open-mouthed and confused, looking to his mother for an explanation. 'Edward has to put all of those pieces together, sweetie, before it'll fly.'

'Yeah, shouldn't take long.' Edward was already laying the pieces out on the coffee table. 'Then we can go and fly it, eh, buddy?'

Charlotte left them to it and went to make drinks for them both. When she returned, Edward had already snapped into the fearsome concentration with which he approached almost any task, leaving Isaac shifting restlessly from one foot to the other. Charlotte placed his coffee on the table and he nodded absently.

'Thanks… Don't touch those, Isaac, I've put them all out in order.'

Isaac's hand shot away from the metal strut as if it had suddenly become red hot, and he hid it behind his back.

'Come here, sweetie.' Charlotte motioned her son towards her and put her arms around him. 'We'll just watch, shall we?'

Isaac nodded, obviously wishing that he could be a part of the construction project, craning to see what was happening. Edward seemed almost oblivious to the two of them, quickly selecting the pieces he wanted and deftly fitting them together.

They watched in silence. 'Look, sweetie, it's almost ready…' The structure was recognisable as a kite now, and Edward was attaching twine to the steering loops at each side.

Isaac nodded. But as Edward had worked she'd felt the excitement ebb out of her son's body, and now he was leaning against her legs with an air of boredom, his eyes on the television.

'Is it time for my programme, Mum?'

'Which programme, Isaac?'

'You know. *Eddie and the Magic Fish.*'

'Don't you want to wait until the kite's finished?'

'I want to see my programme.'

She saw the hurt in Edward's eyes. 'Okay. Come upstairs. You can see it there.'

There was a television in the guest bedroom, and perhaps it was best to let Isaac watch TV while Edward finished the kite. When they got to the point of flying it—and she was sure that Edward wouldn't be able to wait to try out the magnificent creation—Isaac's interest would be rekindled and everyone would be happy.

She left Isaac sprawled on her bed, clutching Stinky, captivated for the moment by the adventures of the Magic Fish. When she went back downstairs, the sitting room was empty. Charlotte could see Edward in the garden, ranging restlessly along the far end of the lawn, kicking at the inconsistencies in the smooth line between grass and flowerbeds.

Perhaps he needed to be left alone for a while, with his thoughts. He'd work it out; the mathematics weren't all that difficult. Isaac was five, and there were times when Edward's focussed ardour for the task in hand simply left him behind.

But there were elements to this equation that intellect, even one as all-consuming as Edward's, couldn't grasp. Twisting her mouth, and in defiance of all that was logical, Charlotte slipped through the open French windows and walked across the grass towards him.

He was lost in his thoughts, seeming not to notice her. 'Given up, then?' She might as well start with a challenge, if that was the way she meant to go on.

'The kite's finished.'

'Yes, I saw that.'

He turned to her, giving her a speculative look, as if he

was trying to weigh the situation up. 'He didn't like the kite. That's okay. Isaac's free to have his own likes and dislikes...'

'Edward, did you ever go to school?'

He blinked at her, struggling to make the connection. 'As it happens, no. By the time I was five I'd already got a handle on calculus and my parents had me tutored at home.'

There was a note of sadness in his voice.

'That must have been lonely.'

He shrugged. 'I don't have anything to compare it with.'

'When everything's fine, you don't need anything to compare it with.'

There was something dull in his eyes as he focussed on her. 'You're saying I don't play well with others.' One hand clenched into a fist. 'That's not exactly an original thought.'

He just wasn't listening to her. It was as if it had been drilled into Edward that being clever meant that you didn't have a heart. 'Maybe it's just a self-fulfilling prophecy. If you believe it's true, then ultimately it is.'

He glared at her. 'And you have a better idea?'

He turned, as if the conversation was now at an end. He was used to having the last word. Used to being right.

'Don't be so arrogant...' Even before he turned back she knew that she'd missed the mark by about a mile. Edward might look and sound arrogant, but somewhere beneath that there was a lonely child.

'I am what I am, Charlotte. If you want to think that's arrogant, then go right ahead.'

All of his defences were up now. The aloof, unsmiling man, whom no one seemed to be able to get close to, was turning away from her again.

She did the unthinkable. Marched straight up to him and grabbed his arm, pulling him around to face her. 'You don't fool me, Edward. I've seen you with Isaac. I saw you with Mercy the other day.'

Something behind his eyes ignited. Dark blue ice turning to sparkling heat. There was more than enough emotion here. It was just a matter of whether she could deal with it. Whether *Edward* could deal with it, without ducking back into the comfort of his books.

'Mercy opened up to you, not me.'

'Edward! Sometimes I want to shake some sense into you…!'

The provocative twitch of his lips told her that she could go right ahead, if that was her inclination, and she resisted the urge.

'What on earth happened to you when you were a child?'

'You think I was a poor little bright boy, with his nose in a book and no friends? It wasn't like that.' He pursed his lips. 'Not quite like that, anyway.'

'What *was* it like, then?'

'I was different. By the time I was ten I could keep up with a university undergraduate on an intellectual level. On a social level, I wasn't quite ready for women, all-night parties and beer-drinking contests. It was difficult to find my own space.'

'You felt out of step, you mean? Your emotions and theirs?'

He looked at her gravely. Then suddenly he smiled. 'Most people assume I don't have any emotions.'

His look taunted her. Dared her to tell him different.

'That's not true, though, is it?' She dared him back.

'I don't think so.'

The dare turned dangerous all of a sudden. He was waiting for her to kiss him. Charlotte baulked at that one.

'Look, Edward, I know that you're used to being better and faster at everything than everyone else, and that it's a lot easier to do things by yourself. But if you want Isaac to be interested in what you're doing then you have to slow down a bit and do things at his pace.'

He hesitated. 'I'm…not very good at that. As you can see.'

'No one's born good at things like that—you have to learn. You're supposed to be a genius. Can't you learn? Or don't you want to learn?'

'I want to.' The admission was a little stiff, and left Edward nonplussed for a moment. 'Why don't you go and tell Isaac…?'

She glared at him and he grinned.

'Why don't I go and tell him myself?'

'Good idea.'

'Right.' He clapped his hands together, as if he was about to embark on one of the most complex experiments of his life. 'Do you think he'd like his own kite? One that's more his size, perhaps?'

Charlotte almost told him no, that Isaac didn't need a kite. But she knew he'd want one, and Edward needed this.

'I think he'd love that. Go and ask him.'

Edward didn't deal in half-measures. The shop he took them to sold nothing but kites, and on a bright late summer's morning, was full of people. He led Isaac straight to a selection of different coloured children's kites, and the two of them became immediately absorbed in sorting through them. Charlotte decided to leave them to it.

'I'm just going to pop to the chemist, to buy some soap. I won't be long. Stay here with Edward, won't you, Isaac?' She nudged his shoulder with her hand.

Isaac ignored her in favour of the kites, and Edward looked up at her. He seemed to know how hard it always was for her to leave Isaac, even for a few minutes, and he took hold of the boy's hand as a gesture of intent.

'I won't let him out of my sight. Go and do your shopping.'

She decided to take her time, to give Edward and Isaac a chance to buy the kite by themselves. There were some nice apples on display outside the greengrocer's and she stopped to buy three, to go with the packed lunch in the boot of the car.

In the chemist's she ran her finger along the lines of jars and bottles which were beyond her purchasing power, now.

Her old soap, the one she'd used to buy before she'd begun to make all her decisions on the basis of price, was there.

Something from her old life, when she hadn't needed to question every word, every action, every penny that she spent. She so wanted that back.

Charlotte picked it up, hesitated, put it back on the shelf, then picked it up again.

It wouldn't matter if she had something that she wanted for once. The soap smelled nice and felt creamy on her skin, and it wasn't so very much more expensive than the more economical brands. As luxuries went, this wasn't so very ostentatious.

'Come on, Mum…' Isaac broke into the debate, tugging at her arm.

She looked round to see Edward, with a firm hold on Isaac's other hand to prevent any possible escape.

'Okay, just a minute. Did you get your kite?' It was clear that he had, Edward was holding a large plastic bag.

'Yes, do you want to see?'

'Mmm. Yes, please.'

Isaac grinned up at Edward, who delivered the bag into his grasp. Inside was a small blue kite with a blue and silver tail.

'Oh, that's so pretty!' She drew the kite out to examine its tail. 'Those sparkly bits are going to shine in the sun when you fly it.'

Isaac nodded, carefully showing her everything. There was a ball of twine, mounted on a reel, to protect Isaac's hands from any friction. 'You tie it on there—see?' Isaac indicated the reinforced eyelets on the kite. 'With a special knot.'

Charlotte nodded, impressed. 'A special knot, eh?'

'Yes. Edward's going to show me how,' Isaac responded proudly.

Her little boy was growing up. It was almost a surprise to find that she didn't mind that Isaac wanted Edward to help him tie the knots on his precious kite, when it felt only a blink of time since her son had looked to her for everything.

'That's great. Make sure you watch what he does carefully.'

'Can we go, Mum?' Isaac was impatient again, jigging up and down on the spot.

'Yes, let me get my soap and we'll be off.' Charlotte looked up to see Edward, in a world of his own, working his way along the shelf and inspecting the ingredients lists printed on all the soap wrappers. 'Edward?'

He jolted back into the here and now. 'Ah. Yes.' He focussed on the soap in her hand and took a matching bar from the shelf. 'That one smells nice.'

She didn't really need it. The thought that Edward liked the smell of it made her want it, though. 'They're all much the same. I'll get this one.' She put the bar back onto the shelf and reached for the cheaper brand.

'I imagine they're all pretty easy to make...' He still had one foot in that world of possibilities that seemed to know no bounds. He inspected the bar in his hand. 'Pretty standard ingredients.'

'*You* might be able to make it. *I'd* probably blow the kitchen up. It's just soap, Edward.' Nothing was just anything to Edward. Everything fascinated him, from pizza-making to nuclear physics. When she was with him the world seemed bigger, far more interesting.

'Hmm. You like this one, though?' He still had the bar that he'd taken from the shelf in his hand.

'This will do. It's cheaper.'

Before she could reach into her bag for her purse Edward had given her preferred choice to Isaac, along with a note from his pocket. 'You want to get it for your mum?'

She met his gaze. This wasn't anything to do with kites, or soap. It was about whether she had the right to a treat, however small. Whether Edward had the right to give it to her, to claim a place in their little family.

'Okay. Thank you.'

He nodded, grinning.

'At last!' Isaac conferred his displeasure on both of them and ran to the counter.

Charlotte watched as the woman at the cash desk smiled down at Isaac, took his money and put the soap into a bag, counting his change into his hand.

'Hey! Hey, give Edward his change back.' Isaac had pocketed the coins.

'That's okay.' Edward winked at her. 'He might be needing it later for ice-cream.'

Isaac looked from Charlotte to Edward, then back again, waiting to obtain a final decision. 'All right, then. Here—let me zip your pocket up, so you don't lose it.'

She bent and fastened Isaac's pocket, then gave way to the pressure from both Edward and Isaac and hurried with them to the car. The afternoon was bright and blustery, just right for kite-flying, and the three of them seemed in complete accord. No one wanted to miss a moment of it.

CHAPTER ELEVEN

THEY DROVE FOR an hour, right out of London, making a bee-line for high ground. The last five hundred yards had to be walked—or rather climbed—until finally they reached the exact location that Edward wanted.

'It's windy enough here.' The words were almost dragged away on the breeze as soon as they left her mouth.

'Yes. I think this will do.' Edward looked around with an air of satisfaction. 'Which kite shall we try first?'

'The big one!' Isaac was jumping up and down with excitement. 'I want to see the big one…'

'Okay.' Edward grinned, laying the large kite onto the ground, clipping together the last pieces of the framework so that it was ready to fly. 'You see, I think that the wind will catch it here…' he indicated the breadth of the kite '…and funnel through this way…' A sweep of the hand to show the anticipated wind direction. 'That should give it extra lift, and the weight of the tail makes it steadier.' He grinned. 'That's the theory, anyway.'

'Will it work?' Isaac stamped his foot impatiently.

'That's what we're here to find out. It's all very well to have a theory, but you always have to test it out… Here, you hang on there.'

Edward gave the kite to Isaac and winked at Charlotte, walking away from them as he unravelled the twin reels of lightweight cord.

He paced out the distance and called back to Isaac, 'Okay, hold it up…'

Charlotte kept a discreet hold on the top of the kite, in case Isaac decided to let go of it before he was supposed to.

'Now, on my count… One…two…three…let her go!'

The kite rose in a straight line, up into the clear blue sky. Isaac shouted at the top of his voice in excitement, and suddenly the only thing to do was to shout with him.

'Nooooo!' The kite dipped erratically and Isaac screamed in horror.

Edward fought for control for long moments and then the kite soared upwards again. Charlotte cheered, and Isaac followed suit, running towards Edward.

'That didn't quite work…' Edward was grinning at her. 'Perhaps I'll just concentrate on keeping it up there at this stage.'

'I want to hold it… Pleeeease…' Isaac was pulling at Charlotte's windcheater in excitement.

'I don't think so, sweetie. It's very hard to control. We don't want you flying away with the kite.'

'Owww.' Isaac seemed to think that flying away was an added bonus.

'What about yours?' Edward reeled his kite in and turned his attention to Isaac's blue and silver kite.

Isaac's face was a picture. Happiness that he was a part of their great enterprise and not just relegated to watching. Pride when the kite soared up into the sky, with Edward kneeling at his side, showing him how to control it.

'Thank you.' Charlotte caught at his sleeve as he stepped back, letting Isaac go solo. 'Thank you so much.'

Edward nodded in satisfaction. 'Every boy needs a kite. I'm just going to make a few adjustments to mine and perhaps you'll help me launch it again.'

A few knots, a little staring into the middle distance as Edward estimated airflow and wind speed, and the kite was up in the air again, this time flying more steadily. Charlotte ran back to Edward's side and he looped his arms over her head.

'Here, you try. Take hold of the reels.'

She pressed her hands over his, trying to stop her fingers from trembling. The wind around them buffeted her, but she was safe in his arms, her back against his strong body, his scent surrounding her and then blown away by the wind.

'That's right.'

His lips were almost touching her ear.

'Pull it a bit to the right.' He guided her arm and the kite dipped to the right, shooting back upwards as the breeze caught it again. 'Ooops. Hang on tight.'

Suddenly he had left her, and was loping across to Isaac, who was struggling to keep his kite in the air.

Charlotte concentrated hard on controlling her own little bit of airspace while Edward restored Isaac's kite safely back above their heads. He made sure that Isaac was happily in control again and then he was back.

'What do you think?' He was surveying the flight path of the kite.

'It's pulling really hard…' Her arms were already beginning to ache.

Edward chuckled, looping his arms around her again. 'Let me give you a hand with it.'

He wasn't helping at all. All that happened was that she melted into his arms, turning to jelly and losing whatever strength she had left. He was controlling not only the kite but her as well. She let go of the kite strings and he strengthened his grip, catching them just in time. Turning in his arms, she faced him.

His rakish half-smile told her that this was just what he wanted. 'Giving up already?'

'You're so much better at it than I am.'

'Think so? You dip beautifully.' He leaned towards her.

She couldn't do this. Not with Isaac just yards away—even if he was paying them no attention.

She ducked out of the circle of his arms, feeling the wind suddenly chill her. 'Are you hungry?'

Edward chuckled. 'Ravenous.'

She fixed him with a glare. Even the thought of Peter's quiet charm, and the way that had worked out, wasn't enough to calm the insistent thunder in her veins. Peter was like a faded shadow of a man next to Edward. Edward was different. Different from pretty much everyone she'd ever met.

'Would you like an apple?' She gritted her teeth and doggedly refused to take any notice of the alternative interpretation of hungry that the curve of his eyebrow suggested.

'In a minute. I've got my hands full at the moment.' His gaze left her, flipping over towards Isaac. 'Steady on, there, chief...'

Charlotte ran to her son, helping him to pull on the string so that the kite fluttered upwards again. 'Enjoying yourself, sweetie?' She whispered the words tremulously in his ear.

'Yes, Mum.' Isaac's attention was on the kite, its tail shimmering and sparkling in the sunshine. He submitted to a hug for a moment and then wriggled free.

'Good. I'm glad.'

She could have cried. The scared little boy who had clung to her when the debt collectors knocked on the door was gone. In his place a child who was enjoying himself so much that he had no time for his mother's cuddles.

'All right over there?' Edward nodded over to Isaac.

'Just fine. He loves this.'

'Yeah. Me, too.'

Edward sat at the piano, his fingers wandering across the keys, playing a soft melody of his own composition. He'd had a great time. The kite had flown better than he'd expected once he'd made a few adjustments to the lines which had altered its angle of flight slightly. Isaac had liked his kite, too, and had insisted on taking it to bed with him. And Charlotte...

He'd planned to give her a great day—help her forget about the troubles of the past week. And she'd shone in the sunshine like a beautiful jewel, full of life and light. But however hard he tried to please her he seemed to end up only pleasing himself, as the echoes of her *joie de vivre* washed over him.

Charlotte. The chords seemed to sing out her name. A sudden slip into a minor key lent an element of yearning to the music that hadn't been there before.

'Why so sad?'

He hadn't noticed her behind him, standing in the doorway which led from the kitchen. He stopped playing abruptly, aware that the music had given away much more than he had ever intended. 'It's a slow piece of music.'

A slight frown of disbelief. It seemed that he could lie to the rest of the world, but Charlotte caught him out every time.

'I recognise it. You've played it before.'

When he'd played it before it had been just a dalliance with the keys. Now it was a full-blown, passionate love affair, full of all the conflicting emotions in his heart. 'It's a work in progress. It changes every time.'

She nodded. Walked over to him. 'Will you play it again?'

'No.' She couldn't lure him in like that. If the music insisted on betraying him, then he'd stick to other people's compositions. 'I mean…I need to think about it a bit more.'

She nodded and he beckoned her over. This time she sat down next to him on the piano stool as if it was the most natural thing in the world.

'Would you like something else?'

'If you want.' She smiled. 'Whatever you want.'

'Your turn to choose.'

She grinned. 'What was it you were playing the other night?' She hummed a few chords, her voice clear and tuneful.

'You've got a good ear. Most people don't get that bit right.' He reproduced the chords she'd sung and she smiled, singing along with the music.

He'd played this song thousands of times before. Kathy had liked this one, too, but it had never felt like this. Never as if he was caressing someone with the music. Never so head-swimmingly erotic.

He hadn't thought about Kathy in years. If asked, he would have said that he'd forgotten her, but it seemed that she'd just lain dormant in his memory, waiting to emerge and reprimand him for having ignored the lesson she'd taught him.

'What's the matter?'

Charlotte was closer now, and Edward realised that he'd stopped playing.

He shrugged. 'This song reminds me of…someone I used to know.'

'Should I be sorry?'

He shook his head. 'I don't think so. It was a long time ago. When I was at university.'

'Which time?'

'The second. Kathy was a medical student.'

She nodded. 'First love?'

He shrugged. 'I suppose so.'

It had been more like a first friendship, really. Kathy had been quiet, studious, so like him that everyone had reckoned they were made for each other and it was just a matter of time before they got married.

When she'd left him, citing a lack of emotional commitment on Edward's part as her reason, it had been proof positive to all their friends that Edward was the cold fish they'd always marked him down as being.

She nodded. 'My first love was Isaac's father. That didn't work out too well.'

'But you loved him once…' The words almost choked Edward.

'You know they say that love is blind?' She looked up at him and he nodded. 'Well, I don't think so. I think that real love sees everything.'

'Do you think you can really ever see everything about someone?'

'I don't know. In the absence of any substantive evidence either way, I'll have to say that it's just a theory. But they say that true love lasts, and I don't love him now.' Her mouth twisted, as if the joke was really on her.

Something inside him raged in bitter triumph. The impulse to tear Charlotte's ex limb from limb de-escalated to wanting to give him a more minor, if acutely painful, set of injuries. If she didn't care about him any more then Edward could live with that.

'You can't regret all of it. Isaac...'

'Isaac's the best thing that ever happened to me.' She laid a finger on his shoulder, as if alerting him to something. 'Good things do come from bad.'

'If you make them.'

Charlotte had that ability. As for himself... Nothing good or bad had come from his time with Kathy. Just a lingering doubt about whether he really could ever commit to anyone. After everything that had happened today that doubt suddenly seemed to matter a great deal.

She was looking steadily at him. That silent interrogation which he found so difficult to withstand. Why didn't she just *ask*?

'How long were you and Kathy together?'

'Three years.'

She nodded. Seemed to be about to ask more, and then didn't. That was as well, really. The nagging feeling of failure whenever Kathy's name was mentioned made him uncomfortable.

'So we're two of a kind, then.' She gave a little sigh.

'What makes you say that?' Charlotte was warm, bubbly—everyone knew without even thinking about it that there was nothing she didn't know about emotional commitment.

'Both still waiting for the right one to come along.'

It felt as if the right one was sitting next to him. But that must be another mistake, because Charlotte clearly didn't think so.

'No. I'm not waiting.' Edward told himself, with less conviction than normal, that he had everything he needed. His work, his books. The textured, multicoloured, harmonic flow of the world around him, perfect in all its intricacies.

'Better watch out, then.'

He was aware that her gaze was on him.

'Why?'

'That's when things sneak up on you from behind. When you least expect them.'

He turned to tell her that she was wrong—one smooth movement which began with a shake of his head, and ended with her lips. She gave a little start of surprise and then... Then she kissed him back.

Soft...slow.

Edward was taking it gently, giving her every opportunity to draw back from him, but that was the very last thing that Charlotte wanted to do. When he brushed his fingers against her neck, his thumb caressing her jaw, she felt her breath quicken.

He was all for the moment. Each touch was special and not to be rushed. Every breath was one they wouldn't take again, unique and remarkable. His fingertips found hers, touching, sensing, and then wrapping around her hand, drawing it upwards. Holding her gaze, he brushed his lips against the back of her fingers.

There was more. Simmering beneath the surface. Waiting. He took the pace up a notch, just one, his hand on the nape of her neck, pulling her in for another kiss. This time there was an edge to it, a promise of so much more if she could only stand this long, slow preamble.

He didn't call out her name. Made no profession of desire, or love, or even friendship. He didn't need to. It was all there in his kiss, the heat banking and flaring until she felt herself begin to tremble.

They broke apart. Charlotte's heart was thudding in her chest, her lungs pulling in air.

'Does that make any difference?' he asked.

'What do you mean?' Of course it made a difference. Edward's kiss made all the difference in the world. Fear clutched at her.

'I mean does that make you or me into different people? Change any of our views on life?'

She wished it did, but all of the old doubts were still there, the dread that she might fall back into disaster again. 'No.'

'Then I guess we'll say that there's someone out there for you, and someone for me. Leave it at that.'

So this was the way he wanted to play it. Just a kiss between friends. *Like hell it was.* That had been the first step on a path which led straight to two naked bodies and mind-blowing sex. They needed no words to know that.

He was right, though. Sex with Edward, if she ever managed to survive the intensity of the foreplay, would be like jumping from the frying pan into a searing fire. She couldn't afford to be fooled again by quiet charm and hidden depths. She wanted—needed—everything to be in plain sight.

'Yes. That would probably be sensible.' It seemed almost wrong to stand up now. Like the biggest lie of all to deny what had just happened. But she did it. 'I'm going to…'

Saying that she was going to bed would sound like a come-on. And his gaze was still so very enticing. Charlotte was under no illusions about whether she would be able to say no to him if he reached out for her now.

His slow smile was laced with all of the intentions that neither of them seemed able to follow through on. 'I'll leave you to it.'

'Thank you.'

What was that for? Starting things? Stopping things?

She leaned forward and planted a kiss on his cheek, drawing back again. 'Goodnight. I'll see you in the morning.'

CHAPTER TWELVE

IT HAD OCCURRED to Edward to burst into her room, carry her off to his, and make love to her until the raging in his blood let up. That might well have been a long and exhausting process, but that wasn't what had stopped him. It was what came afterwards—the falling in love and realising that he couldn't give her what she needed.

He was older now, and perhaps a bit wiser. He'd seen more of the world. Met Charlotte. Maybe things could be different. But *maybe* wasn't a good enough word for someone like Charlotte.

No emotional commitment. The words on Kathy's lips had puzzled and upset him. If he dared to make love to Charlotte, then those words on her lips might just kill him.

So he wouldn't. Instead he'd carry on as normal.

More or less normal, anyway.

It was with a pang of unusual regret that he rose from the kitchen table at seven the following morning and began to scribble a note for her, saying that he was going to catch up on some work he had to do at the Hunter Clinic and wouldn't be in for lunch.

'You're up early.'

Her bright morning smile interrupted him, almost choking him with desire.

'You, too.' The house was still quiet, and Edward wondered whether he'd made a mistake in not following his instincts last night. If Isaac was asleep, there was still time…

'Oh, I've just taken the opportunity to come down and make some sandwiches. Isaac's playing in his room. He'll be racing around wanting to get dressed soon.'

'Ah. I'll leave you to it, then…' It looked as if the Hunter Clinic was his best bet after all.

'We're going to the park this morning. Some of Isaac's friends go boating on the lake on Sundays. I'll leave you a salad for lunch…'

'There's no need…'

'Or you could come with us if you'd like?'

Charlotte, Isaac and Edward. Almost as if they were a family.

Edward picked up the note he'd been writing, screwed it into a ball and dropped it into the kitchen wastebin. 'Yes, I'm at a loose end today. That would be nice.'

The summer sunshine sparkled on the water like diamonds swept up from the bed of the lake in the wake of the small boats which bobbed on its surface.

'Mum… Mum, they're already here. Quick!'

Isaac was running back and forth, trying to hasten the easy pace which she and Edward had fallen into.

'There's plenty of time. Don't you want to go and find Sam first?' Sam was Isaac's best friend from school. 'Look, there he is.' Charlotte waved to Sam's mother and Isaac ran off across the grass, leaving her and Edward to follow in their own time.

'It's a nice day for it.' Edward was surveying the water.

'Yes. It gets a bit crowded sometimes on Sunday afternoons, but if you come before lunch and bring a picnic—' Charlotte broke off, shading her eyes against the glare. 'What are those two boys up to?'

A small boat was rocking precariously as two boys in their early teens took it into their heads to start a mock- fight in the deepest part of the lake. One caught the other with a flailing fist and they both crashed into the water, the boat rocking wildly and threatening to capsize.

'Edward...' She caught his arm and then started to breathe again as two heads bobbed to the surface of the lake and the boys started to doggy paddle towards shallower water. 'Those kids—they could have hurt themselves... Where's the attendant?'

Heads turned as the park attendant jumped into a boat, quickly pushing off towards the boys. Then a shrill wail floated across the still air.

'What's that...?' Charlotte scanned the water and located the source of the scream. She'd thought that the boys were alone in the boat, but there was also a shock of blonde curls just visible inside of the boat. 'Sit down!' she screamed at the child, even though it was unlikely that her voice would carry that far, much less be heeded.

The child managed to get to her feet and the boat bucked wildly.

'Edward, she's going to fall in...'

Her words met thin air. The bag he'd been carrying lay where he'd dropped it, and Edward was already powering down the steep slope which led to the lake, throwing off his jacket and shoes. By the time the other adults gathered around the lake started to notice the little girl he was already wading into the water, then swimming towards the child with long, easy strokes.

The little girl had calmed down now, and it seemed as if he would soon reach her. Charlotte glanced quickly in Isaac's direction and saw that Sam's mother had both him and Sam firmly in her grasp, stopping them both from running down to the lake's edge.

Edward was nearly there. Only another fifty yards.

It was fifty yards too much.

The wake from another boat made the craft wobble and

the child screamed again, panicking, throwing herself from one side to the other. The boat capsized, taking her with it.

No time for the curse of disbelief which sprang to her lips. Charlotte ran to the waterside, one eye still on Isaac. Sam's mother shouted a reassurance that she'd look after him and Charlotte hitched up her skirt and began to wade into the water.

Edward had reached the spot where the upturned boat lay in the water and was looking around for the child.

'Edward… She's under the water.'

He didn't turn his head, but he must have heard. His body seemed to rise in the water, and then disappeared as he dived beneath the surface.

Long moments.

The water was almost opaque here at the edge of the lake, and Charlotte could only hope that it was a bit clearer further out. He had to find her.

How long was it now? Thirty seconds? A minute? Charlotte knew that Edward wouldn't come back up until he'd found the child, and prayed that it would be soon.

The surface of the lake erupted in a frenzy of bubbles and water as Edward broke the surface. He struck out immediately for the shore, not stopping to take a breath although his lungs must have been screaming for air. As soon as the water was shallow enough he gained a footing and waded, the little girl clinging tightly to his neck.

For a moment all Charlotte could feel was relief. Water was sluicing from Edward's chest and legs and the child moved in his arms, leaving a watery red stain on the shoulder of his white shirt.

'Edward…' She waded further into the water, meeting him as he strode towards the bank. 'You're bleeding…'

'It's not my blood.' He nodded quickly towards the little girl, who was whimpering now, holding on tight to his shirt collar. 'Clear a space for me, will you?'

Charlotte stumbled, splashing up onto the bank. 'Some

space, please, guys. My friend's a doctor—give him some space.'

Two women assumed the responsibility of moving everyone back, and someone threw a waterproof sheet down onto the ground. Edward dropped to his knees, ready to examine the child, but she wouldn't let go of him.

'All right, honey. You're such a brave girl, and you're safe now. Let me look at your arm…'

He gently tried to move the child and she hung on even tighter. Charlotte could see a gash on her forearm, which was gushing blood.

'Okay. That's okay.'

Charlotte expected him to use his vastly superior strength to free himself, but instead he held the child closer, motioning to Charlotte.

'Looks as if you're going to have to look at her arm *in situ*…'

Charlotte dropped to her knees next to him, gently lifting the little girl's arm. 'She's got a nasty cut, and it's bleeding badly. She'll definitely need to go to hospital.' She looked up, and almost simultaneously half a dozen mobile phones appeared.

'We'll just need the one ambulance.' She grinned at the knot of people around them. 'Are her parents here?'

Sam's mother's voice sounded above the general hubbub. 'Dave, call an ambulance. Everyone else—see if you can find her mother. Who are those boys she was with…?'

Charlotte left Maggie to it, with only the briefest glance in her direction to check that she was still holding firmly onto Isaac's hand.

'I'm going to have to wrap something around her arm to stop the bleeding.'

'All right.'

The little girl screamed as Charlotte gently wrapped her own scarf around the wound, pressing firmly and extending the arm upwards.

'It's okay, honey. I know it hurts, but you're all right.' Edward's voice was almost painfully gentle, and the screams subsided to a whimper. 'You're doing really well.'

She couldn't tell whether the child understood his words, or his manner. Whichever it was, she was beginning to calm.

'What's your name, sweetie?' Edward managed to disentangle himself sufficiently to ask the question face to face, rather than direct it at the top of the child's head.

'Laura.'

'Well, Laura, you're safe now. I expect your arm hurts, but we'll put a bandage around it and it'll be better in no time.'

Laura nodded up at him. It occurred to Charlotte that she might like to remind Edward of his own words on the subject of his ability to communicate with patients, and she promised herself she'd do it later. He might not want to admit to being so very wrong in front of all these people.

'What happened? She was under the water for a very long time...' Charlotte had half expected to see Edward bring Laura up unconscious.

He grinned at her. 'She instinctively did just the right thing. When the boat capsized she ended up in an air pocket underneath it, and she held on to one of the seats. The biggest problem was getting her to let go of it and hang on to me instead.' His free hand patted Laura's back. 'You've got a great grip, there, young lady.'

Laura looked up at him, favouring him with a tremulous smile. At that moment the knot of people around them parted as a woman came stumbling through.

'Laura...' The woman fell to her knees in front of Edward. 'Laura, I'm so sorry... Is she all right? They said you're a doctor...'

'She's okay.' Edward delivered Laura into her mother's arms while Charlotte kept a tight hold on her arm. 'She has a cut on her arm, and needs to keep it elevated until the ambulance arrives. She'll need a few stitches, but the main thing is that she didn't stop breathing.'

'Laura...' The mother held her daughter tight, her eyes squeezed closed.

Charlotte knew just what scenes were playing in her head. She'd had her own share of them with Isaac recently.

'It's fine. You have a very resourceful young lady for a daughter, there.'

The woman's eyes opened and tears spilled from them. 'I only left her for a minute... The kids wanted ice-cream and I told Trevor to look after her.' One of the boys who had been fighting in the boat stood beside her, soaking wet, bedraggled, and not a little shamefaced.

'She's fine. That's the main thing. Her head was only under the water for a few moments—'

He broke off as tears coursed down the woman's cheeks. Someone proffered a handkerchief, but she wouldn't let go of her daughter for long enough to wipe her eyes.

Edward turned to Charlotte. 'How's that cut doing?'

'I think it's stopped bleeding.' She loosened her grip on Laura's arm and blood began to seep between her fingers. 'Ah. Not quite.'

'Okay. Can the ambulance get to us here?'

'Yes, the park gates are wide enough for them to get through, and they can use the service road that runs through the park, right there.'

He nodded. 'Good. We'll just sit tight here, then.'

The paramedic from the ambulance returned Charlotte's scarf to her with a wry smile. 'Try washing it in cold water...'

'Thanks.' Charlotte took the scarf. Hot water would only fix the bloodstain and it would never come out. Cold water might do the trick.

'I should have offered to rip my shirt up for a bandage.' Edward's voice sounded behind her. 'It's already ruined.'

Ruined it might be, and bloodstained and dirty from the lake, clinging to his shoulders and chest in the places where the sun hadn't dried it, but it was still better on than off. Marginally. When he'd emerged from the water the white lawn fabric had left very little to the imagination.

'Probably best you keep it.' She grinned up at him. 'We don't want to get all the mothers talking. I have to face them at the school gates, remember.'

He gave her a hurt look. 'I'm allowed to rip up my shirt for bandages, aren't I? I thought it was practically par for the course when a doctor has to improvise.'

'Only when there's nothing else to use. I'm a nurse, remember, and I had a scarf handy.'

'Hmm. Shame to spoil it, though.' He caught the end of the fine material through his fingers. 'It's pretty.'

It was her favourite. It went with her blouse, and she'd chosen both from her wardrobe this morning because they were a little smarter than the T-shirts she usually wore at the weekend. If she had allowed herself to examine her motives for that choice she would have had to admit that Edward had played a major part in it.

'It'll wash out.'

'Hmm. You've got a spot of blood on your cuff, as well.'

'That'll wash out, too.' Charlotte rolled the sleeves of her blouse up a little, to hide the stain.

'Yeah. Look, I'll take it home with me and put it in a bowl of cold water. Sam's father...'

'Dave?'

'Yeah, Dave. He's offered to run me home to get a change of clothes. We'll only be half an hour.'

'You'll be coming back?'

'Of course. We haven't eaten our picnic yet.' Edward watched as Laura's mother climbed into the ambulance, shepherding her son with her. 'His ears are going to be ringing tonight.'

'I imagine so.' It was so easy. You only had to take your eye off them for one minute... Charlotte shook her head.

'Isaac's okay.' He pointed towards Sam and Isaac, playing together in the grass under Maggie's watchful eye.

'Yeah, I know.' Still she couldn't help the terrible feeling of foreboding.

'I can understand your fears. With everything that's happened. But no one's going to let anything happen to him.'

'No.' She had to be content with that. With Edward's promises, his father's reassurances. 'Look, you're shivering. You must be freezing.' His hair and shirt were beginning to dry, but Edward's jeans were still soaking wet.

He shrugged. 'I could do with getting those dry clothes. Will you be okay here with Isaac?'

'Yes, fine. See you later.'

He grinned. 'I wouldn't miss this afternoon for the world.'

Charlotte sat with Maggie on the grass, hugging her knees in front of her.

'So, Edward's…a friend of yours…?'

'Yes, I work with him.'

'Ah. A colleague. Well, it was lucky he was here today. He was a real hero.' Maggie laughed. 'I told Isaac and Sam that I thought he was a hero, and Isaac asked if that made him a hero, too. Since Edward was his friend.'

Charlotte grinned at the thought. 'What did you say?'

'I said that it did. Then Sam wanted to know if he was a hero, too, as he was Isaac's friend…'

'I reckon it's catching, this hero business.'

'Definitely.' Maggie leaned towards Charlotte confidingly. 'Mind you, even my heart skipped a beat when he walked out of the water carrying that little girl.'

'Yeah?'

Charlotte's heart had almost stopped. Edward's jeans, moulded tight around his strong thighs… His shirt clinging to a broad, muscled chest which had been heaving from the effort of getting to Laura in time and pulling her from the lake… The droplets of spinning silver that had scattered as he shook his head… It was an image that she wasn't going to forget in a hurry.

'Guess mine did, too.'

'It's instinct. Man saves child. Guaranteed to pull at the heartstrings.'

Head, heart and all points south. If Laura hadn't been the most pressing priority she would have had little choice but to fling herself into his arms.

'Yeah.' She turned to Maggie with a bright smile. 'And it all ended well.'

'Yep. Thanks to you two.' Maggie lay back in the grass. 'I think it's going to be a great afternoon.'

'So, if you ever tell me again that you're no good at reassuring patients…'

Charlotte was grinning at him, as if she knew that Edward was expecting something of the sort from her. At least she'd left it until Isaac was safely tucked up in bed.

'Okay.' He looked up from his book, holding his hands up in mock surrender. 'You just had to say it, didn't you?' But it had felt good to be the one who gave comfort for a change. He could see the extra dimension that it added to Charlotte's job.

She laughed. 'Do you mind?'

'No. I'd mind if you hadn't noticed.'

Charlotte's approval was becoming more important to him than he was strictly comfortable with. It was one thing to gain satisfaction from trying out a new approach and finding that it worked, but that didn't mean that he'd changed. He might be older, and a bit wiser, but were Kathy's words so very wide of the mark?

She jutted her chin at him. 'So you admit that you've underestimated yourself?'

The phone interrupted any possible answer to that, and Edward reached for the handset. He heard his father's voice, with a quick enquiry about how he was doing and a request to speak to Charlotte.

'Here.' He spun the handset across the coffee table and she caught it adroitly. 'It's my father. He wants to speak to you.'

He couldn't have asked for a better illustration of Kathy's point. Even his father seemed to be captivated with her, and somehow found far more to chat about with Charlotte than he did with Edward.

He retreated into a book, hardly hearing what Charlotte was saying on the phone. After half an hour she replaced the handset into its cradle.

'Everything okay?'

'He wanted to set up a meeting for this week. I'm going to see him on Wednesday, after work. He's got some things for me to sign.'

'Good. Anything else?' That would have accounted for about two minutes' worth of their conversation.

'He asked me if I knew anything about the different cuts you can get on precious stones.'

'Really? Do you?'

She nodded. 'My father was a jeweller. The old-fashioned kind, who knew how to make pieces as well as sell them. So I know a little.'

'I imagine he's got their fortieth wedding anniversary in mind—that's only a few months away now.' Edward wondered whether he should follow his father's lead and enlist Charlotte's help in choosing a gift for his parents.

'Mmm. He wants to get something really special. I'm going to give him the name of an associate of my father's who deals in rubies when I see him. He does very fine work. I used to have a necklace that he made for my mother.'

Her voice was matter-of-fact. Just the smallest hint of regret.

'Used to have?' Edward hoped against all reason that the necklace was somewhere tucked away safely—the one thing that Charlotte hadn't sold.

'I sold it. It gave me a few thousand to put towards the deposit on my house.'

'I'm sorry you had to do that.'

She shrugged. 'They're only pretty sparkly things. I remember my parents, and that's the thing that really matters.' She pulled her shoulders back, as if telling herself for the hundredth time that it really didn't matter. 'Anyway, I know a good ruby when I see one. I'll make sure that your father gets a really nice stone.'

'Thank you.' She was quite unselfish in her generosity. Even though she'd lost everything herself, she wanted to make sure that another woman had the perfect gift. 'So, do you need someone to look after Isaac on Wednesday evening?'

'I can have the childminder pick him up from school. That's what I usually do.'

'I've got a free afternoon. I can pick him up and bring him back here if you like.'

She nodded. 'If it's not too much trouble. I don't want to...'

'If you were going to say that you don't want to impose, you can save your breath.' He kept the stern glare up for about two seconds, until she flushed and it melted. 'You're not imposing. It's been a pleasure having him around.'

She grinned, a hint of mischief in her eyes. He could get lost in that mischief, let it bend and break him...

'You two are getting to be quite a gang...'

'Yeah?' Edward had never been in a gang before, even if this was an exceptionally small one. He quite liked the possibilities that it opened up. Going fishing for tadpoles. Wearing their ties like bandanas around their heads.

'I just... Well, I hope that he's not been too demanding. Of your time.'

For someone who seemed to know pretty much what he was thinking for a good proportion of the time, Charlotte could be shockingly unperceptive sometimes. 'No. I think I've been demanding of *his* time, haven't I? It'll be my pleasure to pick him up from school on Wednesday.'

CHAPTER THIRTEEN

EDWARD WAS PLEASED to see that the school made him submit to a thorough check, to make sure he was who he said he was, before they would let him take Isaac. He'd been worried that Charlotte's husband might try something, and it seemed that his father had, too, because when Edward had broached the matter quietly with him he'd told him that was all seen to.

'So. What shall we do, then?'

The feeling that he was playing hookey was almost overwhelming. He wasn't, of course. The clinic knew exactly where he was, and he was just taking a few hours from the hundreds he was owed. But Edward didn't let that spoil the fantasy.

'What would *you* like to do?'

He dumped his keys and phone onto the hall table, and extricated Isaac from his backpack and coat.

'We could play a game on the internet. Or play football. Or perhaps you'd like to go to the park?'

Isaac nodded. He, too, had an air of being about to embark on an adventure. 'The park.'

'Okay. Do you think we should take some supplies with us? In case we get lost? You never know what might happen.'

Isaac smiled. 'Stay with me. I know my way around.'

'Okay. But perhaps we'll take some juice. And one of those fruit and nut bars your mum bought.'

'Mmm. Good idea.'

They rambled together through a small wooded area, picking up fallen branches to swish on the path in front of them. Edward turned over stones with his foot, and they both inspected the creatures which lived in the damp darkness below them.

'Look. A piece of flint.' He held out the broken pebble for Isaac to see.

'What's that?'

'Flint's a type of stone. A long time ago cavemen used to make axes and arrowheads out of flint. It's very hard.'

Isaac inspected the stone carefully. 'Can we make an axe out of this?'

'Maybe. It's a little small. Let's find a bigger piece and perhaps we can take it home and give it a try.'

They searched together and found a bigger piece of flint. Edward put it into his pocket, and then saw a couple of flat, circular stones on the ground. 'Hey, look at these. Do you know how to skim stones?'

'No.'

Edward grinned. 'We'll collect some of these up, then, and I'll show you.'

The house was quiet when Charlotte got back home. The meeting with Edward's father had been longer than she'd thought it would be, and she was tired. She didn't much feel like cooking straight away, but she was going to have to.

'Hey? Guys…?' She called into the silence and only silence answered her. Perhaps they were out in the garden, playing football. She walked through to the kitchen and opened the back door.

No one there. Edward's car was parked in front of the house, and his suit jacket was slung over the bannisters. He must have walked down to the school.

Even if he had they should be back by now. He'd been due to collect Isaac more than two hours ago. Charlotte pulled out her phone and checked it. No calls or texts from the school. That meant that everything had gone to plan. Flipping through her address book, she found the entry for Edward's mobile and called it. Tapping her foot while the call connected, she then let out a huff of exasperation when the tones of his mobile chimed out from the hall table.

'Edward. Where *are* you?'

She wasn't sure whether to be cross or worried. She dropped her bag onto the hall table, slung her jacket over the bannister, and wandered into the sitting room, sinking down onto the sofa.

'Where are *you*, Isaac?'

'Yeaaah!' Isaac jumped up and down, cheering. 'Six!'

Edward straightened, smiling with satisfaction. 'I think the smooth ones do better, don't you?'

Isaac nodded. 'Those big flat ones are the best, though.'

'Hmm. Less air resistance. Larger surface area.'

Isaac nodded sagely, although it was doubtful that he understood the finer points of it. Actually, for once, Edward wasn't much interested in the finer points. Just in counting the number of times their stones skipped across the water out loud with Isaac.

'I'm hungry.'

'Are you? We've had our drinks and…' Edward looked at his watch, his heart sinking when he saw the time. He felt in his pocket for his mobile and realised that he must have left it at home when he changed his jacket. 'Isaac, we've got to get going, mate. Your mum will be waiting for us.'

The list of possibilities was endless. A car accident. The lake. Surely Edward couldn't be so irresponsible as to take Isaac out on the lake—not after what had happened at the weekend. She couldn't think about that any more; it was making her feel sick. Peter's face flipped up into the void that not thinking about a freak accident had left. Could *he* have taken Isaac? Perhaps Edward was out looking for him?

She was being alarmist. They were probably out some-where together. But Edward was normally so responsible. Charlotte couldn't imagine that he'd possibly become as in-volved with a game of football as he did on a day to day basis with his piles of papers and the intricate problems that his patients posed.

One of them had been taken ill. Perhaps she should call the local hospital. But wouldn't Edward have called? Left a message for her on his own home phone if he couldn't re-member her mobile number? She checked the answering ma-chine again. Nothing.

Where were they?

Edward had hoisted Isaac up on to his shoulders, was strid-ing out as fast as he could without dislodging the boy from his perch. He should have left a note for Charlotte, telling her where they were. Or remembered to bring his mobile with him. That would have solved the problem. It was too late now. All he could do was hope that she wasn't worry-ing about Isaac.

He loped up the drive, gravel scrunching beneath his feet. There was no opportunity to pull his keys out of his pocket because the front door flew open. He could see from the way she rubbed her hand across her face that Charlotte was upset, but by the time he reached her she seemed to have regained some of her composure.

'Isaac! How was your day, sweetie?' Her eyes were red, but she was smiling, trying to pretend to Isaac that nothing was the matter. He let Isaac down and the boy ran to her to give her a hug.

'We had a brilliant time, Mum. We've been skimming stones. We've got a special method.'

Her gaze flipped up towards Edward at the mention of the special method and her lips pursed. Before he had a chance to apologise she was smiling at Isaac again.

'That's great. You're going to have to show me how you do that.'

'We've got a piece of flint, too.' Isaac twisted his face up towards Edward. 'Edward's going to make it into an axe.'

Right now, putting an axe anywhere within Charlotte's reach might not be such a good idea. She shot him another glare, and Edward put his hands into his pockets. He didn't particularly want to go into the house, or to be anywhere near her at the moment. Generally speaking, keeping out of the way until it all blew over was his preferred modus operandi in these situations.

'What's for tea, Mum?'

'Wait and see. Go inside, now, and take your coat off.' She stood aside as Isaac ran past her and into the house, then directed her gaze at Edward.

He already had his car keys in his hand, and had pressed the remote to unlock the doors. She stood, arms folded, in the doorway. 'And where do you think you're going?'

Nowhere. Anywhere. 'I've…um…got to pick something up from the hospital.'

'Something important, no doubt?'

'I guess it must be.' He turned towards the car and heard the safety catch on the front door flip. Felt her hand catch in the crook of his arm, spinning him round.

'Afraid?'

'Yep. Terrified.'

He faced her at last. She was trembling with an emotion that he found hard to identify. A cocktail, maybe, of all the feelings that he didn't much want to think about at the moment.

'And running's the best option, is it?'

'I'd prefer to call it a tactical retreat.'

'Call it whatever you like.'

Her chin jutted provocatively. Eyes golden in the early evening sunshine. Her hair was slightly mussed, as if she had dragged it out of the neat knot that she usually wore it in for work and not bothered to comb it.

'Look. You're angry…' It was a very old cliché, but she was one of those people who became even more beautiful when angry. 'I'll let you go and see to Isaac…' He wanted to kiss her.

'Unless you hadn't noticed, Isaac's perfectly capable of switching the TV on by himself and sitting in front of it for ten minutes.' Perfectly on cue, the sound of a children's song washed through from the living room and Isaac's voice joined in with the melody.

'All the same…'

'Don't you dare…'

He felt her hand brush against his and the hairs on his arm stood on end. She pulled the car keys out of his hand and flipped the locking mechanism. Two beeps and a flash of the headlights told Edward that his car had just changed sides and was firmly in her camp now.

He didn't much blame it. She was difficult to resist. Throwing a backwards glance at the treacherous machine, he stalked into the house.

Isaac's head popped up over the back of the sofa. 'Edward. Come and see…'

All his resistance melted. That cornered feeling, which he usually dealt with stony-faced and emotionless, didn't matter any more. 'Hey, buddy.' He strode into the sitting room and plumped himself down next to the boy. 'Have you washed your hands?'

Isaac inspected his grubby fingers. 'No.'

'Well, you'd better do that. Mine could do with a wash as well.' He led Isaac into the kitchen, kicking the plastic box that he stood on to reach the counter-tops in front of the sink. He squirted a dollop of soap into Isaac's palm and then soaped his own fingers.

'Is Mum angry with us?' the boy whispered conspiratorially.

'Nah. Not with you.'

'You?'

'Don't you worry about that. I'll handle it.' Edward didn't bother with any details of exactly how, on the basis that he hadn't formulated them yet.

'Do you want to borrow my ray gun?' Isaac twisted round to face him, splashing water onto his shirt.

'Thanks. But I think I'll manage.' He bent down, keeping his voice low. 'We don't want to hurt her, do we?'

Isaac shook his head, taking the other end of the towel that Edward was drying his own hands with.

'I'll tell you what…' There were no signs of food preparation in the kitchen. Charlotte had clearly been spending her time glued to the front window, waiting for him to bring Isaac home. 'Do you like Chinese food?'

Isaac nodded.

'Okay, then. I'll go out and get some.' Isaac shot him a questioning look. Clearly takeaways didn't figure much in his experience. 'I'll bring it home and we can eat it here.'

'You don't need to do that. I can have something ready in half an hour.'

Charlotte's voice sounded from the doorway. If she'd heard the bit about the ray gun she was clearly undaunted by it.

If she was so keen on him staying in, then she was going to have to put up with the consequences.

Edward reached for the takeaway menu, taped to the door of the fridge, and handed it to her. 'There's a nice place just around the corner. I'll phone in our order and go and pick it up. We can be eating in fifteen minutes.'

She gave a little huff and unfolded the card. The strains of another children's tune floated in from the sitting room and Isaac dropped his end of the towel and ran in to see what was happening on the television.

'Okay.' Edward closed the door into the sitting room behind the boy. 'You want to talk.'

* * *

She didn't really. But when Edward had started to retreat back into himself, his face losing all the animation that she saw whenever he talked with Isaac, she'd panicked. It had been as if she was losing him back into the realms of considered thought and few words.

She twisted her lips together, pretending to read the menu. He came closer.

'Afraid?' He plucked the menu from her hands and held it behind his back.

'Terrified.'

'Good.' That tantalising half-smile. 'I won't be needing the ray gun, then.'

'If you want to get a takeaway you'd better do it. Otherwise it'll be no quicker than if I cook.'

'If it's an apology you want…'

'No.' She'd overreacted. She was the one who ought to be apologising.

'I'm sorry. I should have let you know where we were. I lost track of time and you understandably got worried. It won't happen again.'

'It's okay. It doesn't matter.'

His blue eyes. You could always tell what was going on in Edward's head by those eyes. Now they were dark, as if an old anger had seized him.

'It does. I know that I can't really understand because I'm not a parent….'

'What?' Where had *that* come from?

'I'm not stupid. I know what people think of me.' He turned away from her, one hand slicking his hair back across his head. 'That I'm too bound up with my books to even notice what's going on under my nose.'

Not that again. 'Face me, Edward.'

'Is that better?' When he turned, his face was brooding, angry from the hurt that seemed to have steeped in his soul for a long time now.

'A little bit.'

This was like a crazy game. Each trying to drive the other away, protect themselves, and yet fascinated by each other.

Unable to resist the temptation to dig deeper. Charlotte stepped forward. 'Touch me.'

He looked at her as if she'd gone stark, staring mad. If she'd taken a moment to think about what she'd just said then she would have agreed with him completely.

'Like this?' His fingers trailed the line of her jaw. 'Or this?'

His other arm snaked around her waist in a strong, domineering motion and suddenly she was pressed against him. She should have known better than to taunt Edward.

Charlotte reached up, cradling his jaw in her hands. Not even the fact that Isaac was in the next room could stop her now. 'Now. Listen to me.'

'I'm listening.'

He was listening all right. She had every piece of his attention, from the strong curl of his body to the ever-fascinating eddies of his mind. It was all-encompassing, irresistible.

Charlotte took a deep breath. 'You should have let me know where you were, but I should have trusted that Isaac would be safe with you.'

'And…?'

His anger had subsided and she could feel the tautness of his frame relax against hers. Melting, almost…

'I just…'

'Find it hard to trust?'

Was she that transparent? 'Yes. I suppose I do. It's a big world out there, and Isaac's starting to be interested in it. My job is to keep him safe, make sure that he's got what he needs, and…'

'Let him go. Just a bit, maybe.'

'Yeah. Just a bit.' She reached up and touched the side of his face with her fingertips. 'Who says that you don't understand?'

He let her go abruptly. Probably just as well. Their bodies seemed to have taken on a life of their own. Moving against each other with an almost imperceptible but blissful friction.

He shook his head as if to clear it. 'It's not rocket science. You've had to fend for yourself and Isaac for a long time, now. Isaac's father, the one person who should be helping you, is only making things worse. You've had to struggle to make ends meet, and been chased out of your home by debt collectors. I would think that trust issues go hand in hand with that.'

'Hmm. Life's a bit more complicated than rocket science sometimes.'

Edward leaned back against the kitchen counter, his hungry eyes still on her. 'Rocket science isn't really that complicated. One of those illustrations that doesn't stand up to too much scrutiny.'

For a moment Charlotte could see the lure of his books. Something that was constant in an ever-changing world. If she could have seen the same beauty in numbers and science that Edward did...

Damn the books. They couldn't give him this.

She stepped forward and found him there, ready. His body seemed to mould to hers—a close fit that left no room for anything else to come between them.

She kissed him. She couldn't help it. And once she'd brushed her lips against his she couldn't help but go back for more. His response was thrilling, strong and tender all at the same time.

One hand travelled lightly down her back. Across the rise of her hips and to the top of her leg. This was too much. She'd bitten off far more than she could chew.

'Isaac...' She just managed to get the word out.

'Yeah...'

His grip on her loosened, but Charlotte couldn't bring herself to pull away.

'He's just in the next room.'

She wasn't telling him, she was telling herself. Giving herself the one and only reason that could stop her from keeping going until all the pent-up frustration came screaming from her lungs.

'We should stop.'

Edward seemed as disinclined to bring this to a close as she was, but he was the stronger. He gave her one last, head-spinning kiss before he gripped her shoulders, carefully propelling her backwards, away from him.

'That's…sensible.' Her cheeks were burning, and she still couldn't quite catch her breath.

'Yes. I'd better go and get us something to eat. Before…'

'Before we get too hungry…'

'Yes.' He pulled the takeaway menu out of his back pocket. 'What would you like?'

'Anything. Surprise me.'

His lips twitched into a half-grin before he straightened his face. 'All right. I'll be fifteen minutes.'

Enough time to splash cold water on her face and take a breath. 'Have you got chopsticks here?'

'No, I'll get some.'

He opened the kitchen door and disappeared into the living room. Charlotte heard him exchange a few words with Isaac, and as the front door slammed she shook her head. It was going to take a lot longer than fifteen minutes to get Edward out of her system.

CHAPTER FOURTEEN

'Is it so very wrong to feel like celebrating?' Charlotte wondered if she sounded cold-hearted.

'No.' Paula swirled her herbal tea thoughtfully in her cup. 'It's exactly the right thing to do. You've got to look forward, not back.'

Paula clearly thought that Charlotte was being brave about this. It was nothing of the sort. Ever since she'd received the Decree Absolute this morning Charlotte had wanted to do nothing but dance. And, finding herself alone with Paula in the employees' lounge, she'd been unable to contain her news.

'Actually, it's quite a relief. I was afraid my husband…' Charlotte couldn't help smiling '…my *ex*-husband would make some kind of objection somewhere along the line.'

'From what you've said in the past…' Paula looked at Charlotte thoughtfully. 'Okay, so you've asked for no maintenance. Your ex didn't ask for any rights to visit Isaac. Am I right in thinking that this guy was bad news?'

'Between you and me…?'

Paula nodded. 'Of course.' Paula might gossip, along with the rest of them, but she knew how to keep a confidence.

'Yeah. Very bad news. He hasn't seen Isaac for months, even though I've asked him time and time again if he'd come.'

Paula snorted in disgust. 'What kind of slug doesn't want to see a cute little guy like Isaac? No wonder you want to celebrate. You want to come down to Drake's tonight? We could crack open a bottle of champagne.'

'I'd love to. But I've got to go and pick that cute little guy up.'

Paula nodded. 'And the cute big one?'

'There's only one guy in my life who's even remotely cute. And he's three feet tall…' Charlotte told herself that you couldn't really call Edward cute.

'Yeah, right. You're either blind, or crazy, or…' Paula grinned, her words taking on a sing-song intonation '…you're telling porkies.'

'I'm just out of one bad relationship. I think I'll take some time to pause for a breath.' Charlotte shrugged. 'Twenty years or so.'

Paula leaned towards her. 'I wouldn't leave it twenty seconds if I could get my hands on Edward North.'

'Who says I can?'

Only about half the clinic. And the other half reckoned she already had. Keeping secrets about what you did out of hours was easy enough. Keeping secrets about how you felt about the people you worked with was nigh on impossible in such a small community.

Paula had the grace not to remind her of the gossip. 'Whatever. But in another four hours' time it's going to be the weekend. Tell me you'll find *something* to do to celebrate, eh?'

'Yes, I will.'

Paula nodded. 'Life's too short to worry about what other people say. Even me.'

'Thanks, Paula.' Charlotte looked at her watch. 'I've got to go. I've a clinic in twenty minutes.'

'Edward North?'

'Yes, Edward North—if you must know.'

* * *

'Two more to go?' They were in one of the Hunter Clinic's plush consulting rooms.

'Yes.' Charlotte flipped through the notes. 'April Ashe is next. She's just coming in for a follow-up visit.'

'Ah, yes, April. Have you seen her yet?'

'Yes, she's in the waiting area.'

'How is she?'

Charlotte laughed. 'Isn't that what she's here for? For *you* to say how she is?'

'You know what I mean.'

Yes, she did. And it was a question that Edward wouldn't have asked just a couple of weeks ago. 'She looks great. She's got a new dress on.'

Edward searched her face for some clue. 'How would you know that? Or am I intruding into a knowledge base that's for you to know and the male of the species to wonder about.'

'You'll have to wonder.' Charlotte grinned at him. It was simple, really. When Charlotte had admired April's yellow and white summer dress her mother had said it was new. But it was good to keep Edward wondering from time to time.

This time April walked into the consulting room alone. 'Hi, April.' Edward got to his feet. 'You look very nice today.'

April nodded. 'Thanks.'

Charlotte wondered whether he would ask, but he didn't. Instead he set to, examining the skin on the side of April's face. 'That's healing very nicely, April. What do you think of it?'

'It's…different. Good… It itches a bit still.'

'Yes, that's natural. It itches as it heals.' Edward smiled. 'You've been massaging the oil that Charlotte gave you into it? And I can see you've been keeping out of the sun.'

'Yes.'

'Good.' Edward returned to his chair. 'Well, I don't think that I need to see you again.' He smiled at April and she grinned back.

Experience had taught Charlotte that this was the point where she stepped in.

'You will, of course, be seeing Charlotte again, and she'll monitor your progress. But I was wondering whether you had any questions for me.'

Okay. This was new. Usually he left the questions part to the nurses.

'Um… Not really…'

'Hmm. So what's this question you don't *really* need to ask, then?'

April smiled self-consciously at him. 'Well, I'm going to my end-of-year party at school in a couple of weeks' time.'

'Ah. That might be a little out of my area of expertise.'

He looked at Charlotte and she raised her eyebrows at him. So he was going to leave her something to do, at least.

'I think that April would be interested in knowing whether another couple of weeks is going to make an appreciable difference to the look of the scar. And whether she can use a little make-up. Is that right?'

April nodded. 'Yeah. There's someone I…'

'Yes. Of course. Well, the wound's been dry for a while now, and there's no reason why you shouldn't start to use light cosmetics occasionally, as long as they don't irritate your skin. Charlotte can advise on which types to use and so on. As to the look of it…' He paused, thinking for a while. 'Generally speaking, I'd expect that area to look better in two or three weeks' time than it does now. May I ask you a question, April?'

'Sure. What is it?'

'Well, it's a long time since I was your age…' He paused, as if waiting for a contradiction.

'Mmm,' April agreed.

'But I can certainly remember it.' He shot a stern look at Charlotte, who was barely repressing her laughter. 'And I have to say that any young man who disregards your smile and your personality, and who only sees a scar, isn't worth your time.'

'That's what my mother says…' April gave him a wry look.

'Well, it must be right, then.' Edward snapped his notepad shut with an air of finality.

'But…' April looked at him thoughtfully. 'But when I said I wanted my scar done she was all for it. So was my dad.'

Some of Isaac's questions prompted that very same baffled look from Edward, but he regrouped almost instantly. 'I look at it like this. What I do can't change who you are, because you're already special. My aim is to give you what you deserve.'

A slow smile spread across April's face. 'Nice one. Thanks.'

'You're very welcome, April.' Edward rose from his seat. 'Well, I can see that you ladies have some…um…things to talk about. Is your mother outside? I'd just like to have a quick word with her.'

April nodded and watched him go, before turning to Charlotte. 'You know, I thought that Dr North was a bit standoffish. But he's really nice, isn't he?'

Charlotte laughed. 'Yes, he is. Really nice.'

Charlotte wished Paula a good weekend and watched her go through the doors to the outside lobby. She waited for a few minutes and then made for Edward's office. She'd been saving her good news until they could talk uninterrupted.

'You got it, then?' He looked up when she tapped on the door, pushing the papers in front of him aside.

'How did you know?'

'I saw the courier delivery for you on the reception desk this morning.'

'Okay.' Charlotte sat down. 'So I had a delivery. It could have been anything.'

'That's just the first of my observations. The second was that the envelope was my father's stationery.'

'So you went to the Sherlock Holmes School of Medicine, did you? You'll have to do better than that. It could have been a letter from him telling me that there was some kind of problem.'

'Ah. Yes, it could.' Edward leaned back in his chair, the tips of his fingers touching to form an inverted V. 'But then you wouldn't have been looking like a cat that's just got the cream all afternoon.'

'I haven't!' That Edward had noticed the letter and known where it was from was hardly surprising. That he'd noticed *her* was still a new enough experience to make her shiver with pleasure.

'Yes, you have.' Edward gathered up some papers and stuffed them into his briefcase. 'Let's go.'

He picked up the heaviest of her shopping bags and ushered her out of his office.

He nodded a goodnight to Ethan Hunter, who had appeared from the lobby, and kept walking when Ethan spoke.

'Do you have a moment, Charlotte?'

'Yes, of course.'

It was all very well for Edward to walk on ahead, as if they both just happened to be leaving work at the same time, rather than together. But the canvas shopping bag with 'Smart Girls Recycle' emblazoned across it was hardly going to be his.

'Mrs Ashe asked to speak with me before she left.'

'Is there a problem?' Charlotte had thought that the session with April had gone well, but generally clients stopped to complain, rather than praise.

'She was very pleased with the way that April's procedure has been handled, and she especially mentioned how well you'd looked after her. I hear you even gave her some make-up advice. Well done.'

'Oh! Thank you, Ethan.' Perhaps it was relief, but she thought she saw a flicker of warmth in Ethan's normally impassive face. 'It was very nice of Mrs Ashe to take the time to speak with you.'

'She mentioned that Edward was very kind, as well...' Ethan was clearly a little perplexed by the concept.

'He always does his best for every patient.' Now probably wasn't the time to go into any apparent change in Edward's demeanour.

Ethan nodded. 'Yes, of course. And it's always good to hear that our clients value our people as much as we do. Passing their praise on is one of the more pleasant duties which falls to me when Leo's not around.'

'I appreciate it that you did. It means a lot.' Charlotte smiled up at Ethan and made a move towards the exit.

Ethan walked with her. 'You have a son?'

He'd clearly decided that this was one of those getting-to-know-you moments that a good employer should take with his employees. Charlotte wished he'd chosen a time when Edward hadn't been waiting for her outside.

'Yes. Isaac's five.'

'Must be quite a handful, then. Was he the boy I saw Edward playing with in his office a couple of weeks ago?'

'Um... Yes.'

'I've never seen Edward look so animated.' Ethan was smiling now. A little distant, as if he was thinking about something else at the same time, but definitely a smile. 'You and Edward make a good team.'

Charlotte swallowed hard and decided to interpret *good team* in a purely professional context. 'Isaac has a way of involving people. I suppose all children do...'

'Yeah. I guess they do. But Edward's a pretty tough nut to crack.' The smile faded and was replaced by Ethan's usual thoughtful look. The one that implied his thoughts on the matter were not particularly happy ones.

'No one's that tough.'

Ethan raised one eyebrow. 'I wouldn't go as far as to say

that.' He stepped forward, opening the door to the lobby for her, and Charlotte walked through.

Edward was waiting there, her shopping bag nestled against his own briefcase at his feet. He nodded briskly at Ethan, who returned the nod and disappeared along the hallway.

'Everything okay?' Edward waited until Ethan was out of earshot.

'Yeah, fine. Mrs Ashe told Ethan that you and I had done a good job with April, and he stopped to say thank you.'

'That's nice.'

'He said we made a good team.'

'Well, we do, don't we?'

That slight quirk of Edward's lips told her that he, at least, didn't have his mind completely on the professional. 'Why are you looking so glum? You've just had a vote of thanks from the boss. Ethan doesn't say these things unless he means them.'

What Ethan had really meant was beyond Charlotte. He'd seemed genuinely pleased for the little family unit which was forming before his eyes, but somehow... Charlotte sighed. If Ethan thought that it was beyond his own reach, then Charlotte was inclined to think it was beyond hers, too.

'What? What's the matter?'

'Nothing. Let's go home.'

She'd pushed the boat out and bought steak for dinner, cooking it in a peppered sauce with home-made chips. Edward and Isaac had tucked in with an almost identical glee, and been unanimous in their praise.

'I've been thinking.' Edward was helping her stack the dishwasher while Isaac played in the garden.

'Oh-oh. That generally means trouble...' She smiled at him.

He shot her a look of amused reproach. 'Would you like to go out tomorrow evening? To celebrate...or perhaps to commiserate. Whatever you feel like doing, I'll keep you company.'

'I feel like… No. Let's not do anything, eh? My marriage is over now, and I don't want to look back. I want to look forward.'

'Fair enough. So why don't you just let me treat you, then? My mother's coming over tomorrow afternoon, and she can look after Isaac for the evening if you'd like. We can go somewhere nice.'

Going out. On a Saturday night. It was years since she'd had the money to go anywhere, nice or otherwise, let alone pay for babysitters and… 'I don't really have anything to wear…'

He shrugged. 'You have clothes. We'll go somewhere where clothes are *de rigueur.*'

She couldn't help but laugh. 'Okay. Thank you. I'd love to.'

His smirk looked far too much as if this had been a plan and not an off-the-cuff invitation. 'Good. Mum'll be here about three tomorrow.'

It all seemed to go like clockwork. Edward's mother arrived on the doorstep at five to three the following day, and burst into the house like a friendly tornado. She kissed Edward, hugged Charlotte as if she'd know her for years, and made a beeline for Isaac, who was sitting on the floor playing with a construction set.

'That looks interesting.' Penny North had sat down on the sofa and was now looking hard at Isaac's handiwork.

'It's a spaceship.' Isaac looked up at her.

'Well, of course it is. Silly me.'

Isaac made his decision and opted to trust this stranger with some more information. 'Look, this is the engine.'

'Oh, I see. How clever.'

Edward nudged Charlotte. 'You want to leave them to it?'

His breath caressed her neck and she shivered. Suddenly it all seemed real. She had a date for tonight. Not just any old date, but a darkly handsome, sophisticated, talk-all-night date. And it looked as if Isaac was making his own arrangements for the evening.

'Yes. Let's go and make a cup of tea.'

After Kathy, his mother had seemed to give up all hope of seeing a woman, let alone a child, in Edward's house. Charlotte had gone upstairs to change and he sat with his mother on the patio, watching while Isaac ran around the garden. He liked this more than he was prepared to admit. His mother was clearly overjoyed, and had exceeded all expectations in her enthusiasm for both Charlotte and Isaac.

'Can't you take her somewhere nicer than that, Edward?'

'I like it there.'

'Yes, but a girl wants to be taken somewhere glamorous.' His mother waved her hand, encompassing all the glitzy nightspots that London had to offer. 'Somewhere she can kick her heels up and forget about everything.'

'Like Dad did with you?'

'Yes, now you mention it. Your father wined and dined me until I was far too giddy to say no when he asked me to marry him.'

'Don't jump the gun, Mother. We're just friends.'

'Yes, and that's all you'll ever be if you carry on like this. Just call upstairs, tell her to put her best dress on, and get on the phone and book somewhere nice....'

'She doesn't have a best dress. She's been living hand to mouth for the last few years...'

His mother let out a tut of disapproval. 'Well, couldn't you have taken her out and bought her something?'

'I could have tried, but she wouldn't have let me. She's... proud.' *Proud* wasn't really the word for it. Charlotte didn't have a lot of trust. But Edward didn't want to go there with his mother. 'And she looks great anyway, with or without a new dress.'

His mother nodded in satisfaction at the assertion. 'Well...

yes, all right, then. I can see the difficulty. But for goodness' sakes tell her how nice she looks, won't you? You can't expect women to just know what you're thinking.'

That was the thing. He'd thought that Kathy had known what he was thinking—if anyone should have done it would have been her. And she'd said he had no emotional commitment. Those words had been seared into his brain and had stayed there, like the ultimate condemnation.

'I don't expect anyone to know what I'm thinking.'

His mother quirked a smile. 'Well, that's just as well, dear. You'd already lost me by the time you were about ten. But this is different. We're not talking about advanced mathematics. We're talking about...' His mother groped for the right word.

'Emotions?'

'Yes, exactly. We all have the same emotions, irrespective of whether we can do complex equations in our heads.'

That was a matter of opinion. But Edward was saved from the rigours of that particular debate by Isaac, who tripped over his own feet and suddenly toppled, flat on his face, onto the grass. In a movement that was rapidly becoming instinctive Edward rose and hurried towards the boy.

'Hey, there.' Edward inspected him rapidly for any damage. 'Okay, mate. You're all right.'

Isaac didn't seem to think so, and clung to him, crying. Edward gave him a hug and his sobs subsided. 'There you are. Just a bit of a shock, eh? Have you hurt yourself?'

'No.' Isaac seemed ready to start careening around the lawn again, but then his attention was drawn to the patio.

Charlotte was wearing a simple white dress, with a lacy bodice that showed the curve of her shoulders and upper arms. Her light brown hair tumbled around her shoulders, shining in the sun. He wasn't close enough to see her eyes, but Edward knew that they would be shining, too.

'What do you think, mate? Doesn't your mother look gorgeous?'

Isaac nodded and Edward let him go. The boy rushed towards her, shouting at the top of his voice.

'Muuuum! Edward says you look gorgeous.'

Well, that was one way of doing it. His mother obviously approved, and Charlotte went pink with pleasure. He almost didn't dare go any closer, in case she captured him in some kind of spell.

'Well, thank you.' She was holding both of Isaac's hands, trying to keep them away from her dress. 'I'll just go and clean him up…'

'That's fine.' Edward hoisted the boy upwards, tucking him under his arm, and Isaac squealed with delight. 'We don't want to get your mother all dirty, do we?'

Finally they were alone. Instructions had been given, telephone numbers written down, and Charlotte had elicited a promise from Isaac to be extra good for the whole of the evening. The taxi had arrived, and she had allowed Edward to help her into it.

'This is nice.'

She seemed excited, even though she didn't yet know where they were going. Edward wondered whether it would be appropriate to put his arm along the back of the seat, and decided that he should probably wait until the way home.

'I didn't want to worry about parking. Or having a glass of wine if I felt like it.'

She nodded and smiled at him. That warm, bubbly smile of hers which so lifted his spirits when he saw it at work. Here, combined with the fact that she smelled absolutely wonderful, and with her skin just inches away from his touch…Edward was lost

CHAPTER FIFTEEN

THE TAXI LET them off in Soho. Bubbling with life, on a warm summer's evening, the atmosphere was going to Charlotte's head. Edward took her hand, easing them through the crowded pavements.

'Where are we going?'

'Here.' He stopped suddenly, then descended a set of steps which seemed to run down to a basement. Opening the door at the bottom, he gave his name to a woman, handed his jacket over, and they were waved through.

She already knew what this place was. Soft jazz was floating towards them, beckoning them into a small auditorium. They were shown to a table and the waiter gave them each a menu, and left.

The place wasn't posh, or glitzy, nor was it sleazy. It was the kind of place that no one other than a real jazz enthusiast would know about, and its clientele didn't come here to be seen, but to listen.

'Is this okay?' He leaned across the table, his mouth almost touching her cheek. 'We can go somewhere else if you don't like it.'

'It's wonderful. Can we stay?'

He nodded in satisfaction. 'Of course. What would you like to drink?'

The long cushioned seats were comfortable, and the wine that the waiter brought to the table was excellent, but it was really all about the music. A three-piece band played smooth, moody melodies, which made everything seem so very easy. She slid along the seat, closer to Edward, so that they could exchange a few words without distracting anyone.

The band finished their set to enthusiastic applause and a great deal of crashing about as they left the small stage.

'Would you like something to eat? We've got about half an hour before they bring the next band on.'

The waiters suddenly seemed to leap into action as they were beckoned by one table or another.

'There's going to be another one?'

'More than one. Until about four in the morning, usually.' Edward grinned at her.

'And how many times have you stayed until then?'

'Once or twice. I used to come here a lot, but not so much lately.'

'Can't do the late nights, eh?'

He shrugged. 'Not really. But you can come in here, have a glass of wine, go home early and be tucked up in bed by ten. It's more a state of mind.'

He did seem younger here. As if his quiet manner was more a result of relaxation than introspection. 'Are we going to stay for the next set?'

He nodded. 'As long as you like. The plan doesn't go any further than this.'

'What plan's that?'

'The plan for the evening. It ends here. We're on our own now.'

They weren't, of course. Charlotte knew that they had to get back at a respectable time so that Penny could get on home. But for a few sweet hours it seemed as if there was nothing else in the world. At some point Edward's arm seemed to have snaked along the cushions behind her. She appeared to have moved a little closer to him, and now she was in the circle of his warmth, talking to him, listening to the music with him.

The spell hardly broke when they left the club. The streets were dark now, lit by the glittering lights of Chinatown, and they strolled together through the crowds until they reached Oxford Street, where Edward flagged down a taxi.

The roads were clear of the daytime traffic, and it was starting to rain. Yellow light streaked the windows of the cab as they reached the leafy suburb of Hampstead. A sudden left turn, which would have thrown her against Edward if she hadn't already been leaning against him, and they were home.

'He's fast asleep.' Penny was smiling and seemed in a hurry to be off. 'I gave him some tea and he ran around in the garden until he dropped. Then we watched some TV together and he was out like a light when I put him to bed.'

Charlotte could hardly get a thank-you out before Edward had kissed his mother and was walking her to her car. He watched her out of the drive and then turned back to the house.

It was suddenly very quiet. And Edward was abruptly the only focus of her attention.

'Would you…um…like a cup of tea?'

'No.' He moved a little closer. 'Would you?'

'No. Not really.'

She knew what was coming next. It was drawing her in, like the dark, unknown depths of his eyes, with a force that she couldn't resist. Didn't want to resist. However unsure she was, however hard it was to trust Edward, tonight she didn't seem to recognise any of that. All she saw was him.

'I'll…I'll just go and check on Isaac.' Maybe he was awake. Maybe that would solve the debate that was going on in the back of her mind about what to do next.

'Okay.' He backed off, and flopped down onto the sofa.

Isaac was sleeping soundly, Stinky clutched in his arms, and Charlotte walked slowly back downstairs. That was it, then. It was just her and Edward.

'Is he okay?'

His voice was low, like honey on her senses.

'Yes, he's fast asleep.'

'Just you and me, then.' He motioned her to come and sit down next to him.

'Yes. Just the two of us.' She perched herself on the edge of the sofa, her legs tucked under her. For a moment it seemed that they would simply sit like this for a few minutes and then say goodnight.

Then he reached forward, curling his arms around her waist, almost lifting her onto his lap. His movements were so slow, so deliberate, that they might be mistaken for hesitancy, but there was no uncertainty about him. It was just Edward, doing what he did best, squeezing every last drop from each moment that passed.

'I had a great evening.' She leaned towards him, speaking quietly into his ear.

'Had?'

'Am having. Are you being pedantic?'

'No. Just working out where I stand.'

'This is where you stand.' She kissed his jaw.

He said nothing. For a moment she thought that she'd done the wrong thing, that this wasn't what he wanted. Then he turned and kissed her. Long and deep, leaving her breathless and melting in his arms.

'I've been wanting to do that all evening.' One hand rested lightly on her leg, travelling upwards towards her thigh.

'I've been wanting you to…' He didn't let her finish, before he kissed her again. That was okay. She'd said all she needed to, and now all she wanted was to be part of the strong, flowing tide of his passion.

'Come upstairs.'

'We'll have to be quiet. Isaac…'

'That's okay. We won't disturb him.' He kissed her again, his lips so soft on hers. So demanding. 'I'll stop if you get too *fortissimo*.'

'Funny man. What happens if *you* get too loud?'

'You'll just have to crack me over the head with a table lamp. Or suffocate me with a pillow. Plenty of options...'

A whole world of options, if those still waters ran as deep as she thought they might. More options than Charlotte really know how to deal with right now. But even that couldn't stop her.

'I'll bear it in mind.'

He smiled, that quiet half-smile which seemed touched with every possibility that she could think of, along with a few that she didn't know how to imagine. Then he gathered her close in his arms, lifting her effortlessly and making for the stairs.

Even though she'd been living here for two weeks now, Charlotte had never been inside his bedroom. She'd glimpsed pale, creamy walls bathed in sunlight when she passed by in the mornings, but had never dared to even put her head around the door. The first thing she noticed when he flipped on the lights was that, unlike pretty much every other room in the house, there were no books. Built-in wardrobes ran the full length of one wall, and a wide bed stood opposite the window, ready to catch the morning sun. It was like a soothing blank canvas for the rich pattern of Edward's thoughts.

He set her down onto her feet and closed the door quietly. Then he kissed her, backing her slowly towards the bed. 'Do you have...?'

'Yes.' He moved away for a moment, flipping open a drawer and taking out a box of condoms, putting it onto the small table by the bed.

'Thank you.' He made everything easy. Thought of the things she needed as well as the ones she wanted.

He reached around her, undoing the buttons which ran down the back of her dress. He slipped it from her shoulders, kissing each inch of flesh as he uncovered it. The fabric fell to her feet and she stepped out of it, kicking her sandals off.

'Say something, Edward.' She suddenly felt small and fearful in the shadow of his bulk.

'What can I say? You're beautiful beyond words.' He ran his fingertips down her arms. 'I want you more than I know how to express.'

'That's…' she gulped '…that's just fine.'

'Good.' His fingers again, tender on the side of her face. 'Because you put me at a loss, Charlotte.'

'That's just where we're supposed to be. If we weren't, then we wouldn't need each other to find the way.' She reached up to unbutton his shirt, pulling it open and off his shoulders.

She guessed she had his swimming to thank for the hard, muscular physique that was so good to look at, so warm and enticing when she ran her fingers across his chest. Each time he kissed her it was hotter. Deeper. Each time he laid his hand on her it was a little more demanding.

Before they even got to the bed they were both naked, trembling. He sat down on it, pulling her down onto his lap, astride him.

'Here.' He reached for the condoms, handing her one.

Slowly she rolled it down, loving the way that he gasped when her fingers touched him. Loving the warm feel of his skin when he pulled her close, lifting her. And then it went past loving, or adoring, or any of the other words that had seemed like something to aim for. Pure feeling washed over her when he lowered her slowly down, sliding inside her as he did so.

'Edward…' His name was the only thing on her mind.

'Charlotte…' He choked her name out, his hands twisting her hips so that they both gasped.

His hands, his mouth, caressed her. It was beyond bearing. Her body knew what to do, but he was holding her firmly in his lap, not letting her move the way she wanted to.

'Edward…please.'

One hand slipped between her legs and she almost cried out. He was intent on wringing every drop of pleasure from each moment, and the only doubt in Charlotte's mind was whether she was going to be able to bear it.

'I...can't...take much more of this.'

'Really?' His hand moved to her breast.

'Really. Edward...'

He didn't reply. He rolled his body round, until he was pinning her down on the bed, and with a look of unutterable tenderness slid inside her again. She felt her body mould to his, her hands grabbing at the sheets. Was that a moan? She put her hand to her mouth, biting hard on her knuckle.

He twisted his hips and her head spun. He caressed her, capturing her gasps in a kiss, and she was his. No thought, no fear, just feeling flowing through her, washing her clean of everything other than him. She gazed into his eyes, because they were the only things that made sense any more, and saw them darken. Felt his body stiffen and knew that he, too, had finally reached the point where he was as lost as she was.

Suddenly he was all fire. Coaxing her on, raising the temperature to boiling point. Stronger, sweeter, until her body arched of its own accord and waves of pure feeling washed through her.

Edward couldn't trust himself to speak. If he did he would say he loved her, that he would do anything for her if she'd just stay with him. And that was surely just the heat of the moment.

He felt a cool trickle of sweat trace its way down his spine, pooling in the small of his back. She was so beautiful. So giving. Her body was still quivering, little jolts still shaking her after the one great explosion of feeling. Then, as he watched her face, seeming to find endless fascination in the ever-changing detail, she broke him completely. A single tear trickled from her eye.

'Okay, sweetheart?' Perhaps he had been too demanding. He hadn't been able to help himself.

She gave him a slow, lazy smile which said that everything was better than okay. 'Yeah. Just fine. Happy tears.'

Charlotte wound her arms around his neck, pulling him

close, and he rolled over onto his side, curling his body around hers. Perfectly happy. Perfectly... Just perfect, really.

They woke in the night and made love again, but when he opened his eyes in the morning she wasn't there. He hadn't really expected her to be. Isaac couldn't know about this just yet. Maybe one day—if they lasted that long.

He showered alone, and dressed, drawn downstairs by the sound of her voice and Isaac's. She looked up as he stood in the doorway of the kitchen and smiled.

'Good morning.'

'Yes, it *is* a good morning.' His whole body felt as if it had been bathed in sunshine.

She flushed a little. 'Did we wake you?'

He shook his head. Isaac raced out of the kitchen, ready to attack the day, and Edward took his place at the table.

'I was going to bring you breakfast in bed as soon as I'd finished with Isaac.' Her mouth twisted in an expression of regret.

'Just as well you didn't.' He pulled her onto his lap and kissed her on the cheek. 'If I'd woken up and found you there I wouldn't have let you go.'

'No? Even if I'd had fresh coffee?'

He weighed the question up. 'Maybe if you'd had coffee... Is there any?'

'Right here.' She went to stand up, but he pulled her back down again.

'Charlotte, I know we have to keep this away from Isaac...'

'Yeah. I'm sorry. I just don't want to confuse him...'

'Don't be. I understand.' It didn't mean that he liked it, but he wouldn't hurt Isaac for anything. 'But that doesn't mean I won't be waiting for you. Tonight.'

She gave him a smile. 'Tonight it is, then. In the meantime, do you want some coffee?'

CHAPTER SIXTEEN

EDWARD WAS SMILING to himself. He could see Charlotte from his office, passing and re-passing the nurses' station. Something about the way she moved sent memories of last night and the night before pulsing down his spine.

He shouldn't be doing this. There were things to do—cases to review, patients to see. Admittedly there wasn't actually anything to do at this moment, but he was slipping. He hadn't touched the paper he was writing for a week, nor had he been swimming. He badly needed some thinking time.

The phone rang and Edward glared at it. He was far too busy interrupting himself at the moment to encourage anyone else to do so. He snatched up the receiver.

'North.'

'Edward, it's Ethan. I've a case here that I think you might be interested in.'

Something tingled at the back of his neck. The excitement of a challenge. He could do with that at the moment—before the tilt in the balance of his life became a catastrophic slide.

'I'll be right there.'

Edward was, indeed, interested. The surgery was slated for a couple of months hence, and it would be complicated, demanding, and require painstaking preparation. It was just the thing.

Their review of the notes was interrupted by the phone.

Ethan's brow darkened. His habitual cool courtesy when dealing with the clinic staff was clearly being tested.

'Can you take a message please? I've asked for all of my calls to be put on hold for the next half-hour....' Someone spoke urgently at the other end of the line. 'Ah, Helen, it's you...' He listened again, and then nodded briskly. 'Okay. Yes, thanks, Helen. You were right to let me know. Put her through, please.'

Edward made to leave, but Ethan waved him back into his seat. 'I have to take this, but I won't be long.' He turned back to the phone. 'Olivia...?'

A pulse was beating at the side of Ethan's brow, but his face was fixed, impassive. The look of a soldier about to go into battle. He listened, concentrating on the phone and the notes that he was scribbling. 'Repeat that, please... Okay, got it. All right, consider it done. We'll courier all the paperwork out to you.'

He placed the phone back gently into its cradle. Ethan seemed deep in thought and Edward didn't ask.

'Can you do something for me?' Finally Ethan spoke.

'Of course.'

'That was Olivia Fairchild. Leo's away, and there are some problems with a visa for one of the kids she's sending to the clinic. I'm not sure quite what's involved, but I think there's just a declaration of some sort to be made from our end. Olivia will be travelling with the girl and her mother, so we can send any necessary paperwork straight through to her.'

Edward nodded. 'Leave it with me.' Was that relief he saw on Ethan's face? It probably wasn't anything to do with the legal complexities involved, because there weren't any. 'Give me your notes.'

'Thanks.' Ethan made a few more jottings on the pad in front of him and handed the paper over to Edward. 'Appreciate it.'

* * *

It was like leading a double life. A triple life, actually. There was the persona that she adopted at work—the one that hardly noticed Edward was even there unless he was giving instructions of a medical nature. The one that she had fallen into at home, being a part of the unlikely family that she, Edward and Isaac seemed to have made for themselves. And there was the one which lasted from the time that Isaac went to bed through to the early hours of the morning.

Evenings spent by the piano, talking together or just keeping each other company. Or reading together, their limbs entwined, Charlotte with her book and Edward with his. Early nights, when they had the opportunity to do all the things that they dared not talk about during the day, and which were increasingly bleeding into her thoughts at the most inappropriate times.

'Where's Edward?'

She and Isaac were having tea in the kitchen together. Edward had made it back home only just in time to say goodnight to Isaac for the last three evenings, and Isaac had missed playing with him after tea.

'He's at the hospital, sweetie. He's got to stay and make sure that the people he's looking after are okay.'

Isaac frowned. 'What people?'

Good question. But her own uncertainties weren't the issue here. It had been less than two weeks since she and Edward had first spent the night together, and it had taken only a week before the slow, subtle sense that he was withdrawing from her became apparent. When he was there he was still as committed, still as quietly loving. He just wasn't there as much as he used to be.

'People who are sick, sweetie.' She leaned across the table towards Isaac. 'There's a little boy, about your age, who's had an accident and lost his thumb. Edward's going to give him a new one.'

Isaac regarded his own thumb thoughtfully. 'A bionic thumb...?'

'No, a real one.' Charlotte decided to skip the bit about how the child had lost two other fingers as well, and that the reconstruction of one side of his hand was ground-breaking in its complexity.

'Is that what Edward's doing now?'

Difficult to say. She'd heard about this particular case from one of the other doctors, not Edward. 'The operation's tomorrow. I expect he's preparing for it.'

'And Edward will make the boy better?'

'Yes, he will, sweetie.' Charlotte could give that assurance, at least, with a clear conscience.

'Good.'

Isaac seemed satisfied, even if Charlotte didn't share his confidence. Isaac was too young to remember the excuses that his father had made for being out every evening. Things to do at work. Client entertaining. She reminded herself that Edward was doing something worthwhile, and not running up debts that he couldn't pay.

She heard a noise at the front door and Isaac slipped down from his seat, running into the hallway. So different from the child who, just four weeks ago, had nearly jumped out of his skin when someone knocked on the door.

'Hey, buddy.'

She heard Edward's voice and suddenly all of her fears and uncertainties seemed unreasonable. Not that they stopped pinching at her heart, but for the time being they receded to mere what-ifs instead of painful certainty.

'Is he better?' Isaac was perched against Edward's side, tugging at his shoulder to gain his attention.

'Is who better?'

'That boy...?'

Edward's querying gaze lit on Charlotte's face.

'Isaac was asking where you were.' Charlotte hadn't dared ask, thinking that it was assuming a bit too much. 'I told him that you were making another little boy well. The one you're operating on tomorrow.'

'Ah.' He turned to Isaac. 'The boy's not better yet, but he will be. We're taking good care of him, and he's going to be just fine.' He set Isaac back onto his feet and sat down.

'Would you like something to eat?'

He looked up at her. That dark blue gaze made everything else seem beside the point. The smile overrode every other sensation apart from pleasure.

'No, that's fine, thank you. I've already eaten. I've still got some more to do tonight, but I came home to see Isaac before his bedtime.'

Charlotte turned quickly. She wasn't being fair. He had things to do. He didn't take her for granted, as Peter had done, expecting his dinner to be on the table whatever time he came home.

'Coffee, then.' She smiled brightly at him. 'You'll have some coffee? And I made cheesecake.'

'That sounds fantastic.' He caught Isaac's eye. 'Hey, are you having cheesecake, too? Or are you just going to run around the kitchen while I eat?'

Isaac swooped towards the table, flapping his arms like a pair of wings, and sat down next to Edward. For the moment, at least, before Edward retreated again into his study, the world was as it should be.

The operation must have finished hours ago. It was ten o'clock, and Edward still wasn't home. Charlotte had tried his mobile and it went straight to voicemail. She didn't dare try again, because a list of missed calls from her would look as if she was crowding him. There was only one thing to do, and that was call the hospital.

It took a while to pluck up the courage to do it, and then another five minutes of waiting on hold before she got to speak to the right person. Then she wished she hadn't. It was only a twenty-minute drive from the hospital at this time of night, and Edward had left at nine.

'Not to worry. Thanks.' She smiled into the phone, as if that might give some believability to her words. Of course she was going to worry.

'He said he was going to check back in again when he got home... If there's any message?'

Charlotte pursed her lips and then went for it. 'Can you tell me whether he's done that yet? Checked back in?'

'Yes, hold on...' A keyboard clicked into the silence on the line. *'Here it is. Yes, he called in about twenty minutes ago. Said we could reach him on his mobile if there was any problem.'*

'Thanks. I'll try that, then.'

Charlotte hung up. So what was she going to do now? Edward obviously hadn't been in an accident on his way home because he'd called in. And he obviously didn't want anyone to know where he was.

She knew exactly what she *wasn't* going to do. She'd been here before and refused to believe what was staring her right in the face. The cold, hard proof of the credit card statements that her husband had kept hidden for so long. The affair that he had denied for so long. It had almost broken her.

Not again. Edward was a man with secrets, and she wasn't going to sit around, waiting for them to shatter her life. This time she'd protect Isaac—and she'd protect herself.

The following day was a Friday, and he was home early for the first time that week. Last night Charlotte had been unable to sleep until she'd heard the front door close quietly at two a.m. and Edward's footsteps on the stairs, disappearing along the hallway and into his room. She hadn't slept much after that, either, and in the morning Edward had left for the Lighthouse Children's Hospital before she was out of bed.

'I've been thinking.' She'd waited until Isaac was in bed before she spoke with him.

'Yeah?' He looked up from the papers that he was reading.

'I think it's time for Isaac and me to go home.'

He set the papers to one side, blank shock on his face. 'Is there something the matter, Charlotte?'

Everything that she could imagine. Edward was tired of her and didn't know how to tell her. He had another woman somewhere. He was too self-absorbed to really care about her or Isaac. One or more of those, in any combination. Or something else, perhaps, that she hadn't thought about.

'We were only going to stay for a few days. It's been nearly a month and…' She took a deep breath. 'I'm so grateful for everything you've done for us, Edward. But we can't stay on here indefinitely.'

This would be the time for him to say that they weren't overstaying their welcome. That he wanted her and Isaac to stay. They'd have to talk a bit—about how he seemed to have drawn back recently—but perhaps there was an explanation for that.

He stared at her. 'You want to go?'

Disappointment curled around her heart. 'I think that we should.'

She could see him changing before her eyes. The lover who had turned her world into something that was closely akin to magic was turning into a man. One who accepted her leaving as if it had been inevitable all along and wouldn't say one word to persuade her to stay. Cold grief began to trickle into her heart.

'And us?'

She was almost ready to beg him. She would have done almost anything to keep him just for one more day. One more day when anything might happen, when she might find a way to penetrate the icy shell that seemed to be forming around him. Then she thought of the way she'd worried about him last night. The way Isaac had fought to stay awake so that he could say goodnight to Edward.

'Edward, I have no hold on you. Whatever you were doing

last night is none of my business…' He opened his mouth and she held up her hand to stop him from speaking. 'No. Really, I don't want to know. It can't work between us, and I think it would be better if we just accepted that.'

He could rage against this. Tell her that she was crazy—that he'd been called away to some medical emergency and hadn't been able to call her. At this moment she would have believed lies, excuses—anything. But tomorrow she'd wake up and hate herself for allowing a man to betray her again.

He ran his hand through his hair and a few dark spikes fell back across his forehead. 'Okay. If that's what you want… I'll help you move back over the weekend.'

'That's all right. You must have things to do…'

He shook his head. 'No. I brought you here and I'll take you home.'

She didn't have to say it. He'd heard it before, and Kathy had just been proved right. *Emotionally unavailable.*

Edward couldn't argue with her. She needed more than he could give and so did Isaac. Scratch that. They both *deserved* more than he could give. If breaking his heart was the only way they were going to get it, then so be it.

He hadn't slept much last night, and more than once he'd gone to the door of his bedroom, ready to march along the hallway, gather her up and bring her back. Plead with her—beg her, even—or make love to her until she changed her mind. But each time the futility of such a course of action had stopped him. She didn't want him.

She clearly didn't believe him when he went out early on Saturday morning, with the excuse of having to go to work. Unable to set his mind to anything, he wandered the busy streets, fed the ducks in Hyde Park and dropped in to one of his favourite restaurants for a solitary meal. By the time he got back, late in the afternoon, she had packed hers and Isaac's things and explained to the boy that they were going back home.

Then it was time for them to leave. They somehow managed to stay civil with each other, for Isaac's sake, but they were like actors in a soap opera. As soon as the cameras stopped rolling the smiles fell from their faces and there was no emotion, no more to say. Nothing.

He loaded up his car with their bags and they made the short drive to Charlotte's house in silence. She opened the front door and Isaac ran inside, but it seemed from the way that she blocked the doorway that Edward wasn't welcome. He put her bags down on the doorstep and went back to the car to fetch the rest of them.

She called for Isaac and turned towards Edward. 'Thank you. I'm so grateful for everything that you've done for us.'

Yeah, right. And she was showing him just how grateful she was by leaving. Blocking her own doorway as if he was one of the people that he'd protected her from. The words were on the tip of his tongue when he saw a tear, perched in the corner of her eye and ready to fall.

'If there's anything else you need...'

There was no point in even saying it. They'd lost their opportunity of being friends. He'd blown it—hadn't paid enough attention to the woman he'd thought might be the saving of him—and now they had to part. Better now than some time down the line.

She nodded. 'Say thank you to Edward, Isaac.'

He almost couldn't bear this. Charlotte's cold determination was one thing, but Isaac seemed genuinely sad at their parting. He dropped to one knee and the boy flung his arms around his neck.

'Thank you, Edward. I've had a good time.'

'Me, too.'

'Can we come back to see you again?' Isaac turned his questioning gaze up to Edward.

'Yes, of course. Any time you like. But I'm going to be working hard for the next few weeks. We might not see each other for a little while.' Isaac would probably forget all about him in the space of those weeks. He wouldn't make this more difficult for Charlotte than he had to.

Isaac nodded. 'Okay.'

His trusting acceptance of the lie almost made Edward choke, and he hung for dear life onto the thought that at all costs the child should be protected from the mistakes of his elders.

'Thank you.' Charlotte's face was flushed and she was a moment away from tears.

He should go. Her tears didn't make any difference, and the tearing pain in his chest didn't either. Whatever he felt, whatever he did, it wasn't enough. He didn't have it in him to give any more, and more was exactly what she deserved.

'Take care, Charlotte.' He turned on his heel and walked down the front path without looking back.

CHAPTER SEVENTEEN

CHARLOTTE HAD BEEN dreading returning to work, but it seemed that Edward had dropped out of the life of the Hunter Clinic almost as effectively as he'd dropped out of her own. Even when he was there she wasn't part of his patient care team, and she wondered whether he'd had a quiet word with someone to make that happen.

Perhaps it would be a good idea to look for another job. It was going to be awkward, being faced with the possibility of seeing Edward day in and day out. Particularly since this feeling didn't show any signs of going away. If she had to grieve the loss of the man she'd hoped might be everything to her, then she'd rather do it in private.

She made a few calls and managed to get Friday off. She presented herself at an employment agency at nine o'clock that morning, and by ten she'd been interviewed, the consultant had reviewed her CV, and had promised that she'd be able to find her another job easily.

It was the first step. The next step was to go and see Edward's father, explain the situation to him and ask whether he'd take payment for all that he'd done. It might take a while, but she'd pay that debt off even if she couldn't pay the one she owed to Edward.

When she called his office, his secretary said that he was out all day and took a message. On to step three. She hurried home, changed into an old pair of jeans and T-shirt, and went up to Isaac's room. He'd been so good this week, obviously missing the extra space to play and Edward's large, widescreen TV, but he hadn't complained. Isaac was playing with a friend this evening and she wouldn't be picking him up until eight. She had plenty of time to finish off the little treat she had planned for him.

She surveyed the blank wall opposite Isaac's bed. It wasn't Edward's garden or his TV that Isaac missed. Her son was feeling the same way that she was. He missed Edward. The way he played with him, the way they laughed at the same jokes, how he'd been there for him when things got tough.

'Stop it.' She admonished herself as harshly as she could. Every spare moment she'd had for the last week, whenever she'd been alone, she'd spent the time crying. It was time for her to face facts and get on with it. She'd gone into this with her eyes open, knowing full well that a quiet guy with things to hide was going to cause her pain. Now she'd just got what she had asked for.

She looked at her watch. Eight hours before she had to go and pick Isaac up this evening. She'd better get moving. She hurried to her bedroom and pulled the box of paints and the carefully cut stencils out from under the bed. Time to get to work.

Edward didn't need to think too hard about what he was about to do. He'd already thought it to death, and the one thing he needed to do now was to act. His diary was clear for the day, and he'd hoped that he could make some progress on the research paper that he was writing, but when he'd heard that Charlotte had taken the day off he'd grasped his opportunity.

When he drew up outside her house he noticed that the front window was open. She must be home. He knew that she wouldn't go out without locking the place up securely.

He pressed the doorbell. Flipped the letterbox open and heard the sound of music coming from somewhere. Looking upwards, he thought he saw some movement behind the thick muslin curtains that shaded what must be her bedroom.

'Charlotte…' He called through the letterbox and waited.

Nothing. The music seemed to have stopped and the house was quiet. He slipped the package he'd brought through the letterbox. That was hers, and if she wouldn't let him in he could at least make sure she got it.

The first part of his plan was achieved. The second would be a little more difficult. He straightened up, wondering whether he should go and wait in his car. She had to come out sooner or later.

His gaze lit on a small arched alleyway which ran between Charlotte's house and next door's, giving access to the back gardens. At the far end were two gates, the one on Charlotte's side slightly ajar.

The gate opened into a small, neat garden. There was washing on the line, and when Edward twisted the handle of the back door it opened.

'Charlotte?' He poked his head inside and called to her, not wanting to frighten her. 'Charlotte, it's Edward.'

'Go away. Please.' Her voice sounded strained and insistent.

Maybe she was upstairs with someone. Another man, perhaps. Edward shook his head. He knew her better than that.

'Charlotte, I want to speak to you.'

Silence.

'I'm coming upstairs, Charlotte.' He called up the stairs and in the absence of an answer kept walking. He could hear the muffled sounds of movement now, coming from the bedroom at the back of the house.

The door was closed and he knocked, left it a moment and then twisted the handle. The first thing he saw was the plastic taped onto the carpet along one wall. There were pots of paint on the floor, and the start of what looked like a mural on the wall—a giraffe which grinned towards the bed. Then his heart lurched. Charlotte was sitting cross-legged on the floor, in the corner of the room, crying.

'Charlotte. Please don't cry. I only want to talk to you.' He knelt in front of her, afraid to touch her.

She raised her face towards him. Stained with tears and flushed with defiance. 'So much that you broke into my house to do it?'

'Well, technically I didn't break in. The back door was open.'

'Edward!' Her cheeks bloomed a shade redder and she jumped to her feet, almost knocking him backwards. 'It doesn't matter. I want you to go.'

He stood slowly. He needed a moment to debate what to do next, but she wasn't going to give it to him.

'Just go!' Her outstretched arm pointed the way for him.

'No.'

'I could call the police. You told me that.'

'Fair enough. It's your right to do that. But I'm asking you not to.'

'Why should I listen? You're not listening to what I'm saying.'

'Because I love you, Charlotte.' He'd blurted the words out without thinking. He stepped forward until he was almost touching her, but his head was cool now. 'I love you.'

'Don't!' She dissolved into tears, sobs racking her body. 'Stop it…'

'Can't do that.' He had to go through with it now, because after this he sure as hell wasn't going to get another chance. 'Won't do it.'

'I can't trust you, Edward.'

'You mean you can't trust anyone. You just can't let go, can you? You might just as well still be married to that husband of yours.'

One sharp intake of breath and she raised her hand and slapped him. Edward had never been slapped by a woman before, and he'd underestimated how much it would sting.

'That might be construed as assault.'

Her hand had flown to her mouth in horror at what she'd done, but she still wouldn't back down. 'You're in my space. I'm just defending myself…'

'I know. You don't need to, Charlotte.'

'What do you know about it?' She pushed him away. 'He did nothing but lie to me—all the time. He told me that he was working when he was out spending every last penny, putting us in debt. He had a mistress and I never even knew about it until their child was three years old…' Tears were beginning to streak her face.

'And you gave him the benefit of the doubt and believed him.'

'Yes. And I'm never going to do that again…'

'Then we're done, Charlotte.'

Edward had never seen himself as a gambler. He weighed up the chances, took the safest route. He'd never before staked everything on one precarious throw of the dice.

Her nerve broke first. 'All right, then. So where were you that night when you didn't come home until two in the morning? Don't tell me you were at the hospital, because I know you weren't.'

'How do you know that?' The old guilt pushed back into his heart. Why did no one ever seem to understand that he needed to be alone sometimes?

'Because I phoned there. You left at nine and said you were going home.'

'I had some work to do at the clinic and I popped in there…' Edward shook his head. This was never going to work on lies. However much he was ashamed of the truth, it was that or nothing now.

He'd had a taste of nothing, and he didn't want to go back to it.

'I went to the clinic and took a swim. Then I went out for something to eat and…just walked for a while. Sometimes I need to regroup.'

She stared at him. 'What's so bad about that? That you couldn't just tell me?'

Suddenly the room seemed too small. Even with the windows open the pressure of their emotions was intolerable. But he couldn't leave. Mustn't leave. If he did that then he would only prove that he couldn't fight for her.

He took a deep breath. He'd start from the beginning and he'd get it right this time. 'When Kathy left me she said I was emotionally unavailable. That's stayed with me, and I let you go because I didn't believe that I had any right to ask you to stay. I was never sure that I could give you and Isaac the commitment that you both need.'

She opened her mouth to protest and he brushed his finger across her lips.

'Please. I have to say this. I'm older now, and a bit wiser. I know that I can change, and it's time for me to do just that if I've got any hope of you taking me back.'

She shook her head in disbelief. 'No. Oh, no. You don't need to change. Edward, I see right through you. You have feelings and emotions just like the rest of us. You just need to say what they are—not hide them away in case someone doesn't understand you.'

'I think…that's one of the nicest things you've said to me.' She'd said a lot of nice things, and he couldn't be sure.

'What? That you have feelings…?'

'No, that you see right through me. If you do, then you'll know how much I love you. How happy you make me. That I'll never let you down.'

She stared at him. This was everything she'd ever wanted. All she had to do was take it.

'You have to trust me, Charlotte. You told me once that I could learn. So can you.'

'I…I'm not such a quick study as you… I'm going to be rubbish at this.'

'Fair enough. We can both be rubbish together. Do you

believe that I can give you my heart? And that it'll be enough for you and Isaac?'

It felt as if she was making a solemn vow. 'Yes, I do.'

'Well, then it follows that you must trust me.'

She took hold of the end of his tie. Tugged a little. He moved closer. 'We're two sides of a coin, aren't we? Very different.'

'Yeah, but it's the same coin.'

'Back to back?'

That smile that Charlotte loved so much. Sexy, thoughtful, provocative.

'I prefer face to face.' His hands moved to her waist, and she melted into his warmth. 'Although...'

She stopped him with a look. There was time to talk sex later. This was more important and she couldn't wait any longer to say it. 'I love you.'

'I love you, too, Charlotte.' He glanced around, as if looking for some way to prove it. 'I love you so much that I'll help you finish that mural for Isaac. Even though I'm wearing an Italian silk suit.

'You could go home and change.' But suddenly she didn't want him to go anywhere.

'I won't get that twenty minutes back again.'

She was going to have to get used to feeling this happy. At the moment it was too heady, and she could hardly breathe. 'I could come with you.'

He nodded. 'That's a great start.'

CHAPTER EIGHTEEN

'When do you need to pick Isaac up?' He was carefully putting the finishing touches to his part of the mural.

'Not for another couple of hours. He's gone to play at a friend's house. I have to pick him up at eight.'

'I'll take you, if that's okay. I've missed the little guy.'

'Of course it's okay.' A thought occurred to Charlotte. 'I always wondered…'

'Yeah?'

'Why do you have a child's seat in your car?'

He chuckled. 'I got it for when my sister and her little girl came to stay with my parents. She only used it once. I was going to take it out of the car that weekend, but then it came in handy for Isaac.' He paused, his hand hovering over the last delicate part of a lion's eye. 'What? You thought that I had a child tucked away somewhere?'

'No, not really. I just didn't know. Was it okay for me to ask?'

He chuckled. 'Yep. And, in the interests of complete transparency, there's something I need to know too.'

'Fire away.'

'Why does Isaac call that blue rabbit of his Stinky?'

'Ah. The blue rabbit. I seem to remember he was the one that started everything…'

'That's why I feel such an attachment to him.'

'Well, he was originally called Rabbit.' She grinned at him.

'For obvious reasons. Then Isaac threw him into the pond at the park, and when I'd fished him out again I told Isaac he'd need a good wash because he was really stinky.'

'Ah. Makes me feel so much better to know that there's a logic behind it.'

She laughed. 'Anything else you need to know?'

'Not at the moment. You've got paint on your nose.' He closed the distance between them and swiped at her nose with his finger.

'Better?'

'Not really. I just seem to have smudged it.' He grinned, looping his arms around her waist. In the last few hours all the barriers between them seemed to have disappeared. At some point, while they were painting the bright, colourful mural, all the promises they'd made, the honesty and the trust, had turned from just words into reality.

'Do you think he'll like it?'

'Well, *I* like it.' Edward grinned. 'I think he'll love it. The monkey's great.'

'And your lion. He looks a bit like you.' She pulled at one of the dark spikes of hair that had fallen across Edward's forehead, which mirrored the slightly rakish look of his lion's mane.

He laughed, sweeping his hair back off his forehead with one hand. 'He's more like you.' Edward kissed her eyelids. 'Golden eyes…' he loosed her hair from its bonds at the back of her head, smoothing it over her shoulders '…golden hair…'

'A nasty roar…?'

'That's one of the things I love about you.'

'What else?'

'Let's get cleaned up. Then I'll tell you.' He backed out of Isaac's room, pulling her along the hallway. 'You'll have to hurry. There's a lot to get through.'

They showered together, his strong, gentle hands soaping her clean as if they were washing away what had gone before, starting again. Then they made love. As if it were possible to actually create and mould love into the shape and texture that fitted both their hearts, feeling it grow and flourish between them.

Charlotte had wondered whether there could be anything better than the slow, almost silent build of heat that Edward gently nurtured until the fire in him broke loose and roared through them both. Now she knew. When he told her everything that he was feeling her heart spoke back, sharing the warmth, sharing the longing. Body and soul. He made love to her body and her soul.

They lay together, perfect and still, a fine sheen of sweat covering their bodies. Even that seemed to be something shared…his scent covering her skin. She knew that she was never going to be able to wash it off.

'It'll be time to go soon.' He smoothed a strand of hair back from her face. 'However much I want to see whether next time can be as good as the last.'

'Hmm… Me, too. Will you stay for something to eat tonight? Isaac would love to have you read a bedtime story for him.'

'I'd love that, too.' A thought seemed to occur to him. 'What did you do with the packet that I put through your letterbox?'

'The one with your father's practice logo on it? I thought that came in the post?'

'No, I left it there.' He grinned at her. 'Go and get it.'

Edward knew that she'd torn the wrappings from the parcel as she walked back up the stairs because he heard her gasp of surprise. She walked back into the bedroom, tears streaming down her face and her mother's ruby necklace in her hand.

'Edward. Where did you get this?'

'Put it on and I'll tell you.'

Her hand flew to the neck of her silky dressing gown. 'I'm not really dressed for it.'

'Then take that off.'

She laughed, jumping onto the bed and handing him the necklace to fasten around her neck. 'So tell me where you got this.'

'I had help. You put my father in touch with the guy you sold it to. Luckily he keeps good records, so he was able to forward our letter on to the woman he'd sold it to.'

'And…she sold it back to you?'

'Well, I didn't break into her house and steal it, if that's what you're worried about. I told her how much I wanted it, and why, and she sold it to me. And now it's back where it belongs.'

'Edward… It must have cost you…'

He silenced her. 'I wanted to undo what's been done. Give you some reason to trust.'

Her eyes filled with tears. 'You're the only reason I need.' She clasped her hand to her neck. 'I love that you've done this for me, but I don't need anything other than you.'

'You have me.' He held her close, revelling in the sound of her heart beating beneath the thin fabric of her dressing gown. 'There's nothing to stop me from giving you more, is there?'

'But I have nothing to give you in return.'

'You and Isaac have already given me everything I'd ever want. More than I ever thought I could have. But there is something you can do for me.'

He wondered whether he should really ask this of her. Charlotte had said she trusted him, and he believed her, but perhaps this wasn't the time to be testing that out.

'What is it?'

'There's something I have to do tomorrow and I can't tell you about it. That'll be the last time you don't know where I am.' He watched her intently, looking for any signs of suspicion in her eyes.

She took his hand and laid it over her heart. Then kissed him. The taste of happiness, right there on his lips. 'I'll see you on Sunday, then.'

'You can rely on it. Eleven o'clock.'

* * *

At five to eleven on Sunday morning Isaac jumped down from his perch at the sitting room window and thundered into the hallway. 'He's here…'

'Open the door, then.' One last look in the mirror at her hair and make-up, and the pretty white top that she'd splashed out on yesterday, and Charlotte hurried downstairs to find Isaac and Edward deep in conversation in the hallway.

His smile, when he caught sight of her, told her everything she needed to know.

'You look gorgeous.'

'Thank you. You look pretty gorgeous yourself.'

Edward grinned, pressing on with what was clearly a well-planned preliminary to their afternoon. 'I've just been asking Isaac, as the man of the house…' he glanced conspiratorially at Isaac '…whether it's all right to kiss you.'

Charlotte could feel the happiness radiating from her. 'And what did he say?'

'I said yes. That will be quite all right.' Isaac seemed to be taking his duties seriously.

'Good.' She grinned at Edward and he took a step forward, kissing her lightly on the lips.

'Is that all?' Isaac sounded disappointed.

'You think I should kiss her a bit more?'

'Yes.'

Edward took the hint. Taking her in his arms, he bent her backwards until she would have slipped over if he hadn't had her safe in his embrace. He kissed her on the lips until she was dizzy.

'Better?' He set her back on her feet.

'Much,' Charlotte whispered into his ear.

'Yes.' Isaac gave his blessing to the proceedings. 'Can we go now? I want to fly my kite.'

Edward laughed. 'That's all part of the plan.'

They drove to the same spot where they'd flown their kites the last time, carrying their bags up the steep slope to the summit. Laying a rug out on the grass, Edward opened the picnic basket she'd prepared, inspecting its contents.

'Strawberries?' He grinned up at her.

'Yes. And I've saved some more for later. When Isaac's in bed.' She grinned back at him.

'That I like the sound of. Come here.'

They sat together in the sun, watching Isaac, who was running around in circles, emulating one of the gliders they'd seen in the sky.

'I still can't believe it.'

'What can't you believe?'

'That you're here. That I love you so much.' She shifted into the circle of his arms. 'You and Isaac. I don't think I could ask for anything more than the both of you.'

'Shame. You won't be wanting any of this, then.' He reached for the cool bag he'd brought and drew a bottle of chilled champagne out of it.

She chuckled. 'Well, maybe just a glass. But won't it be a waste? You won't be able to finish the rest; you're driving.'

He shrugged. 'We can finish it when we get home.'

The cork popped out of the neck of the bottle and flew spectacularly through the air. Isaac's head followed its trajectory and he ran to pick it up, stowing it in his pocket before resuming his imaginary flight up and down on the grass.

Edward turned towards her, handing her a glass, his own only half full. She tipped hers against his, smiling. 'To today.'

'And all the others to come.'

'Yes.'

She took a sip, aware that he was watching her intently. 'This is nice.'

He nodded. Took a sip from his own glass, never taking his eyes off her.

'What?'

'You're so beautiful.'

He made her feel beautiful. She leaned forward and kissed him.

'I love you, Charlotte. You and Isaac.' His gaze was still on her, dark and intent. 'You've shown me how to live my life, and I won't let you down.'

He seemed to have something on his mind. 'What's the matter, Edward?'

'Drink your champagne.'

She lifted the glass, and as she tipped it something solid slid against her lips. Jumping, she emptied the glass onto the grass beside her. 'What was that?'

Edward started to chuckle, flopping onto his back on the blanket, as she searched in the grass.

'Don't laugh—there was something in my drink...' She searched in the grass to find whatever it was, and then she saw it. Sparkling in the sunlight.

'That didn't go quite the way I planned.' He was still lying on his back, laughing.

'Did you put this in my glass?' She leaned over him, holding the ring in front of his nose.

'Yep. I thought it might be romantic. You know—finding a ring in your glass. But you weren't looking at what you were drinking.'

'That's because I only have eyes for you.'

He chuckled. 'Clearly.' He wrapped his arms around her and she leaned in for a kiss. 'So now that I've messed that up completely...'

'No, you haven't. You couldn't have done anything nicer.'

'Well, will you? Marry me? I meant everything I said, Charlotte. About loving you and looking after you and Isaac...'

'I know. I love you, too, Edward. And, yes, I'll marry you.' She handed him the ring, wanting more than anything for him to slip it onto her finger. 'Was this what you were doing yesterday?'

'Mmm-hmm. Do you like it?'

'It's perfect.'

She looked at the ring in his hand. Three large diamonds.

One for each of them—the family that she'd so wanted. Her heart was going to burst if things got any better.

Isaac skidded to a halt next to Edward and flung himself across his stomach.

'*Ooof.* Steady on, mate, I was just having a conversation with your mother.'

'What about?'

Edward laughed, giving in to the inevitable. Heaving himself upright, taking both her and Isaac with him, he held the ring up for Isaac to see. 'I've asked her to marry me.'

'Do you love her, then?'

Charlotte smiled. Isaac seemed instinctively to know the only thing that mattered.

'Yes, I do.'

'Does she love you back?'

'Yep. I think she's crazy, but she loves me.'

Isaac looked from Edward to Charlotte and then back again. 'Will we come to live with you?'

'What do you think about that?'

'Can I have animals on my wall? At your house?'

Edward chuckled. 'Well, it'll be *our* house if you come to live there. And you can definitely have animals on your wall. I'll paint them for you myself.'

'Okay.'

Isaac watched as Edward slipped the ring onto her finger. It fitted perfectly.

'Well, that's a relief.'

His smile said it all. Charlotte wanted to see that smile for the rest of her life.

'Are you going to kiss her again?' Isaac was clearly interested in doing things properly.

'You know what, mate? I think I just might.'

* * * * *

200 HARLEY STREET: THE SHAMELESS MAVERICK

LOUISA GEORGE

To Kamy Chetty, thanks for all your support, positive words and help with the icky medical details (any errors are totally mine) xx

And to Jane Beckenham, without you I just wouldn't be here writing this – thank you so much for all your support, enthusiasm and words of wisdom and for introducing me to the world of romance books... this one's for you! xx

CHAPTER ONE

'MAKE SURE TO get my best side, won't you now?' Declan Underwood joked to the army of paparazzi camped on the front steps of Princess Catherine's Hospital as he parked his motorbike and removed his helmet.

He smiled towards his clicking, whirring audience, who clearly had nothing better to do than chase ambulances on a sunny summer morning, and tried to hide his growing irritation. The last thing he needed was more unwarranted delays, today of all days. He was not in the mood to be polite.

Making his way up the pale stone steps, he batted away questions like a tennis ace.

'Is Princess Safia here?' someone shouted from behind a long lens. 'Is she going to make a full recovery? Will she be scarred for life?'

'Now, come on, give a guy a break. I can't hear one for the other.' Toeing both the clinic's and his own staunch professional line, Declan exhaled slowly and waited for them to settle. 'As you know, ladies and gents, my hands are tied. There's a young girl's privacy to think of. I just can't make any comment.'

Note: make sure the blinds are closed at all times. Move her to a higher floor. Increase security.

Sure, both the Hunter Clinic and the hospital affectionately known as Kate's relied on positive press to further their reach and their work, but this was way too much interest in a young girl fighting for her life, regardless of her background.

Small wonder the Sheikh's staff had been definitive in their demands to uphold their privacy. If any of Declan's family had been involved in a tragedy such as this he'd want to protect them too.

He shuddered and damped down the tight squeeze in his chest. *Had* protected them, for all the good that had done.

'Come on, Declan, it's no coincidence that you—the country's foremost burns reconstruction surgeon—are here and there's a private flight scheduled to arrive from Aljahar any minute.'

Was that Fi...something—the journalist he'd spent a few dates with not so long ago? Trying to use her inside contacts to get more information? Tut-tut. Declan flashed her a particular smile. Similar to the one he'd given her as he'd left for the last time, whenever it was, that said, *Hey, don't push it.*

With all the smiling his jaw muscles had begun to ache, but he knew that the Hunter Clinic boss, Leo, wouldn't want his second-in-command to jeopardise the clinic's new positive relationship with the media. 'I'm so sorry, but you all know that I'm in no position to confirm or deny any rumours. You all know too that even if I did have any idea as to the whereabouts or condition of Princess Safia I couldn't tell you a thing. The Sheikh, quite rightly, is very keen on confidentiality. But I'm sure he and his family appreciate all the concern and will issue a statement as and when appropriate. Now we need to leave the family alone to recover. And I need to go to work. Thank you so much.'

Closing the door behind him to a barrage of more camera flashes, he exhaled deeply and headed towards the burns unit. Two extensive surgeries, an afternoon clinic and an evening meeting amidst a swirl of media frenzy about a royal with devastating facial burns loomed ahead of him.

It was going to be a very long day.

'You. Yes, you. Stop. Wait.'

A heavily accented raised male voice out in the hospital corridor drew Declan's attention from the notes he was reviewing at his desk over his hastily snatched lunch break.

'What's all that noise on the street? The photographers? Newspapers? His Highness specifically said he wanted Sheikha Safia's arrival to be discreet. His daughter is suffering and she needs peace and quiet. She is devastated about her injuries...'

'Yes, I understand entirely,' an unfamiliar voice with an Antipodean twang replied. 'I have already spoken to Security and they are planning to transfer the Princess through the back door.' Despite the clipped tones the voice was remarkably calm, smoky. Distinctly feminine. Declan put down the papers and listened.

The male voice cut in. 'We understood Mr Underwood himself was going to oversee every detail.'

'Of the surgery and treatment phases, yes, absolutely, but not everything on this list...'

She paused. Declan heard a rustling of paper.

'He's not responsible for the sheet thread count, or the menus or the quality of the glassware... I'll get the services manager to check through all of that...'

'And lilies—we asked for white lilies to decorate her room.'

'Of course. The lilies. Item twenty-two.'

Not an ounce of agitation.

'Unfortunately we don't allow fresh flowers onto the burns unit. It's an infection control issue.'

'No?'

Agitation rippled off the man's voice in streams enough for both of them.

'But for the Sheikha you can do such a thing. She never stays anywhere without lilies. Be warned: His Highness expects high standards and he will get them. His daughter is the very most precious thing to him and he hates her to be upset. I insist you bend the rules.'

'And I insist you leave the medical professionals to *implement* the rules, sir. We have them for a reason. No fresh flowers. The pollen can infect the wounds and make our patients very sick. It's something we're very strict about. No exceptions.'

Declan's interest was piqued. Management had certainly stepped up their game by employing her. He smiled, imagining a stare-off between the mystery woman and the Sheikh's aide.

'Is there anything else? *Sir?*'

'Do not take that tone. The Sheikh is very powerful and can have you removed from your position with just one word.'

The smile was wiped from Declan's face. No one spoke to a member of staff in that way—whoever she was, and however spirited.

He scraped back his chair and walked into the corridor, watching the exchange from a distance, ready to pounce and squash the man if anything got out of hand. He got the feeling the woman wouldn't thank him for interfering and for what that might imply: that she couldn't handle it. When she clearly could. Bringing up his younger sisters had taught him to leave them alone with their arguments and only get involved if things got physical.

'Well, I have a few words I could use too...but I won't.' With a voice so prickly, he hadn't expected the woman to be so young and soft. She had her back to him, but something about her rang bells in Declan's brain. Familiar bells. Warning bells.

The ponytail of light blonde curls, the neat curves in an ice-pink silk blouse and a straight black skirt that skimmed her knees—just. Sky-high black shoes with a razor-sharp heel that surely no one could feasibly walk in but which made her legs look impossibly long and... deeply sexy. A back as straight as a blade, and that voice...smoky...yes...Australian...?

'Let me assure you, sir,' she continued, 'that Safia will receive the finest care in the world here. And if, instead of dealing with your...housekeeping requests, I could finish my preparations for her admission and initial medical assessment, and then actually deal with the injuries she has sustained, we could all make Safia's stay a lot more comfortable.'

The aide stared at her as she rallied.

'I'm sure His Highness would not like to hear that the medical team were held up due to lilies? Glassware? I thought not. We are done here?'

Oh, God. The headache that had bloomed after Declan's sister's early morning phone call threatened to return. This woman was on his medical team? Since when? And why had no one consulted him about it? Declan didn't like surprises. He always liked to know exactly what he was dealing with, and he'd made that damned clear to the powers-that-be.

The Sheikh's aide blanched and bowed slightly.

'Of course. I'm sorry. Of course, Doctor… You know what's best.'

'Yes. Thank you. We do.'

As she turned to watch the aide scuttle away her eyes locked on to Declan's. Her smile slipped completely, and a tinge of pink hit her cheeks. 'Oh.'

The first time she'd shown any hint of bother. But then, within a nanosecond, she'd regained her composure. *Kiss me.*

A rush of heat and a swirl of memory shook through him. A gold-coloured ballgown that had complemented the colour of the soft curls falling down her back, those startling green eyes commanding his attention, that infuriatingly cocky mouth drawing him in to the most sensual kiss of his life. Only she'd had a sheen of sadness about her too when he'd met her at the bar, knocking back shots. He'd turned it into a game, just to make her smile, which had then turned into something infinitely more interesting.

When was that? Six months ago? The hospital ball? A kiss he'd never found an equal to since, and a woman he'd caught tantalising glimpses of around the surgical unit, at Drake's Bar, and once, possibly, he thought he might have caught a brief whiff of her perfume at the Hunter Clinic. The woman he'd never quite caught up with.

Or even tried to.

And definitely hadn't wanted to.

Because—well…because talking to her, laughing with her, kissing her, had made him want something more. And Declan Underwood never did *more*.

'Good afternoon, Mr Underwood. Adding spying to your list of legendary talents?'

'You are standing right outside my office. It's hardly a covert operation.' Had he ever even known her name?

'Why are you frightening the life out of my esteemed visitors and masquerading as a member of my team? And where the hell is Karen?'

Karen. The timid but efficient junior surgeon who didn't have a bewitching mouth and a dangerous sparkle in her eye.

The woman's mouth twitched. 'White lilies, indeed. If they're all like him we're going to have our work cut out. By all accounts Safia's a little diva. Didn't you hear? Karen's been called away to a family emergency and I've been shifted over to assist until she gets back.'

'Whoa! Slow down. To assist *me*?'

She smiled, but it didn't look as if she was very pleased about the scenario either. He wondered if she was thinking about that kiss too, and how she'd suddenly lost her cool, or her nerve or both, and left him standing on the dance floor trying to work out which tornado had just hit.

Just the thought of it set off a burst of inconvenient heat swimming through his veins.

'Yes, the luck fairies have sprinkled dust on us both today. I'm on your team until Karen gets things sorted.'

Judging by his all too regular experiences of family emergencies she could be away for weeks. His stomach hit his boots. Regardless of what his body might want, mixing work with pleasure was something he avoided at all costs. So he'd be sticking to strictly business.

'And which genius came up with this idea?'

'Ethan Hunter. He called me this morning, said he'd had a call from Karen and was going to run the idea by you, but you were unavailable. He left you a message, apparently. So did she.'

No doubt while Declan's oldest sister had been bending his ear about his middle sister's new boyfriend, the youngest's less than satisfactory university grades and his mother's upcoming birthday plans. He was definitely going to have to set more limits around his personal private time. Sure, hadn't he been trying to do that for the past seventeen years?

'So I miss a call and now I don't get a say about who works with me on one of the most high-profile cases we've had in years?'

'What would you prefer?' Her hands hit her tantalising hips. 'It's me or no one. At least I have a good deal of burns experience. There isn't any other option, with Leo and Lizzie on honeymoon and this place being almost in lockdown with the Sheikh's arrival.'

'No?'

'You could do it all by yourself, but somehow I can't think you'd want to do the junior tasks. Admissions paperwork? Organising bloods?' Her voice rose at the end of every sentence, making it sound as if she was asking an endless list of questions.

'Yes, thank you, I have a full understanding of what is needed. And, it's not that I don't want to do them. I just don't have time.' Stepping up to run the Hunter Clinic in Leo's absence meant he needed more junior staff, not less.

Unbelievable. Declan ran a hand across his neck as he realised he'd been backed into an Antipodean corner. Well, hell, she'd better be as good in surgery as she was at kissing, because he couldn't take any chances—not with his reputation and a young girl's future at stake.

Great. His day had just got a whole lot longer.

'So I hope we don't have a problem here?'

'Absolutely not.'

Oh, but they did. At least Kara did. Declan's Irish lilt curled around her clenched stomach and stroked. Softly. Smoothly. Sexi— *No.* She wasn't allowed to think that.

The man was her boss. And an amazing kisser. *Boss.*
Kisser. *Boss.* He tipped his chin to one side and gave her
the slightest hint of recognition. A nod, perhaps, to their
last…*connection*…?

She felt the blush start at her toes and spread, fast,
to the top of her head. If only she'd explained her quick
getaway—the reason dancing with him had been such a
dumb move. Her surprisingly hot bodily response to the
first man to hold her in so long. No—it had been a direct
response to him and his strong arms and smooth, deep accent. And then, as reality hit, her suddenly very cold feet.

He leaned against his office doorjamb, folded his arms
and eyed her with ill-disguised caution.

Shame, because she'd really, really enjoyed that kiss.
However wrong. However badly timed. However just
damned stupid. And he clearly hardly even remembered
her. But then the man had a following of women who
thought they could change his commitment-phobic ways.
That kiss was probably not a stand-out for him. Luckily
she'd put it far behind her.

She summoned every bit of confidence—or at least
the show of confidence she'd learned to wear whenever
she was in a difficult situation. Eyes forward, shoulders
back. Last time she'd felt the need to summon strength
she'd been staring down into a casket. The memory rolled
off her in waves.

'It's Kara.'

Just in case he'd forgotten her name. Had she even
told him it? She remembered looking up. The sight of
him standing there in a tuxedo, his hair a messy non-
chalant scruff, had stripped the breath from her lungs.
She remembered too the way he'd smelled of something
spicy and promising as he'd leaned in, the hot shock of
an unexpected desire that had matched hers in his deep

brown eyes. The earth tilting slightly as he'd spun her in his arms.

'Kara Stephens?'

'Are you asking me? Because if *you* don't know then we really do have a problem.'

Idiot. She decided to speak slowly just so he could understand. Poor puppy. 'My. Name. Is. Kara. Stephens. Only you don't look very happy about something. And I can only assume it's me.'

Seeing as he was staring right at her. All six-foot-too-much, with his arrogant stance and toned body. Even in scrubs she could see the outline of the sculpted abs she'd pressed against, the biceps she'd held as he'd slow-danced with her. The shoulders she'd wound her arms around as his mouth had covered hers.

Heat skittered through her abdomen like a lit fuse wire.

Boss.

Oh. Yes. The first kiss she'd had in too long and it had been off-limits in so many ways. Alcohol, guilt and lust were a heady combination she'd done her best to avoid ever since. Along with him—Mr Break-Your-Heart Underwood.

And now he would refuse to allow her to join the team. Not just for her handling of a tense situation but because of that damned kiss.

'There's a lot at stake here.' He exhaled sharply. 'What do we know about you? Where did you train? What burns experience do you have?'

'Med School in Melbourne, then Perth, then a stint at the Croftwood Institute, Sydney.'

'The Croftwood? Impressive.'

'Yes. And I aced every exam.' Even so, just thinking

about her last few days there was like a swift punch to her heart.

But she wouldn't look back. London had been a fresh start, and getting onto this rotation had been an absolute dream job—and then the chance to work alongside a world-class reconstructive surgeon. Until one out-of-character misdemeanour came back to bite her.

Well, kissing the boss certainly wouldn't be happening again. Kissing *anyone* wouldn't be happening. Ever.

'So, what *is* this? A corridor interview? I've helped out at the Hunter Clinic before now. If you want a copy of my CV or references just ask.' Irritation tripped up her spine. 'And, besides, Ethan's already arranged everything.'

Declan's eyebrows rose. 'Without consulting me first. Has he ever actually spoken to you? Seen you in full throttle? Because I listened to a lot of that conversation just now, and the way you—'

She jumped in to defend herself. 'Look, I don't believe in taking risks with clients just because someone who has a lot of money or power asks me to. There's not just Safia to think about, but the other patients on the unit too. Money can buy a lot of things, but it won't buy my professional standards.' She studied his face for a reaction but he wore a mask of impartiality. 'Of course I hope I employed more diplomacy than that.'

He nodded and looked at her. Really looked at her, as if trying to work out a puzzle. 'To be honest, I thought you handled him very well—and you stuck to your guns. It's easy to be swayed by people like that and it's rarely for the good.'

Wow, praise from him now? That was surprising. He had a reputation for being a smooth lover and a competent and exacting doctor, leaving his patients satisfied and women always wanting more. Which he steadfastly refused to give.

'If you can handle a skin graft as confidently as you did that aide, then you'll go far.'

The laugh slipped easily from her throat. 'You know, really I just wanted to tell him where to get off.'

'Yes. Me too.' He winked, visibly relaxing. 'But *A*— you didn't. And *B*—you reassured him of your competence and professionalism by not caving in to his demands.'

'I tried my best.'

'Good. I imagine you've more than earned his respect. You need to gain that too when dealing with the Sheikh and the press, which is a necessary role with such a high-profile case. We're a small team with a big responsibility. Are you up to it?'

'Yes. Absolutely.'

'I would suggest you soften a little for the Sheikha, though. Diva or not, she's had a very rough time, she's used to having things her way, and this accident will have knocked her sideways.' Something passed behind those chocolate-coloured eyes and his sharp edges melted away a little. 'Her life has changed forever. She's going to be frightened and in pain and will need a lot of help and re-assurance. Not just today but ongoing. Gently.' He eyed her suspiciously. 'You *can* do gently?'

'Of course. Of course.' Hell, she could do roll over and beg if it meant she got to work with someone so talented. Relief flooded through her and she tried to show him her best gentle smile. 'So I'm in, then?'

'For now. It seems I have no choice—and we have to attend to Safia. I'll review your place in my team later.'

'I come highly recommended. Phone the Croftwood and check. I can assure you, you won't be disappointed.'

'No…I doubt that very much.' Declan laughed. 'But, heck, you're a straight talker.'

The same words he'd used at the ball too, when she'd outright demanded he kiss her, right there on the dance floor, when she hadn't been able to stop thinking about how those lips would feel against hers. When she'd wanted something…*him*…to exorcise the past.

She snapped her eyes closed, hoping to goodness he didn't remember that. When she opened them again he was looking at her strangely. Strangely *interested*. The ghost of that kiss hovered between them as his eyes fixed on hers. Yes, he remembered. And if the brief flash of heat was anything to go by he remembered how good it had felt too. That warm glow in her abdomen returned.

She doused it with a quick shot of reality as she began to walk along the corridor towards the burns unit High Dependency ward. The last time she'd got carried away by hearts and flowers and physical desires she'd ended up married. Then endured a swift lesson in a run of all the emotions from *A* to *Z*.

She'd packed a lifetime of hurt into those few years and she had no intention of making the same mistakes again. So much had sent her reeling, trying to work out how something that had started out so pure had ended so damned soiled. Focusing on her career was a lot less painful—but then, that was what had caused all the trouble in the first place.

'It comes from my upbringing, I guess.'

'Oh? What?' He fell into step beside her.

'Forthrightness. I'm an army brat. Always moving around. If you don't say what you think straightaway you'll be packed up and on the move before you get another chance.' There'd been a lot of lost chances before she'd learnt that lesson. 'Although it can get me into trouble.'

'I imagine it can.'

It already has, his look said. On that dance floor.

His dark pupils flared. 'Australian army?'

'Yes. My parents met as new recruits and both followed military careers.'

'Exciting? Interesting?'

'Difficult...for them both, I think. One member of a family in the military is hard enough, but both parents trying to work up the career ladder meant a lot of discussing, juggling, arguing, vying for priority. What their child wanted came at the bottom of the pecking order.'

She'd learnt to speak loudly and fight hard to get heard.

'Constantly moving and growing up on bases makes you grow a thick skin and a quick mouth. But, hey, I can shoot in a straight line and hit a target at a hundred metres.'

'Me too.' At her frown he illuminated, 'Farm boy.'

Now, *that* was a surprise. He oozed class and rubbed easy broad shoulders with a rich and famous clientele. 'Irish farm boy to Harley Street surgeon? That must be an interesting story.'

'Not really.' His smile disappeared and he looked at her as if she'd stepped over some imaginary line. Shoving his hands in his pockets, he quickened his step. She got the message—working together was okay, even kissing wasn't a step too close, but sharing intimate details...? Never. And that suited her just fine. The less she shared about the life she'd left the better too.

As they entered the unit Kara observed an atmosphere of calm chaos—a feeling that matched her stomach. Although being surrounded by busy people was much less intense than being alone with Declan. She knew how to act here. There were protocols and policies, standards and codes. Out there in the real world, the dating world, the rules were far too confusing.

She breathed out and put her professional hat firmly on. 'So, all the staff are up to speed with privacy requests, and everyone has been told not to comment at all to anyone phoning in, regardless of who they say they are.'

'Excellent.' He nodded, walking into the room he'd personally had allocated to Safia. 'This looks perfect, but keep the bed away from the window.' He peered through the blinds down to the road outside. 'No one should be able to see her here on this floor. As soon as she arrives we'll need to check her pain levels and medication. I don't want her to be scared we're going to hurt her when we remove the dressings. Then I'll need an immediate blood screen to make sure she's haemodynamically stable. Then...then we can take a good look and see what we're dealing with.'

'No worries.' She picked up the clipboard on the end of the bed and checked all the correct paperwork was in place.

'So.' Declan glanced around. 'What's her ETA?'

Kara glanced at her watch. 'Ten minutes.'

'Excellent.'

Although this was a devastating case, he looked wired and ready. This was another side of him she'd heard about but hadn't yet encountered: his infectious enthusiasm for his work. It seemed the man had many sides apart from his infamous charm, and yet—as she'd witnessed— a mysterious unwillingness to open up about anything personal.

Which was fine. Because she would not let that kiss get in the way of her job. Or let that body of his distract her from her purpose. Or those eyes… Her stomach did a little cartwheel… Those eyes staring at her with playful teasing.

'So, Kara Stephens, it looks like we have just enough time to check out the sheets.'

'What?' Her pulse rocketed.

The smile he flashed her was nothing less than wicked. 'Thread count?'

'Oh. Yes. Of course.' And she blushed again, because one mention of sheets and their thread count was the furthest thing from her mind.

CHAPTER TWO

'I SAID, DON'T touch me.' A pair of dark, frightened eyes, trying desperately hard to be brave, peered out through a face covered in bandages. 'Go away.'

Kara leaned in to the bed and lowered her voice. This was getting precisely nowhere, but she could not and would not rush her patient. 'I'm sorry, Safia, but we are going to have to remove the dressings sometime so we can see your burns and then treat them. We just want to help.'

'What part of *go away* don't you understand?' Her muffled voice was thick with the tears the teenager steadfastly refused to allow. 'Leave me alone.'

'Does it hurt? I can give you some more medicine to take the pain away. You must tell me if you need more.'

The girl shook her head.

'I'll do it slowly and carefully. I promise.'

But Safia raised a heavily bandaged arm and pulled the sheet over her head. The spaghetti of tubes reverberated at the swift move. An alarm rang out.

Kara took a moment to compose herself, checked the drips were patent, reset the machines and tried again. And she would continue trying until the poor girl agreed. However long it took. The theatre was booked from eight tomorrow morning. That gave her about eighteen hours. She hoped it would be enough. 'Your Highness…'

'Let me try.' Sheikh El-Zayad of Aljahar, the girl's father, stepped forward. 'For goodness' sake, Safia, do as you're told. We've been waiting for twenty-five minutes for your bandages to come off and it's getting past a joke. The doctors can't do their job and you won't get better.'

'I'm never going to get better. This is it. Scarred for life. So get used to it.'

The Sheikh frowned. 'Do as the doctor says. Stop behaving like a child.'

She is a child. Kara bit that thought back. He had just endured the worst thing any parent could live through—watching his child suffer—and no doubt wanted her full co-operation to get better. But seventeen was barely mature, and the ramifications of such injuries would surely make anyone scared and fractious.

She shot a look over to Declan as he finished his conversation with the Sheikh's wife, psychologically prepping her for the forthcoming procedures and long-term treatment plan. Throughout the long thirty minutes of cajoling and waiting she'd felt Declan's eyes on her, assessing, weighing her up, his playful teasing forgotten, cemented now into something much more serious.

'So to recap—' He leaned forward to speak to Safia's parents. 'We're planning to do a series of operations over the next few weeks. Because Safia's wounds are of differing severity and depth each one will be in its own individual recovery phase. Some wounds, I understand from her notes, are ready for closure or grafting tomorrow. Some will have to wait for closure because they need debriding. I'll keep you fully informed as we proceed.'

Declan's demeanour was one of total calm and efficiency, yet he commanded an authority that stood him apart as he spoke.

'Now, it's getting a bit hot in here. Perhaps Your Highnesses might like a tour of the facility? There's a particularly nice view out over the river from the roof garden. It's very private up there and shouldn't be busy. In fact, I can make sure it isn't. And I can organise some tea for you both.'

Safia's mother nodded and wafted in front of her face with her hand. 'Oh, please. Yes. I need some fresh air.' Leaning in to her daughter, she whispered, 'That is, of course, if you don't mind, darling Safia? We won't stay away for long.'

The sheets moved a little. 'Go. All of you. Leave me here. Forever.'

A quick phone call later and Safia, Kara and Declan were alone.

But now what? Even without her parents in the room it was going to be tough convincing Safia to comply.

Kara was just about to broach the dressings conversation again when Declan laughed. 'Well, would you look at that *eejit*.'

'What? Where?' Kara frowned as she looked over to him. His focus was on a pile of magazines on the table. The latest teen heart-throb was emblazoned on the front cover of *BFF!* magazine, which had been covered in pink glitter hand-drawn hearts. 'Oh, that's Liam from Oblivion.'

'I don't care where he's from,' he continued. 'He looks like he needs a decent feed and a new belt. Are those his grandaddy's trousers he's wearing? Because they don't seem to fit.'

Kara looked up again and noticed he was watching the sheet move down. Just a little.

She joined in. 'How can you say that? Don't break my heart. Liam is hot, hot, *hot*. And what do you know, Mr Fuddy-Duddy? Those baggy trousers are all the rage. Maybe you should get a pair.'

'Maybe I should. D'you think all the girls would come screaming after me then?' He gave a very poor rendition of Oblivion's number one hit. '"That's what makes me looooove you…"'

'Screaming to get away from you, more like. Save our poor ears and stick to the day job.' She leaned closer to the sheet that was now making little noises that sounded a lot like hesitant surprised laughter. 'Great doctor, really, don't let the singing put you off. I heard that Oblivion's doing a tour soon—they're playing in London in a few weeks.' And going to see her favourite singer might well give Safia the motivation she needed to get better.

The girl sighed. 'He played at my sixteenth birthday party. He said I was beautiful.' Safia slowly pulled the sheet back. 'But he wouldn't say that now.'

Declan sat next to the bed and looked at her. Kara wondered what on earth he could say to make her feel better. 'Don't you know you've gorgeous eyes, Safia? Beautiful. A boy could lose himself in there.'

'Once, maybe. But not now.'

'Oh, definitely now.'

Safia met Declan's gaze, still cautious, but she didn't tell them to leave.

Seizing this moment of calm, Declan reached out and began to remove a dressing with painstaking care. When Safia put her hand out to stop him he gave her a quick shake of his head and a reassuring smile. The girl lay back and closed her eyes.

Kara opened another dressing pack and covered the bed as he kept his focus on his patient and smiled softly and gently, as if she was the most beautiful person in the world, the only person in the world. As if the horrendous discolouration and raw melted skin didn't make his heart jerk or his professional eye wonder how in hell they could ever restore her back to her previous beauty.

She'd heard about his slick surgical skills and knew how well respected he was. Heck, the Sheikh had personally requested Declan did the surgery—and judging by his extensive client list both here and at the Hunter Clinic he was well sought after. So she hadn't expected a doctor as talented as Declan to have such grounded humanity.

'There. There. Nearly done now. You're doing grand, sweetheart. Just grand. It's not nearly so bad as I thought it'd be.'

He spoke in a mesmerising, soothing voice that felt as if he was stroking the raw wounds back together again. Kara didn't think she'd ever seen anything so touching.

'I bet you've broken a few hearts already, Safia?'

The girl opened her eyes and gave him a sad smile. 'Yes...you mustn't tell my father.'

'Cross my heart.'

'But I never will again. Who's going to love me with a face like this? Skin like this?' She lifted the arms she'd tried to shield her face with and showed him the skin that had been so damaged. Finally tears began to fall. 'Don't tell me that beauty's skin-deep. Or that scars are sexy. Because they're not. And please don't tell me that looks don't matter—because in my world they do.'

And that was the heart of the matter. A young girl's life was broken and no one could truly fix it.

Kara's throat closed tight.

Declan ran his hand over the girl's hair. 'Ah, now, sweetheart. That's it. That's it. I know. Believe me, I know. Let it out. Just let it go.'

'I'm…so…tired…of being brave,' Safia sobbed. 'Of trying to pretend it's okay when it's not. And all they do is make promises that I'll be back to normal soon. How can I?' She looked up at him, eyes pleading but with a glimpse of trust. 'Can you make me better, Dr Underwood?'

'Call me Declan, please. Actually, call me Dec if you like—my sisters call me that.'

'Okay.' Safia nodded and smiled again. 'Dec.'

'Listen, Safia, I will be honest with you because you deserve that at the very least. I can't ever make it go away completely.' His voice caught a little as he thumbed away the girl's tears.

A few months ago Kara had watched him smooth his way across a dance floor, his charm and flirtatious manner catching her in a moment of weakness. But there was a genuine depth to him that she hadn't imagined.

He cleared his throat. 'But I promise I can make it a whole lot better. Will you let me try?'

'At first glance, Safia's burns are a mix of partial and full thickness—some will need further debridement and then grafting,' Declan said to Kara as they grabbed a coffee en route to the media room.

His head was a whirl of the emotions that always shook through him at this stage of assessment—emotions he had a tight hold of and would never allow to interfere with any professional judgement. Flashbacks from seventeen years ago haunted him each time he removed a dressing, but they made him more determined to improve his skills and techniques.

Another woman damaged. It made him sick to his stomach.

His new junior surgeon took a sip of coffee, oblivious

to what was going on in his head. Which was a damned
fine thing—no one needed to know his motivations, just
his achievements. She smiled and his gut tightened. He
put it down to stress.

'So, Declan, do you prefer autograft or zenograft?'

'It depends entirely on the situation. We can get a better look at the viability of the skin and the underlying bed
tomorrow in Theatre and take it from there.'

Eyebrows peaked. 'We?'

'Yes. Okay, you can scrub in tomorrow. You did well
in there. Teenagers are often the most difficult cases to
deal with. They don't know how to act—they're kids at
heart but trying desperately to be adult. We have to get
the next few days right. How we deal with these burns
will have a huge effect on the rest of that girl's life. Both
physically and psychologically.' From his experience the
mental scarring was often the worst and could change
the very core of an injured person for life.

Kara nodded, eyes alight, blonde curls shivering.
Something unbidden shivered through him too. She'd
been damned good at handling Safia, so he was pleased
to have her on his team. But…really it was more than
that. She was a weird kind of unsettling—and yet settling at the same time.

Her eyes narrowed. 'I can't believe the admitting hospital staff didn't think of offering her some anxiolytics
to help raise her mood. Maybe we could have a chat with
her about that too?'

'I guess they were dealing with her immediate issues,
like keeping her alive.' He held the door open to let her
through. Which was an action he immediately regretted.
The barrage of flashing bulbs that had greeted him that
morning met them as they stepped into the room, catch-

ing her unawares—but he was interested to see just how well she could handle this part of the job.

'Is Princess Safia here now?'

'What can you tell us about her condition?'

Next to him Kara stood tall, her shoulders snapped back, confident. Declan held back a smile as he watched her survey the room with a tilt of her chin. She wore her army upbringing in her stance, and he had no doubt she would answer the press's queries with aplomb and professionalism, but he wasn't game enough to test her with that just yet. In fact he wasn't game enough to do anything that involved any more contact with her than he had to. The woman was mysteriously alluring. So that meant avoiding her at all costs.

No doubt a better man would probably not even allow her to assist him when his hormones were acting as if he was eighteen years old again. But he had stopped being a better man a long time ago—the day he'd lost all faith in love.

Kara's scent wove around him…something exotic that reminded him of brilliant blue skies and endless heat and the tang of flowers on the breeze. His abdomen tightened as seemingly endless heat rippled through him too.

He took a step away and glanced at the floor, trying to take a moment to focus. But all he could see were those ridiculous but sexy shoes, slender tanned ankles leading up to the hem of her skirt, and farther on up to a place where his imagination ran wild.

He ran a hand through his hair and shook that image from his head. *Damn fool.* Since when had he allowed a woman to distract him at work? Since the second he'd seen her firing back at the Sheikh's aide? Or was it that kiss?

He quieted the audience with a raise of his hands and

a smile. Keep them on side and they might actually let him have time free to do his job. 'Thanks for coming to this meeting. We didn't want you getting chilly out there. We're already busy enough without dealing with hypothermic journalists as well. Hope you enjoyed the tea and biscuits.'

Laughter rippled round the room. He waited for it to stop.

'Thank you for your patience, everyone. I have permission from Safia's family to confirm that she is indeed now here at Princess Catherine's Hospital and that I am treating her as an in-patient. I'm sure you are all aware of the car accident she had a few days ago. I can confirm also that, thanks to the great care she received at Aljahar Hospital, she is now in a stable condition, but her injuries mean that she will be under my care for some time. The family again asks for privacy. Thank you.'

'What does the Sheikh think about this?'

'Naturally His Highness is devastated about his daughter's injuries, but he is working with us to get the best possible outcome. Of course we are deeply honoured to have him here.'

'How long will Safia be with you?'

'That depends entirely on her progress and response to treatment. It could be a few weeks.' He paused for effect. 'Okay, I don't think there is anything more we can tell you. Either myself or a member of my team…' He indicated to Kara and she stepped forward and smiled, self-confidence rippling off her. 'This is Ms Stephens, who will be working with me. Either one of us will be updating you on Safia's progress as and when appropriate.'

'They don't teach you that at medical school.' Kara joked as they walked towards the afternoon out-patient clinic. 'They should have "Dealing with the Press" lessons. Confidentiality is such a thorny issue—especially when you're treating someone famous.'

'No one wants to know about you if you're not. But this is a high-profile issue and we have to deal with it—it's just another part of the job. You have to be careful not to give away too much information but just enough to keep the hacks satisfied.'

'It's a bit of a tightrope. I can see I'll have to be careful.'

'I can fix you up with our in-house Head of PR, Lexi, at the Hunter Clinic if you like? She could give you some pointers if you think you might need them.' Why, oh, why was he even thinking of getting further involved in this woman's life? 'But I reckon you'll be fine.'

'Really?' Her smile was genuine. 'Thanks. I'll see how I go.'

That compliment sat between them as they neared the clinic. He'd have to be careful about that—giving her the wrong impression. But something about Kara drew him to her. Even with his internal alarm bells blaring.

As he tried to walk down the narrow corridor without brushing against her and risking an escalation of his already over-excited libido she spoke. 'So, how many sisters do you have?'

'What?' He stopped short, still getting used to her forthrightness. Maybe it was an Aussie thing. No, maybe it was just a Kara thing. 'Sorry?'

'You were telling Safia about your sisters. *"They call me Dec,"* you said, or something.'

'Why do you need to know?'

Her forehead furrowed into a deep V and her eyes sparked with humour and intrigue. 'I don't *need* anything. I was just making conversation. It's what human beings do to fill that very long gap between birth and death. Communication.'

She held his gaze and it felt as if she was throwing down a gauntlet. One he could run with or one he could walk away from.

'Only, I don't have any siblings, and I always thought it'd be nice to have some. It's just a chat, Declan, as we while away the minutes. Not an interrogation.'

She was right. It was just talking. It wasn't exactly baring his soul. And he'd always been a sucker for gauntlets. 'Well, if I were you I'd rejoice in your single-child-dom, Kara—because, trust me, you do *not* need four sisters.'

'Four? Wow.'

'All younger. All a giant pain in the ass…'

She laughed. 'Growing up amongst that must have been busy. But fun, though?'

'It was messy…crazy…loud. Very loud. And awash with wayward hormones.' Remembering the madcap phone call that morning, he shrugged, smiling to himself. They might well be irritating, but they were his. 'Still is.'

'But it explains how you can deal so well with kids like Safia.'

'I don't know about *well*. The way I see it, all girls want to be treated like princesses. It just so happens she *is* one. But underneath they're generally the same. They worry about how they look, who they're becoming, what they want to do with their lives. Love. Boys…yeah, boys mostly, if my lot were anything to go by. Trouble all round.'

He'd had the job of being the man of the house thrust upon him way too young and had had to make sure they somehow had the basics, like enough food to eat, even when they hadn't had the money to buy it. Then as they grew up he'd watched his sisters have their hearts broken and wanted to kill the culprits, but decided not to. He had negotiated conversations about teenage pregnancy and underage sex, about dating rules and bedtimes, had nursed sisters with period pains and migraines and tummy aches of dubious origin. And finally he'd escaped only when he'd known they were all grown up and relatively safe. *Escaped* being a geographical rather than a psychological term.

And yet with all his experience he still couldn't fathom the workings of a woman's brain. Except that he definitely knew when it was time to leave—which was around about the time she started talking about a future.

Kara laughed. 'But I can see the pride in your eyes and hear it in your voice. You love them all, clearly.'

'Yes, I probably do—but don't ever let them know that or they'll take even more advantage. And I chose a job hundreds of miles away from them just to put a good stretch of Irish Sea between us.' He laughed along with her. 'Thankfully none of them are any good at swimming, most of them get seasick, and they can't afford the airfare—otherwise I'm damned sure they'd be here. Making my life hell in England too.'

But in reality he might as well be living back home, seeing as they couldn't or wouldn't make a single damned decision without him. Which was why he kept his tiny slice of private time simple. No getting involved on any kind of scale. His life was already too full of responsibilities and women without taking on another one.

Kara smirked as they entered the out-patients' reception. 'I guess you have to go where the work is.'

'Is that what you did? It's a long way from Sydney to London, and you didn't have four sisters dragging at your heels.'

'I needed a change. Coming here was a good move for lots of reasons.'

The way she said that didn't convince him that her move to London had been a positive choice. She rubbed her thumb around the base of her left-hand ring finger as her eyes darted upwards. She seemed to be searching for an answer. Not the truth, just an answer.

Seemed everyone had their demons. And he was inexplicably intrigued, even though he'd made it his life's purpose never to be drawn into a woman's dramas unless he had a failsafe get-out plan.

She peered up at him and his world tilted a little. He wasn't used to scrutiny, or to someone pushing him for more—or wanting to give it. So why would she have this effect on him?

'And you, Declan? Why choose burns reconstruction when you could have the glory and financial reward of cosmetic surgery? Breast augmentation? Tattoo removal? Enhancement of the rich and famous? Why specialise in burns?'

The way she adeptly deflected the conversation told him she didn't want to delve deeper into her reasons for coming here and he could respect that.

But, hell… His chest tightened by degrees. The questions she was asking. Questions people asked him periodically, but not usually straight after a conversation about his family. Or after a consultation with a badly scarred woman. Questions that he didn't want to answer. Wouldn't answer. Wouldn't no matter how much her sharp green eyes reached down into his soul and tugged.

'Ah, you know…it's just how it worked out.'

And with that he turned and walked away.

CHAPTER THREE

SO THE GREAT Declan Underwood had walls so high even a simple conversation couldn't penetrate them, Kara mused as she scrubbed up the next morning. She would do well to remember that.

She should have remembered it last night too as she lay in the dark and thought about the way she'd fitted so neatly into his arms on the ballroom floor all those months ago. And the way he'd tasted—of something fresh and new, of an experienced man. Not like the previous kisses she'd experienced from the kid she'd known her whole life. The way Declan's big broad shoulders—a match for any Aussie rugby league player's—looked as if they could carry the weight of a million problems. But she hadn't wanted to share hers. No, she'd had other things on her mind. Nice other things. Naughty other things.

And she should have remembered it too when Declan's face had been the last thing she'd thought of before she'd fallen asleep. Almost the first thing to flash through her brain as her alarm clock blared. The very first thing, as always, had been the thick thud of loss. The reality of how much her life had changed. The tiny slash of almost white skin where her wedding ring used to be.

But this morning the sharp sting of regret hadn't been quite so harsh.

Even so, she still hadn't thought about the barriers Declan had erected, or the way he'd turned his back on her. She'd simply remembered how sweet it had felt when he'd hammered against her barriers with one scorching touch of his mouth.

The same mouth that was now grinning at her as he walked into the scrub room. She put the little heart jig down to excitement at the forthcoming surgery and nothing to do with the sudden scent of soap and spice, or the soft brown eyes, or the way his biceps muscles lengthened as he reached for the tap.

The V neck of his top bared a tantalising amount of suntanned chest and she imagined what might be underneath the navy cotton scrubs... Sometimes a working knowledge of anatomy did a girl nothing but harm. Especially first thing in the morning.

He opened a sterile pack and laid it on a trolley, put on the surgical cap and mask and began washing with the nailbrush, rubbing small circles over his fingers, hands, up his arms.

'Good morning, Ms Stephens. Sleep well?'

'Hi. Um... Yes, thanks.' *Liar.* Sleeping and thoughts of Declan Underwood were not satisfactory bedfellows.

She dried her hands, pulled on her gown and snapped on her gloves. Took a quick check in the mirror and relaxed. There was no way there would be any kind of sexual vibes happening today—hair in a cap and body in oversized scrubs really didn't scream goddess or available. Or any kind of *hot-for-you*. Thank God.

'And shouldn't it be top of the mornin'?'

'A whole millennia of culture reduced to the diddly-diddly. Sure, and we're all leprechauns.' He laughed, his eyes crinkling at the corners.

That tall, broad body was the furthest thing from a leprechaun she could imagine.

'And shouldn't it be g'day?'

'Cobber. If you're going the whole reductive stereotype, it should be g'day, cobber. Or sheila. And don't forget the cork hat.'

'Same language but not a lot of commonality, eh? That's a shame. A real shame.' He dried his hands, gowned up and smiled. 'Perhaps we should try to forge some middle ground, Kara? There's a whole lot more I could teach you about Irish culture... In the interests of international relations. Obviously.'

'Obviously.' Was that a come on? Or just a joke?

Aaargh. Having been a one-man woman for so long, she didn't understand the language of flirting.

No matter. She didn't have time to compute. At that moment he stepped back, catching her unawares in the tiny airless room. His hip brushed against hers and she turned too quickly, slamming body to body against him. Tingles ran the length of her spine as her heart continued a jig that was *all* diddly-diddly.

'Oh. I'm sorry.'

His gaze met hers and for a split second, maybe two, he watched her. Some weird connection tugged between them. His eyes misted with something akin to confusion, along with an unmistakable heat that seemed to whoosh all the oxygen from her lungs.

His arms were splayed high in front of him, so as not to desterilise them, but that made his face closer to hers. Damn lucky he was wearing a mask or his mouth would have been in frank kissing range.

The heat coming off him was electric, almost palpable. He smiled. Or at least she thought he did—hard to tell under that mask, but his forehead crinkled and laughter lines creased at his temples.

'Nothing to apologise for, Kara. No harm done. In fact…I like it.'

So did she. And, oh, if it wasn't enough just to have that soft accent tug on her heartstrings.

She swallowed through a dry throat, pushed the Theatre door open with her hip and gestured for him to walk through in front of her. How the hell would she spend a morning in surgery staring at those eyes, listening to that voice, looking at that body, and get out whole? He was going to reduce her to a hot mess of unruly hormones.

So she would take a leaf out of his book and refuse to engage in conversation about anything other than the task at hand.

Forcing words out was harder than she'd expected. 'So. How's Safia doing? When I popped up to see her an hour or so ago she didn't say much. I got the impression she was hanging out for you to visit.'

He shrugged. 'She's okay, I suppose. She's scared about the operation. Actually, she's scared about the pain. I did warn her about the initial sting of the graft sites, but we talked about pain relief and I've discussed it with Paul, the anaesthetist, so she should be well covered when she wakes up. I've warned her we can't fix it all today, and that she'll have negative pressure dressings on and to expect lots of tubes.'

'Great. And the parents? They seemed to think you were going to restore her to her former beauty.'

His left shoulder hiked. 'I had a long and honest meeting with them last night and showed them the digital blueprint we mocked up of how we hope Safia will look after the surgeries. They understand that we can only do so much, and that a lot is dependent on how Safia heals, the kind of scarring we get, whether she complies with physio. Although I still think they're a little unrealistic. My main concern is that she maintains function in those hands. But she's here and agreeing to treatment and that's the best we can hope for right now.'

He turned as the technician wheeled Safia in.

'Okay. Let's go. Hands first and then her face. We'll start with debriding.'

It was like watching an artist at work. A study in concentration, he was efficient but thorough. Instead of the brash rock music favoured by a lot of surgeons she'd worked with Declan chose something that was uplifting but gentle. There was a positivity to it, something that soothed yet entranced.

Or was that just him? Kara couldn't tell.

Even though he was the senior member of staff he treated everyone in the room with the same respect and took his time to explain his procedures.

'See here?' He gestured to Safia's damaged cheek. 'If we want to get a good result we have to consider the whole area as a unit, not just the part that's damaged, otherwise the scarring will be ridged. It's a multi-thickness burn—only second degree here, but here, where her face hit the dashboard, it's deeper. So I'm going to have to use a split thickness graft.'

'And attach it with absorbent stitches? Or glue?' She passed him some gauze just as he reached out for it. The third time she'd anticipated his next move.

'In this case, I'd say stitches.' He shook his head, as if trying to get rid of a wayward thought. 'What did you do in Sydney?'

'Oh, this and that. Music concerts, swimming, going out with friends. My husband was away a lot so I was able…to…study…' She slowed right down and noticed all eyes were on her.

Surgery.

That deep, luscious voice was asking about the Croftwood's choice of surgical closure techniques—not about her private life. Her chest tightened. *Duh.* There went her credibility.

'Er…usually stitches. But glue if we thought the dressing wouldn't be knocked or slip easily. Really it depended on the patient and the damaged area.'

She flatly refused to look him in the eye. Flatly. But she knew she was the single beacon of bright red in an otherwise white and sterile environment.

'Husband?'

The accusation hung in the air along with the ghost of that kiss. As she turned to look at him his eyebrows rose.

God. She focused instead on the tube of antibiotic ointment in a dish to her left. Did he really think she'd have kissed him if she'd had a husband? When she'd entered her marriage it had been with an innocent and pure belief in forever. Too bad forever couldn't happen.

'Not any more.'

'Okay.' Declan's voice was impassive. 'Great work, team. Thanks for your help. She's good to go to recovery. I'll head up to have a chat with Mum and Dad after the next surgery.'

The technicians got busy taking Safia out and preparing for the next patient, leaving Kara alone for snatched minutes with Declan. Goddamn, the man stirred a smorgasbord of emotions in her. Right now it was a huge dose of embarrassment.

'Er… About before…'

'Kara…'

He glanced up from the surgery list he was reading. *About what?* his look said. *The kiss? The husband?*

He removed his surgical mask, his mouth tipping up halfway to a wry smile. 'Your life is your life. You don't have to explain.'

'I shouldn't have rabbited on.'

'Oh, no, to the contrary, we were all riveted. Concerts? Swimming?'

The omission of *husband* made her faux pas even more mortifying.

She shrugged. 'What can I say? We're a nation of water babies. Sydney's by the ocean.'

'And it gets very hot and there are snakes and spiders and lots of things that could kill you. I know.' His voice had developed a harder tone now. 'It's also a very long way from here and people can get lonely.'

Was that what he thought? That she'd hooked up with him because she was homesick? Because she missed her husband? Because she regretted everything that had happened?

Well, wasn't it? She didn't know any more.

Four days later Declan was sitting at his desk making a poor show of doing the paperwork, checking staffing levels for the Hunter Clinic and keeping track of patients' results.

He exhaled long and hard as the paper stack wobbled. It had been a very long week so far and tomorrow promised no let up. There were more surgeries booked, no doubt a scuffle through the media camped outside and a report due for Leo when he returned from honeymoon.

So why the hell, when he was supposed to be working, was he daydreaming about soft lips and green eyes? About a junior surgeon who anticipated his every move in Theatre, whose scent he could recognise at fifty paces, who seemed to have a direct line to his brain.

And his groin.

And was married. Or had been. Still, she wore no ring, and she'd been adamant that it was over.

He smiled at the thought of her ill-concealed blushes. She had a cool exterior, and could handle herself very well, but there was an unexpected softness about her too. A vulnerability that she hid, or tried to hide.

So he'd stayed out of her way as much as possible, because she was a heady mix of things that seemed to attract him more than they should. But avoiding contact with her hadn't worked; he couldn't get the damned woman out of his head.

'Hey. Just passing by en route to an emergency surgery. All good here?'

Friend and colleague Ethan Hunter stood in the doorway, his usual reluctant smile playing hooky. Dressed in scrubs, he looked primed for action. And Ethan always took that very seriously.

He'd been offered the position of Hunter Clinic head in his brother's absence but had somehow managed to persuade Declan to take that particular mantle, talking up Declan's silky PR skills. Declan had agreed—it was all good management experience. And, given the trauma Ethan had been through and his fight back to health, Declan hadn't wanted to refuse.

But this was also the guy responsible for Kara invading his thoughts. Declan could either tell him the truth—that she was quietly driving him mad—or get on with it. The very private Ethan wasn't exactly the kind of guy to confide 'deep and meaningful' to.

Declan shuffled some paper. 'All good, I suppose.

Trying to get to grips with the accounts for when Leo gets back.'

At the mention of his brother's name Ethan stiffened. 'I'm sure you'll manage fine. Hey, how's Kara fitting in? I've heard good reports.'

Declan shrugged, trying not to give too much away. If he was struggling with anything he wouldn't let anyone know. And surely Ethan knew about their kiss at the ball? It was public knowledge.

'Okay. But I'll be happy when Karen gets back. She knows the routine—how I like things.' And she didn't pre-empt everything he did.

But the way Kara's eyes had swirled with a zillion different emotions—none of them warm and fuzzy ones—when she'd spoken about her husband had drawn him to her even more. Having nursed his sisters through enough broken hearts to add more than a few grey hairs to his head, he knew better than even to ask Kara what her story was…but for some reason he was beyond intrigued.

'Hmm. I did wonder about allocating her to you, but short-staffed is short-staffed…'

So Ethan must know about the kiss. It was Declan's own stupid fault for mixing work with fun.

Ethan frowned. 'It's not like you to not gel with someone…'

Oh, yes. He gelled okay. Too damned much. Gelling wasn't the problem. *Un*-gelling was. 'Ah, well, you know…'

'I presume you've had the setting the guidelines talk? Taken the "this is how *I* do things" approach?'

'We've been busy. You know what it's like with a media circus on your doorstep.'

'So demarcate some time—take her for a quick coffee, a drink. There's nothing wrong with her medical practice, though?'

'Hell, no. She's an excellent surgeon. But as it's probably only a short rotation with me I don't think we need bother with all that *getting to know you* stuff.'

'No?' Ethan ran a hand over his jaw. He looked tired. And hassled. 'Try to get on with her, Declan. There's been too much bad blood running through this place for too long.' He checked his watch. 'A drink. A coffee. I don't care what you do. Just do it. I want to hear things are going smoothly, right? I could do without the stress of more work-related worries.'

Declan guessed Ethan was referring to the complicated relationship between the Hunter brothers.

'Okay, boss.'

The man must have been a force to be reckoned with in the army. Fighting the urge to salute, Declan slammed the laptop shut and shoved it into his backpack, made his way to the hospital exit and breathed deeply, filling his lungs with disappointingly stuffy city air. What he needed was a good long ride on his bike to clear the cobwebs. A cosy chat be damned. What he needed was a Kara-free life.

Thankfully the car park was devoid of journalists, leaving him a clear path towards his motorbike. He strode ahead, helmet in hand, the evening sunshine glinting off the chrome handlebars.

Out of the corner of his eye he caught a movement. Someone else leaving the hospital, heading quickly—or as quickly as she could in a pair of red satin stilettoes that made his heart stutter—towards the bus stop. Not quick enough, though, as the bus sailed past, leaving her stamping her pretty shoes against the tarmac.

At closer inspection he confirmed it was Kara, her

hair loose down her back, which drew his eye to her slim waist, nipped in by a fitted cardigan and then lower, to her perfectly shaped backside encased in skinny black trousers. A shot of heat fizzed through him as if someone had flicked a switch in his body.

So he should have just ridden away. But before he knew what he was doing he'd strolled right on up to her.

Ethan's orders, right? Taking one for the team for the sake of no bad blood. 'Hey. Dr Down-Under.'

'Watch it!' She jumped round to face him, at the same time lunging at his throat in a well-practised self-defence karate chop move, her palm almost connecting to his chin.

In a knee-jerk reaction he took a step back and grabbed her palm. He didn't think for one minute she'd have a qualm about trying to floor him and using her stiletto as a weapon. 'Hey! Overreaction, much?'

'Oh. It's you. You nearly gave me a heart attack.' She shook her hand free from his grip and frowned.

'Lucky we're outside a hospital, then.' A short, hot kiss of life sprang to the forefront of his mind.

'Do you often jump out at women from dark corners, wearing…'

Her eyes widened as her gaze travelled over his dark grey T-shirt and jeans. A suit and tie were all well and good for an office day, or a riding the underground day, but not for a bike to work day.

Her throat bobbed up and down as she swallowed. 'Wearing…a leather jacket…'

'Only on special occasions.' When she'd stopped staring and had seemed to gather her wits again he grinned. 'You missed the bus.'

'Thank you, Einstein.' A deep V formed along her

forehead. 'He must have been blind not to see me. I was waving enough.'

'Blind, indeed. Any man worth his salt would have stopped just for those shoes. But you were quite a distance from the bus stop—maybe trainers might be a better choice for running next time.'

She looked down, raised an ankle and turned it this way and that to look at her shoes. He followed her every movement, mesmerised. She had damned fine legs.

Purely an objective observation. Obviously.

An eyebrow peaked. 'Ah, come on—never, *ever* compromise fashion for practicality. Oh…' Her eyes toured his body again and landed on his jacket. 'You just did.'

But he could tell from the hunger in those startling green pupils that she liked what she saw. 'Steady, now. This jacket saved me from a skin-to-tarmac pebble-dashing after a collision with a drunk driver. It's my favourite.'

'Ouch. Lucky escape.' She ran her hand up the zipper and regarded the scuffed black fabric. 'By "favourite," I suppose you mean old?'

'Some things you should never get rid of. Now…'

A drink, Ethan had ordered. A chat. Guidelines. He could do that.

'I don't suppose you've time for a quick drink? Coffee? I'd like to have an informal meeting…a chat about our patient list, Safia, the surgery, guidelines…' *And the kiss. And the husband.*

Hell, he knew too much about Kara Stephens, and *so* not enough. And his drama-free night fizzed into nothing under the cynical watchful eye of the sensible part of his brain.

Kara's teeth bit along her bottom lip as she toyed with

his suggestion. 'Maybe I'm already going out some-where? Maybe I have plans?'

Why wouldn't she? A beautiful woman like her was bound to have plans. 'Okay, well, that's fine. Another time.'

'I don't know...' She stared up at him through her long blonde fringe. 'I guess we should have a debrief, at least. Where would we go? Drake's?'

'Ah, no, after the day I've had I feel like taking a spin. A little farther, maybe? Somewhere I can breathe fresh air, away from the city. Blow out the cobwebs.'

'Not too far. I have an early morning start tomorrow, with a hell of a grumpy boss.'

Walking back to his bike, he handed her a helmet from the top box and grinned. It wasn't the early morning he was imagining...it was a late night...

Whoa, his libido was in super-drive. *Getting to know you* had suddenly got interesting.

Which was a pretty damned stupid idea, given she was already infiltrating his every thought. There were some guidelines he needed to be setting for himself too—e.g. a Kara-free life.

'Okay, so how about Hammersmith? There's a little pub there down on the water's edge, just near Furnival Gardens. Not quite Darling Harbour, I guess, but it's a decent spot and shouldn't be too busy.'

She stopped and regarded his bike with a grimace. 'I don't do bikes.'

'You've got to be open to new experiences, Kara. It's how we grow as people. It's just a bit of fun. What have you got to lose?'

'Skin? I know enough about plastic surgery to never go on a motorbike. *Ever.*' Weighing the helmet in her hand, she eyed him suspiciously. 'Do you always carry a spare helmet?'

'Not always. Just so happens the luck fairies have been busy sprinkling again. I'll be careful—and besides, London traffic is so slow we won't get above twelve miles an hour. Come on. Live a little.' Climbing on, he gestured to the back of the bike. 'I promise not to bite…unless you want me to.'

'Oh, no…biting is way off-limits.'

But she held his gaze and he caught that flicker of desire, those green eyes probing deeper into his soul. And he didn't miss the catch in her voice, the breathy sigh. He wondered, briefly, what was within her limits…

'So, are you getting on or not?'

'Seeing as you asked so nicely. Good to see that chivalry's not dead.'

'Wait. Wear this.'

Shrugging out of his jacket gave him a second to rethink this whole scenario. Man, he needed his head looked at—inviting her out when he should have been going through the Hunter Clinic's quarterly accounts instead of pandering to Ethan's demands. But his friend had been right. The least Declan could do was to lay down some ground rules. A quick drink. A work chat. Then make sure she got home safely. That was chivalry. Not giving in to feral instincts.

Unlike his father, who had given in to too many of his own needs, leaving everyone else to deal with the fallout of his selfishness.

And Declan was nothing like his father.

'It can get cold on the bike and wearing this is safer. Like I said—my lucky jacket.'

He wrapped the jacket round her shoulders, held it while she slid her arms into the sleeves. It dwarfed her willowy frame and she looked like a hot rock chick, not a surgeon. An image that zinged straight to his groin, sending ripples of heat shimmying through him. He flicked her hair out from the jacket collar and slipped the helmet over her head, tightening the strap under her chin, drawing on every reserve not to kiss that pouty mouth.

'Okay, you're good to go. Hold tight.'

He held her hand as she lifted one red shoe and straddled the back seat. Held his breath as she slid her hands around his waist.

And he prayed to the luck fairies that she wouldn't hold on too tight. That his body wouldn't betray him again by reacting to her touch. That he could keep control of his libido long enough to get her safely home. Alone.

CHAPTER FOUR

So much for *professional distance*. Kara climbed up behind Declan and placed her hands tentatively on his waist.
Then, too close for any kind of sensibility, she let go and
held on to the back of the bike.

'Okay,' she shouted as her helmet tapped the back of
his. 'Hammersmith!'

'I'll take the scenic route—give you a bit of a tour.'

He grinned, giving her the thumbs-up and gunning
the engine. A quick jolt as he accelerated made her inhale
sharply and instinctively grasp round his waist again.
Right round.

Now her sharp intake of breath wasn't purely surprise,
but was infused with a good dose of fire as her hands
slid over cotton that slid over muscle. Beneath her fingers
she felt the outline of his abs, lean and taut. Her mouth
watered. If she'd been crazy blurting out her stupid answers in Theatre, it was nothing to the foolhardiness of
hugging against him as they whizzed through the streets
of west London.

At the touch of her breasts against his back awareness flowed through her. Famous city landmarks passed
her by in a blur. She thought she might have seen Kensington Gardens ablaze with flowers, the Royal Albert
Hall and queues of people waiting outside, the dazzling

array of trendy shops in Kensington High Street, but she definitely saw the musculature of Declan's arms as he steered, the tightening of his thigh as they waited at lights, the dips and lines of his shoulderblades.

The traffic flowed remarkably well for rush hour, and he wove the motorbike expertly in and out of the lanes. The warm breeze rushed into her face. The powerful throb and roar of the engine as they sped along gave a power-punch to her chest. Declan was right—this was definitely the way to blow out cobwebs. Her heart thumped and her body ached, but the only thing she knew for sure was that once this ride had ended it would take a lot of convincing for her to get off.

Although not once had she felt any shift in Declan's focus, any kind of reaction to her hands on his body. Maybe she was dreaming that there was a connection between them? Maybe he truly did just want a conversation about their caseload?

In which case she would be fine. She could do professional. She could definitely do hands-off—just as soon as they stopped. For now, though, she was content to hold on tight.

Then, in too few wonderful minutes, they were pulling up outside a beautiful but tiny Tudor-style pub on the banks of the River Thames. Hanging baskets dripped pink and scarlet flowers over mahogany balconies; a smattering of people sat at round tables outside.

He helped her off the bike and unclipped her helmet. 'There we go. Fun, yes?'

'Wow, yes.'

Although not necessarily in the way he was thinking. Her legs felt a little unsteady as she stood, and she didn't think it was all due to the bike.

'I love it. Nothing can beat it. Oh, wait—maybe riding back in the dark, seeing London all lit up.' He secured their helmets in the top boxes, then pointed right along the paved riverfront. 'Should we take a walk first? There's a little pier farther down I like to explore.'

'Oh? Okay.'

She turned to take in the rest of the sights. To their left the green iron latticework of the Hammersmith Bridge dominated the view back towards the city. On the slow-running water members of a rowboat team practised strokes under the watchful eye of their cox. They paused briefly and waved.

Kara waved back. 'Seems like a lot of hard work to me.'

He laughed. 'I prefer rugby myself, but there's a rowing club just down the way. This place gets busy at the weekends, with people hanging out watching boat races and the like.'

'Do you play? Rugby?'

'When I have the time. I play for an Irish club based in Kilburn.'

That explained the toned body she'd run her fingers over. She forced words through a suddenly dry throat. 'What position?'

'You know about rugby?'

How many hours had she stood on the touchline and watched Rob get battered and bruised? How many years of bolstering his flailing ego when they were beaten? Too many to count. It wasn't a memory she wanted to conjure up—or relive.

'Not really.' She changed tack. 'Being a consultant, I thought you'd be more of a wine bar, white tablecloth and fancy grog kind of guy.'

'Grog?'

'Remind me to bring a phrasebook next time. Grog is what we Aussies call beer.'

'I see. It sounded like you had something stuck in your throat.' He laughed. 'I enjoy bars like Drake's, for sure. There's a good crowd in there and it's friendly enough. But sometimes I like a little anonymity—being where everyone knows all your business is like being back home.'

'Or on an army base. Or at boarding school. Both of which I've done.'

'And didn't enjoy, by the look on your face.' He started to wander down the shrub-lined path. Thyme and lavender scented the air. 'I also like to go to places I can pop into wearing my leathers if I see fit. Drake's doesn't really fit that bill.'

'I'm sure they wouldn't mind.' *I wouldn't.*

She sniffed the leather jacket. Got another lungful of Declan. Steadied her heart-rate.

Across the river Kara saw large oak trees, a sports field, people jogging. Next to her Furnival Gardens was in full late-summer bloom, the flowers a little faded now, but bright still, very pretty and so typically English. It was a long way from Sydney's exotic botanical gardens. With no large bats eyeing her suspiciously or flapping their great grey wings over her head. Now, *there* was a bonus.

Ah, Sydney… Her heart stuttered just a little. But she calmed it down again. This new life, so many miles away from the place she'd tried desperately to call home, was going to be stress-free. So long as she kept her heart out of her decision-making.

They walked on towards a cluster of brightly coloured houseboats adorned with a variety of quirky ornaments: gnomes, Buddha statues and pots and pots of flowers. A family of ducks waddled past and slipped into the water.

She breathed the scented air deeply and relaxed her shoulders. 'I can't believe we're still in the middle of London. The air seems fresher here—better than the confines of the city and the hospital's disinfectant smell.'

'It's a good place to clear your head. Sometimes I sneak down here at lunchtime for a run, just to get perspective. It's my guilty secret.' He stopped and turned to face her, looked straight into her eyes. 'What's yours, Kara?'

Oh, God. She forced the still air into her lungs and swallowed deeply. He was looking at her the way he had at the ball. As if he wanted to kiss her. Right now. Suddenly she realised she wanted to be his guilty secret, and him to be hers. To kiss those lips. To curl into his arms.

Dragging her eyes away from his, she glanced downwards. 'Shoes. They're my guilty secret.'

'Ah, yes. Of course. Although there's not a lot secret about that pair. They scream for attention.' He grinned, clearly liking what he saw. 'You sure you can manage a walk in them?'

'Definitely.'

At that moment a jogger ran past and Kara stepped sideways to let him through. Her feet sank into damp grass, ruby-red heels and all. Unless she wanted to hobble across the lawn as if she had some kind of terrible affliction she needed to admit defeat.

'But I think I'll just take them off to save the heels from being ruined.'

He waited as she sat on a bench and unfastened one shoe, then twisted to do the other one. Her hands shook a little as she tried to undo it.

'Damn thing—the strap's caught…'

'Do you need help?'

And there he was, in front of her again, bending down

and peeling the second shoe off, oh, so slowly, his hand on her foot, her ankle, her calf. Her abdomen squeezed at the briefest touch of his fingers on her skin, at the tender way he slid the shoe over her toes, his head dipped in concentration. She almost reached out to run her fingers through that mess of hair. To pull him to her and breathe him in fully. She wondered how the hell someone she barely knew could fire such sensations within her.

Then, as if he'd only just realised the intimacy of such an act, he jumped back and stuffed his hands into his pockets. 'Better now?'

So she'd just discovered that ankles were a definite erogenous zone. Wriggling her toes into the soft lush grass, she smiled. 'Yes. Thank you. Beautiful they may be—but, boy, they feel even better off.'

He laughed, sitting down on the grass opposite her. It seemed the man was at ease wherever he was—operating on complex surgeries in Theatre, in front of the media, roaring through town or sitting peacefully catching the dying rays of sunshine.

'You're as bad as Niamh. She's always buying the most ridiculous shoes—even ones that don't fit properly—just because they're *works of art*, as she calls them.'

'She has good taste, then.'

'Or more money than sense.'

'Niamh?' She knew she was treading on tricky ground here, but she asked anyway. 'Is she one of your sisters?'

'Yes. The oldest of the girls.'

'And then…?'

He shrugged.

She nodded for him to continue.

His smile was hesitant. 'Then there's Aoife, Briana and Roisin.' He counted them off on his fingers.

'I hope there won't be a test, because I'm so going to

fail at remembering them all.' *Efor?* 'There's a lovely musical ring to the names. What do they all do?'

'Apart from get under my feet?'

'There you go again—saying the words, but your face is all soft and filled with affection.'

'Ach, no, I was just squinting because the sun's in my eyes.' He laughed again.

Laughter came easily to him. She liked that. Liked that he found the fun in things. After the past few years she'd struggled to find the fun in anything much, and when Rob had come home all they'd done was argue. But Declan's smile was contagious.

She relaxed into the conversation as he chatted about his family.

'Let me see…you sure you want to hear this?'

'Of course. Like I say, I always wanted to have brothers and sisters.'

'Okay…well, don't say I didn't warn you… Niamh's married and has four kids. Aoife's engaged, for the third time, and has a little one—Declan.' He winced. 'Yes, after me, and not after the hapless idiot who got her pregnant. He disappeared into the ether at the mere mention of a baby. That was a big drama, as you can imagine.'

'Having a baby is always a drama one way or another. And Bri… Bri…?'

'Briana's talking about a wedding next year. Hasn't even met the poor fella yet. And Roisin is causing trouble at Trinity College in Dublin, training to be a doctor.'

Like her big brother. It was all so very different from Kara's life. Declan belonged to something bigger than himself—something full and lively—and he clearly adored them all, regardless of what he said.

A big fist of loneliness curled into her gut. She breathed it away. No point in wishing. All her life she'd tried to fit somewhere—and she'd never found her place, or herself. She'd tried the marriage and profession bit—it hadn't worked because something had had to give and it had ended up being her relationship. Now she just focused on her job, being useful, saving lives, putting people back together again. Taking any further kind of risk with her heart was just not on her horizon.

'How on earth do you keep track of them all?'

'Niamh is an excellent communicator, unfortunately. I think she has me on speed dial.' He rolled his eyes. 'Then there's texts and social media—it doesn't matter where you hide, they can always find you somehow.'

She laughed. 'And your mum and dad? Where are they?'

'Mam still lives on the farm…or rather… Ah, look, never mind.' Dark storms clouded his face. 'My dad… he's gone.'

'I'm sorry.'

'Not dead…just gone.' He offered her his hand and pulled her from the seat, shaking off whatever ghosts flitted at the back of those brown eyes. 'Come on.'

There was more to his family life than he was letting on. Something wasn't quite right. She knew enough about him not to push, but she wanted to ask him about his father. But that would be prying and probably intrusive. She didn't want that in *her* life, so she wouldn't inflict it on someone she hardly knew.

'Now, are you hungry?' He picked up her shoes and put his arms out towards her. 'Shoes or piggyback?'

'Oh, you're really getting the hang of the chivalry thing.'

But she shook her head, imagining how easy it would be to allow some fun into their working relationship. Getting physically close to him again would only make her think or feel something she'd regret. She wouldn't trust her heart to anyone again. So resolutely no piggybacks. The journey home, slammed up against him on the motorbike, would be hard enough.

'Thanks, but I can manage.'

She kept her distance as she walked barefoot into the pub and upstairs to a window seat overlooking the river.

Declan sat opposite her, that sexy mouth teasing her resolve. 'So, Kara, are you planning on staying in Burns and Plastics? Which particular area are you thinking of specialising in?'

'To be honest, I don't know. I love it all, but I'm not sure yet as to exactly where I'd fit.'

'What made you choose it in the first place?'

'I was amazed by the army medics my mother worked with—seeing how they could change someone's life after extensive injury made me want to do the same. So I guess I lean more towards reconstruction than cosmetics.'

'You didn't want to follow your parents into the army?'

She laughed, imagining herself taking orders…and failing. 'God, no, that was never on the cards. I like dealing with clients from all walks of life and different scenarios.'

He took a sip of beer and watched her for a moment, his brown eyes peering deep. 'And has it lived up to your expectations so far?'

'Oh, like all aspects of medicine there's plenty of times when it's devastating and frustrating—'

'When patients don't make it, or don't want to comply? Or when you know the causes of their injuries were avoidable?' He shook his head. 'Believe me, I know.'

'But I still get that mad buzz when someone leaves in a better condition, both physically and mentally, than when they came in. There's not a lot that can beat the high of success.'

'Oh? Really?' Declan put down his beer and leaned across the table. 'Use your imagination, Kara. I can think of a few things.'

She didn't need to ask him what he meant. Those eyes caught on hers again as he smiled, slow and lazy. Sexy too. Very, *very* sexy. An unspoken buzz fizzed between them. Something that was intangible but clear.

Again with the blushing. She couldn't remember Rob ever making her blush, or making her feel this weird mix of fear and excitement just by talking. She wanted to touch Declan. To smooth down that unruly mop of hair. To feel the rough edges of his jaw against her palm, her cheeks, her mouth.

Oh, boy.

'Anyway, am I still on the team, then?' she asked, trying to keep a work focus as the waiter brought their food—a Thai chicken salad for herself and steak for Declan.

In between bites of the most succulent lemongrass-marinated chicken she'd ever tasted she chatted on.

'Do I meet your extremely high standards?'

'I guess I can put up with you. You seem to have exemplary surgical skills and an uncanny knack of knowing what I need even before I do. Which is weird…but I can live with it.' His mouth twitched. 'So we do indeed have an early start tomorrow. I want to check in on Safia before our surgery list starts—make sure she's coping with the pain and the new dressings. Then we're over at the Hunter Clinic to review a couple of private clients in the afternoon. Somewhere in between you can regale the team again with your exploits in Sydney.'

Her cheeks remained heated. 'I'm sorry about that. I

don't usually talk about my private life in the middle of an operation.'

'That's a very good policy to adopt. There's a wicked gossip machine here and it can get you into all kinds of trouble. I find it's best to try to keep a private life well away from work. It stops things getting messy.'

'And who needs messy?'

Messy didn't begin to describe her marriage—it had started out so beautiful, so…naive. Messy had only begun somewhere about the time she'd determined she was going to study full-time, and messy had certainly come to full iridescent bloom at the funeral service.

She gave Declan a tight smile. He was renowned for keeping his relationships clinical. Short. Uncomplicated. And if ever she was going to have sex again that was her game plan too—but he definitely didn't figure in her picture of casual sex partner. Sleeping with the boss would be messy and then some.

She knew better too than to get into a conversation about anything other than work, but she'd muddied things by blurting out details of her life in the middle of an operation. She really did need to make sure he knew that kiss had been fully consensual, and had nothing to do with her memories of Rob or loneliness. And that it wouldn't happen again.

'I like to keep things as uncomplicated as possible. My focus is wholly on my job and I can't see that changing any time soon.' She took a large drink of wine and steadied herself. 'I should tell you, though, just to be clear, that my husband died.'

She could say the whole sentence now without the catch in her voice. She'd come a very long way.

Declan's eyes widened and he put his glass down.

'Oh, God, I never thought… Divorce, perhaps. Separation. What the hell happened?'

'He was killed in action in Afghanistan. Full military honours funeral—quite the hero.' She fought back the rising feelings of guilt, loss and sheer disbelief that had rocked through her for so long. This new start of hers included leaving the sadness behind too. Although that was so much harder to achieve than she'd thought.

'So he was in the army too?'

'Yes. I spent the best part of my teens rebelling against it, but ended up marrying into the firm after all. It was all I ever knew, really. I was very young—too young at eighteen—and I wanted the whole wedding fairytale. Oh, and a career and a family too. Just like every other girl I know.'

She thought back to the struggles they'd both had adjusting to married life, reasserting their individual dreams and trying to mesh them somehow so they could both be fulfilled and happy. She'd wanted a place where she could belong. Finally. Truth was she hadn't found it with Rob either.

Declan's hand covered hers. 'I'm so sorry, Kara. How long ago did he die?'

'Eighteen months.'

He did the maths. 'So the hospital ball must have been close to—?'

'The year anniversary. Yes.' She drew her hand away from his and watched him frown. She didn't want his pity or his sympathy; she just wanted to clear the air. Then she could move on. *Again.* 'But I think I know where you're going with this… Rob dying was devastating, and I'm not sure I'll ever be the same again, but that kiss you and I shared had nothing to do with him. Seriously.'

Declan ran his fingers across his scalp. There were

times when she knew exactly what he was thinking. There were times too when he became closed-off and distant. Right now she wasn't sure what he was thinking at all.

'Yes, Kara, about that kiss…'

CHAPTER FIVE

FINALLY THAT PARTICULAR ghoul was out of its box. Its spectre had hung over them for the best part of twenty-four hours. Or, in reality, six months.

As she put her knife and fork down and sat back in her chair the shadows under Kara's eyes melted away a little. 'It was a mistake,' she asserted.

'Hmm…' Declan disagreed with her. 'Losing your car keys is a mistake. Getting drunk and disorderly is a mistake. Kissing someone like that is no mistake.'

'Well, okay, it was just downright foolish. And it can never happen again.'

'No.'

But, heck, he wanted it to—even now. Even after hearing about the heartbreak she'd been through. She was over the death of her husband? The army hero? *Yeah, right*. Declan knew that loss never left you; the pain dimmed over time, sure, but it still ached in your bones, resurfaced at moments you didn't expect. It snatched clean away the ability to be carefree and left a distrust that life could ever be the same.

But she was clear that their kiss and her mourning her husband's death were separate—perhaps that was what she wanted to believe.

That night at the ball she'd been soft and yet sharp

in his arms, vulnerable and yet defiant as she'd laughed and joked and drunk and danced. And very, *very* sexy. There were layers to her—a fractured beauty about her that intrigued him.

He didn't know how to react to this. Was it wrong to want her after everything she'd been through?

It would be wrong to follow through, he decided—she'd been hurt enough, and he wasn't the kind of man to give her what she needed. But even so he ached to finish what they'd started. The more time he spent with her the more he wanted to kiss her again. And again. To take things to their natural conclusion—bed. Because he could do that very easily.

It was the rest of it—the promises and commitment, the *love* he couldn't do. After the heartbreak he'd seen his mother go through he would never make himself weak and vulnerable—never leave his heart open to such hurt.

So he usually had fun with women who were on the same page as him. Not women who had already had one long-term, this-is-for-life relationship and who clearly deserved another. With the right man. Not him.

'No. You're right. It can't happen again.' That was the right thing to do. The sensible part of his brain cheered from the sidelines.

She flicked her hand nonchalantly. 'We have to work together.'

'Yes.'

'And you're my boss.'

'Yes.'

'And…' Her eyebrows knotted. She obviously couldn't think of another reason why they shouldn't kiss again.

Even though he thought he might be able to persuade her to the contrary, he put his own wants aside. 'And I don't do relationships. And you just came out of one.'

'Hardly. It was a long time ago.'

'You're still hurting. That much is obvious.'

'I'm not. But you don't have to convince me, you know. I *do* get it. We're not doing anything again.'

She looked stung by his words.

'And, yes, Rob's death knocked me for six, that's for sure, but I am in control of my emotions now. I was totally in control back then at the ball too.'

'Knocking back shots was fully in control? Man, I'd love to see you let loose.' She'd been intent on getting wasted and had invited him to join her. Which he had done quite happily, until... 'So why kiss me then run away?'

'Let's just say that in a dim attempt to forget what the occasion was—i.e. the anniversary of Rob's death— I had decided tequila would be the memory-eraser of choice. And I was having a jolly time. Great company.' She winked. 'But suddenly, in a blinding flash of sobriety, I realised that instead of impressing my new bosses I was snogging one of them. And that anything more would be a really bad idea.' Finally her mouth curved into a smile and she pointed at him. '*You* were a bad idea.'

Still no mention of the sizzling static that had crackled between them. The same sizzle that snapped in the air between them now, like a firecracker.

Kiss me.

Oh, yes, he wanted to. '*I* was a bad idea? That's new.'

The smile played along her lips as her eyes brightened. 'Well, you've got to be open to new experiences, Declan. That's how we grow as people.'

'Oh, and we have a comedian in the building. Very clever, Ms Stephens.'

'What's the matter? Is your ego having trouble reconciling that you weren't who I wanted to spend the rest of that night with?'

'My ego is thoroughly intact…' He leaned towards her, unable to resist the allure of that smile. 'Because I don't believe you. You want to know what I think?'

'Not really,' she said

She was smirking in that sarcastic way girls had that was strangely sexy and infuriating at the same time. If she'd been one of his sisters he'd have been hard pushed not to tap her cute ass.

'Oh, do go on. The suspense is killing me.'

'I think you wanted that kiss as much as I did. And that you wonder just what might have happened…'

'I know exactly what would have happened.'

And he could see that she was heading the same way right now too. They both were. Dangerous enough for a fledgling work team. Even more so for a woman whose heart had been shattered and for a man who had no heart left to give. So what the hell his wayward mouth was doing, flirting and teasing, he didn't know.

But he just couldn't help it. 'You never thought about a re-run?'

'Never.'

Her eyes met his and despite her words to the contrary the truth shimmered there in pupils as green as the fields back home.

Home. Reality hit. 'Okay, we should probably be going. Have you finished? Where do you live? I'll give you a lift back.'

'Shepherds Bush.'

She told him the address and for a moment he thought about asking her who else lived there. Did she have flatmates? Was she on her own? Did she need company? He wasn't used to dropping and running. He was used to the sweet magic of commitment-free sex and the un-spoken agreement that it was a one-night thing. But not pushing Kara for anything more felt respectful, right… and way out of his comfort zone. It seemed there were a lot of things about this Aussie whirlwind that sent him off-kilter.

He led her out, helped her on with the helmet, watched as she again sheathed her body in his jacket, washing it in her own sweet perfume. He climbed onto his seat and held his breath as she settled in behind him. This time she didn't hesitate to wrap her arms around his waist.

Many times he'd given rides to his sisters and their friends, to colleagues and to dates. Many times a woman had wrapped her hands around his waist but he had never felt so twitchy and so hot. *Damned* hot.

Kara's legs straddled his back. Those shoes either side of his bike were like some goddamned teenage fantasy. Her breathing was sketchy and shallow, her heat fused to his skin and his hormones hit red alert. Gripping the handlebars as if his life depended on them, he accelerated into the night-time traffic, hoping that the brief journey and the night air would cool things down.

No such luck. When he pulled up outside her apart-ment his gut swirled with a mixture of relief and regret. Laughing, she grabbed his hand and wiggled off the seat, rocking slightly on those take-me-to-bed heels as she straightened up.

So she didn't have to struggle further, he unclipped her helmet and brushed down her hair. The kind of thing he'd do any time for Niamh or Roisin. But the way his groin tightened at Kara's sexy smile of thanks was any-thing but brotherly.

After he'd removed his own helmet he ventured a question that he hoped she'd refuse. He needed to get away, and fast. 'Do you want me to come up with you, or wait here until you're safely inside?'

'Thanks, Declan, but you go home. I can manage. I'm a big girl now.' She found a key in her bag and paused on the steps up to the grandiose Georgian facade of newly refurbished apartments. 'Thanks heaps for the meal and the bike ride. It was fun.'

'No problem. See you tomorrow. Nice and early.'

He made himself turn around, forced the next few steps away from her, but when he reached his motorbike he felt the soft weight of her hand on his shoulder.

Caught the hitch in her breath.

Heard her whisper once more. 'Kiss me...'

'Kara...'

Her name on his lips sent hot sensations skittering through her abdomen and down her shaking legs. God knew what she was saying or doing, but she couldn't let him go without tasting him again. Could not breathe him in, feel the pressure of his body between her legs on that motorbike, could not hold him tight against her and then *not* feel that mouth on hers.

She'd lied. She'd thought about a re-run of that kiss too many times to count. And now she was going to make it happen. Because if she didn't she might just die. Was it possible to die of desire?

He turned, his look of shock similar to the way he'd reacted to her at the ball. The message in his heated pupils was the same too.

He palmed her cheek and smiled. 'What happened to never again?'

'Never say never.'

Her hands found their way to his jacket collar as she lifted her mouth to his before her courage left her. For a moment she thought he was going to resist or reject her, that maybe she'd read all those signs woefully wrong, but then he pressed his lips against hers, his hands framing her face, his touch heart-meltingly tender.

He tasted of something exciting, of adventure, and of a mysterious heat that seeped into her skin. This was nothing like the kiss they'd shared at the ball—this was deeper, sexier and filled with six months' worth of wishing, of relentless holding back and scorching dreams.

'God, Kara.'

His hands ran down her back as he pressed against her, his heart beating a raging tattoo that matched every beat of hers. And even when she knew this was the most foolish thing to do she pressed harder against him. Even when she knew that this was going nowhere she slid her tongue into his mouth, heard the groan in his throat, smiled as his breathing quickened.

She brushed her foot against his leg and he groaned again, in that deep voice that reached into her insides and stroked. 'Those are the sexiest damned shoes I have ever seen. Whatever happens, do not take them off.'

'Aye-aye, sir.' She wiggled against his hips, leaving him in no doubt as to her intentions.

The energy around them was supercharged. The kiss became hotter and more urgent. It was the kind of kiss that you searched for the whole of your life and rarely did you ever find it. Unexpected, exciting. Perfect.

She ran her fingers over his back, down to the waistband of his jeans, and pulled him closer, arcing her body to fit to his, feeling the swell of hardness between them. His mouth was on her neck now, tracing a soft trail to her shoulder, nibbling, teasing, biting.

Her fingers bunched in that scruffy mop of hair as her breasts pressed against him, her nipples hardening as they brushed against his body. Sensation after sensation rippled through her as his hand swept across her ribs, over her bra. Under her bra. Right there on the city street. And then he was sitting her on the motorbike, steadying himself in front of her, his legs straddling hers.

This was the most sexy, the most alive she'd felt in too long. The most amazing. The most thrilling. And if they didn't stop soon they'd be making love on that black and chrome steel.

Was she crazy?

Yes. She probably was. But she needed this, needed him, needed a night when she could be a sexy woman instead of a grieving widow. When she could feel and be held and be wanted. When she could take what she wanted, be herself instead of trying to fit into someone else's mould. Where she could have Declan Underwood in her bed.

She put some space between them—just enough so she could speak. Her hands didn't leave his body; her eyes didn't leave his face. She barely recognised her own voice, 'Do you want to come upstairs? For…?'

He stilled and closed his eyes for a second, knowing that coffee was not on the menu. When he opened them again she knew his answer before he even said the words.

'I should go.'

No. 'But—' The heat coursing through her veins ran cold with embarrassment and disappointment. He didn't want this after all—didn't want her. And she'd made yet another fool of herself in front of her boss.

His palms stroked over her shoulders. 'Go, Kara. Go now, before we do something we'll both regret.'

'Right. Thanks.' Rubbing a hand across her swollen mouth, she held back the sarcastic laugh. She didn't think she could ever regret spending the night with him.

'You know what I mean. We agreed this would be very unwise. Look, I'm not easy to get on with. I don't answer calls. I don't make promises. I'm not there when I'm needed. Except in my job. I'm always there for my job. The truth is, you don't need me in your life.'

'It was just a kiss, Declan.' Although she got the feeling that their kiss was just the tip of the breath-sapping, heart-stopping, wet and wild iceberg.

'And very nearly something else.'

He gave her a wavering smile. Not a let's-get-naked smile. Not a promising-three-times-a-night kind of smile. The kind of smile, she suspected, he gave his patients before he broke bad news. Or the kind of smile he'd given to one of his sisters when the pet goldfish died. It was not the smile she wanted.

'Go to bed. I'll see you tomorrow. Nice and early.'

And before she could answer he'd pulled on his motorbike helmet and disappeared into the night. Leaving her hot and definitely bothered and with no clue how she was going to face him in the morning.

She needn't have worried. He was far too engrossed in his work to bother about the events of the previous night.

They stood in a large group in Safia's room, trying to get the teenager to vent her feelings. No such luck.

Clean-shaven, hair wrangled into smart submission, and wearing a dark charcoal suit, crisp white shirt and silver-grey tie, Declan looked as if he'd stepped out of the cover of a magazine. Kara remembered how his rough jaw had felt across her cheek, how he'd smelt of leather and heat, the way he'd tasted of adventure, the way he'd whispered her name into the night. How his eyes had blazed with a heat that had threatened to engulf her.

Today, however, he looked rested, calm and perfectly

unaffected. Kara, on the other hand, was well aware she had dark smudges under her eyes from a restless night. From dreams about getting hot and heavy under sheets of a substantially lower thread count than the Sheikha was used to.

His voice was soft as he spoke to their client. 'So, Safia, how are you feeling today?'

Dressed in casual clothes, rather than her country's traditional heavily jewelled dress, the young girl sat in a chair and stared out of the window, her arms elevated for optimum healing. So far this morning she'd refused to speak or even to look at the surgical team. Thick tears ran down her face and she made no attempt to stop them.

Kara relayed what she'd learnt from the nursing staff earlier that morning, 'Safia didn't have a great night. She reports having little pain, but she's...well, she's generally not having the best of days. Temperature's fine, though. Bloods are normal. There's no sign of infection. Physically she's making good progress.'

'Ach, Safi...' Declan drew up a chair and sat next to her. 'Everything is going well. So what's the matter?'

'You wouldn't understand.'

'No? Try me.'

He ushered out the attending nurses, the medical students, the physio and even the Sheikha's parents. Kara waited for an indication of what he wanted her to do—stay or leave. God, a re-run of the night before.

This time nothing flashed behind those eyes that made her feel she should be embarrassed, but there was no re-assurance there either. He was nothing but the consummate professional. Heat rose to her cheeks and she picked up her papers and made for the door.

What the hell had she been thinking?

Nothing. She'd thought of nothing past touching her

mouth to his, being wrapped in those arms. Nothing about her responsibilities to the team, to Ethan, to her patients. To her job. To everything she'd sacrificed. She'd been willing to throw all that aside and give in to temptation without a thought for the next minute, never mind the next day, just to have one more kiss with Declan.

Well, it wouldn't happen again.

Out in the corridor a nurse stopped and asked Kara to sign a prescription chart. Then a patient's relative asked for an update. Seemed everyone wanted to talk to her except Declan.

She turned for one quick look back into Safia's room and something about the way he was sitting close to his patient, his voice so gentle, rooted Kara to the spot.

He leaned close and took the girl's hand, looking out across the city and not directly at Safia. A ploy, Kara thought, not to stress the girl out by focusing on her too intently, but to cajole her somehow into talking.

'I see a lot of things in this job, Safia. I see people who have survived terrible accidents, who have lost everything except the ability to haul breath into smoke-damaged lungs. And some are not even capable of that. I see carelessness that leads to injury and I see beautiful people who believe they can't go on but who still have the rest of their lives to live, somehow. And it makes me sad.'

'So why do you do it?' The Princess blinked and wiped her bandaged fist across her eyes, wrestling control over the sobs that had racked her chest. 'Why don't you do something else for a job? Although don't try singing— you do really suck at that.'

'Yeah, I know. Liam's job is safe for now. Truth is, there's nothing else I want to do.' He smiled and turned to her. 'Because when someone can't stay strong for themselves they need someone else to help them along. I kind of see myself as doing that. I stay strong for you until you can find the strength in yourself.' He shrugged. 'Oh, and it just so happens that I'm a genius with a scalpel too. That definitely helps.' He winked at her. 'You're doing fine, Safia. You *will* be fine. This is the hardest bit, you know. Coming to terms with it all.'

'I don't want to come to terms. I want it to have not happened at all.'

He shook his head. 'Ah, sweetheart, I know you do. I know how hard it is. Trust me, I know.'

'How? How do you know? You're a doctor. You're not burned. You don't look like…this.'

Kara squeezed a folder to her chest and watched as emotion bled from his face.

But he didn't shy away from Safia's question. Instead he ran a hand across the back of his neck and nodded. 'Okay…I don't tell everyone this, but it might help you. I hope it does…' He inhaled sharply. 'When I was thirteen we had a fire at our house. I got the little ones out safely, but I just couldn't get to my mammy—my mum—in time…and she got burnt, like you, on her face and her hands…'

Oh, God. Kara's heart thumped and squeezed. She imagined Declan as a young, innocent kid, fighting to save the lives of his family, going back into a burning house to save them. How utterly terrifying.

Blinking back tears, she focused on the blurry piece of paper in front of her. *'Temperature normal. Blood pressure within normal limits…low mood…healing well…'*

Her own reasons for becoming a surgeon paled into the background as she learnt the real reason he fought every day to save people, to try to piece them back together again. And every day the horror of that fire must be somewhere in his mind, spurring him on. She imagined he'd almost lost them in the black smoke and the heat, and realising he hadn't managed to save his mother from being hurt must have bitten deep.

For a man like Declan that would have been a failure. But instead of running away from those demons he forced himself to face them every day.

But he was in London, not back home in Ireland. Had he moved here so he didn't have to face her every day instead? And what about his father? Declan hadn't mentioned him. Hadn't mentioned his dad's role in all of this.

So many questions buzzed around her head.

'So what happened after that?' Safia's voice had lost a little of its self-pity as she stared into Declan's face. 'Is she okay now?'

'She spent a lot of time in hospital and she was very troubled by everything that happened and more. They were hard times, Safia. How she looked on the outside greatly affected how she felt on the inside.'

He waited until the ramifications of that statement settled on Safia's face.

'She wouldn't do her physio, she wouldn't try any more treatments, so her hands and fingers got stiff and sore. She basically lost the strength to carry on. For a long time she let her appearance and her residual pain rule her life.'

Safia's eyebrows rose. 'That's very sad.'

'Yes, it was. She struggled to find that strength within her to make the best of things. That's why I have to be strong, eh?'

He gave her the kindest smile Kara had ever seen.

'But you've got the whole of your life to look forward to. You have very important things to do—I know this— and a happy life to grasp. You *will* get through this, Safia, believe me. You will get through this with dignity and grace and you will make a wonderful life for yourself.'

And until she could he would be there for her...being strong when she couldn't find strength within herself.

Small wonder the young girl looked up at him now with something akin to adoration. 'I'll try.'

'Promise me?'

'Yes. Yes, I promise.' It was a small voice but a big victory.

Kara breathed out slowly. It seemed that the more she learnt about Declan Underwood, the more involved she wanted to become. So she was grateful that he'd stopped talking, because if he was as damaged as she thought he was—and even half as damaged as she was—she could open herself up to a whole new world of hurt.

He turned and caught Kara standing there watching. His mouth opened in surprise, then tightened into a thin line. A torrent of emotion swam across his gaze and so-lidified into anger.

'Ms Stephens?'

'Yes? Sorry. I...er...' She wanted to tell him she hadn't heard, but he knew she had—knew she'd been listening to him bare his soul. And that, she surmised, was like rubbing his wound raw again.

Then he shook his head and with that swift action flicked the anger off. His shoulders were smoothed down, his features took on their normal ridges and planes.

'Okay, Safia, so we'll be back later to see how you're doing. In the meantime I'll send the physiotherapist in and you can start some gentle exercises to help regain the range of movement in that hand. Now, Ms Stephens, we have a surgery to do.'

'Yes, of course.'

Kara hurried in front of him and headed to the operating theatre, where she could bury herself deeper in her job and forget about the red-hot desire burning through her. Forget about the flash of pain and his subsequent refusal to acknowledge it.

Then, when she was finished for the day, she would work out the best way to stop herself from falling head-long into disaster.

CHAPTER SIX

'YOU WANT TO request a transfer? Are you mad?' Declan exhaled long and hard. Now his day was definitely going to the dogs. His day *never* went to the dogs. Work was the one thing he could control in his life: easy, predictable, calm.

He couldn't help thinking this downward trajectory had all started with the appearance of a certain Kara Stephens. The way she'd looked at him after he'd spoken about his mother... God, such pity in those green eyes. He didn't do this—didn't open up old wounds, didn't want sympathy. Never.

Damn. What was she doing to him? What the hell was *he* doing?

He didn't want drama. And no doubt that was what he'd have got if he'd blathered on any longer. That and memories causing a fist of pain under his ribcage.

He'd been trying to help a young girl, not much younger than his sisters, who reminded him of their feisty spirit, who had got under his skin a little. And along with helping her he'd blown open the secrets of his heart.

Damn. Damn.

So much for escaping to London and putting his troubles behind him.

He glared over the sleek smoky glass desk in his

Hunter Clinic office, barely able to comprehend what Kara was saying. Or to reconcile his rapid tachycardia and the thud in his stomach as she spoke in that cute accent that dipped and rose like the County Dublin hills.

'I know it's going to be difficult and will leave you short-staffed, Declan, but I just thought it might be better if I went back to my old team.'

'You're out of your mind.' But, really, he must have been too, to have kissed her back so completely. So totally and completely. And to be sitting here now, wanting to do it again regardless of the fact she'd seen him raw and open.

He didn't want her to leave. Okay, to be brutally honest, he wanted to have her, here in his plush white and light office. To slowly peel off her cream silky top, to strip off her tight black skirt…leaving the beige heels on, though… Man, his thoughts were X-rated…

He was at *work*, goddamn it.

He leant back in his chair. It had been a long day of holding back and he was reaching the end of his self-control. 'So why do you want to transfer?'

'Because of last night.'

'You want to leave because of one kiss?'

'Two kisses, actually.'

She held up two fingers, as if to ram home the point. A lesser woman would blush or shy away from the subject, but this was Kara and it seemed she always tackled things head-on. He thought he saw a smile waiting in the background there too, in the slight twitch of her mouth and a startling sparkle in her eyes. But then it was gone, replaced by steel.

'Two. Kisses.' She shook her head. 'I kissed you twice.'

'I know. I mastered counting single numbers in reception class. Personally, I thought they were pretty damned good.'

He rested his chin on his hands as his eyes met hers. If this wasn't such a serious conversation he could have some fun here. Hell, it had been hard enough to walk away yesterday and now here she was, trying to make it easier for him, and all he could think of was that he wanted more. A lot more. A lot more of everything. Particularly those slender legs, that tight nip of a waist. That cocky, forthright mouth.

What the hell was happening to him? She made a mockery of his self-control and a challenge to every promise he'd ever made to himself about getting in too deep.

'But a kiss is definitely not something I'd want to leave my job over.'

'I would hardly be leaving my *job*. It's just a sideways move to a different consultant and team. Don't get me wrong, Declan, the kisses were great. But I think we're struggling to draw a line here. This is work, our jobs... we can't stuff that up. If I go and work with someone else then we can put a stop to this...*kissing thing.*'

'Whoa...so, let me get this right. You want to leave me high and dry, with no junior surgeon and a heavy caseload, at the beck and call of a royal family, with a frightened patient who has developed a great rapport with you...' God forgive him for using Safia in this '...just because we had a kiss? In our free time? As consenting adults?'

'Two kisses. And I'm trying to do the right thing. The professional thing. What happens if this...attraction spills over to work? We can't afford to let it distract us.'

It was too late for that. And why he suddenly felt a need to defend their actions he didn't know.

'It won't. People have work liaisons all the time and it doesn't interfere with their ability to do their job.'

'No? Do you want to kiss me now?'

He checked his watch. 'It's after five and we're not technically required to be here… And you're an attractive woman. Any man would want to kiss you.'

'Not helpful. We're supposed to be having a meeting. At work.' She frowned. 'Safia is almost headed in the right direction now, so she doesn't need me, and besides it's you she has the real rapport with anyway. I'm sure they can find a replacement. I'll swap with someone. There are plenty of doctors who'd jump at the chance of working with you.'

'But you're not one of them.'

Her shoulders slumped forward. 'Of course I am, and I've loved every minute of it. But, come on, Declan. We both have jobs to do and this could get in the way. This… this is crazy.'

And the rest. He never spent more than a few minutes thinking about a woman. His life had no space for this. His heart certainly didn't.

Fun, yes—a little playful, harmless fun. But nothing more. And with Kara he had a feeling she wanted more. With what she'd been through she certainly deserved more.

'And if you do leave? Then what?'

She held her hand up. 'I just want to put a huge wedge of space between me and temptation. My life's been stuffed up too many times already.'

Which wasn't exactly a ringing endorsement of his kissing talent. He should have been relieved. He wasn't.

'I have to warn you that my first impulse is to say no. Things aren't going well for Karen's mum and she's requested further time off. If you transfer out it will leave the clinic in difficulty.'

'Oh. I see.'

'Look, I need a good junior surgeon and I have one. Why would I give that up for the sake of temptation? I don't intend to allow my work to be compromised.'

His private desires could go to hell. Was it really because he would be short-staffed? Or was it because he was being selfish? *Gah*, he hated that thought—that he would use his needs to make someone do something they didn't want to.

If that was the case he was no better than his dead-beat father, who had fed his own pathetic needs before putting food in his kids' mouths, forcing a boy to do the work of a man. Who had betrayed the love of his family, his wife. His son.

So, no, he didn't want to be selfish—but he also didn't want to be short-staffed to the point that something had to give. With the desperate needs of his patients and the reputation of the clinic in his hands he had too much at stake right now.

He bit down on the flare of heat as she glared at him. A challenge. But not, he suspected, with the kind of result she was expecting. Because instead of annoying him it fired him.

'Okay, well, leave it with me. I have an urgent report to write in what's left of this evening. I'll see you in the morning. We can talk more then.'

Scraping his chair back, he stood and walked to her side of the desk. She stood too, picked up her bag and slung it across her body—a very chic leather barrier. Slamming down the venetian blinds, he turned to her, watched the steel in her pupils melt into hazy heated green.

She could have left. For that matter so could he. But the only direction his feet moved in was towards her.

He ran his fingers through a loose curl of her hair, reached out and pulled the messy ponytail down until her blonde hair pooled over her shoulders. Then he grasped a handful of it and breathed in the sweet scent of freedom and heat.

He looked into her face, at the smattering of freckles over her nose, her perfect full lips glistening with a pale, barely there lip-gloss, then into those eyes that searched his soul. His thumb ran a trail down her cheek, landed on her mouth, and she bit gently down on the soft pad and smiled. His groin tightened as spasms of heat shimmied through him.

She gasped, but she didn't pull away. 'Two kisses, Declan…'

And both times she'd asked him. Now it was his turn.

He leaned into her neck and whispered, 'Kiss me.'

And he could tell by the way her body softened towards him that she did want that. More than anything. That this buzz between them tugged hard, and that she was struggling to fight it. But he didn't wait—couldn't wait—to do what he'd been aching to do since he'd forced himself to walk away last night. He lowered his mouth onto hers, felt the hesitation, the sharp intake of breath, then felt the heat and the need spiral through her.

She wound her hands around his neck as the kiss deepened. And he should have stopped. He should have allowed her to go, to walk away from his team and to stop this *kissing thing*… But he couldn't. Something about Kara Stephens made him want to hold on and never let go.

A sharp knock at the door had them jumping apart. Kara stepped away from Declan on jelly legs and hung on to the back of a chair, her grip as white as the expensive upholstery. She didn't want to look at him, but she stole a glance to see how he was reacting.

Instead of being in any way embarrassed or flustered, like her, he looked triumphant as he held up three fingers. 'Three. Kisses.'

Kiss number three had *so* not been in her plan.

What was it about him that made her want to kiss him so thoroughly? And so many times?

His story and his humility had touched something deep inside her and that reaction had frightened her. The only logical thing she could do, she'd thought, was to move away...not kiss him again. Every contact she had with him dragged her deeper and deeper under his spell. This wasn't just about a purely physical attraction, and that realisation scared her more than anything.

Her cheeks and body ablaze, she inhaled and searched for inner serenity as Ethan Hunter walked into the room. When all she could find was inner chaos she gave up and threw the head of the Hunter Clinic's charitable arm a wobbly smile, hoping that, if nothing else, she could at least project a semblance of calm. 'Hi, Ethan.'

'Kara, hello. How are you?'

She'd heard rumours about Ethan's temper and mood swings, but so far her dealings with him had been only professional. However, well used to being around army veterans, she could spot the invisible wounds, the need to be treated equally, especially after being damaged both emotionally and physically—as Ethan had been—and the refusal to accept any weakness.

Although he clearly believed he hid them well, Ethan wore the scars in his limp and in his stubborn refusal to use a walking stick, and in his absolute unwavering dedication to his reconstructive work on wounded soldiers and war victims alike.

It had been Ethan's suggestion that she join Declan's team, so now would be a good time to mention that she'd like a transfer…and then start tomorrow as far away from Declan as physically possible. But as she opened her mouth to speak her courage flailed and then collapsed in a puddle.

Was leaving the team the right thing to do? Or should she just wrestle her stupid wayward emotions into some kind of order? Was she just a wobbling mess of overreaction?

'I…er…I'm good, thanks.'

Ethan gave her a small smile. 'Thanks for moving across to work with Declan's team. You helped us out of a big hole there.' He nodded towards Declan. 'He has a lot on his plate, holding the fort here while Leo's away, on top of his workload and other commitments. Lucky for us he knows just how to pander to royals.'

'I like them. They're just as frightened as the rest of us when it comes to surgery, and they all need our help. Besides, Safia can't help her background. Kara's been great with her, though—settled her down…got her to open up…' Declan grinned, fully aware of Kara's discomfort. 'I don't know what I'd do without her if she left. Anyway, what can I do for you, Ethan?'

Declan offered him a seat, which he ignored.

'A drink?'

Ethan glanced over to the decanters but shook his head. 'No, thanks. I just wanted to have a quick chat about cover for Mitchell and Grace's leave… As you know, their wedding's coming up so we'll be two more surgeons down, leaving us short-staffed to cover on-call responsibilities at the clinic. If anyone else goes we'll be in big trouble.'

Declan turned to Kara and raised his eyebrows. 'Actually, Kara was just saying—'

'That I'm more than happy to stay on until Karen gets back.'

She threw Declan a look that she hoped would convey how frustrated she felt. What was the use in arguing? Clearly there was a lot riding on her placement here, and creating personnel issues wouldn't leave them well disposed to writing her a good reference.

And who in their right mind would walk away from working at the glamorous Hunter Clinic? Its client list was a who's-who in movie world cosmetic surgery, and Ethan's charity work brought in heartbreaking yet challenging cases from war-torn areas. As a place to hone her craft it was the very best in the world. It was too good an opportunity to give up just because of a kiss.

Three kisses.

Three kisses going nowhere. She was over trying to save things that were going nowhere. Like her marriage. And as it looked as if she was stuck working with Declan she'd keep her heart well out of it. She could do that.

She could.

A flurry of footsteps tapping on the marble floor out in the corridor had them all turning towards the door. Kara breathed out, grateful for the added distraction.

'Here you all are! Makes a change for me to be crashing into someone else's room.'

The Hunter Clinic head, Leo Hunter, stalked in, wearing a huge grin. Following right behind, her hand firmly in her new husband's grip, came Lizzie.

'Thought you'd all be home by now—it's getting late.'

'Just catching up on things.' Declan strode over and shook his friend's hand warmly. 'Good to see you. Good honeymoon? Or shouldn't I even ask?'

'Great. I think it was France, right? Didn't get out much…far too busy…' Leo winked as he shared the joke with Declan, but then his smile slipped a little as he looked over to his brother, Ethan, who cautiously smiled back. 'Hello, Ethan.'

'Hi, Leo. Lizzie.' Ethan walked over, his face serious and his shoulders hitched. He grazed his sister-in-law's cheek with a hurried kiss, shook his brother's hand quickly, then stepped away.

Kara watched with interest as the family dynamics came in to play. With his broad smile and easy manner Leo was clearly pleased to be back at the clinic he'd worked so hard to salvage from scandal and near ruin. Whereas Ethan's response was…*guarded* to say the least.

Again, the gossip machine had informed her of the rift between the brothers that was slowly healing but was not quite mended yet. For two people so passionately involved in putting lives back together they had resolutely failed to fix their own. There had been difficult scenes, terrible arguments and times when the brothers had clashed spectacularly. But after Ethan had been best man for Leo and Lizzie's wedding there had been some new, more friendly ground covered. Although, as far as Kara could see, the smile Ethan gave them still didn't quite reach his eyes.

Declan stepped forward and kissed Lizzie's cheek too. Warmth emanated from his smile. The contrast between him and Ethan was startling.

'You look great, Lizzie. Tell me, how was Paris?'

'*Très* amazing, thank you. Just…amazing.' She turned

to Leo, her eyes shining brightly. 'Can we tell them? Please?'

Her husband gave her an indulgent smile, his love evident in the protective arm round her shoulder and pride shimmering in his face as he looked only at her but spoke to the room. 'Okay...so, we have news.'

'I'm pregnant!' Lizzie blurted out, running a hand over her still flat stomach. 'We're having a baby.'

Leo kissed the top of her head. 'Yes. And we couldn't be more happy.'

Some people could have it all—work, marriage, love. As flutters of sadness whirled through her gut Kara forced out a smile, feeling, she thought, exactly the way Ethan looked right now: empty. Hollowed out.

But still he stepped forward and again shook his brother's hand, almost as if he was doing what he knew was polite rather than what he deep down wanted to do. 'Congratulations.'

'That's great news!' Declan gave them all a broad grin. 'Really fantastic. Seems it's all weddings and babies at the moment. Do you think there's something in the water?'

'Oh, yes, it's Grace and Mitchell's wedding in a couple of weeks, isn't it? Exciting!' Lizzie positively glowed with happiness. She glanced at her watch. 'Gosh, look, we really should go. We haven't even made it home yet, but Leo wanted to pop in here just to let you know we're back. You know what he's like—this clinic is his baby and he couldn't possibly drive past and not say hi.'

'You mean he wanted to see if the place has managed to survive without him? I think we've coped. Just.' Declan laughed. 'But you must be tired after your travels. Take your wife home, man. You have another baby to think about now. You can play surgeon-in-chief tomorrow.'

'Okay. Okay. I'll be in first thing tomorrow, if you can spare the time for a hand-over?' Leo looked at both Declan and Ethan, who nodded in agreement.

'Of course.'

And with that bombshell Leo walked his new bride out, their excited chatter resonating off the walls as they wandered down the corridor. Ethan followed a moment later, muttering something about a case arriving from Afghanistan in an hour or so and how not everyone needed to wear their hearts on their sleeves. Leaving Kara alone again with Declan, a whirlwind of emotions fluttering through her stomach.

Grateful that it wasn't her own private life in the spotlight, she commented on the scene that had just played out. 'Was it just me or did Ethan not seem particularly thrilled at the prospect of becoming an uncle?'

'He's had a rough ride, Kara. You of all people should understand that.'

Yes, she knew enough about rough times. About loss and grief. About the way dreams didn't become reality. That no matter how hard you tried to love someone, sometimes it wasn't enough. 'I guess…'

'Having seen first-hand how traumatic injuries affect soldiers…'

'Oh, yes. Of course.'

Declan shrugged and walked her towards the door, his hand on the small of her back, its heat sending her mind into a fuzz.

'But I think it's more than that. Between you and me, I think Ethan might be a touch jealous of Leo's happiness. It's something he's not been able to find for himself.'

'I heard they don't have an easy relationship.'

'There were issues between them in the past… That's why he joined the army, apparently—to get away from the messed-up Hunter family dynamic. And that, in turn, is why he's like he is now.'

She thought back to the way Ethan's jaw had tightened at the pregnancy news, the shadows that had formed under his eyes, the hollows in his cheekbones—jealousy? Without a doubt.

But she also knew that you had to dig very deep and get through tough times—find another focus, like work, and bury yourself in it. There was no point dwelling on what you couldn't change. It seemed Ethan, with his devotion to his work, was following the same mantra.

'Hey, are you okay?' Declan touched her arm. 'You seem a little quiet.'

If he'd just move his hand she wouldn't feel like leaning against him. Confiding in him. Asking him to kiss her again, fourth time lucky.

'Is that so strange?'

'Actually, yes. I never thought… All this talk of weddings must hit a raw nerve for you.'

The wedding hadn't been the problem. It had been the marriage. 'My wedding was a long time ago…it was a perfect day, exactly how I'd planned it. It's just a shame everything turned out the way it did in the end. But I'd never begrudge anyone a bit of happiness.'

'Fair play to you, Kara. That's my girl.'

His voice softened as his hand ran up her spine in a tender gesture that made her want to rest her head on those broad shoulders and just stop. Stop fighting this attraction. Stop trying to do the right thing when she wanted so desperately to do the wrong thing—with him.

'And you're staying on the team? No more talk of leaving?'

She pulled herself away from him. She'd managed perfectly well on her own up to now and she could do it again. And again. Unlike his mother and Safia she didn't need Declan's strength. She had enough of her own. She knew not to rely on anyone else because when it came down to it their promises pretty well amounted to nothing. Especially men like Declan—players; men who wanted everything but gave little in return. Well, he could have her one hundred per cent work commitment and that was all.

'I guess you boxed me into a corner there. So, yes, I suppose I'll stay. Even though now Leo's back you won't be so busy.'

'I'm always busy. I like it that way. Besides, he'll need time to catch up.' He gave her a wicked smile that threw her a challenge. 'Think you can keep your hands off me?'

'Oh, don't worry, Declan. I *know* I can.' Even though it would take a huge effort. 'Good night.'

Then she walked out of his office without looking back. Truth was, she had no idea how she was going to get through the next few weeks with any scrap of sanity left.

CHAPTER SEVEN

ALL WENT WELL for the next two weeks. Kara managed to maintain a respectable distance and Declan appeared to be trying too. Not once had they shared another kiss, or even a proximity that might generate one, even in the moments they spent together going over their cases.

Although the heat flickered between them like a smouldering fire—one small, wayward spark and she had no doubt things could get way out of control—she kept a lid on her emotions during the day. Only at night did she allow herself to relive those moments of closeness she'd shared with him.

So it was good to get some perspective now, on a rare day off, on her own out in the fresh air, taking in some of London's famous sights.

Having taken way too many photographs of the magnificent Globe Theatre, she wandered along Queen's Walk by the Thames. Barges glided past, and a cruise tour boat with people hanging out of open windows, cameras snapping, pointing and laughing. The river was as busy as the land on this bright sunny day.

In the distance the iconic sand-coloured Westminster Palace and its famous clock tower, Big Ben, dominated the view. She wandered along the paved walkway, weaving through the clusters of tourists taking photographs, past buskers and living statues, dodging jugglers and Latin American street dancers that added an exotic pulse to the atmosphere. The park was just a little farther along, next to the London Eye Ferris wheel, where somehow Mitchell and Grace had managed to land permission to hold their wedding reception.

Seemed most people from the Hunter Clinic had wrangled a day off to join in the festivities. Thank goodness she hadn't followed through on her request to transfer; she would have missed being here with this group of people who had invited her into their sophisticated yet welcoming world.

Some of her colleagues stood in the corner, laughing, chatting. Kara began to approach, but just at that moment she saw Declan join them.

Heart thudding against her ribcage, she turned away.

With a toned body like his, encased in a dove-grey collared shirt and smart black trousers, he was bordering on illegally sexy.

Oh, please bring back the scrubs.

So much for perspective. How the heck could she get an ounce of that when he was within touching distance?

Keeping her back turned to Declan, she waved at the beaming bride and groom and at Mitchell's adorable daughter, Mia, who was the absolute darling of the piece. And, no, not once did she feel a pang of nostalgia for her own wedding—although she did fight back the sting of tears at the smiling faces, the sweet beauty of the love-conquers-all message.

Because she knew, deep in her heart of hearts, that sometimes love just wasn't enough to keep two people together. Which was so *not* how she should be feeling at a wedding.

She plastered a smile to her face, which wasn't too difficult because Grace and Mitchell's love shone through. 'Congratulations! Happy day! You look gorgeous!'

Voices behind her grew louder. One of them was Declan's. Her back stiffened.

'Oh…er…I'll be off now,' she heard him say. 'Got to go.'

'Wait,' the other male voice said.

Was it Ethan? Leo? She didn't dare turn to take a look.

'Is that Kara on her own? Come and say hi.'

God, no. Her heart dropped.

Declan's voice grew louder. 'No, seriously, I should go. I've got things to sort out.'

So he didn't want to face her either. And why did that not please her as much as it should?

The not-as-smooth-as-Declan's voice shouted, 'Kara! Hey!'

All well and good to avoid proximity in the busyness of work. But out here, in the sunshine, when she'd been caught alone, they were destined to at least talk. Anything less would appear rude.

Drawing a deep breath, she turned. Declan was standing in front of her on his own now, eyes blazing with frustration, his friend having disappeared into a huddle of suited men shaking hands and laughing.

He shrugged and raised his beer bottle. 'Hi.'

'Hi.'

'Nice day for a wedding,' he said politely, picking his words carefully.

The tiny hairs on her arms prickled at the voice. Warm and thick like Irish whiskey, it soothed her to the pit of her stomach. But also, like the strong dark liquor, it made her giddy and excitable.

'Yes.' She drew a breath and steadied her nerves. 'I thought I'd come along and take a sticky beak.'

His smile was breathtaking. 'There you go with that foreign language again. A what?'

'A look. A nosy. My flatmates have gone away for a few days so I was at a loose end. I just took a stroll along the riverfront. I never knew there was so much along here.'

He glanced down at her wedge sandals—honestly, they were only a few inches high...

'Really? Strolling in *those*?'

'Yes, Declan, what else would you do in them?' She held up her hand at the glint in his eye. *Do not take them off.* Suddenly her imagination ran riot with images of him naked...her legs wrapped around his. Heat seeped through her. 'Do not answer that.'

'Don't worry, we're in a public place—I do know how to behave.'

His voice lowered into a growl that simultaneously made her laugh and stoked something hot and needy in her stomach.

'I've been behaving for the past two damned weeks.'

So he was suffering too. That gave her a short blast of something wild and exciting. To have a man have to control himself around her gave her a sense of strength—power too. Something she hadn't had for a while.

'And so you shall continue.' She looked up into his dark brown eyes and thought that out here in broad daylight she was very unlikely to kiss him. Especially when they would be surrounded by people from the clinic. Despite how much she was drawn to that mouth. 'We're going to stick to safe subjects...like work.'

'Really?' His shoulders slumped forward. 'Dull.'

'Safe.'

'Dull.'

'Shut up. Actually, I was wanting to talk to you about

Safia while we have a few minutes. I'm still worried about her.'

Kara had been meaning to catch up with him about the Princess for a couple of days, but an emergency case had taken priority.

He became serious in an instant. 'Me too. She's healing well, but my pep talk didn't really help.'

'Oh, it did. It was exactly what she needed to hear.'

And it had certainly helped Kara get more insight into the workings of his mind. Flirty and funny he might be, but he held people at an emotional distance, carrying baggage almost as big as hers, along with a huge responsibility for a family he tried hard not to care for.

'She's definitely more motivated, but she's still very down. Her parents got her tickets for the Oblivion concert and she didn't even show a flicker of interest.'

'When a girl stops showing interest in a sex god there is something very wrong.' He smirked and held his arms out, puffing his chest and smoothing his fingers through his hair. 'I should know.'

He was a sex god?

Spasms of lust rippled through her as he laughed. Yes. He was a sex god.

He was driving her crazy with his easy nonchalance, his wicked humour, his sexy talk. Crazy and just a little bit sexually frustrated. She took a bottle of water from her handbag and had a long, refreshing drink, hoping the cold might wash some sense into her. It didn't.

His eyes followed the movement in her throat as she swallowed. His gaze was bordering on insatiable. 'You are way too cocky, mate.'

'You just don't know what you're missing.'

Oh, but she did. Knew it with every single second she

spent with him. Knew too that keeping a distance was definitely the only path to take.

She tried to relax and move the conversation to less shaky or sexy ground. 'Funny how life works out. I never thought I'd be working in London, walking alongside the Thames on a day off, visiting places where Shakespeare had been.'

'You had a different life planned?'

'Yes.' Rob was supposed to have left the army. They were supposed to have had a family, settled down. Found somewhere to belong, to fit. 'But here I am, a long way from that.' Making her new life fit around her instead.

He walked her slowly to a patch of grass. Laying his jacket out, he indicated for her to sit. 'Your poor feet need a break. I have about five minutes, then I really do have to go.'

Good, setting out parameters.

Glancing around, she saw that most people had sat down in little huddles, or couples, spreading out in the park. Everyone seemed relaxed, paired off, settled in the sun. To interrupt them by barging into their groups would seem rude. Not to sit down for five minutes would too.

She determined to stay just long enough to be polite. 'What about you, Declan? Did you always want to come here? Where is it you're from again?'

'County Dublin.'

'Do you miss it?'

'Not really. I miss the fresh air, mostly, but you can't beat London for excitement. I love it here. No pressures. I like to be free. No ties.'

No ties. Like her. And yet whereas he clearly wanted to cast his ties off, she'd spent a good deal of time over the years trying to forge them one way or another. It was just that she'd tied herself to the wrong people.

'I've always wanted to visit Ireland—it sounds wonderful. I think somewhere back in our family's past we have people from there.'

'Most folks do.'

His hand brushed against hers and it would have been so easy to grasp it. But instead she shoved her fist in her dress pocket and let herself be carried away by his voice.

'It's a grand place to bring up kids. I can see that now, living in a big city like London where there's noise and pollution and crime, but I couldn't wait to escape. There were times I didn't think I'd ever leave the village I grew up in.'

Was this a good time to broach the subject? Unanswered questions swirled in her head and she felt compelled to know more and more about him. He seemed relaxed, just chatting.

Her heart thumped a little as she asked, 'Was that... because of the fire? Was she badly hurt...your mum?'

'She was close to not making it. Not just physically but emotionally.'

'I can't imagine how bad that was for you all. What about your dad? Was he hurt?'

His eyes clouded like dark storms. But it wasn't grief, it was anger. 'Not badly enough.'

Wow. Bitterness flowed from him. 'What do you mean? What happened?'

'That's a lot of questions, Kara.' He put his hand on her shoulder. 'I prefer to look ahead now, eh? No point in dwelling on all that.'

She looked up into those clouds, saw fear there too, and hurt. She wanted to wrap him in her arms and wipe away that pain. But he would never let her do that—he was too proud, too closed-off.

'You mean, back right off.'

'Yes, I do. Leave it alone.'

At least this time his tone was gentle—but she'd over-stepped the mark. In lots of ways he was right. There was no point dwelling on the past, even if it did tinge every-thing you felt—your dreams, your plans. Taking a long deep breath, she looked ahead.

Adults laughed and chatted, children of all ages played together, teenagers swung toddlers around, made daisy chains, chatted happily alongside each other.

With a sorry heart she thought about Safia in her hos-pital room, so far away from her friends and surrounded by stuffy aides and parents who desperately wanted to make her feel better but were at a loss as to what to do.

But as she watched a thought crystallised.

Declan lay back on his elbow and gave her a lazy smile. His hair kind of flopped over his eyes just a little, and once again she found herself fighting the urge to run her fingers through it. The clouds in his eyes had passed through and she saw only light in them now.

'I have an idea.'

'Oh?' His eyebrows peaked. 'Should I be worried? Scared? Excited?'

'All of the above.' She winked. 'Brace yourself.'

Declan sat up as Kara smoothed her pale yellow linen dress around her. He'd thought he'd been doing quite well, sticking to safe conversations and being on his best be-haviour. And, truth be told, he'd spent two whole weeks reining in his libido to the point of utter frustration—and, man, he'd been good. In Theatre, on the ward rounds, in meetings, he'd maintained a professional distance, had kept his dirty mouth in check, had not touched her. Not once.

And while once upon a time if his libido had been

bouncing like this he'd have gone out and got laid with a like-minded woman, recently he just hadn't had the appetite. But now the sight of those long tanned legs and cute *kiss me* mouth made his heart jump more than a little.

'So…' She gifted him a smile, which turned the heart-flip into a full-scale bungee. 'Now that she's had her second lot of surgery do you think Safia is well enough to be in a shared room?'

'Work, work, work. Of course.' He tipped his head back and laughed.

The woman was either work-obsessed or choosing her conversation topics with absolute care. Judging by the pink tinge to her cheeks, and the resolute way she would not look him fully in the eye, he guessed it was a bit of both.

'Yes, she's healing well, but her parents have specifically requested for her to be on her own. They are very strict on privacy.'

'Yes, I understand that. She might be a princess, but really, as you say, she's just like any other girl. She wants to be with friends, to chat and laugh and squeal over boys. I think she's lonely, and I think she needs normal.'

'And moving her to a shared room would give her company, distract her from her burns. Genius.'

It was a simple idea, but often they were the best ones. He'd been so focused on keeping the girl safe and her parents happy that he'd skipped past Safia's basic needs. Companionship.

Hell, the more he thought about it the more he could apply that logic to himself. But he'd never wanted companionship before—at least not past the bedroom door—so God knew why suddenly he felt as if he'd been missing something…he didn't want to think about what.

'What about the cross-infection risk?'

Kara leaned forward and he caught a flash of pure white lace under the halterneck dress. His mind whizzed into overdrive. The trouble with halternecks was the sheer amount of skin exposed. Her neckline, sun-kissed shoulders, a wide expanse of back that made him want to stroke his fingers down that spine.

But the best bit about halternecks was the amount of skin exposed…the neckline, sun-kissed shoulders…

Yes, he knew exactly what he'd been missing. And looking at those long limbs, that easy smile, the curve of her breasts, he could only guess what else he was missing too.

As if he'd ever dreamt that a loudmouthed Aussie might fill a gap in his life that he didn't even know he had. Confused wasn't the half of it.

He dragged his eyes away and reminded himself of their conversation. *Cross-infection risk.* 'Minimal, I'd say. At least at the moment while she's still on prophylactic antibiotics. She should be fine. We'd just need to keep an eye on her temp and wound sites. I'll talk to her parents and run it by them. I'm not sure they'll be very happy at the prospect of moving her.'

'But we're talking about her mental health here, not just physical. Surely they'll see that?'

'I'll discuss it with them. That's all I can promise.'

His cell phone rang. *Damn.* Not today.

Her eyes flicked to his phone, lying on the grass next to him, but truly he didn't even need to check to see who was calling.

'Aren't you going to answer it?'

'Nah. It's just family stuff.' He'd deal with it later. He took a long slug of his beer. *Later.*

'Then surely you should pick up?'

'Look, I'm having a good time.' The ringing stopped. 'See. She'll leave a message.'

It rang again.

Kara's gaze hooked on to his. 'It might be important.'

'It's Niamh. It won't be.'

Kara's eyes narrowed with suspicion. 'How do you know? How do you even know it's Niamh?'

'She has a special ringtone so I know when to answer. Or rather, when not to answer.' He laughed. 'You know, they're great, but, man, *so* needy. I'm at a friend's wedding, for goodness' sake. This…' He indicated the setting, the weather, his beer. *Her.* 'This is nice.'

Days off were scarce; spending them outdoors with a beautiful woman were rare indeed.

His phone rang again.

'It's okay. Pick up. Seriously, I don't mind.' She reached for the phone and glared at him. But her smile was sweet and she was laughing. 'Declan, come on, it might be important. What if it was and you missed something? Family's important. Just be grateful you have one that cares.'

He saw the flicker of hurt as she flapped a hand in front of her and shook her head. *Don't go there.* But he remembered the bitter words she'd used back in that corridor weeks ago. *What their child wanted came at the bottom of the pecking order.*

She'd clearly had a bad run, with parents who cared more for their careers than for her needs. And her husband had left her a widow so young.

Hell, his family might irritate him but he knew he was loved—even if it was to the point that it felt suffocating.

'Okay. Okay. But I know I'm going to regret this.'

He huffed out a breath and snatched her hand away, grabbing her fingers and holding them. She playfully pulled back, but she didn't wriggle from his grip. Her skin was warm on his. Every single nerve-ending fired into action.

And there…right there…that second…the electricity between them sparked into life again. Need slammed into him. She felt it too, he knew. He could just see the playful teasing in her eyes melt into something dangerous and hot. Her smile wavered into the bite of her teeth on her bottom lip, the reddening of her skin, the quickening of her breath.

She didn't want this. But she did. And, *God*, he wanted her like nothing and no one he'd ever wanted before. He'd held back and held back…

He caught her chin with his hand and tilted her head to his. Her mouth was only inches away. Her tongue darted out and wet her lips as if she was about to eat something delicious.

Kiss me.

And he was going to. As he lowered his mouth towards hers the earth twisted on an axis he couldn't fathom and the breath was stripped from his lungs. And, sure, his whole damned workplace was here, watching again. Like before—that first time on the ballroom floor.

And just like that first time he couldn't stop himself—couldn't stop the pull of her lips, of her fragrance. He just wanted her in his arms. There was a connection—not just a base physical attraction, something more—that drew him to her.

He was going to kiss her once more, just to get her well and truly out of his system. Then he was going to put a stop to these flirting shenanigans and focus on his life and responsibilities.

'Declan?'

She fitted so perfectly into his arms. Her breath was

on his throat like a butterfly kiss. Her voice was hoarse, and he definitely caught the sexy catch.

'Aren't you going to answer it, then?'

The phone. The damned phone.

He exhaled and kept his voice steady—this time not from frustration but from pure, blatant, feral need. Clearly his sister didn't need to hear that.

'Niamh. This had better be important.'

'Hello to you too, Dec. Now, I was just planning ahead awhile… You know Mammy's birthday's coming up…'

Please. Really? Mid-pash? 'Can this not wait?'

'Why? What the hell are you up to on a fine Saturday afternoon?'

He growled. 'You don't want to know.'

'Wrong, Declan. I *do* want to know. What's her name?'

Was nothing private? 'None of your business.'

'Sure, that's an odd name for a girl. Now, tear yourself away and talk to me about Mammy's birthday. She'd love to see you here…'

He listened to his sister blather on and his blood pressure started its usual upward hike as his libido crashed into his boots. 'I'll see what I can do, but you know what it's like. I do have work to do.' He dragged his hand away from Kara, stood and took a few paces away so she wouldn't hear the drama. 'We're fierce short-staffed as it is.'

'It's always work with you, Dec. But I think seeing you would be a real tonic for her.'

'I have to work, for God's sake.' What more did they want from him? He sent home a good amount of money, and it was a far cry from what he'd been forced to do as a kid just to get some food on the table. At least he was on the right side of the law now. 'How the hell else do we pay for the things you all want? Look, I'll see what I can do.'

In reality, he didn't want to face the endless questions that Niamh seemed to think were perfectly acceptable for a girl to ask her brother…and added to five-fold by the rest of his siblings and his mother.

When are you settling down?

What about babies?

Found a nice girl yet?

Despite her own experiences his mother seemed to think that the answer to life, the universe and everything was finding a nice girl. He'd found plenty. He just hadn't loved any of them. And didn't plan to any time this side of the millennia.

'Look, I'll get back to you. I have things to do.'

'Okay, big brother, think about it. Be good. And be careful. And if you can't be careful…you know the drill. Buy a pram.'

Yada. Yada.

He flicked the phone into his pocket and inhaled deeply, trying to find the equilibrium that had been shattered first by a sexy siren and then by his stroppy sister.

Once calm, he turned back, ready to start again with Kara. 'Now, where were we…?'

But she'd disappeared.

He searched the crowd and saw her walking back to the main wedding group, being led by a pair of too-cute little girls in party dresses that reminded him of happier days with his sisters—before the fire had maimed their mother, sent their feckless father running away from his responsibilities and catapulted Declan into being the main breadwinner when there were no jobs for a scrawny kid, no way of earning money to pay for things.

And still, so many years later, they relied on him for everything.

As if she could sense his eyes on her smooth, straight

back, Kara turned and scanned for him. Once she'd found him she shrugged a little, her eyes bright but her smile regretful. Regretful about what? he wondered. That things had nearly got out of control again? Or regretful that they hadn't?

And then, as she wandered through the wedding party, he thought perhaps Kara's feelings were all mixed up with her own past. Did she regret coming to a wedding that would surely bring back memories of her own and of her war hero husband? Was that why he'd felt her tiny shift towards temptation? Did she just need comfort?

And why the hell did he care? Because the last thing he needed was another woman to worry about.

CHAPTER EIGHT

'SAFIA IS PROGRESSING very well indeed, at least physically.'

True to his word, Declan was presenting Kara's idea to Safia's parents in the burns unit family meeting room. Their first meeting since the weekend was going well so far.

No, their first meeting with *Safia's parents* was going well…but Kara was struggling with the near-kiss thing, and how easily she fell under Declan's spell every darned time. A lucky save by that pair of darling girls had put an end to something before it had started, but she was losing self-control with every touch, every look, every minute she spent with him.

Especially when he was dressed, like today, in a smart dark suit and an open-necked camel-coloured shirt. One tiny glimpse of his chest and she was a quivering mess of hormones. And it was way too early in the day for that.

'We have completed phases one to three of her management so far. She is alive and thriving, her burns are now all in a closed healing phase. She is having regular therapy to prevent contractures and she is responding well to that.'

The Sheikh nodded. 'Yes, we are delighted with your care. We are most grateful. She is getting better.'

'Well, yes. Her wounds are healing.' Declan leaned forward and frowned. He seemed to be choosing his approach carefully. 'But I'm concerned about her low mood.'

'She is sad, but she'll feel better soon.' Safia's mother had clucked around her daughter like an anxious mother hen from the minute they'd arrived. And who wouldn't? Who wouldn't fight for their child's life? Love for her daughter shone through, but it was a little…stifling.

'Until a few years ago burns specialists spent a lot of time and emphasis just on treating the burns and keeping the patient alive. Now survival is much more likely that we have to look at how patients like Safia are going to fare in the future, once they've been released from hospital. That's why we've been giving her physiotherapy since the day she arrived.'

'But I don't know what to do with her. She just sits and stares out of the window.'

Declan nodded, his hands clasped in front of him, his eyes soft and gentle. 'I know. I know. And I understand how upsetting it is for you to see her like this. We need to get her interested in things again. What does she like doing?'

'Make-up, clothes, horse-riding. She…you know… *hangs out*. In our country obviously she studies, goes to parties…shopping…friends. But she won't let them come to see her. We'd fly them in, but she refuses to see anyone.' The Sheikha nervously toyed with the edge of her beaded shawl. 'She's always got an opinion on everything. She's a handful at times. But now she doesn't seem interested in anything.'

'Ms Stephens has an idea we want to run by you.'

Declan's eyes fell on Kara, making her pulse jump in a skittering dance. *Damn. Stop it, already.*

'We thought, perhaps, that Safia might benefit from sharing a room with other people her own age?'

'Absolutely not.' Sheikh El-Zayad's voice filled the room. He was a man used to getting his own way, who commanded everyone and everything. 'I appreciate your concern, Mr Underwood, and I'm very grateful for your help in her progress, but my daughter shares a room with no one. She is the Sheikha of Aljahar—a princess. She does not mix with other...ordinary people. We have paid for privacy—it is very important to us.'

Declan shot a quick look over to Kara. No one else would have noticed but his jaw had tightened just a little. He took a deep breath and smiled, his voice now soothing, but with an authoritative edge.

'We could compromise. Perhaps she doesn't necessarily need to share a room—but she does need stimulation. It's very important she has contact with people her own age—not just your aides and...yourselves. The physiotherapist is happy to come and attend to her in her room—but I do think she needs to be occupied for the other hours of the day. At the very least she should come out and join in some activities, eat her meals with the others. Long-term psychological effects on people with burns injuries are well documented. We need to keep her motivated.'

Kara knew he wasn't just talking about his professional experience. So his actions and his words were oceans apart. Because, yes, even though she'd tried hard not to listen in to his private conversation with his sister she'd caught snippets.

He was refusing to go and visit them—and using work as an excuse. Maybe it was easier dealing with someone who wasn't a relative than having to face your own realities at home.

'With all due respect, Your Highnesses…' She smiled to them both, knowing her voice was rising just a little. 'Integration is a huge part of our therapy here. I don't want to alarm you, but I know you appreciate honest talking…' She waited until she'd received a positive response from them. 'Safia won't get better unless she sees some normality in her life—she's had enough of pain and being shut in that room on her own. I'm concerned about the risk of depression. She needs to be engaged. And she needs, really, to be part of this discussion.'

'Thank you, Kara.'

Safia's voice had them all turning quickly to see her standing in the hallway. Dressed in jeans and a baggy sweatshirt, she looked like a regular teenager apart from the left side of her face and her hands which were covered in dressings.

She was pale and unsmiling. 'Talking about me again, Daddy?'

Declan stood and brought Safia into the room, offered her a seat. 'Hey. Thanks for coming by. It's nice to see you out of that room for a change. It must be boring on your own all day?'

'*Duh*. Of course.' Safia shook her head, her black curls bobbing round her shoulders.

As a member of a famous royal family her photos had graced the newspapers from an early age; her face was well known. She'd been a pretty girl—a beautiful teenager. Kara's heart clenched at what the future held for Safia now. She couldn't begin to imagine the grief and loss the girl felt.

She watched as Declan and Safia sat across from each other, saw his generous smile and a concern that went beyond his professional obligation. He pointed through the glass door to the ward where, as luck would have it, a seventeen-year-old boy who'd been brought in after a freak lightning strike had burnt his back, walked past. Wearing teen trademark baggy-bottomed trousers that hung off his hips, and a sideswiped fringe, he stopped and gave Safia a hesitant smile. Then a sort of half-wave before he disappeared into the ward.

Declan watched this with interest, a hint of a smile playing over his lips. 'But I bet you wouldn't be interested in spending time out there, Safia? Although Jack's got an interesting story to tell.'

The girl shrugged, but there was a spark in her eyes. Finally they'd got her interested in something. 'Anything's got to be better than sitting around with you lot.'

Declan grinned. 'Feeling better already?'

'Maybe.'

Kara glanced to Safia's parents, who looked at each other and shook their heads. They murmured quietly in a language Kara didn't understand and finally Safia's mother sighed. 'Okay. If you think so. Do it.'

'Wait—' Sheikh El-Zayad tried to speak, but his wife stopped him, patting him on the knee.

She turned to Declan and winked, 'Don't worry. Leave him to me.'

It was very early days but Kara took the wins as they came. Safia needed to be stimulated and motivated—whatever it took. 'Okay, as soon as there's a bed free we'll move her in. Until that happens, how about we take a little stroll down through the main ward and see who's hanging out?'

Please be there, lightning boy.

'Yes.' Declan nodded his thanks to the Sheikh and Sheikha and bowed them through the door first, then followed with Safia. 'There's a games console over there. You fancy your chances against me?'

The Princess frowned. 'A video game?'

'Why not? It's great therapy for those thumbs.'

'Daddy would have a fit.'

She gave them her first real smile for weeks. But then surely anyone would have to smile with the offer of a few more minutes in Declan's company?

'You're on.'

It was late when Kara eventually managed to snatch time to write up her case notes for the day. Hiding out in Declan's offices at Kate's, she'd dodged the Sheikh's aides with their endless questions about maintaining Safia's dignity in the face of such intrusions as sharing the patients' TV room. Funny, what most people took for granted they'd had to fight for, for Safia—just some friends, a little hope…

Kara's feet ached—but then that was nothing new. Her head ached—but that was becoming a habit whenever Declan was around. Too much arousal could do that to a girl. The sooner she was home and out of the Declan Underwood temptation zone the better. Gathering her paperwork together and stuffing it in her bag she finished up.

The phone rang. *Damn.* She looked round for someone to answer it, but of course his secretary had left for the day, and Declan was consulting next door. Who the hell would ring his rooms so late?

Sighing, she picked up. 'Mr Underwood's phone.'

'Can I speak to Declan, please?' The voice was soft and sweet, unmistakably Irish. Niamh? Aoife? Briana? Roisin?

'I'm afraid he's consulting at the moment. Can I take a message?'

There was a frustrated sigh. 'Sure. But it won't make

a blind bit of notice. Tell him Niamh rang and he must call me back…*immediately*. It's very important.'

'You could try his mobile phone?'

'It's rung and rung to the voice mail a million times. The man's either got cloth ears or he's avoiding me. I'm resorting to underhand tactics and phoning him at work.' There was a smile in her voice. 'He hates that.'

The smile was catching, Declan's sister seemed warm and friendly—the kind of sister Kara would have liked if she'd been lucky enough to have one. 'Don't worry, I'll tell him. Oh, wait—he's just here.'

He'd come through the adjoining door.

'Still here? It's after five…'

He grinned and her heart melted. His eyes glittered, and the soft upward curve of his lips was like a promise.

'You know what that means.'

The five o'clock rule. Kissing was apparently allowed, according to him. Not her.

Dragging her heart back behind its steel barrier, she pointed to the receiver in her hand. 'Niamh's on the phone. She says it's important.'

'It's always important.' He threw some files onto his secretary's desk and shook his head. 'Tell her I'll call her later.'

Kara grinned. 'He's just coming, Niamh. He's—'

'Hey, I can wait all night. Just don't, for God's sake, try making excuses for him. He's a terrible liar. Tell him I've got more willpower than he'll ever have and I can keep ringing until he answers. And I will.'

Kara had no doubt that Niamh was just as willful as Declan.

They clearly all loved each other in a very definite sibling kind of way. Kara covered the speaker and held it out to Declan, shaking her head. 'She said she's had to resort to underhand tactics…'

She looked at the tired lines around his eyes, the tight clench of his jaw. Here he was, at way too late o'clock, still at work, planning his Theatre list for tomorrow, seeing clients after hours to make sure he could fit them into his schedule, attending to the needs of everyone but himself. And now this.

With a shock she realised how much she wanted to see him smile again. To feel the warmth of his smile on her, his breath, his touch. And soon.

'Do you always inspire such devious strategies in women?'

'Sadly only the ones I'm trying to avoid.' Glancing at the phone he let his eyebrows dip into a frown. Then he looked back at her.

She saw the mirrored need in his eyes—a raw need that fired something deep in her, something that shivered through each nerve-ending. Heat pooled in her gut, and lower, and then he was next to her, one hand in her hair, the other on her back. His mouth was on her neck.

'Declan.' She thrust the phone towards him. 'Your family loves you enough to be bothered. Talk to your sister. Be nice. That is all.'

'What is this? Secrets of the sour, sassy sisterhood?' He let out a contrite sigh. 'Ah, hell, give it here.'

Damn. Declan grabbed the phone, once again torn between the woman in front of him and his family's needs. He'd been too close to grabbing her and having her against that wall. To losing himself in her.

'Niamh. This had damn well better be important.'

'Hello to you too, Declan.' His sister lowered her voice. 'So, are you sleeping with her yet?'

'What?' His eyes popped as he strode across the room, out of Kara's earshot. 'No.'

'But you want to—she sounds nice. Won't take any crap from you, I wouldn't think.'

'Niamh, what do you want?'

'Apart from a big brother who shows his face every now and then? Sure, Declan, I can't remember what your ugly features look like these days.' She sighed. 'Is she pretty?'

He glanced at Kara, who now appeared to be nose-deep in a patient's notes. He looked at the soft golden shine on her hair, the way her lips twitched, that mouth that tasted of sunshine and sweetness.

'Yes. Very. Now, this is exactly why I live in London—to get away from all this…interrogation.'

'No, you live in London to get away from all those poor broken-hearted Dublin girls who wanted to make a decent man of you… And to avoid the truth.'

The truth that he would never be a decent man, because every time a woman had made those happy-ever-after kind of ministrations he'd run a mile. A sea. A country.

'Niamh. Leave it.'

'Will you come over for Mammy's birthday? Please? She won't be happy until she sees you again.'

'She won't be happy until I'm married off to the lowest bidder.' His heart squeezed. Poor Mammy…all she'd ever wanted was for him to be happy—but in her book that meant marriage.

He wasn't convinced. He'd seen the destruction marriage, and the end of it, had wreaked on *her*.

'I'll send her something. I can't—' Couldn't face going back. Couldn't look at her and know he'd failed her—in every way. He hadn't saved her from being hurt, and now he couldn't give her what she wanted most—hope. 'Yep. I'll send her something.'

'She doesn't need your flowers. She needs to see you. It's her sixtieth and she needs something to celebrate. When did you last come home? Can you even remember?'

No. Shame hit him in the gut. Working in London meant he could earn more cash than he ever would back home—which in turn meant he could support his family and have a life.

'I don't know—I can't face all those questions…' He turned his back and whispered, 'She's forever on my back.'

Niamh laughed. 'She just wants to know you're happy all the way over there. A bunch of flowers doesn't tell her that. Why don't you bring someone? That'd shut Mammy up. Hey, what about that girl? The one who answered the phone—?'

'Who? Kara?'

As he spoke Kara's head popped up. 'Yes?'

'Oh, sorry. Not you…' He pointed to the phone. 'It was…it's my sister.'

Niamh laughed again. 'Tongue-tied? You? Wow, you have it bad, big brother. Go on—ask her to come.'

Kara's eyes narrowed. She stood and picked up her handbag. 'What's she saying?'

Don't leave. Stuck in between two determined women, that was all he needed. But he wouldn't be taking her anywhere near his home.

'That…that the weather in Ireland's very warm…'

Kara waited, her eyes blinking innocently. 'The weather? Why—?'

'Coward!' Niamh hollered. 'Ask her. It'll get Mammy off your back.'

'Hmm…' He supposed his sister could be right. Having Kara there would be a delicious distraction. He could mix family with…a little pleasure. Would she? Could it work? How would it work? Hell, he didn't know, but it was a heck of a plan. Kara in his house… A man could think of worse ways to spend a couple of days.

Maybe it was time to go home.

He huffed out an exasperated breath. 'Niamh wants you to come visit Ireland.'

Kara stared, her hand on one hip. 'Your sister wants me to go to Ireland?'

'Just for a weekend. My mum's birthday. Sure, why not? You said you'd always wanted to visit the place.'

'No way.' Her hands were physically up in front of her. She didn't want this. She really didn't want this.

Niamh's voice crackled down the phone. 'Did she say yes?'

'Niamh, for heaven's sake leave us alone for a minute. She's thinking about it.'

Kara's cheeks reddened. 'Do you Underwoods always work in packs?'

'Believe me, my sisters could teach the army a thing or two about stealth operations.' But the more he thought about it, the more it became a perfect plan. '*They* want me to go back for her birthday. They said you should come too. *You* said I should be nice to my family. Bingo—everyone's happy. Say yes?'

'Emotional blackmail doesn't wear well on you, Declan.' She fiddled with her necklace.

'No ties, no strings.' At her frown he thought he'd better just be honest. 'Look, I just want to give Mammy some hope—to think that I'm off her hands. I…we… need her to stop worrying about us all and focus on her own life. There'll be the hassle of my sisters…but they're not so bad really.'

'No.'

But she'd released her grip on her bag. Was looking down at her magnificent shoes, out of the window, at the floor. She was wavering, he could tell.

Time to strike.

'I've tried my whole life to make her better—and the only thing she's ever said she needed was to see me settled and happy. She would love you, Kara. It's just a weekend. Two nights. Two. Nights.'

He held his fingers up just the way she had with her *Two kisses* quip. He saw the flash of recognition and the rush of desire on her face—not just in her eyes, but in the flush of her cheeks. And, goddamn it, in the ghost of a sexy smile.

He imagined what he could do to her—with her—in two nights. Hell, he'd settle for just two hours. Naked. Shoes optional. Actually, shoes definitely on.

'It's gorgeous at this time of year. The leaves turning golden, the rolling hills. Ireland…land of your ancestors.'

Then for a fleeting second he realised what a stupid plan it was. Because above the pretence and the joking he knew that he was actually falling for her. That some part of him wanted Kara in his chaotic life—and that was the maddest thing he'd ever thought. He wanted ties and that made him scared as hell.

Because after the weekend he couldn't offer her anything apart from a return to this—late-night meetings in his office, early mornings in surgery and the craziness of hospital life in between. Just colleagues. And then she'd be gone anyway, back to her team, and he'd be left with catching the scent of her in corridors, fleeting glimpses across the cafeteria…

His voice wavered a little as the reality of the plan sank in. 'But if—'

She smiled. 'Oh, okay, what the hell? Why not? I'm going to regret this, I know, but when you describe it like that how can I refuse?'

CHAPTER NINE

KARA STARED OUT of the hire car window as the Dublin countryside flew past. Pink clouds melted into rolling hills, ten shades of green, as the sun began to set around them. It was nothing...*nothing* like the endless red dry earth of her childhood, the heat, the bright, cloudless blue skies.

Here, lush fields carved by stone walls as ancient as the earth itself spilled out in front of them to the left and right as far as she could see. Cows grazed lazily, and ignored their momentous arrival in Declan's home county.

Momentous? Sure. What kind of far-side-of-madness idea was this? Panic rolled through her in waves.

This weekend was going to be sheer torment—not least because she would have Declan within the temptation zone for forty-eight exhausting hours. But then, she couldn't deny she wasn't a teensy bit intrigued to see where he'd grown up and what had made him the complex man he was today. Even if the reason she was here was to cajole his mother into believing he was happy and settled.

She wondered if Declan was having second thoughts too as he stared ahead with eyebrows furrowed, his jaw fixed. His mood was hard to read—but he definitely wasn't in his happy-go-lucky, carefree place. The silence between them since they'd checked in at the airport had stretched and stretched, interspersed by brief words and *über*-politeness.

As he drove he glanced over to her and she must have looked either a fright, or frightened, because he managed a smile.

'Hey, don't look so worried. It'll be fine.'

It was more a question than a statement, and she wondered just who he was trying to convince.

'I know. I know. I'm just a little nervous about meeting everyone.'

'Ah, they'll love you. How could they not?'

'Okay.' She wanted to run her hand along his leg and pat it and smile, tell him she was okay and looking forward to it all—do the kind of things you'd do to a friend or a lover. But she couldn't because, really, she was neither.

And the frightening truth was, deep down, that she didn't want to live something over the weekend and later want it to be true. But it was already too late.

He pulled up outside a large farmhouse and she could see, in the dimming light, a number of smaller outer buildings dotting the acreage. With walls the colour of thick clotted cream, wide picture windows edged by pink roses, the house took her breath away. She imagined Declan as a child, running around, up to his neck in mud, playing and working on the farm.

He opened the car door for her and she stepped out into a surprisingly warm gentle breeze.

'Wow. It's so gorgeous. It's like a dream house. You grew up here?'

'Well, on the farm, yes.' His eyes darkened. 'But there was the fire, obviously…and so we built this.'

And there her images of him morphed from innocent

to troubled. Her heart thudded. This place must bring back so many bleak memories for him. No wonder he barely wanted to visit.

'Ach, *Declan* built this.'

A thin, pretty woman with long dark hair stepped out through the front door, folded her flour-dusted arms and grinned.

'Not with his bare hands, you understand. Although he tried to in his weekends off from medical school. But he's a surgeon, not a builder—mighty fine with a knife, but we were deeply concerned about letting him loose with bricks and mortar. I'm Niamh. Pleased to meet you.' She stuck out her hand. 'Thank you for bringing him.'

'I...er...I didn't. He brought me, really. But nice to meet you too.' Kara shook Niamh's hand and immediately liked the warm, friendly welcome that put her a little more at ease.

'It was you on the phone, right?' At Kara's confusion Niamh explained, 'I recognise the accent. Australian? Kiwi?'

'Aussie.'

'I thought so. And I do get the feeling he wouldn't be here if you weren't. So you've done a grand job already.'

'Hello? I *can* hear you, you know.' Declan growled as he gave his sister's cheek a peck.

'Tosh, what do we care? And smile, Declan, it's only for a couple of days.' Niamh laughed. 'You certainly took your time getting here. And I don't mean the journey from the airport. Because that doesn't take a year and a half.'

Kara wondered what else Declan's sister thought behind those perceptive Underwood dark brown eyes. And, indeed, just what Declan had told her about the nature of her and Declan's relationship.

And then from behind Niamh came a roar, high-pitched squeals and a loud stamping along the wooden floor as four small children ran out and grabbed on to Declan's legs.

His face changed in an instant. His eyes lit up brightly and his smile stretched. 'Look at you all.' Swinging each one round in turn, he plastered a kiss on each plump cheek. 'Aine—pretty as a picture. Fiona—my, what a smile you've got. Saoirse—look at you.' Lastly he reached down between his legs and caught hold of a wee grinning boy. 'And Declan Junior—whoa, you've grown, my man. This is my friend, Kara. Say hi.'

'Hi, Kara,' they chorused, their curls bobbing in time with their words, and Kara's heart just about melted.

'Hi, everyone. Very pleased to meet you…er…Aine, Fiona, Saoirse and Declan.' If she repeated the names she might have a hope of remembering them.

She bent to shake their chubby hands and before she knew it was almost bowled over by sticky fists and warm bodies pressing close in a sort of clumsy, grubby scrum.

'You talk funny,' Aine whispered.

'So do you.' Kara gave the girl a big smile and tapped the end of her cute snub nose with her finger. 'And you're gorgeous.'

'Well, come in, come in. The others won't be long.' Niamh ushered the children back into the house and was just turning round herself when she glanced down to Kara's feet. Her hand went to her chest. 'Oh, my…'

Kara followed Niamh's line of vision and lifted her foot up, all the better to see her beautiful red suede ankle boots with black ribbon ties. 'Oh, yes. These. Totally impractical, I know. But just for the journey…'

'I think I just fell in love with your girlfriend. Clearly we're going to be great friends,' Niamh quipped to Declan as she led them into the house. 'You must tell me where you got them from.'

'Sure, I'd love to see you milking the cows in those,' Declan snapped, expertly avoiding the girlfriend comment.

But his eyes flickered towards Kara. She just couldn't read what he was thinking and once again she wondered what she was doing here—doing this.

'Come meet my mam.'

Kara's heart-rate trebled. Declan had explained that his mum was shy and very aware of her scarring, so it was important to put a lid on her loud-mouthed, out-there, army brat self.

But when Declan's hand fitted around hers and he walked her through the airy hallway to the large kitchen she stopped thinking and tried to just *be*. Which wasn't hard; being in his firm grip and the subject of his warm gaze made her lose track of her thought processes anyway.

The kitchen was everything Kara dreamt a family kitchen should be. Flour on the benchtop, creamy mounds of dough left to rise, a large wooden table covered in piles of pots and pans, and a warm, herby cooking smell that made her nervous stomach grumble.

Once again she felt out of her depth. She'd never had a home like this—one that felt so welcoming, that smelt of flowers and yeast and clear fresh air, that was busy and chaotic and so full of life. A lump thickened her throat. It was everything she'd ever hoped for growing up, pretty much alone—the career, the husband, the home life. She'd believed she could have it all.

Until hard reality had smacked her in the gut and she'd been left with little more than broken dreams.

Mary Underwood sat in the corner of the room, looking out of the window across the blackening night. As they approached she looked up and inhaled sharply. Tugging down one side of her long grey bob to cover a good part of her face, she stood and offered Kara a shaky smile. 'Goodness, I can't believe you've come home with our Declan. You're awful pretty, Kara. Nice to meet you.'

Kara could see the muted sadness in those dark brown eyes. The same eyes every member of the family had. But all of them shimmered with something different. With Declan it was wickedness, or heat, or cool restraint. Niamh's were tired and yet somehow content, and held a little of the wicked in them. Mary's were filled with an almost tangible love for her son but edged with pain.

The cause was right there on the woman's face. Melted skin pulled down her features into nasty ridges like old candlewax. Her hands too were scarred and lined.

Kara stepped forward, unsure whether to kiss her or shake hands…or what to say. Words felt inadequate. 'Nice to meet you. Thank you for letting me come—especially for your birthday. I'm really happy to be here.'

'You and me both. I never thought I'd see the day.' Mary nodded, relaxing a little with each softly spoken word, but still tugging at her hair. 'Now, Declan, take Kara to the cottage and settle her in. Be sure to be back by seven for your dinner.'

'Aye, Mam, will do. It's good to see you.'

He wrapped his arms round his mother but she batted him away with a friendly smile. 'Away with you, now. Can't you see I'm busy?'

They walked through the encroaching darkness to a small house across a field. Declan opened the front door and ushered her in, shutting out the four sets of Underwood eyes that hung around in the paved area out front. Cute they might be, but clearly his nieces and nephew hadn't got the hang of adult time. And he needed a good shot of that right now.

Actually, he needed a good shot of London right now… with Kara as a chaser.

Yet here he was, for the first time in many months, with a *girlfriend* in tow. What a crazy, mixed-up idea that had been.

She peered up at him through thick black eyelashes, her green eyes piercing. 'Wow. This is so different to the main house. So…stark. And so not the twee cottage I had in mind.'

He plonked their bags down on the whitewashed floorboards and looked round at the clean lines. No frills, no mess. Masculine. His. 'Home sweet home.'

'This is yours?'

'Yes. When I could, I made it my priority to have some space. Sharing with that amount of oestrogen is way too dangerous for my health. So when I come home this is my space. No unwanted interruptions…' He nodded to the giggling coming from the other side of the door. 'Not too many anyway. Ach, they'll get bored soon enough. You can have the main bedroom. I'm just next door. In case… Well, in case you need me. For anything.'

Declan put Kara's bag on the master bedroom floor.

'Oh? And just what would I need you for?'

'You may need help changing for dinner. I'm all yours for unzipping…unbuttoning…unclipping…' He leaned in closer, inhaled the scent of outdoors and coconut shampoo. 'I think you'll find I'm pretty adept at it.'

'I don't doubt that for a second, but I can manage.' Kara gave him a strange half-smile, her hand clutching the hem of her cashmere cardigan. He'd never seen her quite so unsettled.

He liked that. Liked that she was such a mixed bag of emotions, but that she was determined to deal with it herself—not demanding anything from him, not clingy. Nor did she ask about a future for them, or push him into a corner, or cause a drama. That was how he liked things—uncomplicated.

So why the hell he'd invited her here to make things very complicated he didn't know. But he reminded himself they had only two days to do this. Then they would be free to go back to their uncomplicated lives in London.

Only now London didn't seem very uncomplicated either.

'Thanks for doing this. You being here means a lot to my mum. She was so pleased to see you.'

'I think it was you she was happy to see—seriously, I'm just icing.' Kara started to unpack her bag, but kept her voice low. 'Declan, why haven't you done reconstruction on her scars?'

'Don't you think I've tried? Don't you think I've offered to bring her to London and get her the best treatment available? She doesn't want to. She says she's come to terms with it and I just have to accept that. I became a plastic surgeon just so I could help her, but she's not interested.'

And even though he tried to bite down his frustration Kara noticed. Taking his hand in hers, she pulled him to sit on the bed.

'I understand—I do. But I guess you have to let it go. If she's come to terms with it, then so should you. She's not an invalid—she's a grown woman who clearly must know what she's doing if she's brought all you kids up.'

Kara didn't know the half of it.

'It's other things she's struggled with.' And he couldn't

bring himself to explain. He didn't want to even *think* about his father and the legacy he'd left.

Nothing about this place had any kind of reminder of his dad. Declan had made sure of that.

Kara's hand ran down his spine in soft strokes that almost undid him. 'I really hope your family like me. They seem lovely. All of them.'

'You haven't met all of them yet…that will be an experience. You did bring earplugs?'

'For sleeping?'

'No, for dinner. Don't say I didn't warn you.'

He grinned at her knotted brow and ached to smooth it over with his mouth. To wrap her in his arms and lie there surrounded by all the smells and sounds of home— the familiar, but with Kara, so exotic and different.

'It gets busy, but it's a family rule that we all eat together.'

'That's nice. I don't remember many meals like that growing up. It was usually just me and one of my parents, or a nanny, or a grandparent, and then as I got older, when I came home for the holidays, it was often just me and a TV dinner.'

At her words his stomach tightened—because although he'd made a space for himself far away he couldn't imagine growing up sitting at an empty dinner table in silence, or with only the TV for company. For him dinner had always meant chatter and good food and just the occasional argument. No wonder she'd grabbed the chance of marriage so young, to create a feeling of belonging.

She looked around the room, at the high ceiling and the intricate coving he'd designed. 'Did you really try to build this place?'

He laughed. 'Yes. I had a hand in all the buildings. This is a converted barn. It didn't get damaged much in the fire, so I just had it renovated to my specs. But I had more of a go at building the main house. Pretty naive, but when you're that young you think you can do everything.'

'And the great Declan Underwood *can't*? You do surprise me.'

It hadn't been for lack of trying. 'It soon became apparent that it was better for me to work as a doctor and pay someone else to do the physical work. As I earnt more we added more buildings—the barns, Niamh's house out back, the milking shed… But I did some labouring in my spare time.'

Dark memories slid through him. The smoke and the flames, the fear that had gripped his chest, the rough thick clutch at his throat as he'd tried to breathe in a furnace.

Then the days, months, years of dealing with scars, betrayal, grief. And finally restoration.

'Wow, that's some responsibility you carried here. Did you work with your dad?'

'No. He left.'

She frowned. 'So it really was just you? On your own?'

'Yep. Me and the builders, obviously…and the architects…' And the insurance. And the… Hell, there'd been a lot of professionals involved. Just not the one person he'd needed.

'But who did you ask for help? Who gave you advice?'

Would she not let it go? 'I didn't need any.'

'Everyone needs someone to talk things through with, Declan. Even you. Do you still have contact with your dad?'

'No.'

Once he'd been unable to leave his father's side, had looked to him for everything. To learn how to do the practical things for running a farm. How to be a decent farmer. A decent man. And then…

He swallowed back the bile rising in his throat. 'I wouldn't want anything from him now.'

'Why not?'

'Forget him, Kara. I have.'

He'd tried to erase the memories. The ones where his father had carried his boy high on his shoulders. The ones where they'd been fishing, hunting, laughing. Memories he didn't want because they weren't real. Oh, yes, he'd believed them then—but after his father had left he'd realised they were meaningless. Because love wasn't real—it was fleeting and flimsy and disposable. *That* was the one true thing he'd learnt from his father.

He looked at Kara, sitting there, not a memory. She was real, here, in front of him, and he grew hard just looking at that mouth, those eyes, that body. He wanted her, and that urgent feral response threatened to subsume him.

'So all that hard physical work explains these, then.'

Her hand slid to his biceps and a river of desire ran through him. When her hand slipped to his chest and her fingers brushed against his abs he was lost.

'And these too…'

That brief touch was like a spark to an ember. The next thing he knew he was leaning her back across the four-poster bed and planting kisses on her lips, on her cheeks and the sweet sun-blushed skin at her throat. And she was kissing him back—not hesitantly, not softly, but with all the intensity of a woman who needed kissing. Who wanted to be thoroughly kissed.

And that was what he told himself as he stroked his tongue in her mouth and felt her meld her body against his. *She wanted this.* As he peeled away the cardigan and dropped it to the floor, as he undid the tiny buttons on her blouse and unclipped the scrap of pure white lace that pretended to be a bra—because, by God, it was barely covering her straining breasts. *She wanted this.*

When he took her hardened nipple in his mouth and felt her moan into his hair. When she straddled him and rocked against his erection. When she kissed him hot and greedy and needy with her slick wet mouth.

Her hands were dragging his shirt away, her nails scraping along his back. Her mouth was kissing trails down his ribcage, her hair a mess of blonde against his chest. But it was her eyes that told him most, glittering dark like the most precious emeralds. *She wanted this.*

And, *God*, so did he. He wanted to be inside Kara right now—to ride her to the edge and back. To wipe away that half-smile and replace it with a sexy, satiated one. He wanted to watch her come, to taste her, to feel her clamp around him, to wake up with her in the morning. Because they had forty-eight hours to find each other before things were back on an even keel in a world where they didn't do complicated.

But in reality losing himself in Kara wasn't complicated at all. It was the simplest thing he'd ever done.

CHAPTER TEN

KISS ME. SHE was so on the edge of giving herself up to him.

And she didn't want it just to stop there.

But Kara heard the sound of footsteps and giggles outside the door and pulled away from Declan, naked from the waist up. Suddenly she felt cold—and not just physically naked but psychologically laid bare too. Because making love with him would confuse everything. Kissing him like this had already stirred enough chaos in her brain.

She rested her forehead against his and laughed. 'This sneaking around behind closed doors makes me feel like a teenager again.'

'Unfortunately that's the way it is here—no damned privacy. Even this far away from the house.'

He was still hard, she could feel him underneath her, but he didn't appear to mind. He just seemed content to stroke his fingers down the curve of her body.

'But I think it's dinnertime. We'd best get dressed and get down there. Hungry?'

Yes, but not for food. 'You bet.'

Fastening her bra and grabbing another top from her weekend bag, Kara made herself presentable. It was weird having him watch her do such an intimate thing that no one had seen her do since her marriage. Even weirder as he brushed by and kissed the top of her head, sheathing that gorgeous body back into his shirt. It all seemed so natural for him, this playing at being a couple. And for her it felt…strange. Connected and yet disconnected.

One thing was for sure: having seen him semi-naked, she was definitely going to miss that body when she went back to London and back to her old team.

'So, does your mum do the cooking for you all? That must be a mission.'

'Mostly. There was a time when she couldn't manage, so Niamh helped, but she's better now. Well…'

Once again something flickered behind his eyes and she wanted to ask Declan his story. Because while his mother might well be healed he still carried scars in his need to protect her.

'She seems just a little shy, Declan, that's all. But, hey, I don't know her, so I don't want to be talking out of turn.' She changed the subject, not wanting to start the visit off on the wrong footing. 'So, dinner…?'

'Can wait just a few more seconds. I have something much more interesting in mind…'

He pushed her against the door and kissed her again, this time gently, like a summer breeze against her lips, his hands cradling her face. And she kissed him back, determining to enjoy the next couple of days instead of analysing them. They both knew this couldn't go any further than a little flirtation, and she was big enough to deal with that.

The dining room was dominated by a large mahogany table and a selection of matching chairs, bright plastic highchairs and a long wooden bench. A glass chandelier gave off a subdued pearly glow. At one end of the room a large stone fireplace promised cosy winter nights, and all round the room on various dressers and bookcases were photos: a teenage Declan and his sisters, the babies, a selection of gruff-looking mongrel dogs, the farm, visitors.

As none of the pictures was of the siblings when very young, Kara suspected these had all been taken post-fire. 'Did you lose a lot of stuff in the fire?'

'Most everything. The house was pretty destroyed, but there were a few things we managed to save. No photos, though.'

'None of your mum? *Mam?*' Kara wanted to fit in, but the word didn't roll off her tongue just yet. She picked up a photo of Declan aged about sixteen, grinning wildly with a stack of bricks on a hod, then glanced at another of him in graduation gown and cap. 'My, my, how you've grown.'

'I damn well hope so. I was a wiry little whipper back then. And, no, she won't have any taken. She says she doesn't want to ruin the pictures.'

'But that's such a shame.' She bit back a question about Declan's father. No photos of him either.

'Dinner's ready,' Niamh announced, bounding in with a large casserole dish in her hands and a bottle of wine tucked under one arm.

Declan strode forward and took it from his sister. 'Careful.'

'Don't you love the macho? And the manners? Where did they come from? I think you've knocked some sense into my brother, Kara. It's about time someone did.' Niamh leaned towards her. 'So, the others are here. Take a deep breath and then let it out very slowly…oh, and take a big slug of wine to help calm your nerves. Let the chaos begin!'

And within a second Kara was enveloped in hugs and

hands and smiling faces, her ears filled with musical names and lyrical-sounding words. She was found a seat next to Declan, given a plate filled with steaming chunks of meat covered in a dark rich gravy, large mounds of creamy mashed potatoes and a glass of red. And she was smiling with Aoife, laughing at Roisin's tales of medical school, feeding one of the little ones in a highchair, and everything under the protective gaze of Declan. It was exhausting, but lovely.

'So, Declan's never brought a girl home before. Spill the beans…how did you two meet?'

It was Briana, the romantic of the family. She'd already told Kara about her dream wedding dress, the honeymoon, the number of babies she'd have. All she needed to do was find the right man. Kara didn't say anything about her own past, wanting Briana to hold on tight to her dreams, because every girl deserved them.

'At work—well, kind of…'

Declan grinned as his foot connected with Kara's under the table. His toes slid up her leg until she realised she must have been grinning like an…how did he say it? An *eejit*. An intense sexual need ran through her veins.

Then his hand shifted over to her lap and his fingers tiptoed towards her thigh. She squirmed in her seat.

'At a ball, no less. Kara wore a long gold gown and taught me a few Aussie swear words and a drinking game…a lot of tequila was involved. I knew immediately that she was the girl for me.'

And he grinned his goofy grin and made it sound, truly, as if they were made for each other. He never mentioned how she'd left him standing on the dance floor after a searing kiss that had turned her legs to jelly and her brain to mush. And heaven knew what they were doing here—doing this. Because she didn't have a clue.

Except that she wished his hands were running over every part of her.

'Ah, a ball…every girl's dream. So romantic.' Briana clapped her hands together. 'And the wedding?'

Whoa. Kara spluttered into her wine as she felt Declan's grip on her thigh tighten.

'Has not been discussed.'

'Leave it alone, Bri. They don't need you meddling in their business. Remember, Kara's our guest. Be polite.'

Declan's mother's voice soothed the conversation. Kara realised the older woman had been observing, but hadn't actually spoken until now. Everyone stilled and looked at her with surprise. Was it so unusual for her to contribute to a conversation?

'Kara, tell us, have you visited Ireland before?'

'No. Not at all, apparently I have ancestors here somewhere—County Wicklow, I think. I can't wait to have a sticky bea…a good look round tomorrow. Declan said he'd take me for a drive.'

'A drive?' Briana looked horrified. 'I thought he'd be teaching you how to milk cows. You know, in the cowshed…' Now she winked. 'Down and dirty…'

'Briana! You have a dirty mind,' Niamh interjected. 'Er…how about a spot of shopping? I could come with you.'

'We thought we'd take a look at the city on the way back to the airport on Sunday,' Kara answered, turning her head this way and that to speak to them all. 'He knows a good pub that sells great food.'

'Sure, Dec knows all the pubs with the best *craic*,' added Roisin with a wink. As the baby of the family, she clearly adored her big brother.

Uh-oh. Dictionary required. 'What's crack?'

'Craic.' Roisin laughed. 'It means fun. A laugh. There's

plenty of it in Dublin. And while you're there you could come have a look round the Trinity College campus. It's beautiful. Actually, you could give me a ride back there on Sunday.'

'What about a horse-ride? There's a trail over the hills that takes you down to the river—it's pretty special.' Aoife joined in, her hand never leaving that of her quiet fiancé, Ronan, and soon everyone had voiced their ideas of how to entertain an out-of-town guest.

Kara looked to Declan for an opinion, taking comfort in the fact that his hand was still on her lap and that the spotlight had moved on from their nuptials. His smile was slow and made her stomach flutter. She got the impression, with the smouldering heat in his eyes, that Declan's idea of entertaining his out-of-town guest was nothing at all to do with going out and everything to do with staying in.

'Whatever you want, Kara.'

I want you. She swallowed deeply, wondering just how much deeper she had to fall before she could harden herself to him completely. 'Wow, there are so many fabulous things to do here. I'll let you decide.'

When Declan squeezed her thigh…this time higher… much higher…Kara almost choked on her white chocolate and raspberry cheesecake.

Afterwards, when everyone was helping to clear up in the kitchen, Kara offered to help but was flatly refused. Irish hospitality, she supposed.

'Okay, but it's the party tomorrow, is that right? What do we do? What do I need to bring? Do you need help with anything?'

Niamh gently held her by the shoulders. 'No. Absolutely not. Now, we've a few things to do in here, but you go and sit down. Tomorrow you can do some sightseeing, and in the evening we'll have a cake.'

'Here, have another drink. It helps. Trust me, I know.'

Declan topped up Kara's glass while jiggling the small child sitting on his shoulders up and down. For all his self-imposed exile he'd managed to slip right back in and seemed, despite himself, to be enjoying his time here.

Because, whatever Declan said to the contrary, he was a family man through and through. She could see that from the pure joy in his eyes as he piggybacked each child in turn, as he lost himself deep in conversation with Roisin about her grades, as he watched his mother with a look in his eyes that spoke of his regret and a fierce love.

'Wait! Just wait a minute—let me get my camera. I so need to remember all of this.'

Kara dashed out to the barn and back and took a series of snaps of Declan with a variety of relatives and ankle-biters playing the fool, flicking each other with washing up foam. And then one with all the siblings looking reasonably decent and the children smiling. Mostly.

'Now, *that's* one for the album.'

Out of the corner of her eye she caught Mary watching, her eyes guarded, her shyness now morphing into embarrassment about being caught on camera. Kara raised her eyebrows in question…*do you want to join in*? But Mary turned away and shoved her hands in the soapy water.

So Kara got snap-happy with the rest of the family, clicking and laughing and showing the children all the photos she was taking—making them stick out their tongues, pull their best crazy faces, joining in with them to cries of, *'Again! Again!'* It seemed that she'd get tired of it long before they would.

A little later, when Declan approached his mum and she lifted her head to him and smiled, Kara clicked and caught a picture of them that, when she looked in the viewer, made her heart ache. From this angle, even though her face was in full view, the only thing that shone out was the deep love between the two of them. If only Mary could understand that everyone saw past her scars, and that the only person she was hiding from, really, was herself.

Suddenly Niamh grabbed the camera and Kara realised she was in the spotlight once again. 'Wait. Let's get one of the happy couple. Quick, Dec, get your arm around that lovely girl's shoulder. That's right. Great. Now smile.'

Happy couple. The idea thrilled inside Kara…and frightened her to death. Every instinct in her fought against being another half of something—something that might subsume her, something that would spiral out of control. And yet…

'Come here, then.'

Declan wrapped his arm round her and looked down into her eyes. And she could feel herself falling and falling into his gaze and his smile and his heat. She tried to smile too, but the whirl of emotions running through her stretched her too far. She wanted him. Wanted this. Wanted to have the dream, have everything.

But the harsh reality of it was that she'd fallen so hard for someone before…the wrong someone. And her dream had shattered into a million pieces along with her life. She couldn't do that again. Didn't know if she had the strength to pick herself up at the end.

Because how the hell did you ever know who the right someone was?

The walk back to the cottage was filled with things unsaid. The memory of his hand on her thigh lingered, turning from an ache to a need. He was close now—so close she could smell him again, that rich, earthy scent that was just him, mixed with a decent slug of red wine and white chocolate. Irresistible.

And maybe it was the wine, maybe it was the fresh Irish air, but her guard and her sense seemed to leech from her with every step closer to the cottage.

As they reached her bedroom door he looked down at her with eyes that held a zillion promises. 'You have everything you need?'

'Yes. Thanks.' *Except you.*

It was a pure physical ache. She wanted to pull him inside and drag him onto the bed again. But instead she demurely waited for him to invite himself in—it was his house after all. And she didn't know the rules. What would it cost her to be able to give a little of herself for two nights with him? She didn't want to think.

'Thanks for a lovely evening.'

His head was close to hers now, his hand against the door. But he didn't come in and close it as he had before. 'You certainly bowled them over.'

'Oh, you know...I have a gift.'

'So do I.'

He ran a finger down her cheek, making her insides melt. Hot and needy. How could one touch make her ache with so much want?

'Oh...' She spoke through a dry throat, her hand on his chest feeling the sharp erratic rise and fall of his breath. 'And what would that be?'

'You'll have to wait and see.'

'Spoilsport.'

He came into the room and closed the door. She inhaled sharply. Declan. The bed. Night. Reality hit her like a tornado. 'Are you...staying in here tonight?'

'You know, you ask way too many questions.'

His mouth was on her neck, sending ripples of need through her.

'Do you want me to?'

Yes. No. She didn't know. She was scared. Scared about what would happen if she gave herself to him. Scared about what would happen if she didn't.

'Oh, God, that feels so good.'

'You're very tense. Here, relax.' He sat her on the bed, knelt behind her and massaged her shoulders. Smoothly, slowly, rhythmically. Until she rocked under his hands, drifting from pleasure to some kind of daydream until she didn't know which was which.

His breath was on her neck. Heating her. 'I'm sorry, I know we can be a bit overwhelming. But the hard bit's over now—they've met you and you've survived.'

'It's not them. It's…this. I don't know what we're doing.' She went for her trademark forthright and hoped she didn't sound needy. She'd spent way too much time in her marriage trying to fathom out what was going on and never quite being able to work it out. From then on she'd determined never to be left in some kind of relationship darkness. 'Declan, why am I here?'

'Because you are very…very…lovely.' His mouth was on that soft spot of her shoulder that made her curl into him, and it would have been so easy to let him carry on. So, so easy.

She pulled away. 'No, really. That wasn't what I was asking. I don't want you to give me compliments. I want some truths. Really, why am I here?'

Declan's hands dropped to his sides. His eyes closed for a beat. Two. Good question. God knew why she was here, save for the fact he'd wanted something else to think about during the birthday weekend.

He could hear the *thud-thud* of his heart echoing in his ears. He searched for words. Found himself wanting.

But she deserved some kind of explanation. 'All my life I've worked to give them the things they want, that they deserve. The things my father didn't. Everything I did was to provide security and a future. And I'd do it all again in a heartbeat. But being back here always feels so…tying. So claustrophobic. I can't breathe.'

It wasn't just the people, but the memories. Dark emotions filled his chest.

'Sometimes London isn't far away enough…but I thought if I brought you along we could have some fun. Lighten things up a bit. I really do want to show you the place.'

And put some sort of distance between himself and his family.

Her eyes widened and he wanted to jump deep into them and never resurface.

'They're a handful, all right. But isn't that what families are like? Especially big ones like yours. Your mum deserves a medal to have had you all.'

'She deserves more than that. The things she went through…' It made his heart hurt and reinforced his determination never to get close to anyone.

So why he was sitting here, sharing this with Kara, he couldn't fathom. Part of him wanted to tell her everything. The other half wanted to run a mile—away from this proximity, from this feeling that somehow she might fit. Seeing his mother so betrayed by love had made him try to harden his heart. Hell, he hadn't had to try too hard. Watching his father walk away, refusing to turn to his wife's pleas and his son's desperate words, had cemented a block of ice in his chest.

He couldn't let it melt now. Talking to her, sharing things like this with her, would open him up to the risk of being hurt again.

'So tell me, Declan. What happened?'

Nonsensically, and the opposite of what he should have done, he silenced her with a kiss. The feel of her mouth underneath his sent spasms of need zipping through him. He wanted to erase the past, to create a new present that was just Kara and him. Wanted to fill his senses with her. She tasted sweet, like the cheesecake, hot as fire and soft. So soft beneath him. She smelt of freedom and heat and home and a foreign land he wanted to explore.

He pulled her close. When she opened her mouth he thought she was going to ask more questions. Whatever else happened, he was all out of talking. 'No. Not now, Kara.'

'Yes. Now.' Her hands were on his chest, fingers fisting the fabric of his shirt. And he realised, with a surge of heat in his gut, that she was not talking about the same thing he was.

CHAPTER ELEVEN

ALMOST REVERENTLY HE peeled Kara's clothes off. When she tried to unzip his jeans he stopped her hand. 'No. You first.'

And this time there was no embarrassment, no chill, as his hands stroked her from shoulder to waist or when he stood apart from her and looked. Just looked, with such pure intensity that she believed his words. The lump returned to her throat.

'My God, Kara, you are so beautiful. So, so beautiful.'

Then he was holding her close again, lips clamped to hers, and she feverishly tasted him, savoured him. She moaned when he dragged his mouth away. Moaned more when he pressed it against her neck. Her chest. Her nipple.

Silently he scooped her up into his arms and carried her to the bed. Whatever doubts she'd had until this moment were forgotten. She would have him. Because she couldn't not. This moment was meant to happen and she had no strength or desire to fight it. Her thoughts were muddled, but so clear. Bad idea. Good idea. All she knew was that she had to have him.

Her hands moved to his chest, ripping each button apart until she was feeling skin. Hot muscle under her fingers. She leant him back on the duvet and straddled him, relishing the hardness beneath her. Knowing that every single ache in her body was mirrored in his. Mirrored too in eyes that had lost their soulfulness, that were not teasing or playful but intense and dark and urgent.

'Kara, we don't have to—'

'Yes, we do.' She leant forward and kissed him again, arching against the hands now circling her bottom. Slowly, slowly his fingers trailed up and across her abdomen, making her catch her breath in short staggered gasps. Then his thumbs brushed her nipples, followed by his mouth. Hot and greedy, he licked as each bud hardened under his touch.

His jaw was stubbled and it burnt across her chest, and she enjoyed the raw feel of him, stoking a fierce need. Not listening any more to his resistance, she unzipped his jeans, shucked them to the floor and took him in her hand.

'Wait. Kara, wait.'

'I need you.'

She heard the words, heeded the emotion. Didn't care. Didn't care that she had opened herself to him in every way—to hurt, to pain. Because that would be some time in the future and this was now. *He* was now. And she didn't want to think about the past or some time not yet happened. She wanted to live this moment.

'God, Declan. I need you so much.'

Furious and fast, he sheathed, and then she was lowering herself onto him. His body was slick and hard. And she was ready for him. Had been ready for so long. As he entered her she gasped. Heat engulfed her, filled her.

Turning her onto her back, he murmured her name, thrusting deep and slow. Too slow. Too fast. Her mind was a chaotic whirl. Her body was responding to his scent, his touch. This was perfect. He was perfect.

And then he was harder, faster, and more perfect than she could even imagine, and she felt herself falling again. Falling deeper and deeper, and flying higher. Soaring. Until she was…he was…they were lost. Lost somewhere on the edge of forever. Somewhere deep in the core of her heart.

'Now, here's the gift I was telling you about last night.' Declan brought out the large parcel he'd hidden in the bottom of his luggage and handed it to Kara in the farm-yard.

The breeze had dropped and the early morning sun glinted off her hair, highlighting the gold. As she pulled her silver-grey cardigan around her and stamped her skinny-jean-wrapped legs he didn't think he'd seen any-thing so breathtaking.

And yet…

Her eyebrows rose. And was that a flicker of uncer-tainty behind those eyes?

Definitely. The smile she gave him was hesitant. She fiddled again with the hem of her cardigan, as she'd done the evening they'd arrived. Forthright Kara seemed to have developed a little more vulnerability, and she wore it in the dusky smudges beneath her eyes.

This was new ground. Complicated and unsteady. And if she felt anything like he did, then, man, they were in trouble. Because he didn't know the next step.

Friends? Lovers now? What? He'd never wanted any woman so deeply, or taken anyone with such need and intensity. Or wanted to stay and leave at the same time. No, he'd never wanted to stay before, and that was what spooked him the most. But he'd brought her here and he had to give her a good time for what was left of the weekend.

'Well, thank you, Declan. You mean you really do have a gift? I thought you were referring to…those other things.'

'Well, I know you have a passion for *these* kind of things, and I imagine you haven't got anything quite like them. But, believe me, you're going to need them.'

Confusion ran behind those green eyes as she ripped open the box and then tipped back her head and laughed. 'Gumboots? *Leprechaun* gumboots?' She held them up and turned them around and around as she took in the little grinning green men on the boots. 'Will I go all diddly-diddly now?'

'God forbid. The world is not ready for that. Please, stay a diddly-free zone.' He helped her take off her very unsuitable black patent pumps and steadied her as she slid her legs into her new rubber boots. 'Wellies. Top-boots. Waterboots. Not a gum in sight.'

'I love them. But for…?'

She gave him a twirl, kicked up one foot then the other. Pretty damned hot. And since when had he ever thought a woman in wellies could be hot?

'Milking. You don't get to come on a farm weekend for free, you know. There's something needed in return.'

Dark eyes blinked. 'You mean last night wasn't enough?'

'Last night was…more than enough.'

It had left something indelibly etched on his heart. Something he couldn't shake. Something he wanted to shake—because if he didn't he wasn't sure how he'd get out whole.

Without encouraging any more conversation along that line, he led her into a shed and climbed onto a dirt-splattered motorbike. The only way he knew how to clear his head. Then he pointed to the back, small as it was.

'Your chariot, my lady. I'll give you a backie down the field. We herd them up, bring them to the milking shed, then take them down again. Then we come back and hose the shed out.'

She looked at the bike, a little disappointed. 'This is nothing like the one in London. That is big and black and shiny and there's room for two. This is…shabby.'

'It is a bit grubby, I guess. But it's a nippy little fella. Come on—hold on tight.'

'There's no space.'

'Squeeze on. You'll be fine.' He pushed himself as far forward as he dared, and she slid right where he liked her best: hugging tight against his body, her legs wrapped round him, this time with no helmets, her hair flowing free in the wind.

With a roar he took her over the rough terrain, through divets and dips to the highest point of the hill and the deepest part of the valley. Fast. And he heard her squeal and screech, and he felt her arms tighten around his waist as the early morning chill bit into his cheeks.

When they reached the bottom of the hill she climbed off and dragged in a breath, pushing that silky blonde hair behind her ears. 'My God, that was wild.'

'You can drive on the way back if you like.'

'Oh, I don't know. I don't think so.'

'It's okay. I'll show you. It's not difficult.' Focus on something else. Anything to exorcise the confusion swirling in his gut right now. He took hold of the handlebar. 'Hop back on.'

Her eyes were sharp as she watched him. 'Maybe. I don't know. I think I might be better as a passenger.'

'I taught the girls before—you'll be fine. Give it a go.' He twisted the key and started the bike up. 'This side is the clutch and gears. The right side is brake and accelerator.'

He showed her a couple of times, until she got the hang of moving forward in first gear and quickly changing up to second.

'Go.'

Off she flew with a scream, stuttering and bunny-hopping, legs flapping out at the sides, then came to a juddering halt. 'Help!'

'Squeeze gently and slowly—there. See? You're getting the hang of it.'

He watched the flurry of hair, the cosmopolitan dressed form buzzing round the field—his life in London and his life in Ireland suddenly melding into one.

His heart jerked.

She had derailed him. Totally. His body knew how to react, but his brain was definitely, seriously spooked.

When she came back over the hill and drew to a halt her back wheel skidded in an arc. Mud churned like his thoughts, spraying him in dirt. 'Hey! Watch it.'

'Oops. Sorry!'

Not sorry at all, she clambered off, her hand over her laughing mouth, head tipped back. He watched the gentle curve of her neck, the movement of her delicate throat as she spoke.

'Told you I'd be rubbish.'

'No, you didn't. And you're not. You're a natural… Well, with a little practice.'

For a second their eyes caught, lost in the fun, lost in the moment. The urge to kiss her again was almost unbearable. He wanted to taste her, touch her. To put his mouth on those places he'd explored last night. To wake up with her again. But this time he wanted that waking to be joy-filled, not loaded with confusion.

As her laughter died on her lips questions formed in her eyes. Questions he couldn't answer. Questions he didn't want to be asked. And he knew that when they got back to real life nothing would be the same again.

'Okay.' He found his voice. 'So, let's get on with the milking. Everyone'll be waiting for us back at the house.'

Pushing all other thoughts aside, he instructed her in the best way to deal with the cows up close, but he was trying to keep a distance. Trying to keep a goddamned distance between friendship and something beyond intense.

'So this is the place where I grew up. Not much more than a village, really.'

Declan walked Kara along the cobbled main street of one of the prettiest places she'd ever visited.

The road was flanked with quaint shopfronts painted in pastels: pink, blue and white. Tiny flags wove across the road and back again; flowers adorned each windowsill. It was like something from a film, from the last century, from centuries ago.

'Gosh, it's so beautiful. How could you ever leave?'

'Because it's tiny and there's nothing here for me. At least not job-wise.'

'Well, maybe you should have built a hospital as well as your houses and barns.'

He laughed, a little more relaxed now, she noticed, as they'd put distance between themselves and the farm. But there was still an edge there, and she couldn't help thinking it had a lot to do with last night.

'Steady now, girl. I'm not Superman.'

'Well, really? That's a shame. There was me thinking…'

He looked at her quizzically and there was a warning in his voice not to mention last night. 'Thinking what?'

Actually, once again she hadn't been thinking at all.

Not thinking when she'd lain in his arms, when she'd taken him inside her and almost wept at the pleasure. Not thinking about tomorrow, or being back at work, or how she would extricate her heart from all of this when the time came.

Her heart. *Huh*. She tried to put everything into perspective. It was only sex. That was all. Natural and normal. The logical conclusion of attraction.

It wasn't…couldn't…be more than that.

'Ah, nothing.'

Heat flared in her chest at the realisation that it could be, might be, more than that, and she fished around for something to distract her—something that wasn't him and the thought of last night. Of how amazing he'd made her feel.

Glancing across the road, she saw a pharmacy. 'Hey, I've had a thought. Why don't we print off some of those photos I took last night and put them in a frame for your mum? I got some good pictures. I'm sure she'll like them.'

He looked bemused, but shrugged. 'You don't think the scarf you bought her is enough for a birthday present?'

'Well, it can be a thank-you-for-having-me gift instead, then. Or an extra present from you, if you like?' She hesitated to say *from us*. 'I don't want those lovely pictures to go to waste when all they'll do is stay on my laptop.'

She dragged him into the pharmacy and handed over the camera's memory card. Then they meandered through the shops along the main street while they waited for the photos to print.

Presently they came across an antiques shop. Inside was a cornucopia of old-style Ireland. Wicker baskets and old rusted irons, heavy wooden furniture and cloth embroidered in Celtic symbols. Nothing like Declan's place, but everything like his mum's.

Kara pointed to a silver picture frame with spaces for three photographs. 'Look, that's beautiful. Let's buy that.'

'Why?' he asked later as they sat in a café flicking through the prints. 'Why are you doing this?'

'Why not? Declan, you've got a lovely family here. I just want to celebrate it.' She showed him a picture of the little ones sticking out their tongues and laughed. 'How about this? Or this…?'

It was the photo of him and his mum in the kitchen.

'This. This one definitely.'

He shook his head, his mouth a grim line. 'I told you, she doesn't do photos.'

'Why? She looks beautiful in this. Look at it. You can't see her scars—all you can see is a very proud woman who has survived.' Kara's heart squeezed. 'Give it to her, Declan. I'm sure she'll love it. Would you give a decent photo to Niamh or Briana?'

'I guess.' Shaking his head, he hauled in oxygen. 'I just never really…'

'Really what?'

He didn't look at her. 'Could see past those damned scars.'

And if he felt almost responsible for them being there Kara could understand that. But if he was looking for absolution then she wasn't the one to give it. It had to come from within him.

She was beginning to understand just what made it difficult for Declan to get close to anyone. Responsibility wasn't just about giving things to people, it was about risking your heart with them…and he couldn't do that.

He'd been hurt badly, she thought, and he was all about protecting his family. But most of all himself.

'But if you can't see past them then how the hell will she?'

For a few moments he stared into his coffee cup. Kara couldn't read him. The day had been dotted with moments of reflection—him, her. She could see him building the barriers between them again.

'Okay, you're right. I'll give it to her. Thanks.'

She wanted to reach over and kiss a smile back on to his face. She'd lost count now of the kisses. 'So, what's on the agenda now?'

'Ah…' His eyes glittered and he shook off his mood. 'I'm torn between washing down the slurry pit or—'

'No way. You brought me here to do some sightseeing, not deal with cow poo.'

'You didn't let me finish…' Now his eyes positively sizzled with promise. '*Or* we could just go back to the cottage?'

He didn't need to explain any further. An afternoon in bed with Declan certainly appealed. Hell, she couldn't think of anything she'd rather do. There was only one night left, after all, before they went back to being colleagues.

Picking up the pictures, he secured three into the frame and went to put the rest back in the envelope. One dropped out onto the table between them.

The one Niamh had taken. *The happy couple.* Kara gasped. The way she looked up at Declan, her body turned into his, her arm secured around his waist, head tilted…the smile that laid open her heart. And the way his hand lay across her shoulder, possessive—but adoring.

God. Her heart felt as if it was rubbed raw. Was

that how they looked to everyone else? Truly, heart-stoppingly, gut-wrenchingly connected?

Panic rose from her stomach and tightened like a vice. This couldn't happen.

She couldn't feel like that—as if he was meant for her. As if this time—*this time*—things might work.

She couldn't allow her heart to be blown wide-open again.

She cleared her throat. 'I'm thinking horse-riding might be nice. Or we could babysit the kids while Niamh goes shopping.'

Anything. Anything that would stop her getting closer, falling deeper, losing herself further in Declan Underwood.

CHAPTER TWELVE

'MAM LOVES THE pictures. Thank you.' Declan found Kara sitting on a wooden bench in the garden, illuminated only by thick yellow moonlight.

He'd done his duty and given his mum more attention than she'd ever wanted, had helped around the farm and managed a horse-ride with Kara. Now the birthday cake had been cut and eaten and his family had settled down to watch a movie.

And he just needed a little distance from everyone. Except Kara. Seemed he couldn't keep distance from her no matter how much he tried.

Curling her wellie-clad feet underneath her bottom, she smiled. 'See. I told you she'd like them.'

'You know, I never realised just how much stronger she'd become over the years.'

'Well, Niamh would say it's because you don't get over to see her enough. But I'd say it's because you treat her the same way you always have. With respect, but pity too.' Kara shifted as he sat next to her. 'She doesn't need that now.'

'And you're always right?'

She nodded and her hair bobbed around her face. 'Obviously.'

'And smug too.'

'Takes one to know one.' She turned to look at him and wrinkled her nose as she smiled. 'I was meaning to ask you—why didn't you take over the family business, become a farmer like your dad?'

He cleared his throat as he tried to counteract the instinctive stiffening of his muscles at the mention of his father. 'No money in it. Not really. I needed something else, something more. Something…a long way from here.'

'You know, every time I mention your dad you close up just a little bit more.'

Busted. 'Bluntness just rolls off you, eh? You're not exactly one of those meek conformist women, are you?'

She shrugged. 'Believe me, I've tried and tried to fit my big cuboid persona into a round hole. And failed. Too many times to count.'

'Oh?'

She nibbled at her bottom lip and he could see her weighing up what to say. Silence stretched. He understood why she'd prefer to keep her secrets, but that didn't mean he didn't want to hear them.

'Too many times…?'

She sighed and peered straight ahead, her fingers gripped tightly together. 'Rob thought I should have been different… Well, let's just say I was a huge disappointment to him.'

'How could you ever be a disappointment?'

She shrugged. 'We started out wanting the same things, or at least I thought we did. But after he joined up he changed. He became more demanding, more possessive and authoritarian. It was his way or no way. He'd always said he was going to stay in the army for a few years, then get out…but that changed and he wanted to stay on for longer and longer. It was all about him and nothing about what I wanted or the dreams we'd made together. And I wasn't allowed to complain. Just comply.'

'So what? He wanted a divorce? Or…? Don't tell me he hurt you?' Acid rose in his stomach as he fought an intense primal anger at the thought of anyone laying a finger on Kara's perfect body.

She shook her head, her voice unsteady. 'Not physically. But the pressure was there always…to be the perfect wife, to do what was expected, not to ask for anything that I wanted, not to expect better…or more. God, I tried so hard to make it work. I wanted it all so badly. I wanted the dream. It was there, all I had to do was step into it, and yet…it wasn't a dream at all. I thought if I tried to love him more it would be enough love for both of us.'

Declan's gut contracted. The man had clearly been an idiot. 'You were so young, though. How did you even know what you were doing?'

'Yeah. Pretty tragic to realise at twenty-two years old that you've made the biggest mistake of your life and you're stuck. That you are way better at working than you are at loving.' She squeezed her hands together in her lap. 'I believed those vows, Declan. I loved him. I committed myself to him for life.' Her eyes glistened. 'Hard to admit it, but I was—plain and simple—married to the wrong man. It took me a long time to figure it out.'

Hell, he'd seen that before—right here in these damned fields, in what became a pile of smouldering ash. 'You didn't leave?'

Her brows came together. 'I didn't want to face the truth. I had enough trouble reconciling that sometimes love just isn't enough to keep two people together. I couldn't actually put voice to that fact.' She sighed. 'And when he died it all seemed such a waste—he could have been happier without me, with someone else.'

His stomach hit his boots. He imagined her as a teen-ager in a wedding dress, living a dream. The harsh real-ity she'd faced when it had crumbled around her despite how hard she'd worked to save it. So young. Too young.

Declan's heart jittered. He tipped up her chin and looked into her eyes. 'God, Kara, there are good men out there—men who will cherish and love you and who will willingly nurture you. But I do understand. I know enough about selfish men to write the goddamned book.'

'Your dad?' Her hand was at his cheek now.

Breathe. He nodded and stared out into the darkness. 'Yes, but let's just forget him too.'

She gave him a wobbly smile as she slid into his open arms and leaned her head against his chest. This was sup-posed to be about her…just about her. She looked to him for some kind of understanding or absolution.

'Good to know I'm not the only messed-up one.'

'We're all messed up somehow, Kara. You'll be fine. You are more than fine. You're marvellous.' He squeezed her against him, then stood up, pulling her with him. 'Come on, let's walk and clear our heads. Think about what we could do tomorrow.'

He needed to get away from the house he'd tried to build with his bare hands because of a dumb-ass man who'd pleased no one but himself. So he grasped her fist and wandered through the fading light towards the open fields. He'd moved to London to get away from all this… He never shared this stuff—not with Leo or any of the Hunter Clinic guys, not with his friends. Memo-ries were best left alone as far as he was concerned. Until they threatened to overwhelm you.

'Talk to me, Declan. Tell me about your dad.'

'No. It won't make you feel any better.'

She squeezed his hand, her voice less shaky now. 'It can't make me feel much worse. Can it?'

How blissfully ignorant she was. And she should stay that way. 'Look at the stars, Kara. A bit different to the sky in Australia?'

She tipped her head back and stared upwards. 'A little. It's bigger and brighter in Australia, is all. And the constellations are in a different place. Now, stop avoiding it.'

And, yes, that was what he'd done for years. Buried everything deep and got on with making a better life. A life that was so damned full he didn't have time for this… sharing and sentiment and drama. Yes, she had some— as he'd suspected. But instead of being irritating it had cut him deep.

She stopped dead and hugged her arms around him until most of her pressed against a lot of him. 'It's only fair. I've told you my guilty secrets—now it's your turn. And I'm not moving until you do.'

'That's not much of a threat. I like it like this. Very much.'

He took the opportunity to smooth his hands down her back and press her against a lot more of him. And wondered whether getting hard in the middle of an intense personal conversation was against someone's rules. Clearly not against his. But then, he never had personal conversations like this, so he could put it down to rookie error.

She dropped her hold and took two steps back. 'Okay… so no hugs until you talk.'

'Would you ever grow up?'

'No. I don't want to. Growing up sucks. As I found out to my cost.' The smile slipped. 'But I guess I'm the only one big enough to open my heart.'

And even though he knew about this kind of game, because his sisters had played it too many times, and even though he knew not to rise to her challenge, that once he'd started he'd find it hard to lock his anger away again, he felt the words rising within him. Because Kara had that way about her that made you want to tell her the truth.

He looked back up the hill towards the house, saw the light in the kitchen. Remembered how the light had filled him with terror that night. The light and the thick smoke, the crackle, the orange sparks rising into the black sky. An acrid smell that had filled his lungs.

'Dad had gone out for a drink that night—nothing unusual. *"You're in charge, boy,"* he'd said as he'd left. He always did that. It was our...' his voice cracked at the irony '...in joke. I was in my room and heard screaming from the lounge. My mum was yelling at me there was a fire and to get the girls out. Thick black smoke was everywhere. Heat. The smell. But I managed to get to them in the back bedroom and fought my way down with them. One by one.'

Kara's hand cupped her mouth. 'I can't imagine the terror.'

'I thought Mum was outside. But I couldn't find her. I called and tried to go back in but I couldn't breathe. I couldn't get to her. I tried. *Tried.* But the more I tried the hotter the flames and the thicker the smoke became. I couldn't breathe. I thought she'd be dead. I thought...I'd let her die. Then suddenly Dad was there, taking control, running in to what looked like a furnace. And then I thought I'd lose them both.'

And, to his eternal shame, he'd hoped and prayed that if the worst thing happened and only one person got out alive it would be his father.

'Then he strode out with her in his arms.'

Kara stroked his back as they walked down towards the stream at the bottom of the hill. 'You must have been so scared.'

Desperate. But his hero father had saved the day. At that moment the thirteen-year-old Declan had thought he couldn't love his father more.

'Mum was in and out of hospital. She was in pain, grew depressed and withdrawn with her injuries. And Dad didn't help. He couldn't look at her. Wouldn't tolerate her black moods. He began staying out more and more. Left me to do more of the work around the place—stayed out overnight. I wanted to ask him what we'd done wrong, why he didn't want to be around us. But the look in his eyes was so cold. And then one day he took me to one side and told me he'd met someone else so he was leaving. That was the last time I saw him.'

Kara shook her head against his heart. 'After everything you'd already been through…'

'In sickness and in health. That's what he promised. To love her. To love us all. Mum took it badly. She believed he left her because of her scars and it sent her spiralling into a black depression. I thought…I thought at one point she'd never get better. She was damaged. Devastated. And she thought it was all because of how she looked.'

He managed to bite back the bitterness he'd felt for so long.

'You don't walk away from the people you love, no matter what happens. Not if love means anything.'

Declan had grown up loving that man with every cell in his body. There'd been a bond, he'd thought, sacred between father and son.

Something inside him had broken the day his dad had left. And he'd had no idea how to fix it.

So he had buried his anger and disappointment and

tried to turn it into something positive. Determined never to give anyone the chance to hurt him like that.

'But you know what? My mum didn't deserve that, and neither did the girls. If he wasn't prepared to provide for his family then I knew I had to man up and do it instead.'

And had done so every single day since.

The water babbled and gurgled, cutting through the thick silence of the night. His chest heaved as he fought back the memories, the fear and the anger.

Kara ran her fingers over his ribcage. 'I'm sure your dad was devastated too. I'm sure he did love you. Still does.'

'Funny way of showing it.'

Her palm flattened against his chest, her voice thick with sadness. 'I'm so sorry.'

So this was how distraction from his reality had panned out. Delving even deeper into his past. So not what he'd hoped for.

He tried to lighten the moment. 'Sure, it's fine, Kara.'

'It is now, yes. Look at what you've achieved. Just look at you, Declan. A career most people could never hope for. Sisters who are so, so proud of you—and you of them. A farm that provides food and an income, a beautiful house. More…so much more than many people have, and all because of you.'

She curled into him, hugging him close, and he felt the weight inside his chest begin to lift.

'It *is* fine—it's better than fine.'

He nuzzled his face into her hair and just for a few moments he let himself believe it could be.

They lay down on the grass, listening to the eerie night sounds, the fresh country air whispering over them. The familiar smells of his home mingled with Kara's scent. Her heat pressed against him; her hair tickled his chin.

Awareness prickled through his veins.

'You know what I think?' she whispered.

He doubted it was anything like what was running through *his* mind. But a man could hope. 'No.'

'I think we say to hell with them. To hell with everything they made us feel, the disappointment and the hate.' She rolled on to him, straddling him. 'We should let it all go. We deserve better. Much, much better. We need to forget it and take something for ourselves. What do you say?'

She made it sound so easy.

The air around them shimmered and suddenly her mouth was very close. Her breasts rubbed against his chest and he could feel them pebbling as she leaned closer. Her scent enveloped him and he grew hard again in an instant. Very hard. He wanted to kiss that mouth, those breasts, to take her to the edge of oblivion. To do it again and again until neither of them had any memories apart from this, here. Now.

'You have any ideas?'

'Oh, Declan, yes. Yes, I do.'

And then she was kissing him—hungry, hot kisses that obliterated the anger and filled his heart with something else. Something much better indeed.

CHAPTER THIRTEEN

KARA KISSED HIM because she had to get the cruel image of a boy trying to save his family out of her head. His eyes were filled with a lifetime of shadows, of hate and regret and sorrow, and she wanted to erase that too. To smooth down his edges, to change the blackness into light. She kissed him because she wanted to feel something, to be wanted.

And because she wanted him.

She wanted Declan more than anything she'd ever wanted before.

Meshing her hands into his hair, she kissed him with everything she had, told him with that kiss just how much he had touched her heart. And he kissed her back with the same longing, the same promises, the same damned wanting that had fizzed around them since that ball.

He rolled her onto her back and kissed hot trails down her neck, stripped off her top and bra and exposed her nipples to the cooling air. But his heat warmed her, made her dizzy, until she just wanted more of him. And more.

When his palm cupped her breast she arched against him, shocked by the moan coming from her throat, by how much she ached to have him inside her. When his mouth clamped her nipple and a shiver of desire rolled down her spine she thought she could now definitely die happy.

'God, Kara, I want you so much. It's killing me.'

His voice was deep and hoarse, more a growl than words. His eyes had darkened, were fierce and glittering with a need that she knew was mirrored in her own pupils.

'Have me. Take me.'

'Kiss me,' he whispered.

And she did. Again and again. Until her mind was almost numb and her lips were swollen and sore yet still hungry for more.

Her hands met his chest and she dragged off his shirt, buttons popping and flying who cared where. Then she pressed against him, slick skin on skin, and a primal, feral need shuddered through her. Grass tickled her back and the stream played a gentle backing track to his breathing, his words.

'Now these. Off.' He pushed off her wellies. No, he tried to push one off but it got stuck, so he tore himself away from her, knelt and tugged again at the first one, then the other, toppling backwards on the riverbank. His roar echoed through the trees. Somewhere an owl hooted.

She couldn't help the laugh. He looked magnificent, biceps bulging, muscled chest puffed out as he stood above her. All sexed-up because of her. 'But, Declan, I thought you wanted me to leave my shoes on?'

'Don't be ridiculous. Crazy, beautiful woman. How can I get to your jeans if you leave them on?'

He knelt and slid his hand to her jeans button, then he inched them down over her legs. Slowly. Too damned slowly.

'Besides, those leprechauns do nothing for me…but those ruby-red shoes…' He groaned. 'Man, next time…'

He pressed kisses down her abdomen, making her inhale sharply, sending spasms of need pulsing through her.

'Next time you put those on.'

Next time. He wanted a next time and they hadn't even finished this time. Had barely started. And, God, she definitely didn't want it to end. 'Whatever you want.'

'Everything. I want it all, Kara.'

And she could tell just how much he wanted her as he pressed against her. She unzipped his jeans, shrugged them off and took hold of his erection, felt him harden even more, felt the heat surge through him, the shift in his breathing. Until it was almost impossible to breathe herself for needing him inside her.

'Declan, now, please. I need you. *Now.*'

His fingers roamed her thighs, opened her legs and then he was sheathed and over her, entering her, pressing deep and hard. And there was nothing then except the sheer power of this man and this never-ending need.

'Kara. Kara. My God, you are so beautiful.'

Her name on his lips was like music. His mouth was against her cheek, against her ear, in her hair with every wonderful thrust. Hard at first, frantic, desperate until she was so close…so close. Then he slowed the rhythm and looked at her, holding back as the pressure inside her, outside her, over her, started to increase. Slowly, too slowly, not slowly enough, he kissed her with such need, such passion, that nothing else mattered. Nothing but this.

'Declan… I… I…'

'I know… I know…'

She was on the edge and that fired something urgent in him. Declan shifted her hips as he felt her clamp around him, drove deeper inside her, wanting to savour every moment, to ride sensation after sensation. Her hair pooled over the grass. Her body arched as he held her waist and rocked her.

But he held back. It would be too easy to let loose and put his own pleasure first. He wanted to show her that not all men were like her husband and his father—that there were good men too, who would put her needs first. This was for Kara—for everything she'd had to endure.

He put all thoughts of consequences to one side. He didn't know what would happen next—couldn't promise her more than this. Didn't know anything past this moment. He wanted it to last forever, but he was riding an edge and it wouldn't take much to plunge him over.

He slanted his mouth across hers, tasted her again, ran his hands along the smooth soft shape of her curves, gripped her bottom and pressed deeper.

'Declan…' She was panting now, her head rocking back. 'God, yes.'

And he tried to hold on just a moment longer, clasping her close, stroking her hair, looking into those deep emerald eyes misty with satisfaction. But when her hands gripped his back and she pulled him closer, moving her body in perfect rhythm as she moaned deep and long and loud, he was lost. And only Kara could show him the way back.

'So, will you give me a ride back to uni or not?' Roisin grabbed a rosy apple from the bowl on the kitchen benchtop and bit down hard. 'Only I can go with Ronan and he's leaving in a few minutes. Tell me now.'

'Don't be so rude. I'm sure Declan will offer when he's ready.' Niamh smiled at Kara and rolled her eyes. Then winced as she dodged a face full of porridge from Declan Junior's well-aimed spoon. It landed next to Kara on the table with a plop. 'Nice try, sonny. Next time see if you can get your evil Auntie Roisin square on the nose.'

The little boy grinned and loaded his spoon. Kara could see the glint in his eye. Like uncle, like nephew. It seemed the Underwood genes ran deep.

'Nah-ah. Only joking.' This time Niamh made sure the food went where it was supposed to. Then she lowered her voice. 'I can't thank you enough for bringing him over. The first time he brings home a girl…and, well, I'm so glad it was you. Don't be too long coming back again. Any nonsense from His Lordship over there and you get on to me, d'you hear? He might be my older brother but I'm not averse to kicking his bu—' She picked up a large bowl and smiled sweetly to the rest of the family. 'Now, who wants the rest of these eggs?'

Sunday morning and everyone had gathered for yet another meal. The scent of sausages and bacon had drawn Kara from the cottage, but she didn't feel hungry. After a sleepless night she didn't feel anything at all except numb, and yet at the same time overwhelmed.

She'd fooled herself into believing just for a few moments that making love with Declan wouldn't carve a piece of him onto her heart, wouldn't matter.

It did.

His story had touched her. His passion and determination had lit something deep in her. She hadn't just got a slice of him in her heart—she had a gaping hole filled with him.

This wasn't a juvenile infatuation or some kind of wishful thinking. She loved him. In such a short, intense space of time she'd fallen completely for a player who, underneath it all, wasn't a player at all.

He was a man trying hard to carve himself some space

in a life that was full, trying to squeeze some joy from a life that had been tarnished.

She loved him. The realisation hit her square in the chest as she heard his laughter and turned instinctively towards it with a leap in her heart.

She loved him, and instead of being the joyous thing Briana believed in it was terrifying. To lose control of her feelings—to put herself there again. The one thing Kara had tried so hard never to allow to happen.

Swallowing back the ache, she turned away.

'Are you ready?' Declan called to her from under a spaghetti of chubby arms and legs and a lot of giggling.

She wanted to run away, far away, and yet she'd never be ready to leave this. For the first time ever she felt as if she truly belonged somewhere, and knowing she'd never come back was breaking her in two. 'Give me a few minutes to get my things sorted. I won't be long.'

'Okay, well, I'll go with Ronan, then. Finally I get an answer I can understand.' Roisin sighed. 'Lovely to meet you, Kara. Please keep doing whatever it is you're doing to Declan…it suits him. He's actually nice.'

His sister wrapped her into a big warm hug and Kara squeezed her eyes shut.

'And come back soon.'

She couldn't keep doing this. 'Bye, Roisin. Keep up with those studies. If ever you get the chance to come over to London I'd love to show you around.'

'That would be great. I'd love to. You can count on it.'

And then she was gone, along with Ronan. A thick weight pressed in Kara's chest. Two down, another dozen or so goodbyes to go.

Somehow she managed to get a few moments alone in her bedroom to pack away her things and take stock. Although she'd been taking stock for hours—and it had got her precisely nowhere. No matter how much she tried to fill her lungs with fresh country air she still had trouble breathing.

She could not let Declan know her true feelings and she certainly didn't know his—couldn't guess. She couldn't turn a weekend into something more. Couldn't expect him to invest the same kind of emotion she'd foolishly invested.

And besides—they were colleagues. He was her boss and they'd crossed a line. What the hell had they been thinking? She couldn't love him. But she did.

'Time to go, Kara. Give me your bag and I'll put it in the car.'

He was standing in the doorway, but he didn't come in and kiss her as she'd thought he might. He just gave her a faint smile, then turned to wait for her, avoiding eye contact.

Last night they'd stumbled back up the hill satiated and exhilarated. Stopping to kiss every few steps until it had taken an age to get home. He'd cuddled against her in bed and they'd made love again. Then at some point in the night she'd fallen into a feverish sleep. And into regret.

Not regret that she'd slept with him, but that she couldn't...wouldn't...shouldn't do it again.

Now he was decidedly distant. Did he think it had been a mistake too? Was he struggling with *what next*?

It would be so easy to carry on as if everything would be fine. To pretend everything *could* be fine. But she was tired of pretending now. She just wanted to go home. Alone.

'Declan. We need to talk...about us.'

He put his finger against her lips and shook his head. 'Not here, Kara. Not now. We have to go. Everyone's waiting to say goodbye.'

Including him, it would seem.

'Okay. Then let's do it.' With a sigh she closed the door behind her and followed him to the leaving committee, that ache in her chest intensifying.

The hardest goodbye was Mary's. Surrounded by the little ones, Declan's mother wiped away a tear. 'So grand to have you here, Kara, my love. You must come back and visit us soon.'

'I'll try.'

'And I think I might come over to see you and that grand clinic you have.' She touched her damaged cheek. 'Who knows what you could do to make things a little better, right? I think it's time.'

Kara watched with a heavy heart as Mary hugged her son. How long would it be until he came back again? And who would he bring next time? No—she wouldn't allow herself to think that. Couldn't imagine standing back and letting someone else love him. This was, she knew, special…for them both. And very special for Mary. Two women loving one man.

But was it harder to be his mother and have him gone from her day-to-day life, but to be tied to him for ever? Or to be Kara—to have him gone from her life but to see him every day?

Fighting back tears, she settled into the car en route to Dublin. The grey road stretched out ahead and the sky was black with rain over fields that seemed to have changed from lush green to brown overnight. She didn't know what to say, even where to begin.

So she stuck to the mundane, her throat too full of goodbyes to start another. 'Looks like the weather's changed for the worse.'

'They say if you don't like the weather here, just wait five minutes. It's fickle like that.' He shrugged and looked ahead, retreating further and further into whatever black mood he'd created.

She couldn't bear the thought of this kind of pointless half-hearted small talk and shopping and sightseeing and more pretending for the next few hours. 'Declan, I don't think I can face shopping.'

'Okay.'

He glanced across to her, hands white on the steering wheel, his jaw tight. She wanted to hug him close, to look forward to a future with him in it—at work and at home. In a house like his. She wanted to rewind to last night, wanted him to kiss her again and tell her she was marvellous. But mostly, she wanted not to have fallen in love with him at all.

'Shall I see if we can get an earlier flight?'

'Yes. Yes, that would be good, I think. All things considered.' Not marvellous at all. Not even a bit.

His eyes narrowed—and was that a flicker of relief there too? Her heart began to break. There really was no going back.

'Okay. If that's what you want.'

'Yes. Yes, it is.'

So instead of finding the *craic* in Dublin's fair city and seeing the splendour of Trinity College they landed in a cold and dreary Heathrow in the early afternoon. The crowds pressed in as they jostled through Arrivals and all she wanted to do was get home to her apartment and pull her sheets over her head—like Safia had—and shut the world out.

As the underground train rattled towards the city Declan turned to her, his eyes clouded, voice flat. 'Thanks very much for helping me out this weekend. You were amazing. I hope you didn't hate it too much.'

Helping him out. Was that all it was, in the end? Yes.

It was. And she'd been under no illusions—apart from her own.

That damned lump was back in her throat again. 'No, it was wonderful. Thanks for inviting me.'

'You know…it was amazing. Really, the best.'

But… There was a but. There had to be a but.

He hesitated. His face closed in and she thought for a moment he was going to kiss her, but he played with a lock of her hair instead, running it through his fingers, back and forth. Judging by his frown a battle was being fought in his head. She didn't know what or who was going to be the winner but she had a bad feeling it wouldn't be her.

And it was so hard for her to stay quiet…because she always spoke first and regretted it afterwards—but this time, *this time*, she knew it was better to keep her mouth shut and her emotions hidden.

His mouth kicked up at one side. 'But we did agree… You know what it's like in London—so busy, work's full-on…neither of us has time for a relationship.'

He was right of course. She'd trodden that path before and all she'd achieved was misery and regret for all involved. Sometimes loving someone just wasn't enough. The pain in her chest tightened.

'I know what we agreed, Declan. No strings. And that's fine. Actually, that's great. Perfect. That suits me down to the ground. Because, as I said, I don't want anything to interfere with my job.' She forced a smile and fought the tears. She would not show him how she felt. 'Back to normal, then. I'll see you in the morning, bright and early.'

'Not quite.' He looked at his feet. 'I just got a text message from Leo. Karen's mum's well enough to be left, so

Karen's keen to get back to work. You've been reallocated back to your old team. From tomorrow.'

And he'd had to tell her this on a busy train? A sharp fist wedged under her ribcage. There really were no ties at all. Or the man was a damned sight better at acting than she was.

The train screeched to a halt. She glanced up. The next stop was hers. Biting down on her bottom lip, she tried to keep her voice light. 'Okay, well, this is it, then.'

'I'll see you back to your flat.' He picked up her bag.

'No. No, you won't.' She took her bag back from him, being careful not brush against him or inhale any of his scent that drove her wild. Better to say goodbye now, here on a busy train, than on her doorstep, watching him walk away and wishing him back.

At least this way she could be the one to leave and keep some semblance of dignity. Fighting tears, she forced her mouth into a smile. What she didn't want to do was rip open their…relationship…and tear it to shreds, into tiny heartbreaking pieces.

What she wanted to do was throttle him instead—and herself—for letting it get this far. For making love, for allowing herself to fall in love with him.

'I think I'm better going home on my own.'

His nostrils flared. 'I'm coming with you. No arguing. You could get mugged, or attacked, or anything.'

'And you think that risk bothers me?' She could deal with a mugger better than a broken heart any day. 'Declan, leave it. I'm not one of your sisters. You can't tell me what to do, and you can't dictate what happens in my life. I'm going home on my own.'

'But why?' He shook his head as if finally realising this was the end. 'Wait—'

'No, Declan. This is my stop. I have to go. I can't

spend the day going up and down the Central Line.' Or round and round in circles, getting nowhere.

A screech of brakes and a judder. The doors swished open and a rush of hot thick air entered the carriage.

His hand was on her shoulder. 'I'm sorry, Kara.'

'Look, we both knew this weekend was a one-off. What happens in Ireland stays in Ireland, right?'

Her fist tightened around her bag's strap and she concentrated on not letting her voice crack. She could not give in to her emotions. Later, maybe, when she was alone. But not now. Definitely not now.

'Really, there's nothing to be sorry about. We both knew what we were getting ourselves into.'

He lifted his eyes to hers and she saw someone struggling with a host of demons. And losing.

'Did we?'

Damn. Declan kicked the tube station wall and relished the pain emanating from his foot, let the hurt stoke his raging heartbeat. Then he kicked with the other one, just for the hell of it.

In the distance Kara walked down the platform to the escalator, back straight, shoulders taut, hair skimming her coat in a river of blonde curls. Curls he wanted to lose himself in. Hair he wanted to be pooling over the sheets on his bed. *Their bed.* In a future that was filled with her laughter and her sparkling eyes, her forthright honesty.

A few weeks ago he'd been satisfied with the life he'd carved for himself. Relationships that cost little more than his credit card bill. Work that he could invest as much of himself in as he physically and mentally was able. A job he loved. Now his life was brimful of complications every which way he turned. And he didn't know what the hell to do about it.

How could he let himself fall in love?

His heart twisted some more. *Did* he love her? *Could* he love her? The idea was so out there that he couldn't reconcile it. For a man who didn't believe in love the idea was laughable. But what else could describe the chaos in his heart?

Lust. He thought about how his body reacted to her. That was what it was. Lust.

And it was foolish even to want that. The way she'd been behaving all day—so closed-off and quiet—he'd got the message that she'd thought the whole weekend had been a stupid mistake. At least, making love had been a mistake—because that marked the point where everything had changed between them. Become harder, stronger, deeper.

Or was it that she was hiding her true feelings? Because the devastation in her eyes wasn't just at saying goodbye to his family, that much he knew.

He watched as she rose on the escalator, her red suede boots eventually disappearing out of view, and fought the urge to run after her. His heart splintered.

He'd managed just fine on his own until now—always setting the rules, always being the giver. He didn't know how to take something for himself, to rewrite the rulebook. He'd never allowed himself to get in so deep that he'd felt helpless, confused. So goddamn out of control.

Watching her leave was a million times worse than watching his father turn his back on his family. This time he didn't shout and plead. This time he let her go. Because, after all, that was the right thing to do. Before it got too deep and hurt too much.

She'd think he was mad enough having got off at her tube station just to watch her walk away, never mind chasing her down to have a conversation which started and ended with, *I can't. I don't know how. I don't want to love you.*

Because loving her would be too hard. Too easy. Too much.

But, God, he wanted her. The pain in his chest settled into a keen ache. As he picked up his bag and waited for the next train home he exhaled. Tried to shake the headache settling on his forehead. But it hung around, making his brain a hot mess of fuzz. He wanted her, but he couldn't take a risk on having her. He wasn't going to let anyone tread on his heart.

The harsh truth was, the weekend hadn't been a mistake. Falling for her had.

CHAPTER FOURTEEN

DRAKE'S WAS BUZZING. Sadly, Kara wasn't. But for the sake of the team she tried very hard to be. And apparently she was failing.

'Are you okay, Kara?' Angela, the surgical reg, put down a fresh glass of Pinot Noir and squeezed in next to her at the crowded dark wooden table. 'Only, you've been quiet for a long time. And that's just not normal. For you, anyway.'

'I'm fine. Really. Sorry, I've just had a lot on my mind recently.' Declan mainly. Well, Declan totally.

Kara laughed, wishing she'd managed to mask her feelings more successfully. Even during her brief social visits to Safia the girl had been asking awkward questions and raising those dark eyebrows, muttering something about losing the love of your life.

And she had.

Those few weeks with Declan had been the most precious and amazing time of her life. He'd fired something in her. Made her want things out of reach, want the impossible. Allowed her to dream. And now it was gone and she felt bereft all over again, as if something had been physically wrenched from her, and it hurt like hell.

She knew it would take time—but she would eventually heal. She just hadn't thought it would hurt so much. Working long hours on little sleep was stretching her to her limit, but whenever she closed her eyes she saw his face, heard his voice.

No longer. She was through with this. At least she was going to try to be through with it until she really was.

'You know what, Ange? I've decided to hell with it. I'm going to stop looking backwards and start again.'

Again. How many times was she going to start again?

This was definitely the last time. Over the past two weeks she'd fluctuated between *damn the man* and checking her phone to make sure it was still functioning as she prayed for a call from him. For anything. A glimpse of him—something. But he'd been strangely elusive.

So it turned out he didn't want her after all.

And so she'd consigned herself to being just another of his conquests.

Her stomach knotted at what they'd lost.

Inhaling deeply, she drained her wineglass and put it down. No point in wallowing in self-pity. She had a wonderful job, and so much to give to her patients and her career.

Despite everything she'd found a different place to belong—here, at work, doing surgery, saving lives. And while it didn't fulfil every need it kept her busy and rewarded enough not to dwell too much on what might have been. She had a great career path and a supportive team.

'Well, thanks for the drink, everyone. I'm going to head off now. It's been a very long day.'

Tomorrow was the first day of the rest of her life, and she was going to make the most of every second. Declan Underwood be damned.

* * *

Declan assisted the Kate's emergency room staff to lift the badly burnt young man across from the paramedics' trolley to the department's one.

'Cause of the fire?' Declan always liked to know exactly what he was dealing with.

'Faulty electrics. They're living in a squat down on Crawford Crescent. Someone fiddled with the wires so they could have some free juice.' The paramedic shrugged. 'This one slept through a lot of it, so he was hurt the most. We've put an IV line in, started fluids and intubated. Blood pressure dropping. Pulse jogging along at ninety-seven and rising.'

Declan nodded and began a systematic assessment as he resecured the oxygen to the intubation tube. Starting with airway management.

'First off he has nasty laryngeal swelling due to smoke inhalation, so we need to monitor that IV input. I don't want to exacerbate the oedema. Okay, everyone, you know the drill. Cardiac monitoring, urine output, pulse oximetry. I need someone to cut off his damaged clothes and start burn-cooling and irrigation, but keep an eye on his core temp. I need an arterial line…crystalloid fluids.'

He turned to the paramedic again as his team began to carry out his instructions.

'Any signs of drug or alcohol use?'

'You name it, you've probably got it. There were empty vodka bottles around the house entrance and a couple of dodgy-looking packets of white powder in his pockets.'

'That will all impact on pain management. Cheers, mate.'

He watched the paramedic leave, then spoke to his reg, Karen, who was competent and capable. And not Kara.

His heart thudded with disappointment and regret as he met tired pale blue eyes, not vibrant sparkling green ones that could see into his soul.

'So, add in a comprehensive drug screen. Locate next of kin. Tetanus, probably too…'

As he worked on saving the man's life Declan relished every single second he was busy—because being busy meant he had to focus on something other than Kara and the burning hole she'd left in his heart.

'Today, mate, you have me. And there's no way you're going anywhere on my watch—except to the burns unit. Alive. And you're going to stay that way, so help me God.'

Yes, Declan liked to know exactly what he was dealing with. Which was why he'd watched like a useless pudding as Kara had walked away down the tube station platform. Why he hadn't contacted her for two weeks. Why he'd avoided looking for those emerald eyes and skyscraper heels in Drake's Bar or the staffroom or the hospital corridors. Why he hadn't listened out for her laugh. And why he'd been unable to sleep.

Because he had no idea what he was dealing with. But he had a nasty suspicion that it was a lot more than lust.

After settling the stable-for-now John Doe in the intensive care unit he made his way up to the private wing and went to see someone else it was going to be hard to say goodbye to. No matter how much he tried not to get involved, he couldn't help himself.

'Well, well. Look at you now. All ready to go?'

Safia stood in her home country's ornate dress, surrounded by packed suitcases, and smiled her regal smile. A genuine but nervous one. 'Yes. Thank you, Dec. But it feels a bit weird, going out there into the big wide world. Everyone wants to see the scarred Sheikha.'

'You will be fine. You *are* fine—just look at you.'
He checked the reddened skin on her face, knowing that
over time she would have minimal scarring. 'Give it a
few months until everything has settled down and I'm
sure you'll feel better about the results. And make sure
you do the physio and attend all my follow-up appoint-
ments.' He gave her a pretend frown. 'Because I *will*
growl if I have to.'

She waved a hand at him. 'You mean like you have
for the past couple of weeks?'

'I have not.'

'Mr Underwood, you have been acting more like my
dad than the chilled-out cool guy you were when I first
came in here.'

She tapped her fingers on the bedside table and he
marvelled at the flexibility she had there now, in such a
short space of time.

'Missing someone?'

'No.'

'You forget that I might be a princess but I'm also a
teenager. And I have to lie a lot to manage being both.'
She shook her head and rolled her eyes. 'That looked a
lot like lying.'

So what if he had been lying? There was no point
discussing his private life—er…his non-existent private
life—with a young girl. She was seventeen. What the
heck did she know about life or love? But then at thirty
years of age what did he? Absolutely nothing, it seemed.

He might as well be talking to one of his sisters. Hell,
he was surrounded by women who thought they knew
better about his love-life than he did.

'No, I'm just trying to do my job, Safia. Just getting
on with things. I like to be busy.'

Her eyes glinted suspiciously. 'That's exactly what she said too.'

'You've seen her?' His heart did a clumsy jitter.

He didn't need to ask who Safia was talking about. He'd had ample opportunity to see Kara too, just hadn't taken it. He'd needed time and space.

And that hadn't worked either.

'She popped by yesterday to say goodbye and wish me well.' Safia frowned. 'She looked about as happy as you do. And she tried to pretend she was fine too, but she had all the classic symptoms.'

'Symptoms?' Now his heart did a double jitter. What was wrong with her? 'Symptoms of what?'

'In here.' Safia pointed to *BFF!* magazine's front page. '"*How to Know You're Falling In Love: 20 Classic Signs.*"' She flicked open the mag and ran her finger down a page. '"*Loss of appetite.*" She refused a chocolate when I offered it to her. And no doctor refuses chocolates. Ever. "*Sleeplessness.*" She had big dark circles under her eyes. She looked exhausted and her hands were shaky. "*Lack of concentration.*" She kept checking her phone and really didn't have a lot to say…'

'Okay—I don't want to be rude…'

Declan relaxed. The girl was talking about a little dream world she'd created to pass the time while she'd been in hospital. Fair play to her too—whatever helped the healing process was fine by him. But what he'd shared with Kara wasn't the stuff of teenage magazines. It had been very adult. Very intense. Amazing. Life-changing.

And he'd been a damned fool to let her go. But he just didn't know how to get her back. Or even if she would be interested.

'*Perfect,*' she'd said as he'd flailed around for words. '*What happens in Ireland stays in Ireland.*'

'But I don't think—'

Safia held up her hand. She was going to make a very fine wife to any sheikh brave enough to take her on.

'And when I asked her if she was missing someone, she lied too.'

'Safi…seriously….'

'I *am* being serious. Love is a serious matter—especially when you don't admit it. And it makes you grumpy.' She shrugged apologetically. 'Stop frowning. I'm just trying to be strong for you until you can be strong yourself. Everyone needs someone to help them along. Right?'

He hadn't seen that coming. Why were some people just so damned…*right*?

His heart did a little leap. 'And she lied too?'

'Yes. I think she loves you just as much as you love her. I didn't think you were that stupid, Mr Underwood.'

Stupid. Yes. *Eejit.* Yes. He resisted checking the magazine's list for the other signs of falling in love, because if he was honest he knew them well enough by now. He couldn't think of anything else but her. His mouth ached to talk to her, to kiss her. His arms cried out to hold her. His feet wanted to take off in their own direction to find her. His whole body had a physical withdrawal. And don't even ask about his brain…

So, yes. He'd fallen in love with her. And the only pain that love had caused was this—this not accepting it, this fighting it. Not being able to tell her. To cherish her. To hold her. See her. He'd been so scared to feel it. Admit it.

What the hell he was going to do about it, though, he couldn't fathom. He'd let something precious slip through his fingers while he'd been so damned focused on why they couldn't be together.

He missed Kara like he'd miss oxygen. He missed

her crazy attitude and her smile. He missed her scent and her heat. He missed that she knew what he needed even before he did.

And if he was going to manage living a life here in London he wanted her to be in it. Somehow. In fact he couldn't imagine another day without her. He just had to work out what to do about it.

Kara reached the top of the steps to her apartment and fitted the key into her lock. Looking back to the pavement below, she remembered the time Declan had dropped her off on his bike and the kiss they'd shared. Good times. Special times. Even now her skin prickled with awareness at the thought. Like some sort of sixth sense. He'd always had that effect on her—as if her body just knew when he was near.

In the distance she heard the distant purr of a motorbike. Her heart stalled as the awareness intensified.

Don't be silly. There are plenty of motorbikes in London. For goodness' sake, she couldn't keep having that reaction to every motorbike sound. She'd be exhausted.

Kick-starting her foolish heart again, she turned the key and put one foot inside her apartment. The purr turned into a deep, throaty roar. Louder and louder.

It was the kind of roar that only one type of bike made—the kind of roar you recognised. Her stomach clenched.

Could it be?

Sure enough, at the end of the road she watched a shiny black and chrome bike turn the corner, then pull up at the kerb, with a rider who would not look out of place on the cover of a magazine. Suddenly there didn't seem to be enough air to fill her lungs. When she did manage to inhale her breath was stuttering and sharp. Clutching her handbag strap, she felt her hand shake.

Dressed in black jeans and the old leather jacket that had definitely seen better days, but which she loved almost as much as the rider because it had saved his life, Declan looked dangerous and edgy. Far from his usual cool exterior. His eyes flashed with apprehension; a muscle twitched in his jaw. He didn't smile.

What was he here for? Her mouth dropped open. She put a hand to it and resisted the temptation to run down the steps and throw her arms round his neck.

Instead of speaking he climbed the steps, put a finger to her lips and shook his head, closing off all conversation. Then he walked her to the pavement, pulled out a helmet from the top box and fastened it under her chin. His eyes glanced to her legs, to her ruby-red shoes. A flicker of heat warmed the apprehension.

As she climbed onto the back of the bike he took her hand and steadied her as he'd done before. A flash of electricity buzzed between them, making the hairs on her arms stand upright. It would never diminish, it seemed, this attraction, this connection. Even when her heart was broken, when her head knew things could never work out, some parts of her body just would not give up on him.

She wanted to ask him where the hell they were going. What he was doing there so late at night. She wanted to believe this was what she hoped it might be. But as she slid her arms around the body she now knew so well and had ached so much to touch she reminded herself that this was not going to be what she wanted. That she must try to stay detached... But how could she when she was glued to him on a powerful motorbike?

There must be an emergency, a problem, something

serious to do with work, his family. Because why else would he be here?

Resting her head against his back, she clung on to that thought as they sped through the dark streets of London. Faster and faster they flew, the cool autumn wind blowing her hair around her face. And still she didn't know where they were headed, or why. But she knew that for these few minutes she would hold on to some kind of hope.

Soon enough they reached the riverbank. Now, in the dark, it had a different feel to it. Down in the houseboats someone was playing a slow soft tune as yellow lights danced across the water. Different, but equally beautiful. Like Declan. He'd changed. Thinner, maybe. His cheeks had hollowed out a little, making his cheekbones even more sleek and sharp. Guarded, but alert, his eyes danced along with the lights.

He lifted her off the bike and threw his helmet onto the grass. Then he pulled hers off too and his hands were cupping her face, in her hair, pulling her closer until his lips met hers and she couldn't help but melt into his kiss.

So it was indeed something serious. At his touch her body went into overdrive. She'd missed this so much. Missed this closeness, his smell. He tasted of fresh air. Of love. Of a future.

She'd been there before. It had failed spectacularly.

Her heart beat loud and slow against her ribcage. She put her hands on his chest and pulled away. 'Stop…stop. We can't do this. I'm sorry. I need to go. *We* need to go.'

'No…I have to tell you something.'

He walked her along the path where the scent of sweet aniseed herbs filled the air. Around them the breeze dropped, as did the music. And as they left the busyness behind it felt as if they were the only two people in this city of eight million.

He stopped and turned to face her. 'I've been a prize idiot, Kara. I let you walk away from me and I know I shouldn't have. I really should have told you how I felt.'

Her heart seized at his words. Part ecstasy, part regret. 'In what way? *Felt*?'

'Feel. How I *feel* about you. I was hurt badly when my dad left, and I saw what love can do to a person when it isn't returned. It can eat away at every part of you. Can make you mistrust, make you question yourself, your worth. It stripped away my ability to risk loving someone else. So I tried hard not to care. I used it all as an excuse not to get involved and give any part of myself away and it worked fine for years.'

'I know.'

'But then I met you and everything changed. My life changed. And the lives of those around me.'

He stepped back and gave her a cautious smile that reached to the bottom of her heart and spread to every corner.

'I love you, Kara. More than anything. And I want some kind of a future with you—'

'Shh. Stop. I can't.' There—she'd said it. 'I just can't.' Then she turned and stumbled across the grass, headed who knew where, blinking back tears. Why had she let him bring her here to say these things only to break her heart a little more? 'Just go and find someone else to fall in love with, okay? Because I can't do this.'

'Hey, we can do anything we want.' He tugged her arm and pulled her round, seriousness etched across his face. 'I know you're scared. Hell, I am too. I've never done this before…and I know I'm making a huge mess of it right now. But it's from my heart, Kara. We can work things out together. Just the two of us. We can carve our own space. We belong together.'

'No. I can't, Declan.' Her heart shattering, she dragged her wrists from his hands. *Belong?* How much had she ached for that all her life? And now she'd found it, it was beyond her grasp. 'I'm so scared things will change. That we'll get all wrapped up in this bit and not see the end hit us. I couldn't bear it if you fell out of love with me. If I'm not enough for you.'

'You don't think you're enough?' He tipped back his head and laughed. 'Kara, you're more than enough for any man. And certainly perfect for me.' He was reaching into his jacket pocket now. 'Is that why you retreated that day we left my mam's?'

'Because I fell in love with you, Declan. Despite how much I tried not to. You and your damned lovely family won me over. I didn't know what to do after we'd made love. I was so confused. It changed everything— it changed my heart.'

She touched her chest and felt her heart beating a crazy rhythm. Fast and shallow.

'But we'd both agreed there couldn't be more. And you didn't exactly make me feel like you *wanted* more. I don't want to say yes if it'll end in a few years. I can't take that risk. I can't do that again. Not with you. I love you too much.'

He palmed her cheek with his hand and looked deep into her eyes. Never had she seen such passion. True. Stark. Raw.

'Oh, my God, Kara, you think that if something doesn't work I'll chuck it aside? Get a replacement wife and family? If I promise you one thing it is this—I will be there for you, whatever happens. To love and cherish.

In sickness and health. Those vows mean something to me too. I am not my father.'

'No. No, you're not.'

When he hadn't contacted her she'd branded him with the same attributes her husband had had: shallow and selfish. But Declan wasn't like that. He'd shown loyalty and belief and strength to everyone around him. And now he was offering that to her too. It had taken him a bit longer than she'd hoped. But he'd done it. And she didn't doubt his sincerity now. Or his love. Because she could see that in his smile, in his eyes.

'Right now I have something to ask you.' He lowered one knee onto the grass and pulled out a small box, revealing a stunning emerald ring. 'Kara, I love you with all my heart. I don't want to imagine another day without you in my life. Would you do me the honour of being my wife?'

'Oh, my God. *Oh, my God.* That is beautiful.'

Tears pricked her eyes. She pressed her hand against her mouth to stop her lips from wobbling but she couldn't. Couldn't breathe or speak. He loved her. *Her.* And she loved him right back.

'It was my grandmother's. One of the only things we salvaged from the fire. I want you to have it. Mammy wants you to have it. Naimh says she'll kill you if you don't. The whole damned clan want— You get the picture. Please say yes. Or I'll be in a whole lot of bother.'

'Say it again.'

'What?'

'The whole proposal thing…' Her throat ached. 'I just love that accent. It makes my heart go diddly-diddly. Go on, say it again…please.'

He shook his head and rolled his eyes, but he wasn't

angry. He was happy. Very happy indeed. 'Kara, I love you with all my—'

Stamping her feet and clapping, she squeaked, tugging at his shoulder. It seemed that once the right someone came along you knew. You just *knew*. 'Yes! Yes! I will marry you. Yes! Now, get up and come here.'

'Aww. Give me a minute…'

His hand was on her ankle, his fingers running tiny circles around her foot, up her leg. Heat shot through her as he found that point…yes, *there*…that made her shiver with need.

'Now, these are very fine shoes. How about we take a very quick drive home so I can spend a little time getting to know them…?'

'You want me to definitely leave them on this time?'

'Hell, yes.'

She knelt down next to him, looking forward to getting to know him a lot better too. As he smiled at her she reached out and touched his beautiful face, ran her finger down his cheek until it met his mouth.

Then she leaned in close and whispered, *'Kiss me.'*

* * * * *

200 HARLEY STREET: THE TORTURED HERO

AMY ANDREWS

For Carol, Scarlet, Alison, Lynne, Kate, Annie and Louisa. It was fun working with you ladies – let's do it again sometime!

CHAPTER ONE

ETHAN HUNTER NEEDED a drink.

Bad.

After five hours of complicated surgery his legs ached like a bitch and finding the bottom of a bottle was the only sure-fire way to soothe the fiery path of hot talons tearing from thigh to calf.

It was that or painkillers, and Ethan refused to be dependent on drugs.

'We're heading to Drake's, Ethan,' a voice with a thick Scottish brogue said from behind. 'Why don't you join us?'

A sudden silence descended into the male change-room as Ethan turned around to find Jock, the anaesthetist from the surgery, addressing him. He looked around at the four others, who'd all been chatting merrily until now. Clearly none of them were keen on having Ethan join them.

Jock didn't look particularly enthused either.

Not that he could blame them. The longer the surgery had taken, the more his legs had ached, and the more tense and terse he'd become. Accidentally dropping an instrument had been the last straw, and kicking it child-ishly across the floor until it clanged against the metallic kickboard of the opposite wall hadn't exactly been his most professional moment.

He hated prima donna surgeons, but his simmering frustration at his shot concentration *and* the pain had bubbled over at that point.

Even so, he didn't need or want their *duty* invitation, no matter how much he craved some alcoholic fortification. Ethan was just fine with drinking alone.

In fact, he preferred it.

'No thanks, Jock,' he said. 'I've got to get back to the clinic.'

Which was true. There was an important case file he needed to familiarise himself with on Leo's desk. And some classy fine malt whisky to go with it.

He looked around at his colleagues. 'Thanks for your help in there, everyone. Good job.'

There was a general murmuring of goodnights and then Ethan was alone. He sank gratefully onto the bench seat just behind him, easing his legs, muscles screaming, out in front of him. He shut his eyes as the pain lessened considerably and sat there for long minutes as the rush of relief anaesthetised the lingering tension in the rest of his body.

It felt so damn good to be off them!

But he couldn't sit here forever. Work called. He reluctantly opened his eyes and reached for his clothes.

The black cab pulled up in front of the imposing white Victorian facade on Harley Street. Like the many clinics and physician's offices that called Harley Street home, the Hunter Clinic was as exclusive as the address implied.

Ethan's father, celebrated plastic surgeon James Hunter, had founded it over three decades ago, and it had gone on to become world-renowned as much for its humanitarian and charity work with civilian and military casualties of war as for its A-list clients.

Thanks largely to his brother Leo.

Certainly not thanks to their father and the scandal that had not only resulted in his premature death through a heart attack but had almost caused the closure of the clinic over a decade ago.

Again, thanks to Leo's drive and commitment, it had been avoided.

Not that Ethan gave a rat's about any of that right at this moment. Thinking about his father and his previously rocky relationship with his brother always got things churned up inside, and tonight he was barely coping with standing upright.

Ethan paid the driver and hauled himself out of the back through sheer willpower alone. The only thing that kept him putting one foot in front of the other was the lure of Leo's whisky.

Ethan grimaced as he limped through the corridors to his brother's office, holding on to the polished wooden handrails for added support. His badly mangled ankle and knee felt ready to give at any second, and the effort it took for his muscles to support them was bringing him out in a sweat.

Ethan wished he hadn't neglected his physio so much, or ignored Lizzie—Leo's wife and his ex-home visit nurse—when she'd scolded him about not using his stick. He hated the damn stick, and the questions it inevitably aroused, and he didn't have time in his busy schedule for the intensive physio required—but at this moment in time he was prepared to embrace both.

Not that it would help him now.

But what *would* help beckoned just beyond Leo's door, and Ethan had never been so glad to get to his brother's office. It had once belonged to his father, and he'd used to hate being summoned here by the *great man* himself, in a rage over some imagined slight or other, as his father had slowly spiralled downwards into alcoholic depression.

Thankfully those days were gone, but it was pleasing to know that a decanter of finest whisky could still be found within the walls of this office—even if it was rarely touched.

The last ten paces to the bookshelves behind Leo's desk were agony, but ultimately worth it as Ethan wrapped his hand around the satisfyingly full decanter. He splashed two fingers of amber liquid into a glass tumbler that sat nearby and threw it straight back.

Searing heat hit the back of his throat and almost instantly tentacles of warmth unfurled outwards from his belly. He poured himself another one and threw that back too, enjoying how the spread of heat pushed back the relentless creep of pain.

A third glass was poured, but before Ethan drank it he picked up both it and the decanter in one hand and reached for the back of the plush leather swivel chair with the other. Leaning heavily against the solid piece of furniture, he dragged it towards him, thankful for the wheels that made it easier, throwing himself down into it, groaning as the weight came off his legs.

He shut his eyes on a deep sigh as screamingly tense muscles found release. Nursing his drink and the decanter against his chest, he flopped his head back into the cushiony leather headrest, tilted the chair backwards and swivelled gently from side to side, enjoying the rush from the twin sensations of heat and relief.

Ethan wasn't sure how long he sat there, idly twisting from side to side, his eyes shut, his tired muscles almost jelly now they'd been given permission to relax. He just knew it felt good to be non-weight-bearing.

Bliss. Ecstasy. Paradise.

But he *was* here for a reason—apart from the damn good whisky. He dragged his eyes open, knowing he couldn't put it off any longer. Finally acknowledging that was exactly what he *was* doing.

On Leo's desk there was a chart. The chart of a child with a terribly disfiguring condition that Ethan could help.

He could change little Ama's life.

He *would* change her life.

But Ama's case was complicated in more ways than one. Her condition was complex and would require multiple surgeries to correct.

But that wasn't the issue. Ethan thrived on complex.

It was the strings attached to the case that were the problem. Big, fat strings involving someone from his past and the unholy mess he'd made in his selfish, juvenile need to hurt his brother.

Olivia Fairchild.

Olivia's charity Fair Go was sponsoring Ama and her mother and an interpreter to travel from sub-Sahara Africa to London and the Hunter Clinic, for surgery and rehabilitation.

And she would be here—tomorrow.

Olivia who'd loved him. And he'd thrown it in her face by using her to get back at Leo. Flaunting her in front of his brother, knowing how much Leo had fallen for her, taunting him with the woman he couldn't have.

Olivia had been heartbroken when she'd realised. The

look in her eyes that terrible, fateful day... He shuddered thinking about it now. The huge row he and Leo had got into, not knowing Olivia was listening to every ugly word. Him admitting that he was only interested in the sexy Aussie doc because Leo wanted her for himself.

It hadn't been true—not really. At the beginning, maybe, but not at that point. He'd enjoyed her company and there'd been something about her that had made him forget all his *stuff* when he was in her arms. The darkness that had been with him from his teenage years. The anguish over his mother's premature death. His dysfunctional relationship with his father. All had been lifted whenever she'd held him close.

But the damage had been done and his betrayal, his hurting her, had been unforgivable. *Toxic.* That was the word she'd used to describe his and Leo's relationship just before she'd fled back to Australia. And she'd been right. It had been toxic. And a lot of that had been on him.

But it wasn't any longer.

He'd been so angry and self-destructive back then. Angry at his mother for dying and the ensuing scandal over her infidelities, angry at his father for being weak and taking the easy, boozy way out after Francesca's death, and angrier at Leo for playing protector.

Protecting James from himself instead of confronting him over the inept drunk he'd become. And protecting Ethan from his father's wildly fluctuating mental state—from deep depression to manic rage—denying Ethan the opportunity to vent all his anger, frustration and loss.

Ethan cringed as he thought about what a bastard he'd been. He'd taken what he'd wanted with no regard for Olivia's feelings. Just stringing her along, thumbing his nose at her love, knowing how much Leo had had to grit his teeth every time he'd seen them together.

He'd thought himself so far above love back then—that he was immune to it. What a fool! It had taken a small, fierce, passionate firecracker of a woman from a foreign war-torn land to teach him how wrong he'd been. Maybe that was his punishment for Olivia?

Learning what love really meant and having it cruelly snatched away.

Ethan took a deep swallow of his drink, beating back memories of Aaliyah. He didn't need *that* guilt on top of his Olivia guilt tonight.

No whisky bottle would be safe.

Olivia…

Had she forgiven him? Did he even deserve her forgiveness?

He hoped so.

Or at least that they could put the past behind them. Because not only would he be seeing her tomorrow but he'd be working with her too. As a paediatric reconstructive surgeon, Olivia had been given clearance by Leo not only to assist in Ama's surgeries but to scrub in on any of the Hunter Clinic's cases during her stay in London.

The humanitarian side of the clinic, which was Ethan's baby, worked with charities from all round the world—Olivia's charity being just one. Consequently it had a reasonably robust operating schedule—many of the cases were kids. There would be plenty of opportunities for Olivia to keep her skills up to date while she juggled her hosting responsibilities for Ama.

And Ethan knew having another pair of hands—skilled hands—would allow them to do so much more.

But team work was critical.

He couldn't change what had happened in the past, and he was pretty damn sure she wouldn't want to re-hash it either, but he could treat her with the respect she deserved going forward.

He took another sip of his whisky as the questions circled round and round his brain. Questions he didn't have answers for. Questions that could drive him nuts.

That could drive him to the bottom of Leo's decanter.

But he'd come too close to being his father, to taking the easy way out, a while back—he wasn't going there again.

He sighed and reached for the heavy walnut desk, grabbing hold and dragging the chair closer, trying to use his legs as little as possible. And there it was, right on the edge in the middle of the desk, Ama's chart.

Ethan placed the decanter and his glass on the table and pushed all thoughts of Olivia aside as he opened the chart and started to read.

Olivia Fairchild was late. She checked her watch for the hundredth time as she paid the taxi driver. The cool October evening, a far cry from the heat of Africa, closed in around her as the taxi took off and she turned to face the familiar building on Harley Street.

Late or not, she took a moment to collect herself and clear her throat of the emotion that she'd been battling on the cab-ride. She blinked back stupid tears. Getting Ama and her mother settled into their room at the Lighthouse Children's Hospital had been more emotional than she'd expected. She felt flustered and off-kilter rather than cool and professional, which was what she'd hoped to be when she came face to face with her past.

But Ama had got to her tonight—just as she had from

day one. She'd been so apprehensive of her strange new world, and so distressed when her mother had left the room with the interpreter to attend to some paperwork, that Olivia had felt completely out of her depth.

For nine years Ama had known nothing other than a small village in sub-Sahara Africa where she'd been closeted away, not allowed to go to school or play with the other kids because of her disfiguring condition.

London must be terrifying.

Olivia, who had spent a lot of the past six weeks building a rapport with Ama, had tried her best to comfort the girl, but sometimes only mother-love would do and Ama had cried and cried until her mother returned.

And, oh, the way she'd clung had been gut-wrenching!

Olivia had been able to feel the frantic beat of Ama's heart through her painfully skinny ribs as the little girl had held onto her for dear life. And Olivia had clung right back, rocking her slightly, shushing her gently, feeling so inadequate in the face of the girl's anguish.

It had reminded her of the day she'd found Ama and her mother, both wailing and crying in the street, clinging to each other as two men engaged in a heated discussion had grabbed at them, trying to pull them apart. She hadn't been able to bear it.

A passing car hooted, bringing her back to the here and now, and Olivia shivered as the Hunter Clinic came back into focus. She took a deep breath, steeling herself to enter.

Her heart pounded as she mounted the stairs and pushed through the heavy doors. After-hours the clinic was hushed and deserted and she took a moment to absorb it all. Except for the stark whiteness of the updated décor, visible even in the darkened interior, it looked the same as she remembered—exclusive, luxurious, old money. It smelled the same. It *felt* the same.

And yet it didn't. It was familiar…yet not.

Maybe it was because *she* was different? Not the same starry-eyed Olivia who had trusted her heart to the Hunter boys only to be used in their toxic games and have it crushed into the dirt.

Older. Wiser.

Stronger.

It was warm inside and she undid the toggles on her duffle coat as her boot heels tapped on the exquisite grey and black marble floor on her way to Leo's office. It felt like a lifetime ago now since she'd walked these corridors on her frequent trips to see Ethan.

Ethan.

Olivia's heart skipped a beat as her stride faltered.

No. She would not think about him tonight. She wasn't here to see Ethan. She was here to see Leo.

Ethan would come tomorrow. And tomorrow would be soon enough.

Despite only the most subdued light, coming from lamps placed in discreet alcoves, her feet took her to Leo's office without any real direction from her brain. Once there she didn't stop to give herself time to think or doubt, she just reached up to knock on the door, surprised when it swung silently open under the weight of her closed hand.

For a moment, peering into the sumptuous darkened office, with just a desk lamp illuminating the room, she thought the man sitting at the desk, head bent over a chart, looked like Leo and she smiled.

'Leo,' she called from the doorway, her voice hushed

as seemed appropriate in the quietness of the deserted building.

Ethan, who'd been too intent to register the knock, looked up as his brother's name spilled from Olivia's lips, and even a decade down the track he still felt the impact of that mouth.

Wide and sexy, forming a natural pout that had always fascinated him. A mouth he'd kissed.

He'd *missed*.

It was a startling realisation for a man who'd felt dead inside for the past year. And he wasn't sure he liked it.

What the hell was she doing here? Didn't her flight arrive early tomorrow morning?

'Olivia,' he acknowledged, watching as her eyes, always two huge chocolate pools shimmering with emotional intensity, grew even rounder.

He should stand—innate good manners dictated that he should—but his legs felt about as supportive as wet noodles and he didn't trust them. Thankfully Olivia seemed too stunned to call him on it.

Olivia blinked as all the oxygen in the room was sucked right out. 'Oh…'

Ethan. Not Leo. *Ethan.* Her heart pounded in time to the drumming of his name through her brain.

Ethan. Ethan. Ethan.

'I'm sorry, I know I'm late, but…' She nervously checked her watch. 'I'm supposed to be meeting Leo here.'

Ethan hadn't been sure what they'd say to each other when he and Olivia came face to face again. They'd spoken twice on the phone about the case, which had been brisk and professional, but he'd thought it would be different when they were looking at each other. That old hurts might have fizzled out.

Evidently not, judging by the wariness in Olivia's startled gaze.

Her first words were not warm and welcoming. There was no *let bygones be bygones* about her demeanour. She hadn't smiled for *him* as she had when she'd mistaken him for Leo. And, perversely, it bugged him.

There was a wariness, a distance in her gaze. As if they were strangers instead of ex-lovers. And a part of him wanted to snatch her up, taste that pouty mouth again, remind her how good they'd been together.

If only he could get up without falling flat on his face!

'He's at home,' Ethan said abruptly, angry at the direction of his thoughts.

For God's sake, he was lucky she hadn't slapped him in the face. Clearly he wasn't thinking straight. *Clearly* he was just too damn tired to be facing ghosts tonight.

Olivia frowned. 'Oh…'

But…she'd called Leo the moment they'd landed and they'd arranged it. She delved around inside her bag for her mobile phone, pulling it out. Immediately she noticed two missed calls and a text—all from Leo.

Apologies. Something came up. Get Ethan up to speed and you can catch me up tomorrow.

'Something came up,' Olivia said, looking from the phone to Ethan as she relayed the text.

Ethan grunted as a rather unpleasant thought occurred to him. Leo had texted him during surgery, asking him to familiarise himself with Ama's chart—*on his desk*—before the morning. Had Leo set this up so he and

Olivia could get their first meeting over and done with in private—to give them room and privacy to clear the air?

His relationship with his brother was the best it had been in years, but he didn't appreciate being manipulated like this.

'I bet it did,' Ethan said dryly.

Olivia put her phone back in her bag. 'He wants me to get you up to speed.'

Ethan had sometimes forgotten, just looking at her, that Olivia was Australian. Her flawless peaches and cream complexion seemed eminently English, and it was only when she opened her mouth and the flat Aussie drawl came out that he remembered. That and the opal ring she still wore on the middle finger of her right hand—a gift from her parents for her eighteenth birthday.

'No time like the present,' he agreed grimly.

If Leo *had* set them up then it would be foolish not to use the time wisely.

'Come in.' He gestured, suddenly realising she was still standing just inside the doorframe. 'Take a seat.' He indicated with his head for her to take the one on the other side of Leo's desk.

Her movements seemed awkward and unsure as she drew closer. She certainly didn't seem to be in any hurry to reach her destination, and he waited impatiently for her to take her seat, his gaze drifting to the way the denim of her jeans clung to legs still as slender as he remembered.

As she drew level his gaze moved up. Her red turtlenecked skivvy was mostly hidden by the thick navy jacket she was wearing, but it did emphasise the length of her neck to perfection. A neck he'd explored in intimate detail.

Olivia was conscious of his gaze on her as she moved

into the room. Heat flared in her belly as she remembered the way he used to look at her—all intensity and wicked, wicked purpose.

Before he broke her heart.

She was thankful for the thick wool of her coat hiding nipples suddenly taking on a mind of their own.

She didn't have time for recalcitrant nipples.

They were two professionals, working together for the good of a patient. Yes, they had history, but if they kept things collegial, if they kept their focus on Ama, they'd be fine.

She was here to do a job and then get the hell out of Dodge.

She'd been burned by this man before. And fire had already claimed too much of what she'd loved.

Olivia sat, glancing briefly around at Leo's office. It didn't appear to have changed much since the days when it had belonged to his father. All dark and masculine—a stark contrast to the bright modern white outside.

Her gaze returned to Ethan and for long moments they just looked at each other. His lids were half shuttered; his gaze was totally guarded. He looked so...*distant* and she shivered.

He picked up the nearby whisky decanter and splashed some into a glass, silently asking her with a raising of his eyebrow if she wanted any. She shook her head, surprised to see him drinking, knowing how much he'd despised his father for his weakness where the amber liquid was concerned.

Keep it professional, Liv.

'You've changed,' she blurted out.

And it was nothing to do with the drinking. Ethan's eyes were the same deep brown as hers, but he had those amazing golden flecks in them that used to *glow* with fire and passion. He'd been so angry back then that they'd flashed and flared all the time as he'd struggled with his demons—his father's alcoholism, his mother's death and what he'd perceived as his brother's molly-coddling.

But she'd also seen them glow and flash at other times too. At work when he was totally absorbed in a surgery. And in bed...

There was no glow tonight. Just a dull glimpse of what had been. It was as if it had been snuffed out. Suffocated.

What had happened to turn those gorgeous flashing eyes so damn bleak? And his perfect chiselled face so damn gaunt? His severe haircut didn't help. Nor did the weary lines around his eyes. Not to mention that he needed a shave. His shaggy regrowth looked more salt than pepper at the grand old age of thirty-five.

Was he suffering some kind of PTSD from being blown half to hell during his last tour?

'You haven't,' he said, interrupting her reverie.

It was Olivia's turned to snort. 'Yes, I have.'

She'd been through more than her fair share of heartbreak these past ten years, and although she'd come through it stronger it had changed her utterly.

Ethan paused slightly, then acknowledged the truth of it with a nod. She was right. She was more reserved, less carefree. Her gaze was not as open, was more...*distant*.

Had that been his unforgivable actions or just getting older? Life in general?

Or had something else caused the coolness in her eyes?

'I just don't need to resort to whisky to prove it.'

Ethan felt the accusation hit him in the chest with all the power of a sledgehammer.

He threw back the contents of the glass and slammed

it down on the desktop. 'It's been a long day, Olivia,' he said, his jaw so tight it felt as if it was going to crumble from the pressure. 'Surgery is over and I'm off duty. A few glasses of Scotland's best isn't going to hurt.'

Olivia had never been one to beat around the bush and she wasn't about to start now. Clearly something was eating at Ethan—something had snuffed out the light. And, whilst she might not know what it was, she sure as hell knew whisky wasn't the answer.

'I'm sure that's exactly how your father started out.'

CHAPTER TWO

ETHAN'S HEART POUNDED a furious tattoo in his chest. Having his father shoved in his face was always a red rag to a bull, but pure overproof rage surged through his system at her matter-of-fact taunt. If anyone knew the location of his soft underbelly it was Olivia. And she'd never been afraid to call him on his crap.

It was the *Australian way*, she'd assured him all those years ago.

He gripped the edge of the desk and lurched to his feet, too angry even to register the limp protest of gelatinous muscles. 'Go to hell, Olivia,' he snapped.

Her words stung. They stung hard. Because they'd found their mark so accurately. After he'd been discharged from the hospital in Germany and returned to the UK to recuperate from his injuries he *had* drunk way too much.

Trying to block out the pain and the dreams and the guilt.

Leo's email had saved him. The offer to come back to the clinic and head up its humanitarian programme had been just the right bait to wave in front of him and he'd reached for it like a drowning man, knowing that he was treading the same slippery slope his father had trod before he'd slipped away altogether.

But he wasn't that guy any more. And it infuriated him to be pigeonholed after a few minutes' reacquaintance.

She had no freaking idea what he'd been through.

Olivia stood too, refusing to have him standing over her, trying to intimidate her with his height and breadth and sheer masculine presence—which he still had in spades despite his more mature looks.

So, she'd annoyed him—*good*!

Maybe it would make him realise that sitting alone in an office at nine o'clock at night with a decanter full of whisky wasn't the answer to whatever was eating him.

'I'll follow you down, shall I?' she enquired calmly.

Ethan pressed his closed fists into the hard wood of the desktop and prayed for patience. He didn't need her judgement—he could do that plenty on his own.

'I think you can bring me up to speed in the morning,' he said through clenched teeth. He was too tired for this crap. 'I'm going home. See yourself out.'

At least going home was his plan, but by the time he'd taken a few paces the adrenaline from his surge of anger had worn off and the message from his quad muscles that they were too fatigued to hold him upright had finally broken through the righteous indignation swamping his brain.

His legs buckled.

Olivia leapt forward in alarm as Ethan wobbled and then toppled sideways, reaching out for the desk wildly in an attempt to stop himself from falling his butt. She grabbed hold of his arm and between her and the desk they saved him from being a rather inelegant crumpled heap on the expensive Turkish rug.

'What the hell, Ethan?' she said as he leaned heavily

against her, struggling for balance. 'How much *have* you had to drink?' she asked.

Ethan sucked air in and out between his teeth as his muscles protested. 'Not the booze,' he choked out, one hand reaching for a screaming thigh muscle. 'It's my damn legs.'

Olivia believed him. He definitely wasn't drunk. His words weren't slurred and he didn't stink of alcohol. In fact, with her nose damn near the vicinity of his throat, she could say for sure that he smelled the way he always had—of utter hedonism. Total crack for the olfactory system. It swamped over her now in a sweet pheromone cloud, and her body responded accordingly.

Honestly, the man was waging chemical warfare on her body and he didn't even know it, thanks to whatever was going on with his legs.

'Here, come on,' she said, staggering under the weight of him a little as she slung his arm over her shoulder. 'Over to the lounge.'

Ethan didn't have much of a choice. His thighs were trembling now from the effort of just standing and he felt as weak as a kitten. She led and he followed, and he felt about as potent and virile as a postage stamp.

'I'm fine,' he said as soon as they were near enough to the couch to reach for it. 'Let go.'

Olivia eased away as he flopped down onto the firm leather of the elegant Chesterfield and gave a relieved groan, his hands automatically reaching for his thigh muscles, his eyes shutting, his head flopping back as he kneaded up and down their length. She knelt down in front of him, his knees either side of her shoulders, resting back on her haunches, and waited for him to recover.

It took a few minutes for the creases in his face to start to iron out a little. 'What happened?' she asked quietly.

His hands stopped their massaging briefly before starting up again.

'Is it from when you were injured during your last tour?' she prompted, when it didn't look as if he was about to answer her any time soon.

His eyes flicked open and Olivia was struck again by how dull and lifeless they looked. No spark. No glitter.

'How did you know?'

She gave him a half-smile, trying to lighten the mood. 'We *do* have newspapers in Australia, you know. And this new-fangled thing called the worldwide web—which, you know, even goes all the way to Australia.' Her smile died on her lips when it was apparent he wasn't going to join her. 'You'll be amazed at what you can find on it,' she murmured.

Ethan pulled his head off the cushioned comfort of the lounge and pierced her with his gaze. Her honey-brown hair fell in wavy disorder around her face and he remembered vividly how it had felt spread out across his chest.

'You kept tabs on me?'

Olivia sucked in a breath as his low, gravelly voice swept hot fingers along the muscles deep inside her. And was that a flare bursting to life in those golden flecks?

'No,' she said, annoyed that even tired and in pain he could think such a thing.

Clearly his ego hadn't been injured.

'I haven't spent the past decade *pining* over you, Ethan Hunter, if that's what you think,' she clarified, her voice snippy even to her own ears. 'I researched the clinic on-line when I was looking at partnering with you guys. The newspaper articles about how you evacuated an entire hospital that was being heavily shelled showed up in the search.'

Ethan dropped his head back again and shut his eyes against the annoyance in hers and the echo of memories. He'd been meaning to check up on her over the years, but military life had been full-on and there'd always been an excuse not to.

And then he'd met Aaliyah.

Olivia watched him a little longer, the kneading of his long fingers hypnotic. Part of her wanted to take over—the Olivia of ten years ago would have.

This Olivia curled her hands into fists by her sides and said, 'What are your injuries?'

Ethan sighed, lifting his head off the lounge again. 'Legs shot to hell. Right knee and ankle torn up by shrapnel.'

'Have they been reconstructed?'

He nodded. 'As best they could. They're never going to be the same again, though.'

'Do you have some kind of physio regime, because your legs don't seem to be very strong. I'd have thought you'd need some kind of a walking aid—a stick or something?' She frowned, thinking back to the articles she'd read. 'It's been about a year, right?'

Ethan grunted. 'Yes,' he said tersely. 'And, yes, I have a regime.'

It took Olivia a second or two to realise she'd asked the wrong question. 'Do you *follow* it?' She folded her arms. 'Religiously?'

Ethan glared at her. God, she sounded like Lizzie. And Leo. And a lot of well-meaning other people who didn't have a freaking clue about the realities of his injuries.

'It's none of your damn business,' he growled.

'It *is* my damn business if you're going to collapse on the floor in the middle of operating on Ama.'

Ethan bristled at the implication, and at the unflinching demand he saw in her eyes. She was calling him on his professionalism and leaving him in no doubt that she was holding him to account. It rankled. But still, it was preferable to the pity he usually saw reflected in other people's eyes.

The *poor you* look that got under his skin like an army of marching ants.

She didn't seem to give a damn about the fact of his injuries or even how he'd got them—just that he could do his job. She was being a doctor. And it was in equal parts satisfying and irritating

'I'm not going to be collapsing on anyone,' he snapped. 'I just stood for an extraordinary amount of time today.'

'Which shouldn't matter if you'd been diligent with your physio,' Olivia said.

She knew Ethan. She knew he wouldn't respond to her empathy. God knew, the empathy and protection Leo had tried to force upon him all those years ago had driven a huge wedge between the brothers and she'd been just one of the casualties.

She knew he wouldn't let her massage his legs or talk about what had happened. But, having worked out in the field herself, in places no one should have to live, she did know that military men responded best to tough love.

'I've been a little busy trying to establish the humanitarian side of the clinic,' he snapped. 'I do what I can when I can.'

Olivia drummed her fingers against her biceps. 'Well, it looks like it's not enough. You should be stronger than this by now.'

Ethan knew she was right, but…it *had* been an unusual day. He let his head flop back again.

He needed to make time to get stronger in his legs. He'd gone from two months in hospital and multiple surgeries to home and feeling sorry for himself to throwing everything he had into his new role at the Hunter Clinic—none of which had been conducive to the hard yards he needed to do.

As Olivia watched he seemed to melt into the couch, exhaustion in every line of his body, and part of her wanted to lay her cheek on his nearby knee and just sit with him in silence. She was surprised to feel such tenderness for him after what had happened. But then the heat in her belly had been a surprise too, after all these years.

She nudged his knee with her shoulder. '*Have* you got a stick you should be using?'

Ethan lifted a hand off his thigh and massaged his forehead with it. He wished she'd just be quiet, already—she was like Jiminy freaking Cricket. 'Yes…' he said on a sigh.

'And the reason you don't appear to have it with you is…?'

Ethan lifted his head. 'I hate the damn thing,' he muttered.

Olivia raised an eyebrow. Did he realise how much he sounded like a petulant child? 'Does it affect your tough guy image, Ethan? I wouldn't have thought you so vain.'

Ethan snorted. Did she *really* think this was about vanity? 'No, it's just…' He shook his head, shut his eyes, rested his head back again as he realised he was about to admit the truth. 'It…invites conversations I just don't want to have.'

The heaviness in his voice reached right inside her gut and squeezed. *Hard.* She knew all too well how hard rehashing things could be—talking about stuff that sometimes you just didn't want to talk about. Especially with people who had no connection to you.

So many people had wanted to talk to her after what had happened to her parents, had wanted to reminisce, lament, vent. And she'd spent an awful lot of time avoiding them.

Without thinking about it she slid a hand onto his knee. The fine wool of his trousers was soft against her palm, the contours of his knee hard.

'Ethan…'

Ethan lifted his head again as her touch caused a riot of sensations up his aching leg. *Good* sensations. She was barely touching him at all, but still it felt as if she'd injected pop rocks into his thigh. He looked at her neat fingernails and remembered how good they'd felt on other parts of his body. How *good* they'd been together. How much they'd sizzled.

How insatiable they'd been.

His reasons for being with Olivia might not have been exactly altruistic, but they'd been amazingly compatible in the bedroom.

Which reminded him how long it had been since he'd been with a woman. A year.

Not since Aaliyah.

He dragged his eyes off her hand and looked up. Their gazes locked. The worst thing about her touch was how familiar it felt. Here in this clinic, with this woman from his past looking at him with patience and compassion, it would be so easy to grab hold and travel back to a time when he'd been able to lose himself in her and have everything else fade to black.

But it felt…disloyal. To Aaliyah. And he despised himself just a little bit more.

'Just go, Olivia.'

Go before I kiss you. Before I haul you up on the couch beside me. Before I beg you to stay.

Before I use you one more time.

Olivia's belly clenched at the flare of heat that fired Ethan's dull gaze. She'd seen that look before. She knew what it meant. She knew what he wanted. Her breath grew thick in her throat as things south of her waistband stirred and strained, demanding she respond in the most primal way.

His nostrils flared as the silence stretched between them and she could feel the coiled intensity of his muscles. He wanted her. She could see that. Hell, half an hour in his company and she wanted him too.

But, unlike last time, she wanted *all* of him. She wanted his story and his sadness and his shadows. And she wasn't going to settle for scraps. For some quick roll in the hay while he made love to her with dead eyes. Because having sex with Ethan had never been a one-time thing for her and she needed to protect herself better than last time.

She was here for Ama. And then she was leaving.

She was not having sex with Ethan Hunter.

Olivia pushed herself shakily to her feet. She was standing between his knees now and an image of her straddling him played in glorious Technicolor inside her head.

She took a step back. 'Are you—?' She cleared her

throat of its sudden wobble. 'Are you heading home soon?'

Ethan shook his head. He probably hadn't been very capable of standing prior to Olivia touching him; he for damn sure wasn't now. 'I'll sleep here tonight.'

Olivia nodded. It seemed best, considering walking had been a monumental effort. 'Are you...will you be okay?'

'Dandy,' he said sarcastically, annoyed at her distant propriety—a far cry from the heat of the look they'd just exchanged.

Olivia ignored his terseness. 'What time do you want to meet in the morning?' she asked.

'Be here at nine.' His tone was dismissive and he hoped she got the message—*get the hell out.*

Olivia got the message. It rankled, but she didn't want to get into anything more with him tonight. It seemed their incendiary attraction still simmered and she didn't trust that the line between angry and passionate wouldn't blur and they wouldn't do something they'd *both* regret in the morning.

She turned on her heel and headed towards the desk, where her bag had been dumped when Ethan had fallen. She reached for it, her gaze falling on the decanter of whisky. She snatched it up. It could leave with her as well.

Out of sight, out of mind.

'You don't have to take it,' he said derisively from behind her. 'Even if I was capable of hauling my butt off this couch, I'm done with drinking tonight.'

Olivia turned, slinging the straps of her handbag over her shoulder. 'Consider this as my way of delivering you from temptation.' And with that she headed for the door.

Ethan tracked her progress, her clinging jeans, the

swish of her honey-brown hair down the back of her coat way too fascinating for his own peace of mind.

A surge of what felt like good old-fashioned lust swept through his system.

He didn't feel very delivered at all.

Ethan was woken by a hard shake to his shoulder who knew how many hours later? Except where there had been darkness there was now light. *Way too much light.*

Daylight streamed like glory from heaven through the open slats of the dark wooden blinds dressing the window under which the chesterfield sat, piercing like needles into his eyeballs.

'Ugh,' he groaned, shutting his eyes tight. 'Somebody turn down the sun.'

'What the hell are you doing here?' Leo demanded, ignoring his brother's protests as he yanked up the blind, causing a tsunami of sunlight.

Ethan groaned louder. 'It was late,' he said, shielding his eyes. 'I crashed here.'

'I should start charging you rent,' Leo muttered.

Ethan cracked an eyelid open to find his brother lounging against the far arm of the couch. He squinted at his watch. It was six-thirty in the morning. 'Lizzie kick you out of bed?'

Leo grinned, which was way too much for Ethan at this hour of the morning. 'She's not sleeping very well,— has to keep getting up to go to the bathroom. I'm trying to give her as much room as possible.'

Ethan was pleased his brother had found love, but such happiness was a bit hard to take—especially hard on the heels of his less than stellar reunion with Olivia. He sat and swung his legs over the edge of the couch, pleased to feel the strength back in his quads.

'You look like hell,' Leo said cheerfully.

'Gee…thanks.' Compared to last night he felt like a million dollars.

'You going to head home or shower here?'

Ethan ran his hands through his hair. 'I'll use your bathroom.' He always kept spare clothes in his office, and a private bathroom was one of the perks of being the director—or related to him anyway.

Ethan owned the clinic jointly with his brother, but had gladly ceded control to him when he'd decided to leave everything tainted with the Hunter name behind and put his medical degree to good use in the army. Leo had been angry that he was skipping out on his family responsibilities, especially with the clinic in such trouble after his father's scandal, and had spent the next ten years trying to involve his younger brother in the day-to-day running of the clinic.

But Ethan hadn't cared. He'd not wanted any part of lipo and boob jobs on a bunch of movie stars. He'd been doing *real* work and Leo could do whatever the hell he liked to salvage the professional and financial reputation of the once renowned Hunter Clinic.

And then he'd been blown all to hell and Leo had made him an offer he couldn't refuse. An offer he'd desperately needed to stop him from sliding into an abyss of self-pity.

Leo pushed up off the arm. 'When you're done I'll buy you breakfast.'

Three quarters of an hour later they were sitting inside a nearby café, tucking into a traditional English breakfast. They were both on their second cup of coffee.

'So. You saw Olivia last night, I take it?'

Ethan looked up from his plate. 'Yes. Nicely orchestrated,' he said with derision.

Completely unabashed, Leo said, 'How did that go?'

'How do you think it went?'

'Not as well as I'd hoped, by the sounds of it.'

'Let's just say I wasn't in the best shape when she arrived. She pretty much accused me of being one step away from the old man and then chewed my ear off about not doing my physio.'

Leo laughed. 'Still the same blunt old Olivia, huh?'

Ethan grunted, then took a sip of his coffee. 'She is and she isn't. There's a…reserve about her…she's not her usual vivacious self.'

'Maybe that's just being around you?'

Ethan contemplated his brother's observation. *Maybe it was.* 'Anyway…it didn't go well. She has your decanter of whisky too, by the way.'

Leo laughed harder. 'Did you discuss the case at all?'

Ethan shook his head. 'She's coming to your office at nine to brief us both.'

Leo quirked an eyebrow at his brother. 'Am I to be an intermediary?'

Ethan looked at his older brother. His tone was light but their history with Olivia Fairchild was complex. And, apart from one aborted attempt on the day of Leo's wedding, Ethan had never really apologised for his behaviour where that was concerned. He'd not only hurt Olivia but he'd also hurt Leo—deliberately.

Because he could.

He put his coffee cup down in its saucer. 'No. Of course not. About that…about Olivia…about what happened between all of us—'

'Don't worry about it,' Leo interrupted. 'Water under the bridge.'

'No.' Ethan shook his head. 'I was out of line.'

'Yes, you were.' Leo grinned. 'But…I knew deep down she never really liked me—not in that way. She certainly never gave me any reason to think there was anything other than friendship on her behalf. But…she was so gorgeous…my ego got in the way.'

Gorgeous. Yes, Leo was right. Olivia had been vivacious, sparkling, witty. Quick with a laugh and a snappy one-liner.

And utterly gorgeous.

'That doesn't make my behaviour any less reprehensible. You were right. I was using her to get at you and I'm sorry. I was pretty self-destructive there for a while, huh?'

Leo shrugged. 'Losing Mum was hard on you.'

'And not on you?'

'Ethan…we've made our peace. We *both* did things wrong and I don't expect you to spend the rest of your life apologising for something that happened a long time ago which we've put behind us.'

He paused and pierced his brother with a look that Ethan had come to know as his clinic director look.

'And I'm not the one you need to apologise to. That's what you were supposed to be doing last night.'

Ethan grimaced. 'Yeah. That didn't happen.' He glanced at his brother, who held his gaze with unwavering intensity. 'She refused to accept my apology last time. What makes you think she will now?'

'It's been a long time,' Leo said. 'And she's never struck me as being someone to hold a grudge.'

'It was pretty unforgivable.'

Leo nodded in agreement. 'You need to make it right,

though. You'll be working with her again over the next few months. You have to clear the air.'

Ethan knew Leo was right. Once upon a time that would have rankled, as everything about his brother's authority and over-protectiveness had rankled. But he'd done a lot of growing up and recognised good advice when he heard it. 'I know.'

There was silence for the next few minutes as they finished their breakfast. Leo put his utensils down on his plate and looked at his brother. 'I thought you and her might…'

Ethan glanced up from his breakfast. The possibility of he and Olivia glimmered for a moment. Her touch on his leg last night was almost tangible again, the way they'd been together settling around him in a fine mist he could almost taste.

But then memories of another woman—a woman he'd loved, a woman he'd left to die—pushed into the possibilities, beating them back, drowning them in a tide of guilt.

Aaliyah.

Ethan threw his napkin on his plate. 'Let's go.'

CHAPTER THREE

RUNNING EARLY THIS time, Olivia smiled at Leo as she walked into his office an hour later. She'd always had a soft spot for the incredibly hard-working elder Hunter brother and it hadn't been killed by time, distance or past wrongs. Yes, she'd told them their relationship was toxic but that hadn't really been Leo's fault.

Leo had been caught in the middle between his father and his brother and had practically killed himself to do right by both of them.

It was Ethan's bitterness that had been the true destructive force.

She thrust the whisky decanter she'd hauled all the way back in the taxi at him as she neared. 'I relieved Ethan of this last night.'

'Yes, he mentioned it.' Leo grinned taking it from her and then sweeping her into a huge hug.

'I can't believe it's been ten years,' he said as he pulled back. 'How have you been?'

Olivia gave her standard reply. 'Fine.' Because the truth was less than fine, and she refused to give it power over her. 'But now…what about you? Not only married but a baby on the way? I have to meet this girl!'

Easily deflected, Leo chatted for ten minutes about Lizzie and babies and their life together and Olivia was heartened to hear that Leo had found the happiness he'd always deserved. She'd valued and enjoyed his friendship and had been saddened by its becoming another casualty of Ethan's destructive streak.

If she'd only been smarter she would have chosen the older Hunter brother. But the heart wanted what the heart wanted, and from the moment she'd laid eyes on Ethan she'd been officially off the market!

She'd fallen hard for his good looks, charm and intelligence. Yes, he'd been angry, and hurting too, but he'd oozed undeniable potential from every cell in his being. She'd just known that one day he would do great things.

And that had been pretty damn irresistible.

But she would have resisted had she known she was going to cause an even bigger rift between the two brothers. She'd thought she'd be able to help them reconnect, to heal the cracks in their relationship that had been gutting to watch.

Her tender heart had been touched by the suffering they'd endured—their mother's death and the scandalous details of her life that had come to light after, and their father's messy slide into the bottle. Coming from a background that placed family above *everything*, she hadn't been able to bear the thought of what the Hunter boys must have been through growing up and she'd desperately wanted to help.

She'd wanted to show Ethan, and Leo by extension, how wonderful a loving relationship—like the one her parents had—could be. And to bring them back to each other.

But Ethan had been on a different page and she hadn't got the memo.

The light chatter stopped as soon as Ethan entered the room. Olivia was relieved to see him looking much more human this morning. Back to his usual level of *ooh la la* in a suit and tie. He'd hadn't shaved, but the lines around his eyes had disappeared. His gait was strong and sure even with the slight limp as he strode towards the desk.

She'd lain awake half the night thinking about their reunion and the state of his health. He seemed even more messed up than he had been a decade ago. Lucky for her, life had hardened her sappy little heart over the years, and the urge to fix Ethan Hunter had withered and died a long time ago. He was a big boy who could take care of himself.

Leo looked from one to the other as she and Ethan stood awkwardly in front of his desk. 'Let's get down to it, shall we?' he suggested.

'Yes,' they both said in unison, and then glanced guiltily at each other before simultaneously looking away.

Leo sighed. 'Take a seat,' he said, indicating the chairs opposite him, and Olivia wasn't sure whose butt was on whose respective chair faster—hers or Ethan's.

Clearly Ethan was keen to get this over with.

Good.

That made two of them.

Ethan strode into the Lighthouse Children's Hospital just prior to lunch. He'd walked from Harley Street. Last night the thought of walking any distance had been beyond him, but he usually walked from the clinic to the Lighthouse, and also to Princess Catherine's Hospital, time permitting.

The Hunter Clinic and its team of surgeons had operating privileges at both hospitals and neither was far to walk. Still, after Olivia's dressing-down last night he was using his stick, even if he did have plans to abandon it just prior to seeing his patients.

Olivia had accused him of vanity last night and he'd set her straight on that. Drawing attention to himself, to his injuries, wasn't something he was keen on. But it was more than that. A surgeon with a walking stick just sent the wrong kind of message. Especially in the world of plastics and reconstructive surgery. Patients wondered about a surgeon who couldn't heal himself.

Leaving his stick in one of the empty offices, he did his rounds. Being a visiting surgeon, he didn't have any junior doctors to accompany him but always made sure one of the nursing staff on each ward did. Nothing annoyed the nurses more than a doctor coming in and making changes to treatment and then leaving again without informing them.

And Ethan had learned a long time ago never to upset the nursing staff. That nurses were a vital part of the medical team—the interface between the doctor and the patient.

And you annoyed them at your own peril.

He prided himself on having good relationships with the nursing staff wherever he went, and at the Lighthouse particularly.

He left Ama to last. There was a lot that needed to be done before she went to Theatre next week and he wanted to have a clean plate today so he could focus solely on her. Plus Olivia was with her, and for some reason he was unaccountably nervous. It was obvious from her briefing this morning that this case was dear to her and he found himself not wanting to disappoint her.

He'd done that once already and was desperate to make amends.

He made his way to Ama's room by himself, assuring Ama's nurse, who was busy with another of her patients, that he would keep her up to date with the tests and procedures he was ordering. He heard laughter as he approached—Olivia's laughter. With her petite frame she looked as if she'd have one of those light and tinkly girly laughs, but it was surprisingly deep and throaty and it always came out at full roar—coming not just from her belly but from her heart.

He remembered it well from back when she used to smile at him, when she used to laugh.

It evoked powerful memories of a turbulent time in his life. A time when her laughter had helped ease a lot of his frustrations.

She had her back to the door when he pulled up and he lounged against the frame, observing her for long moments. She was sitting on the bed opposite a little girl who sat cross-legged in the lap of an older woman. Their skin was as dark and burnished as the finest ebony.

Ama and her mother, he assumed. Although he could only see them in profile and therefore the defect, which he knew to be quite significant, wasn't showing, given that it was the other side of Ama's face. He also noted the colourful headscarf that Ama wore draped over her affected side, obscuring it completely.

Looked at from this vantage point, Ama looked perfectly normal. But he'd seen the pictures—NOMA had ravaged the right side of her face, leaving her terribly disfigured.

A chequerboard sat between them and they were engrossed in a lively game. A third person—a young woman with skin more of a mocha colouring—sat on a chair beside the bed, also involved, switching between English and an unfamiliar language and laughing as Ama made a run of the board.

'Ama, you are getting much too good at this,' Olivia said, and laughed that full throaty laugh again.

The woman in the chair spoke to Ama in what he presumed was her own language and the girl giggled, her eyes sparkling in absolute delight.

Ethan was struck by how intimate the cosy little circle appeared. They all seemed very comfortable in each other's company. Ama's mother was looking at Olivia as if she was some kind of saint and Ama was smiling so big at Olivia, her eyes sparkling so brightly, it was like the sun shining.

Olivia passed over a red chequer piece to Ama and Ama laughed again, the whites of her eyes flashing as she held on to Olivia's hand for long moments before accepting the spoils and crowning her victorious piece.

Ama said something in her own tongue and the woman Ethan assumed was the translator said, 'Ama thinks she's winning.'

Olivia laughed again, and even with the distance between them, it whispered against his skin.

'Oh, does she, now?' Olivia said with mock indignation. 'We'll see how easy it is for her to win when I'm tickling her,' she announced, raising her hands and wiggling her fingers in Ama's direction before launching a tickle attack on a giggling, squealing Ama.

The chequerboard was upended, but nobody seemed to mind as general pandemonium ensued.

Ethan was struck by the genuine connection between Olivia and Ama and her mother. There was nothing forced or stilted—just an easy familiarity. But there was also an unspoken trust in their byplay, and Ethan knew how hard Olivia would have had to work to gain that trust. To take them out of their own country, away from everything they knew and trusted, and bring them to a strange place with strange people and strange customs.

But most of all it was just a joy to see the return of

the Olivia he'd once known. Last night she'd fluctuated from reserved to distant to tense, and this morning she'd been polite and professional. Hell, even when she'd been angry with him there'd been an aloofness that he'd never seen in her before.

But this was the Olivia of old. The one who got way too close to her patients. Who'd spend time at the end of a very long intern shift playing games or reading books to the kids in her charge, or stopping in at the shop to buy a favourite snack or a goofy toy for a child in her care.

Their bosses had frowned upon it, and he had teased her about it endlessly, but it was what made Olivia so good at what she did—she wasn't just their doctor, she was their friend.

That had, of course, led to tears on occasions. Every death or negative outcome she'd taken to heart. She'd considered herself a partner in a patient's journey and she'd felt it deeply when things went wrong.

Many a time he'd been a shoulder for her to cry on.

And he'd been worried last night, when she'd looked at him with such reserve and distance, that the old Olivia was gone forever. That maybe he'd been responsible for killing her off.

He was glad to see he hadn't.

She might have developed a harder shell, but it was good to know that she still had her gooey centre. It wasn't a particularly smart trait, or conducive to longevity in the profession, but as someone who also became a little too invested in the lives of the people he operated on Ethan recognised, on a subliminal level, that Olivia Fairchild was a kindred spirit.

It was why he'd chosen the army and humanitarian work over the more lucrative field of cosmetic surgery, unlike his father.

Because people mattered.

Ethan took a steadying breath and walked into the room. 'This looks like fun,' he said.

Olivia started at the sound of his voice and Ama, who took her cues in this strange new world from Olivia, shrank into her mother's arms, quickly pulling the headscarf covering the right side of her face closer, patting it, checking its position.

'Ethan,' Olivia said, scrambling off the bed. 'I thought you weren't going to be here until after lunch.' She turned quickly to Ama and smiled at the girl, who was still a bundle of nerves. 'It's okay,' she assured her, and Dali, the interpreter, repeated the assurances to Ama and her mother in their own language. 'This is the doctor I was telling you about. Dr Ethan.'

Ethan smiled as Ama peeked out at him from her mother's shoulder. 'Very pleased to meet you, Ama,' he said, bowing slightly.

The girl's gaze darted to Olivia, and Olivia nodded and smiled again. She moved closer to Ethan, conscious of his tall breadth in her peripheral vision, trying to divorce herself from the sexual pull of him as she placed her hand on his forearm. 'We are old friends,' she said to Ama. 'We did our training together, here at this hospital.'

Ethan nodded. 'We sure did. Olivia used to tell us stories about having a pet kangaroo at home in Australia.'

That elicited a small smile from Ama and Olivia gave Ethan a grateful squeeze on the arm before she dropped her hand. Ethan's bedside manner had always been fantastic, but it had been a long time since she'd been familiar with his doctoring skills. A lot of surgeons tended not to be very good with their people skills.

Olivia introduced Ethan to Dali and to Ril, Ama's mother. He was at his charming best, but she was still

nervous as to how he was going to go forward with Ama.
Olivia knew he needed to see her face, but she also knew
he needed to approach it very carefully.

'You like chequers?' Ethan said to Ama.

She gave a slight nod after Dali had translated.

'Do you mind if I watch while you and Olivia play?'

Ama looked at her mother, as the interpreter translated, and then at Olivia, who smiled. Very slightly she
nodded her head.

'Excellent,' he said, smiling down at Ama.

Ethan drew up a chair opposite Dali on the same side
of the bed. It was the side of Ama's defect and he was
hoping that she'd become engrossed enough in the game
to drop the fabric so he could get a good look. He was
going to need a much closer examination before he operated, but for today he had to build some trust and he
was happy to stay hands-off.

Two hours later Ethan knew a lot more than any photo
could tell him about Ama's defect. Sure enough the girl
had forgotten about trying to shield her face from him
after about fifteen minutes, and he'd been able to get a
much more thorough feel for the mechanics of what he
was dealing with as the scarf slackened.

The extent of the destruction of her facial tissue and
the functional impairment of her mouth and jaw were
clinically challenging. He was going to need extensive
imaging, but he was sure it was going to involve maxilla
and palate losses as well.

It was shocking to look at. Ama essentially had a huge
hole in the right side of her face, exposing the inside of
her mouth, her jaw and nasal cavity. It was all the more

shocking because it was a perfectly treatable condition caught early enough.

He knew from Olivia's briefing and studying Ama's chart that her NOMA had started the way it always did—with a simple mouth ulcer when she'd been four years old. But poor nutrition and poor oral hygiene had led to the ulcer developing quickly into full-blown NOMA. Her cheek had begun to swell and over the course of a few days it had developed blackish furrows as the gangrene set in. It had festered over weeks, forming horrible scabs. When the scabs had finally fallen away, she'd had a gaping hole in her face.

But Ama was one of the lucky ones—she'd survived. Ninety per cent of sufferers—usually children—didn't.

Just looking at Ama as she played chequers with Olivia swamped Ethan with a sense of hopelessness. NOMA *was* the face of poverty in poor, underdeveloped countries. And young children living in such extreme conditions where malnutrition was rife were at the highest risk.

He glanced at Olivia. The jacket she'd worn this morning to the debrief had long been discarded and her pencil skirt had rucked up her thighs slightly as she sat on the bed with her legs tucked up to one side. Her long-sleeved blouse fell softly against her breasts and was rolled up to the elbows. The top three buttons, which had been primly fastened all the way to the collar this morning, were now undone and gaping occasionally to reveal flashes of cleavage.

She looked perfectly at home and one hundred per cent unaffected by Ama's facial deformity as she played chequers. As if Ama was just another of her patients. But he knew Olivia's gooey centre well, and he knew she would be distressed by what this little girl had been through and the suffering she must face on a daily basis.

She glanced at him then and it was confirmed. Her gaze was a melted puddle of warm chocolate and it was begging him for help. To *do* something. To *fix* it.

And in that moment he'd have fixed it with his own bare hands if it had been within his power.

Instead he smiled at her and nodded.

He stood and smiled down at Ama and her mother. 'I'm going to get some tests organised,' he said, nodding reassuringly. 'They'll do them after lunch and Olivia will be with you the whole time, right?' he said, glancing at Olivia who had scrambled off the bed and was standing next to him.

'Right,' Olivia said, also smiling and nodding at Ama. 'I'm just going outside with Ethan for a moment,' she said. 'I won't be long.' She narrowed her eyes and wagged her finger playfully at Ama. 'Don't you cheat.'

Ama grinned.

Olivia was conscious of Ethan's big silent presence by her side as they walked out together. It was just like the old days—walking side by side through the Lighthouse.

Complete with the same old awareness. That delicious little frisson.

Which was pointless and useless and completely inappropriate!

'Thank you,' she said as they stepped into the corridor. 'You were very good with her.'

Ethan brushed off the compliment with a shrug. 'I think she'll be happy with the result.'

Ama was always going to have scarring and obvious skin grafting all her life, but he was confident they could close her oral and nasal cavities so she could swallow and eat properly and look more or less like other girls of her age.

Olivia smiled at him. 'I know she will.'

Ethan sucked in a breath at her full-wattage smile. It was the first one she'd given him in over a decade and he'd forgotten how deadly they were. 'I'll get the X-rays and MRI organised for this afternoon,' he said briskly, trying to dispel the strange tightness in his throat. 'We'll also need a full battery of blood tests.'

She put her hand on his arm as she'd done earlier. 'Again. Thank you. Will you ring me when you have the results?'

The fact that he hadn't yet apologised to her weighed on his conscience as she looked at him as if he'd discovered a cure for cancer. But as they stepped aside to let an orderly with a wheelchair pass Ethan knew that a hospital corridor wasn't the best place for it either.

'How about we go to Drake's for dinner and we can discuss it further there? I can bring my laptop and the images on a stick.'

Olivia blinked. 'Drake's is still around?' They'd been regulars at the bar during their time at the Lighthouse.

Ethan nodded. 'Drake's has been an institution around here for over a hundred years. There'd be a riot at the clinic if they shut down!'

Olivia laughed. Considering how many of Drake's clientele were hospital staff, Ethan was probably right. She hesitated, though. Being back with Ethan amongst so many familiar memories probably wasn't a good thing. Maybe she should try and limit that?

'Come on,' he persisted. 'You want to see the scans, and we've both gotta eat, right?'

Olivia couldn't fault his logic. 'That's true.'

'I'm seeing clients until six tonight, so how about I meet you there about six-thirty?'

She nodded before she changed her mind. 'Okay.'

Ethan waved to Olivia from the booth table he'd claimed when she arrived ten minutes late. He watched her wend her way through the early evening crowd. The cool night air had put some pink into her cheeks, reminding him of strawberries and cream.

He shook his head as the thought lodged in his brain. *Strawberries and cream?* For crying out loud—he'd be writing freaking poetry next!

'Sorry I'm late,' she said as she stopped in front of their booth and stripped her duffle coat and jacket off, revealing the blouse from earlier. His gaze drifted to her cleavage and those three little buttons, still undone.

'No worries,' he said as he forced his eyes upwards. 'I took the liberty of ordering you a glass of wine. You still like to drink Shiraz when it's cold outside?' he asked, indicating the glass of wine.

Olivia blinked at the glass, surprised he'd remembered. She probably shouldn't be—he'd always been a details man. But still, it had been ten years, and given the *true* nature of their previous relationship she was surprised he'd even bothered remembering in the first place.

'Oh, yes—thanks…' she said, settling into the booth opposite, pushing the bitterness aside. It was a long time ago and she was over him and the games he'd played.

Olivia took a sip and noticed the open laptop. 'That the scan?' she asked.

Ethan nodded. 'Yep.'

'Well, show us, then,' she said, placing her glass back

on the table. 'I've been dying to know how fully the NOMA has invaded and the true extent of the damage.'

Ethan looked over the rim of his beer glass at Olivia. The scans were very interesting, and he could only imagine how someone as invested as Olivia would be desperate to pore over them, but first things first.

He shut the laptop lid and took a steadying breath. 'In a moment,' he said. 'There's something I have to say first.'

Olivia glanced at him. His voice was deadly serious and her heart pounded like a gong in her chest. *What the...?*

'I owe you an apology.'

She opened her mouth to say something but Ethan cut her off with a slice of his hand through the air.

'Please, Olivia, I need to get this out.'

He'd been rehearsing it all afternoon and he was grateful that she closed her mouth and let him get on with it.

'I'm very sorry for what happened ten years ago. For my reprehensible behaviour. For the way I used you and hurt you. For involving you in something that I shouldn't have. Basically, I'm sorry for being a total...jerk. There is absolutely no excuse for my behaviour. And I'm not expecting your forgiveness. I don't blame you if you hate me. I just want to be able to clear the air so we can work together. With the budding partnership between Fair Go and the clinic we're going to be seeing each other quite a bit, and I don't want it to be awkward between us. At least not because I haven't apologised, anyway.'

Ethan's heart was pounding when he'd finished and he grabbed his beer for a deep, long swallow as Olivia sat like a stunned mullet in her seat.

CHAPTER FOUR

OLIVIA BLINKED AT the most comprehensive apology she'd ever received. Her fingers tightened around the stem of her wineglass as she was sucked back to the emotional tumult of that time.

He *had* acted reprehensibly. He *had* been a jerk. He'd hurt her. He'd broken her heart. Just…taken it and stomped all over it.

She'd never loved anyone as she'd loved Ethan Hunter.

He'd certainly made her wary of ever letting anyone in again. In fact she'd never really let anyone in since. Sure, she'd dated. She hadn't become some born again virgin. But she'd never given her heart to anyone else. And that was all because of Ethan. Mostly because he'd damaged it so badly, but also because, deep down, she'd measured every other guy against him.

And none of them had measured up.

Yes, the irony that a jerk had been her yardstick was not lost on her. But even though his motives for being with her had been grubby, his treatment of her had always been exemplary.

They'd had so much fun—being with him had been the best time of her life.

Ethan couldn't bear it as the silence stretched between

them and she just kept staring at him. What was going on inside her head?

'Olivia?'

Olivia dragged herself back from the past, her gaze focusing on *this* Ethan. The thirty-five-year-old version. He was seeking forgiveness. Seemed to *need* it, if the intensity of his gaze was any kind of indication. Was it purely about Ama and their having to work together or was there a more personal absolution he was seeking?

'I don't hate you,' she said, picking up the glass of wine and taking a sip.

Even when her heart had been haemorrhaging she hadn't hated him.

'Hate implies strong emotion and the truth is I don't feel anything for you, Ethan. Not any more. It was ten years ago. We're different people, a lot has happened, and I've been over you for a long time. But you're right—we do need to work together, so clearing the air is good and I appreciate your *very* comprehensive apology. Thank you.'

Ethan knew he should feel relieved, and he did. But her admission that she felt nothing for him was startling.

Nothing?

Seeing her again had aroused a whole host of feelings. Nostalgia, apprehension, uncertainty. Hope. Worry.

Guilt.

And when she'd touched him last night—need, desire, lust.

It certainly hadn't been *nothing.* After a decade apart and their turbulent history how was *nothing* even possible?

But she was looking at him with such assuredness. The same old Liv, but different. The emotion and the connection he'd witnessed at the hospital earlier, that she'd been known for, were nowhere to be seen.

Well…if that was the way she wanted to play it. She was, after all, the wronged party.

'No,' he said, reaching out to cover her hand with his. 'Thank you.'

Olivia looked down at their joined hands. She'd used to dream that they'd be this amazing his-and-hers medical team—just like her parents. Living and loving and sharing. Growing old together. She'd been such a fool.

And she wouldn't go there again.

She pulled her hand away. 'Don't,' she said.

Ethan frowned at her abrupt withdrawal. 'I'm sorry… I didn't mean… That wasn't…'

'Accepting your apology does not mean that we're going to pick up where we left off, Ethan.'

Ethan quirked an eyebrow. *Whoa.* 'I didn't think it did.'

Olivia didn't care how egotistical she sounded. She needed to put it out there. Ethan was still as handsome as he'd always been. Probably even more so now life and experience had given his good looks a devastating depth.

Not to mention those fascinating shadows in his eyes.

'I know you,' she said. 'I know how it starts. So just don't…'

Ethan blinked. Did she think he was using his apology as a segue into some kind of pass? He knew he didn't exactly hold the moral high ground with her, but her insinuation was pretty damn insulting. 'Well, surely,' he said, withdrawing his hand and wrapping it around his beer, 'for someone who feels *nothing* that won't be an issue.'

Olivia was surprised at the bitterness of his tone. Had she annoyed him by her deliberate choice of words?

Too bad.

She'd been lying about the nothing, of course. Her body had been in a complete jumble for the past twenty-four hours. She *wished* she felt nothing. The way she had after the tears and the anger and the heavy sense of loss had all passed and she'd gone through life on autopilot. *Nothing* felt far preferable to the other stuff. It hurt less.

She'd gone there too, after her parents had been so cruelly snatched away. She'd craved the pain-free bubble of *nothing* back then. And had spent way too long inside it.

'Just putting my cards on the table. You and I aren't going to happen. Not going there. Not going there ever again. *Never, ever.*'

Ethan had an absurd urge to laugh at her emphatic denials. But he didn't think that would be appreciated. 'Are you trying to convince me or yourself?'

Olivia shivered as the low, gravelly note in his voice slid along the muscle fibres deep inside her belly. Their gazes locked for a brief moment and in those seconds she saw the golden flecks in his eyes flare to life as if a match had been struck.

And she felt a corresponding flare in those muscle fibres as they smouldered, then flickered to life.

'Just promise me it won't happen,' she said, desperate as heat spread through her belly. 'Say it out loud. I need to hear you say it.'

Ethan wanted to reach across the table and yank her sexy mouth right on to his. Okay, she didn't want anything to happen between them, and after he'd screwed up so badly last time he owed her that at least.

But, damn—it was all he *could* think about now.

And he despised himself a little bit more.

'I promise.' And he meant it. He raised his beer glass. 'Here's to *never, ever.*'

Olivia clinked her glass to his, feeling relieved and mollified. 'Good,' she said, taking a decent swallow of Shiraz. 'Now, show me the damn scan.'

They pored over the images for the next half-hour until their meals arrived. They talked about Ama's interesting facial anatomy, forever altered by the gangrenous infection. They talked about the staged repair and the different surgical approaches open to them. About anaesthetic options and the pros and cons of different types of grafting. About the potential complications.

During dinner they discussed timeframes and the team they'd need. They also touched on Ama's long-term recuperation and eventual follow-up. By the time their meals were finished they'd just about talked themselves through every aspect of Ama's care.

Olivia placed her cutlery on her empty plate and checked her watch—almost eight o'clock. If she left now she could be at the hospital before Ama went to sleep.

'You have somewhere to be?' Ethan asked as he drained the dregs of his second beer.

Olivia looked up. 'Sorry…yes… Do you mind? I've been reading some English books to Ama every night. She loves Dr Seuss, although I have no idea how much she understands.'

'I think Dr Seuss transcends language barriers,' Ethan said.

Olivia smiled. 'Yes, I think you might be right. It's just so good seeing her laugh, being a kid, you know?'

Ethan nodded. He'd been in a lot of places where children had to grow up too early. Where going to school and kicking a ball around weren't options. Where the innocence of childhood was usurped by the harsh realities of war and poverty.

His mind wandered to Aaliyah. To how she'd despaired about the children too.

So like Olivia in many ways.

'Yeah. I know.' He stood and grabbed his jacket, shrugging off the memory, refusing to compare. 'Come on, then, I'll walk with you.'

Olivia stood too. 'It's okay, it's not far. I'll be fine.'

'Liv,' Ethan said, 'I'm not going to let you walk the streets of London at night by yourself—especially when the Lighthouse is on my way home.'

Olivia's breath hitched as he reverted to the shortened version of her name. Did he remember when he'd started calling her that? Just after they'd first made love?

Had he even realised he'd done it?

'I've walked these streets many a time by myself, and way later than eight o'clock.' During her year in London she'd walked, bussed, tubed all over, at all hours of the day and night.

'Not when I was around, you didn't.'

And it was true. Ethan always had been the perfect gentleman. Well, except for that one time when he'd dragged her into an alley on their way to her place and had his wicked way with her because neither of them had been able to wait.

She huffed out a little breath, annoyed at her brain for dusting off that particular memory. 'Fine. Lead on.'

They were out on the street in under a minute. It was chilly after the warmth of the bar and Olivia buttoned up her duffle coat, pleased for its impenetrable warmth as they turned in the direction of the hospital. Unlike the thick wool of her tights, it *was* keeping out the cold. Her warm breath misted in the air and she set a brisk pace as icy fingers wrapped around her legs.

'So tell me about Fair Go,' Ethan said, leaning heavily on his stick to keep up with her.

Olivia stumbled a little at the unexpected question and felt his steadying hand briefly at her elbow before he removed it. 'I'm sure if you search for it online you'll find all you need to know.'

Ethan didn't care that she didn't want to talk. He needed to. Because all he could think about at the moment was a particularly steamy incident in an alley not far from here, and that wasn't conducive to a platonic walk.

'And why would I do that when I have the charity director at my disposal?'

Olivia shrugged. 'I started it a couple of years ago... I'd just finished my second stint with *Médecins Sans Frontières*—'

'Wait,' Ethan interrupted, placing a hand on her arm and urging her to stop. 'You worked for Doctors Without Borders?'

Olivia drew to a halt. 'Yes,' she said.

She remembered how Ethan had often talked about wanting to take his surgical skills into conflict zones. She had already been marinated in her parents' humanitarian works, and Ethan's fervour had easily infected Olivia. He'd hated—been embarrassed by—his father's lucrative cosmetic surgery clinic when there was so much suffering in the world, and had been determined to make a difference.

She'd hoped they'd do it together. Like her parents had. And then things had ended and she'd thrown herself instead into her parents' work in remote areas of Australia.

But when they'd been lost she'd needed something more. She'd needed to get away.

To be totally absorbed in something other than her own grief.

'What can I say...?' she said, pulling away. 'You inspired me.'

Ethan let her walk on for a bit, the belt on her royal blue coat pulled tight against the cold, emphasising her petite frame. He'd had no idea she'd followed through with their fledgling plans to join the famed international organisation. He'd assumed they'd fallen through when their relationship had ended.

He should have known—she'd always been strong-willed, her petite physicality belying the strength of her character.

'Where did you go?' he asked as he caught her up.

'Africa,' she said, keeping her gaze dead ahead. It was bad enough that he filled up her peripheral vision with all his sexy, haggard broadness.

'And that's where you got the idea for Fair Go?'

Olivia nodded. 'I saw a lot of kids with terrible conditions falling through the cracks because they weren't classed as *emergency* or *life-threatening*. But they did affect the quality of those kids' lives. And why should they have to suffer because they had the misfortune to be born into poverty? Why shouldn't they have the same expectations as kids in the western world?'

Ethan heard the husky note creep into Olivia's voice as they stopped at a red signal and waited to cross the road. 'I agree,' he murmured.

The Hunter Clinic was working with charities all over the world, trying to redress that balance.

'There are a lot of charity and aid organisations out

there that have a particular focus on certain regions or diseases or conditions or gender. And I get that—I do. There's just not enough charity dollars to go around.'

She turned to face him slightly.

'But it doesn't make it *fair*,' she said. 'I want to be able to give the children who fall through the cracks a chance at a better life too. They deserve a fair go too.'

Ethan nodded. Of course they did. So Olivia Fairchild was going to see to it. Good on her.

'I'm assuming your parents are the main benefactors?' he asked. 'They must be very proud of you.'

Like himself, Olivia came from a wealthy background. It had been one of the many things they'd had in common. Except Olivia's parents had turned their backs on lucrative practices and devoted their time to isolated communities as flying doctors.

Olivia was grateful that the light changed just then and they were able to cross the street as quick, hot tears welled in her eyes. She blinked them back. It wasn't Ethan's fault that he didn't know about her parents' tragic demise. She hadn't told him, and it was hardly as if their deaths had made international headlines.

She swallowed the lump in her throat. 'Yes. I got the money from my parents,' she said. 'And I have some good people I trust looking after the financial side of things.'

Ethan nodded. He knew how important it was to have trustworthy people involved in things like this. 'Well, Ama is very lucky to have someone looking out for her and willing to give *her* a fair go.'

Olivia suppressed a snort. He had no idea. Ama might be happy and bright now, but that was not how she'd been the day she'd first met the girl and her mother on a dirt street.

Ethan glanced at Olivia. Her brow was furrowed. 'You're frowning,' he said, shoving his hands in his pockets. 'Are you worried about Ama? Don't be. Everything's going to work out fine. Trust me.' He grinned as her frown continued. 'I'm a surgeon. And I'm *good.*'

Olivia looked up at him, his chiselled features filling her vision. His smile sucked the breath from her lungs. *Oh, he was good, all right.* They were probably a metre apart but he felt much closer—Ethan and his indomitable confidence had always managed to fill up the space between them.

She *was* worried about Ama. But not about the procedure or his ability to perform it. She had one hundred per cent faith in Ethan's capabilities and she knew Ama would be a very different girl by the time her multiple surgeries were done.

'I know,' she said. 'It's just…afterwards I'm worried about. When she heads back home again. You and I both know she's still not going to look like she did before NOMA, and that makes her…vulnerable.'

Ethan slowed a little. 'You're worried she'll still be ostracised?'

Olivia slowed too. 'Yes. And I'm worried that her uncle will still force her into marriage.'

Ethan blinked. 'What? She's *nine*, Olivia,' he snorted.

'That wasn't stopping him the day I found her.'

Ethan felt a cold fist close around his heart as Olivia's words sunk in. 'I beg your pardon?'

Olivia shuddered, thinking back to the horrible altercation she'd witnessed. She vividly recalled the taste of vomit in her mouth when the interpreter had finally sorted out what was happening.

'The day I found Ama her uncle, who was the head of

her household since Ama's father had died the year before, was giving her away to a man who looked at least forty. She was crying and clinging to her mother, and her mother was crying and begging her brother to reconsider.'

Another rush of emotion filled Olivia's chest. She shook her head against it, tried to push it back, but the memory was still so acute. How could anyone force a *nine*-year-old girl to *marry*? The thought was utterly vile.

Olivia wasn't naive—she knew awful stuff like that happened in places that the world didn't care to know about—but confronting it first-hand had been wrenching. Caught up in the rekindled horror of it, she turned to Ethan.

'You should have seen them,' she said. 'They were… clutching each other in the middle of this…street. It wasn't even a street, really—just this dirt…pathway. They were both so skinny and desperate and…wailing. Ril was wailing and holding on tight as this…disgusting old man with gnarled hands and three yellow teeth pulled at Ama's arm.'

Olivia halted, oblivious to the people walking behind her, caught up for a moment in the heat and utter despair that symbolised so much of Africa for her. It had been horrible. The consequences for Ama had she not intervened were still too much for her to bear.

Ethan gently took her elbow, moving her out of the path of other pedestrians who were bustling around them.

'It was terrible, Ethan,' she said, only vaguely aware that they were standing on the first step of the very grand entrance to one of the many clinics that populated the area. The Lighthouse was only two blocks away now.

'It's okay,' he murmured. The distress on Olivia's face squeezed his gut tight and he wanted to make it better.

Olivia shook her head. 'No, it's not,' she said.

'No,' he agreed. 'I'm sorry. It's not.'

She looked up at him. Muted light shone through the glass side panels of the grand doorway and fell over the planes and angles of his face. 'I couldn't leave her,' she said. 'I couldn't...'

Ethan nodded. 'Of course not.' His hand was still at her elbow and he gave it a gentle squeeze. 'What did you do?'

She shrugged helplessly. 'I gave him all the money I had on me and told him to get lost. And then I didn't let her out of my sight.'

Ethan smiled down at her. The light from inside lit her face and her eyes glittered with indignation. She looked fierce. Like a mother bear. He could just imagine her, furious and fearless, defending a child, standing up to a man in a hugely patriarchal society. Telling him to get lost.

'That was brave,' he murmured.

The compliment slid into all the places Olivia had forgotten about. Places that Ethan had always kept alive and humming. They were standing close on the step, closer than when they'd been walking, and she could smell the beer on his breath and the spice of his cologne.

'Dali called it stupid.'

Ethan chuckled. 'Well, it was probably a little of that as well.'

His low, sexy laugh was just the right timbre to produce an army of goose bumps and a funny little pull somewhere in the vicinity of her belly button. 'I was scared witless,' she admitted. 'But...what else could I do?'

Even now the thought of Ama's fate had Olivia just walked away was too distressing to think about.

Ethan shook his head. Her gaze was so raw and her question so earnest. 'You're a good woman, Olivia Fairchild. You always were.'

And he meant it. It buzzed through his veins, echoed around his head and filled up his chest. He was proud just to know her, to have a chance to know her again, and before he could stop himself he'd stepped in close, slid his hands onto her waist and dropped his mouth to hers.

And it felt good as she opened to him. Easy and sexy and right. Just as it always had. Her lips soft, her taste and her scent stirring old memories, urging him to go deeper, to pull her closer.

And he did.

Olivia temporarily lost her way as the taste and the touch and the smell of him wiped out all her common sense. It was as if she'd been transported back to their first kiss a decade ago. A kiss that had started out as a crazy, tired comfort thing, after a long, harrowing night shift together, and quickly became something quite different.

Something that had made absolute sense.

She slid her palms up the front of his jacket, smoothing and sculpting the muscles she knew lay beneath, clutching at his lapels as she tried to recapture that long-ago crazy/sane moment to take her away from the dirt and heat and poverty of Africa.

The tragedy of Ama and girls just like her.

The tragedy of her parents.

The tragedy of them.

Ethan groaned as Olivia deepened the kiss, opening her mouth wider, her tongue hot, dancing a wild tango with his.

'Liv…' His hands slid down to cup her bottom as his groin caught fire.

Olivia protested against his mouth as common sense wrenched her away from him.

One word.

Just one word and he'd yanked her back to reality.

'Damn it!' She pushed on his chest, stepping back, stepping out of his arms, sucking in air, breathing hard.

What was she doing? What the hell was she doing? Kissing Ethan again. Ethan, who was even more messed-up than he'd been a decade ago. Ethan with the shadows in his eyes.

Ethan whom she had to work with.

'You promised,' she hissed at him.

Ethan's head reeled from the abrupt disconnect. His head buzzed with the sexual high even as shame and guilt flooded over the top, smothering it very effectively.

He hadn't betrayed Aaliyah's memory in a year.

And here he was, kissing an ex-girlfriend on a public street like some grubby teenage boy.

Olivia glared at him, mad at herself but madder still at him. She'd be a bloody fool to get involved with Ethan Hunter again.

She pushed him hard in the chest. 'You promised *never, ever,*' she accused. 'We toasted it!'

'I'm…sorry,' he said, trying to pull himself together for Olivia as he battled his own demons. 'I…got carried away.'

Olivia knew the feeling.

But she was too angry to see his side right now. Too angry with herself. One touch of his lips and her resolve just disappeared.

She had to get away. She had to see Ama, for God's

sake. It was the whole reason they were out on the street together in the first place. Not for some public necking session.

'I have to get to the hospital,' she said tersely.

Ethan nodded. 'Of course. I'll see you in the morning,' he said, knowing the Lighthouse was close enough now for her to get there without his company.

But it didn't stop him watching her as she hurried away without a backward glance.

CHAPTER FIVE

BY THE TIME he entered his apartment ten minutes later Ethan had called himself every name under the sun. He'd kissed Olivia after expressly promising not to start anything. And even though she'd kissed him back it was unforgivable.

It seemed he was destined to behave unforgivably around Olivia.

And what about his vows to Aaliyah? Forgotten in one mad moment. What kind of a man did that make him?

Guilt chewed at his gut as he splashed whisky into a glass. Guilt over kissing Olivia. For *wanting* to kiss Olivia. For forgetting about the woman he'd loved—the woman he'd left behind in a Godforsaken part of the world, whom he'd promised he'd be back for.

Another broken promise.

Ethan's brain seethed and boiled like molten lava in a volcanic cauldron as he stared morosely into the depths of the amber liquid in the crystal tumbler. How could he have betrayed the memory of Aaliyah? Yes, she was gone. She was dead and he was alive. But it had only been a year.

One lousy year.

How could he have forgotten his promise to her the

day he'd asked her to marry him? That he would love her only, be faithful to her always?

And what about the silent pledge he'd taken the day he'd woken up in the hospital to the news of Aaliyah's death? That he was done with love. Done with relationships.

Done with emotion. With feeling. With passion.

Those things had died with Aaliyah and he'd literally felt the bands of cold steel wrapping around his heart as he'd sworn never to get involved again, never to love again. Hell, he'd welcomed them. They and the scars on his legs were his reminder that the women he loved tended to leave him.

His mother. Aaliyah.

He'd resigned himself to a solo life. Was he happy? No. But how could he be after what had happened to him? And where had happiness got him anyway? He was... content. He and Leo were in a good place, he was going to be an uncle soon, and he was doing good work. Important work that meant something to him.

And now Olivia had walked back into his life.

Ethan swirled the whisky in the glass. *Damn her.* Damn her for getting too close. Again. For making him remember what it felt like to be a man.

To want a woman. To want to feel her, taste her.

He hadn't needed that in his life. And he sure as hell hadn't missed it. The desire for physical affection had been non-existent.

Couldn't she just have stayed away? Left him with his ghosts and demons? He'd grown used to them for company and he'd been just fine here in his shell.

And yet with one look and that gut-wrenching shimmer of emotion in her expressive gaze he'd wanted more.

Just like that she'd wormed her way under his skin—
just like ten years ago, when he'd only been supposed
to be using her to throw in Leo's face but she'd come to
mean more.

Even now he couldn't get her out of his head. Couldn't
stop replaying their kiss over and over. He could still taste
her, feel the curve of her waist embedded into his palm.
Feel the tension in his belly and the tightness in his groin.

He shut his eyes, desperately trying to recall Aaliyah.
Her bronzed skin, her midnight eyes, her calming touch.
But all he saw was Olivia.

A surge of anger and frustration welled in his chest
as Ethan fought another battle. The glass felt good in his
hand—heavy. Reeking of money and class. As did the
whisky. And he wanted nothing more than to knock it
back. Have a second. A third. But Olivia was still in his
head. As was her taunt from last night. Packing a bigger
punch than it had already.

'I'm sure that's exactly how your father started out.'
Damn it!

He shook his head, letting the rage bubble up and out.
Swinging wildly around, he threw the heavy crystal glass
at the opposite wall. The crash was loud, as was the inevitable harsh shatter as shards of glass and liquid slid
down the wall.

Ethan stood for long moments just staring at the mess,
his heart pounding in his chest. He didn't feel any better.
He still wanted a drink. He still wanted Olivia.

Damn it!

He stalked to the nearby gym set-up that Lizzie had
organised for him back when she'd been his home visit
nurse. She'd been determined not to just dress his wounds
and check he was taking his medication but to bully him

into doing his physio so he could strengthen his legs and stop brooding inside the house.

Ethan sat at the leg press machine. And took out his frustrations on it.

Olivia knew it was her turn to apologise this morning. After tossing and turning through another sleepless night she knew she was as much to blame for the kiss as Ethan.

No, she hadn't made the first move. But she hadn't immediately pushed him away either. She hadn't told him no or slapped his face. In fact she'd opened her mouth wider, invited him in, stepped in nearer, put her hands on him. For God's sake, she'd grabbed hold of his lapels and dragged him closer!

She might not have asked for it but she'd definitely encouraged its continuation. So *she* would be the one saying sorry, as soon as he walked through Ama's door this morning.

Thankfully he didn't make her wait too long, showing up at the room at eight-thirty in a set of blue Theatre scrubs.

And for a moment Olivia lost her breath.

She'd forgotten how damn good the man looked in blue. It was such a girly, sky-blue too, and yet somehow he oozed masculinity. Maybe it was the way he filled them out. The breadth of his shoulders, the narrowness of his hips… Or maybe it was the rough-looking salt and pepper whiskers at his jaw.

He shot her a hesitant smile and a quick nod before he turned his attention to Ama and her mother. She was watching something loud and animated on the overhead television, scarf firmly in place. There was no way she could possibly follow the plot—it didn't even make a whole lot of sense in English—but she seemed utterly engrossed nonetheless, even bursting out laughing occasionally.

Olivia watched as he pulled up a chair by Ama's bed and sat down facing the television, also taking in the cartoon.

'What's that dog doing?' he asked Ama, and Dali dutifully interpreted.

They chatted back and forth through Dali about the television show, as if he had all the time in the world instead of a Theatre list that probably started in thirty minutes. When an ad break came he took advantage, and Olivia listened as he explained to Ril and Ama, in clear simple terms, what the tests had shown and how they were going to proceed. It was pretty much an abbreviated layman's version of what she and Ethan had talked about last night in the bar.

Before they'd ruined the evening by letting their past rear its ugly head.

'I'm putting a team together now and we're going to do the first surgery on Wednesday next week,' he said, and waited for Dali to translate. 'The second one probably three or four weeks later.'

Ril, who was sitting on the bed next to her daughter, nodded and asked a question.

'Ril would like to know if Olivia will be one of the surgeons,' Dali said.

'Absolutely,' Olivia piped up. 'Let him just try and stop me!'

There was a lightness to her tone, but Ethan heard the undercurrent loud and clear. Did she think he'd try and block her after what had happened between them last night? He knew how much Olivia wanted to be involved—he would never do that.

He turned to reassure her. 'Of course Olivia will be there,' he said, smiling at her before turning back to Ama. 'I seem to remember she was an excellent surgeon and I have every faith she's only got better.'

Olivia, who'd been nervous of Ethan's answer, relaxed. 'I have,' she said with a smile for Ama's benefit.

She'd assured Ama she would be there with her the whole time, and even if Ama was asleep and not aware of her being there Olivia intended to honour her promise.

The questions went back and forth for a while longer and Olivia was impressed that Ethan was prepared to sit and answer every one—not hurrying, just being thorough, which was an exercise in patience when the whole process took twice as long with an interpreter.

When the questions seemed exhausted Ethan looked at the little girl and hoped he'd won her trust enough for his next request. He was conscious of what Olivia had told him last night—conscious that Ama's trust of men, particularly those in authority, must be very shaky.

But he really did need to examine the operative area a little more closely. He'd been careful not to leap into that too early, but he wanted to do some computer modelling over the weekend so it was important to be able to assess the current state of the oral cavity, the health of the mucosa and gums—something an MRI couldn't tell him.

He turned back to face Olivia. He needed her help now. 'I was hoping that Ama might let me have a look inside her mouth now?' he said. He looked at Ama. 'What do you say?'

Olivia took her cue as Dali spoke to Ama. She moved to the opposite side of the bed from Ethan, perched herself on the mattress and took Ama's hand with an encouraging smile for both her and her mother.

'Ethan's going to use a special light, like I was telling you,' Olivia said, 'to have a look inside your mouth so he gets the operation right.'

Ama started to look apprehensive and Olivia gave her hand a squeeze. 'It's okay. It won't hurt, and Mum and I and Dali will all be right here with you.'

Ama looked from Ethan to Olivia then back again, in that solemn way of hers with her big brown eyes. That look always broke Olivia's heart. Ama had eyes that had already seen too much heartache and suffering for one so young.

'See?' Ethan said, pulling a small pen torch out of his pocket and flicking it on, placing it in Ama's hand for her to get a feel for its harmlessness.

Ama looked down at the instrument. She turned it over in her hands and then turned it so the light shone directly in her eyes. She squinted and pulled the light away. She turned to look at her mother, then back at the torch, shining it in her face again. This time she squinted and gave a nervous giggle.

'This is what you'll look like,' Ethan said, taking the torch out of her hand, opening his mouth, placing the lit end against his cheek and then closing it again. His cheek glowed an eerie red and he waggled his eyebrows at her.

This time Ama laughed. As did Ril and Dali. Olivia's throat tightened at his ease with Ama, and for a moment she was transported back to the old days, when the torch-in-the-mouth thing had been one of their favourite games to play with the kids at the Lighthouse.

His bedside manner had always been second to none.

'See?' he said pulling it out, then wiping it over with an antiseptic wipe. 'It doesn't hurt at all.'

Ama pointed to Olivia and said something in her own language. Neither of them needed an interpreter to understand her meaning.

Olivia huffed out an exaggerated sigh, rolling her eyes as she held out her hand for the torch. 'If you insist,' she griped good-naturedly.

Ethan winked at her as he placed it in her open palm. His fingers brushed lightly against her and a little spark of heat ran up her arm. She glanced at him and wondered if he felt it too, but he was smiling at Ama.

Olivia flicked the torch on and popped it in her mouth. The acrid taste of antiseptic was bitter on her tongue but she ignored it, pushing the light into the mucosa of her cheek and closing her mouth around her. Her cheek dutifully glowed red and Ama laughed louder this time.

'Dali. Dali,' Ama said in her guttural accent, and Ethan laughed knowing there was going to be no quick way of doing this as both Dali and then Ril were also subjected to the trick, the torch being cleaned in between.

Consequently, when it came to the examination Ama submitted happily. Ethan was pleased to note that the oral mucosa looked relatively healthy and he took a few seconds to assess and familiarise himself with some of the landmarks he'd noted in the MRI.

But then the fun part came, when Olivia found a mirror and they spent ages flashing the light on and off inside Ama's unaffected cheek. Every time her cheek glowed red she laughed as if it was the funniest thing she'd ever seen. It was sobering to think that, sadly, in Ama's case it probably was.

'Okay, okay.' Ethan smiled. 'I've got to go but I'll be

in to see you...' he waggled his fingers at Ama and the girl giggled '...every day.'

Ama reluctantly surrendered the torch, holding it out to him, but Ethan shook his head. 'It's a gift for you. Enjoy.'

Ama's eyes widened as Dali relayed the message and Olivia felt a wave of goose bumps march over her skin as Ama hugged it to her chest.

Olivia followed Ethan out through the door as he departed. She wanted to get the apology off her chest straight away. A bit like he had last night.

'Thanks so much for that,' she said as they both watched Ama from the doorway, smiling as she flicked the light on and off and shone it on everything. 'Anyone would think you just gave her the sun.'

Ethan shrugged. Olivia was wearing a pair of snug jeans again today, and a fine woollen sweater that fell nicely against all the flesh beneath. It wasn't helping his resolve to keep his hands off. He'd thought about his re-kindling sexual attraction to her a lot last night, and probably limiting their alone time together was wise.

'Plenty more where that came from,' he said.

Olivia nodded. She knew that drug reps alone kept doctors endlessly supplied with such knick-knacks. 'Well, you made her day.'

Hell, given where Ama came from, he'd probably made her entire life! She doubted the girl had ever received too many gifts of such a magical calibre.

Ethan cleared his throat as they both watched Ama continue to play with her new toy. 'About last night—'

'Oh, no,' Olivia said, quickly cutting him off as she turned to face him. 'Let me.'

Ethan eyed her warily. 'Let you what?'

'Apologise,' she said.

Ethan folded his arms. 'Liv...*I* was the one who kissed *you*, remember? After I'd just promised I wouldn't go there.'

Olivia shook her head, trying to shrug off the way he said her name and how it heated all the old familiar places. Unfortunately the way the fabric of his scrubs pulled around his shoulders and biceps didn't help with the heat problem.

With her heart already fluttering, and her cheeks already flushed at the delicate subject matter, heat was the last thing she needed.

The memory of the kiss sat between them like a big guilty secret, and she'd rather crawl over an acre of glass than have to discuss the way they'd erred last night—like a couple of kids sent to the naughty corner by their parents to talk over their behaviour. She was a grown woman and it was an embarrassing discussion to be having.

But she couldn't let him take the fall for it either.

She needed to own her part in it.

'Yes, I know,' she said. 'But I didn't exactly stop you. I was as much to blame. Probably even more so if you consider my *never, ever* carry-on at the bar. I should have pulled back straight away. I should have...slapped your face,' she said, trying to make a joke to ease the awkwardness of the situation.

Much to her relief, Ethan eked out a half-smile. 'It's fine,' he dismissed. 'How about we both take equal responsibility and agree that being alone together is probably something we should avoid?'

Olivia let out a breath she hadn't been aware she was holding. She returned his half-smile with one of her own. 'That sounds like a good plan.'

Ethan nodded. 'Okay, then.'

'So… I take it I'm still okay to scrub in on some of your surgeries, though? I'm really keen to do what I can while I'm here, and now Ama and her mother are settled they're probably sick of the sight of me.'

Ethan grunted. He doubted that. Ama and Ril's faces lit up like a city skyline whenever Olivia entered the room. Given what she'd done for them, he didn't blame them.

He remembered a time when she'd made him light up too. When he'd felt more for her than he'd ever anticipated.

But he had to admit to being curious about how Olivia had developed as a surgeon. And they could always do with more help.

The clinic's humanitarian programme ran on a tight budget—it had to when billing charities was involved. Having a third surgeon in an op was sometimes necessary—as it would be with Ama and other big cases—but usually not.

It was certainly not a luxury they could afford.

And Ethan didn't believe in wasting money—too much of that went on in charity circles as it was. The Hunter Clinic was opulent and wealthy, and the programme was lucky to have the free use of it and all its associated services—including the pro bono time of any of its surgeons.

But the charities involved paid for all the extra stuff that the Hunter Clinic couldn't provide—including any outside surgeons—and Ethan didn't believe in running up their bills like that unless it was completely necessary.

But Olivia was free. And a free surgeon was a gift he wasn't about to knock back.

'I have a big burn contracture release tomorrow. I could use an extra pair of hands with it.'

A little trill of excitement ran through Olivia at the thought of being back at the table again. It had been a few months since she'd picked up a scalpel and she'd missed it.

'Sounds great.'

Ethan nodded. 'I'll be able to introduce you to some of the team that will be working on Ama's op next week as well. Kara Stephens is helping me out tomorrow. She's a junior surgeon—another Aussie who's a real go-getter and has wanted in on Ama's surgery ever since she heard the first whisper about it. And Jock McNamara is the anaesthetist on my list in the morning and I want him for Ama's surgery. He does a lot of anaesthetics for the facio-maxillary ops and really knows his stuff.'

'It'll be great to meet some of the team,' Olivia enthused.

'Good,' Ethan said. 'List starts at eight-thirty at Princess Catherine's.'

'I'll be there.'

There was an awkward moment when they both paused, waiting for the other to say something and then both realising simultaneously that the silence was growing.

'Right, then…' Ethan said. 'See you tomorrow, Liv.'

Olivia felt the emotional whammy again of what had been a very intimate connection between them. Liv had been the name he'd called her behind closed doors. The name he'd chanted in her ear as he moved deep inside her. The named he'd cried out as he came.

She couldn't be Olivia Fairchild if he reverted to Liv all the time. Olivia was a capable paediatric reconstructive surgeon. Olivia was a compassionate doctor who had put her skills and her heart on the line in Africa. Olivia was the director of Fair Go.

Liv was Ethan's friend. His confidante. His lover.

Liv was the woman who knew the depths of his pain and anger.

Liv was the woman who had loved him.

'Ethan.'

Her quiet call stopped him in his tracks and Ethan turned to face her. She hadn't moved from the spot in the hallway where he'd left her. 'Yeah?'

'Please don't call me Liv…' she murmured.

He was tall and dark and handsome and she wanted to run straight into his arms. Being here, in this hospital with him, stirred too many memories. Unfortunately none of the bad ones. None of the things that had broken her.

'It's too…hard…it's too…familiar.'

Ethan nodded slowly. A heat unfurled inside his gut and travelled south. He hadn't even realised he'd said it. The name—the endearment—had come from somewhere way back in the past. From memories rich with laughter. And spoiled by the callousness of his youth.

If he was going to cling to Aaliyah, to the welcome familiarity of his grief and guilt, then Liv *could not* exist.

'I'm sorry,' he said, rubbing the back of his neck. 'I didn't realise…'

Olivia nodded. 'I know.'

Ethan regarded her for a moment or two. 'I don't want this any more than you do, Olivia. I can't.'

She could tell from the dullness of his eyes that he was telling the truth. That his body was betraying him as much as hers was betraying her.

Remember that, stupid foolish heart—he doesn't want this. Neither do you.

'I know,' she said again.

They didn't say anything for a moment, and then Ethan said, 'See you in the morning,' and turned away.

Olivia watched him go, acutely aware of the contrast between a happy Ama to one side of her and the stoic set of Ethan's receding back to the other.

His choice of words intrigued her. *I can't.* 'Can't' implied more than a conflict of choice. 'Can't' implied something out of his control. Had he meant that? Or had it just been a slip of the tongue?

And if he had meant it, what exactly *did* it mean? Did it mean that he actually wasn't able to? Wasn't capable? Emotionally? Or had something happened to him physically on one of his tours? Maybe his injuries were more extensive than just his legs?

Could 'can't' mean that he wasn't able to perform sexually any more?

And why on earth would he think any woman worth her salt would give a damn about it?

Olivia gave herself a mental shake. What did it matter? She wasn't here to get involved in his life. To commiserate about any long-term effects of his war wounds or to kiss him better.

She was here for Fair Go. She was here for Ama.

And Ama was just one of the many kids she planned to bring to the UK for surgery. Several had already benefited, thanks to Fair Go and the generosity of the Hunter Clinic.

And that was what she needed to concentrate on.

Running a charity was a big freaking deal, involving serious money and financial responsibility, and she couldn't afford to drop the ball because some guy from a million years ago—who had, *by the way*, ground her heart into the dirt—looked at her with shadows in his eyes and called her Liv.

Ethan Hunter was a big boy who'd had his chance with her and blown it.

She wasn't his *Liv* any longer.

CHAPTER SIX

ETHAN WAS SCRUBBING up at the sinks in the scrub room the next morning when Olivia bustled through the door.

'God, I'm so sorry,' she said, barely acknowledging him as she pulled up beside him and reached over to remove a mask out of the nearby box, tying it on in record time. 'I underestimated the time it would take me to get here, and the streets…'

She shook her head as she wrenched off her opal ring and shoved it into the pocket of her scrub trousers.

'I don't remember them being this busy ten years ago.'

She opened a sterile packaged scrub brush and flicked on the taps, wetting her arms from the fingertips to the elbows. She turned to look at him as her right hand attacked the nails on her left hand with the brush. She knew the scrub routine back to front and could do it blindfolded.

'When did it get so busy?'

Ethan blinked. Olivia had always been a chatter. Her ability to fill up a silence or engage a total stranger with her intelligent observations on any subject was one of the things that had drawn them together in the first place. She'd always blamed it on her single child status, remarking that chatter had been her defence against loneliness.

Certainly their stilted, awkward conversations over the past few days had been well out of character.

But she was in fine form this morning.

'It's London,' he said, smiling beneath his mask. 'The streets have always been busy.'

Olivia conceded his point as she turned back to inspect her work. A large window in front of them gave them direct visual access to the Theatre and Olivia noted that the patient was already on the table and was being draped.

She switched the scrubbing brush to the other hand. 'Well, it's a far cry from Africa, that's for sure.'

'True. Not a lot of giraffes in London,' he remarked dryly.

To his surprise she laughed. A laugh that came straight from her soul and ruffled the edges of a hundred different memories. Having her beside him like this again, in scrubs and a mask, her expressive eyes dominating—it was as if they'd never been apart.

It felt comfortable. Like old times.

As it could have always been if he hadn't been so angry and vengeful, so damn determined to lash out.

So he did the only thing he could do to distract himself from futile games of *what if.* He started talking about the case.

'Our patient today, Daleel, is a twenty-eight-year-old Somali man who suffered burns five years ago to over forty per cent of his body. Frankly, how he survived I'll never know, because he only had the most rudimentary of medical care.'

Olivia nodded. It was something she'd seen over and over during her time on the front line and working with various aid organisations in conjunction with Fair Go. Men, women and children who survived against all the odds—like Ama—but who were left permanently and hideously disfigured with absolutely no hope of leading a normal life.

'His right arm is fused to his torso, his right hand is badly contracted, and the severe scarring of his face and neck have led to a contracture that's pulling his whole head into a downward flexion.'

Ethan, at the end of his scrub, held his bent soapy arms out in front of him, hands up, elbows down, and dunked them under the spray tap. He watched as the water sluiced from his fingertips down his arms and dripped suds off his elbows into the sink.

'Think you can handle it?' he asked. The soap was all gone now, and he flicked the tap off with an elbow, then held his arms over the sink a little longer, waiting for his elbows to stop dripping.

'I think so,' Olivia said.

He glanced at her and for a moment their gazes met over the top of their masks and the sense of familiarity returned. Ethan straightened. 'See you in there,' he murmured.

Olivia was conscious of him in her peripheral vision, his sterile arms out in front of him, using his back to push open the swing doors. Then through the glass window she saw him emerge into the Theatre, hands still up and out from his body, striding towards the scrub nurse who was already masked, gowned and gloved and holding out a sterile towel for him to dry his hands.

She continued her scrub, watching Ethan go through the familiar routine of gowning and gloving. She'd never known a man to look so damn good in what was essentially a no-frills dress. The plainness of it just seemed to emphasise the broadness of his chest and the length of his frame. Some women got off on men who wore Armani suits. But she much preferred a man in Theatre garb.

And *damn* if Ethan didn't rock a pair of scrubs.

He chose that moment to glance up from checking the tray of instruments that had been placed near the patient, and their gazes locked as he looked directly at her. Olivia blushed, grateful for the camouflage of the mask. Had he been able to read her less than professional thoughts?

Was he remembering her fetish for a man in scrubs?

Did he remember that time she'd admitted to the erotic dream she'd had about him, involving an examination table, some handcuffs, a pair of scrubs and the very inventive use of a scalpel for removing said scrubs from his otherwise naked body?

They never did get round to enacting that particular fantasy…

The other surgeon—what had Ethan said her name was?—leaned in obliviously, asking him a question, and Olivia quickly dropped her gaze.

What the hell was she doing?

She was here to help give a man his life back. Not to have completely inappropriate, unprofessional and *graphic* thoughts about a highly respected surgeon.

Olivia dunked her arms under the water, watching the soapy residue disappear down the drain, and hoped to God her erotic thoughts would follow.

Ethan entered Drake's the following Tuesday night with a spring in his step—not exactly easy to do with his limp. Tomorrow was Ama's operation and everyone at the clinic was psyched about it. The team was in place and raring to go, Kara could talk about nothing else, and he knew Olivia—although she was more subdued than the excitable junior surgeon—was also eager to get underway.

He knew how close she was to Ama's case.

Maybe she shouldn't be. Maybe it wasn't the professional thing to do. If something went wrong… But some cases just got to you—he knew that.

And nothing was going to go wrong.

The surgery tomorrow was complex, but they all knew what they were doing. And Ama's new life was just around the corner.

'Ethan!'

Ethan looked up to find Leo waving at him across the reasonably full bar. He was at a table with Olivia, Kara, and her fiancé, Declan Underwood—a plastic surgeon who also worked at the Hunter Clinic.

He made his way over to the group. He was supposed to be meeting Leo here for an after-work drink and a general catch-up. There'd been a fairly full surgical list the past five days and Ethan had only been into 200 Harley Street for a few hours on the weekend, to do the computer modelling for Ama's surgery.

But Leo liked to have a meeting once a week to discuss general Hunter Clinic business and Ethan had bunked out on the past two. He appreciated his brother wanting him involved now he was an active partner in the business, but Ethan had no doubt that Leo could and did run the clinic perfectly well without his input.

Hell, the man had dragged the sinking clinic out of the scandalous mire it had sunk into after their father's headline-grabbing drunken scene and subsequent death. He'd worked day and night not only to put it back into the red but into the hearts, minds and chequebooks of every A-lister in Europe and beyond.

The only decisions Ethan wanted to be consulted over were those that involved the humanitarian programme. Then he was all ears.

'I hope you don't mind us crashing your party.' Declan grinned, half standing and holding out his hand as Ethan pulled up at the table.

The man's Irish brogue seemed more pronounced tonight, and Ethan assumed it was due to the almost empty pint of Guinness sitting in front of him.

Ethan shook Declan's hand, nodding a welcome at Kara and Olivia, who returned it with a cool smile. 'Not at all. Leo just wants to chew my ear about figures anyway. You've saved me.'

'Hmph,' Leo said good-naturedly. 'As if that would get me anywhere.'

There was general laughter as Ethan sat in the spare chair. It was between Leo and Kara and opposite Olivia, and he glanced at her as he sat down.

'Looking forward to tomorrow, Kara?' Ethan asked.

'You betcha.' She grinned.

Hearing her Aussie accent, Ethan realised the Brits were outnumbered at their table tonight.

'I don't think I'll be able to sleep. I feel like a kid on Christmas Eve.'

Leo laughed. 'That's what I like to see,' he said. 'Enthusiasm.'

Ethan smiled as he glanced at Declan, who was looking at Kara as if she was a tasty little Christmas treat waiting under the tree and he was Santa. Ethan felt a pang in the centre of his chest. He'd known that feeling. He'd *loved* that feeling.

The feeling that you never wanted to be anywhere

else, with anyone else, just wrapped up in a bubble, just the two of you.

'Don't worry, darlin',' Declan said, exaggerating his accent. 'I have just the thing for insomnia.'

Everyone laughed, but still Ethan felt the pang throb a little harder. Leo had the same look as Declan and they were both clearly very contented men. Satisfaction oozed from their pores.

He glanced at Olivia again. Had she ever had anyone special? He realised he'd been so busy these past five days keeping his distance that he hadn't bothered to find out much about her life that didn't relate to work. There was ten years lost between them—maybe the wariness he saw in her expression now was to do with a man?

Conversation naturally flowed onto the case for a while, and it was good seeing Olivia relax again. She was in her comfort zone and the old spark came back. The passion and the fervour she obviously had for what she was doing sent a little buzz around the group and it was hard not to get a little high off it.

Ethan knew that feeling well. He'd got the same kick from the work he'd done these past ten years. Sure, initially when he'd first joined the army it had been the pressure and the danger he'd thrived on. The risks of front line work had made him feel more alive than he'd ever felt back home, with a drunken father and a stiflingly over-protective brother.

But he'd learned the hard way the downside of front line work. That you couldn't save everyone and that innocent people too often paid the price.

Leo had thought Ethan had joined up to spite him, and in some ways he had. But he'd caught the bug—

the thrill of transforming somebody's life. And that was why he did it.

'You're sticking around for the hospital ball?' Kara asked Olivia, dragging Ethan back into the conversation.

Olivia shrugged. 'Oh… I…I didn't know there *was* a ball.'

Kara frowned at Ethan and Leo. 'What's the matter with you two?' She tsked with a smile on her face. 'You're really not very good hosts, are you?' She looked back at Olivia. 'It's the Lighthouse Ball—it's the highlight of the year. It's on in two weeks. *Everyone* goes.'

Olivia stilled with what she hoped was a smile on her face. Oh. *That* ball. Memories swamped her. A fabulous red dress. An exquisite set of matching lingerie. She'd been to *that* ball a decade ago—on Ethan's arm.

'You will come, right?' Kara said. 'Don't make me be the only Aussie there.'

Olivia shook her head. *Been there, done that.* 'I don't know how Ama will be by then.'

'No, Kara's right. It was remiss of me not to mention it,' Leo interjected. 'You should definitely go.' He looked at his watch. 'You should get Ethan to take you. You remember how much Ethan loves to dance, right?'

Leo grinned at his brother, and if Olivia hadn't been so annoyed at Leo she'd have been heartened by how much closer the two men were now, compared to their toxic relationship a decade ago.

'Funny,' Ethan said to his brother. 'You're hysterical.' He looked at Kara. 'I don't dance,' he said.

Olivia nearly snorted at the understatement. He could manage a waltz/shuffle and that was about it. He much preferred to mingle and be charming and to look dashing in a tux and turn every woman's head.

The last thing she wanted to do was go to a damn hospital ball with Ethan.

Ethan in a tux.

She'd had a fantasy about him in a tux involving a scalpel as well.

'Sorry—got to go, guys,' Leo said. 'Lizzie can barely stay up past nine these days.'

'And to think,' Ethan quipped, 'he used to party with princesses till dawn.'

Leo grinned at his brother. 'Totally overrated,' he said, then departed quickly.

Olivia saw Leo's departure as a perfect opportunity to effect her own, but before she could get her goodbyes out Kara was back onto the subject of the ball.

'Are you sure about the ball?'

Olivia nodded quickly. 'I don't have a dress anyway,' she said, hoping that another woman would understand such a conundrum even if it was hogwash.

'Oh, good grief, that's not a problem,' Kara dismissed with a wave of her hand. 'Have you *been* to Oxford Street? With your figure we could find you something in a jiffy. Plenty of places in London to shop for ballgowns. Actually, I even know this great place where you can get some Australian designer stuff.' She paused for a second and narrowed her eyes as she stared at a spot just above Olivia's head. 'You're from Sydney, you said, right?'

Olivia nodded. 'Ah…yes. But my parents were flying doctors so I mainly grew up in the Outback. Not many ball frocks out there,' she said, trying to make a joke.

But Kara was clearly enthused about the idea.

Ethan could see Olivia's lack of enthusiasm a mile away. 'Kara,' he said with mock sternness, 'you're badgering.'

'Sorry,' Kara said, but her grin didn't look very contrite to Ethan and his spine prickled—in a bad way—when she looked speculatively from him to Olivia and then back to him again.

'You just never know, right?' Kara said. 'The craziest things happen at balls,' she murmured, and she slid her hand onto Declan's and they smiled at each other.

Ethan suppressed an eye-roll. He'd already heard from Lizzie about how Declan and Kara had set tongues wagging at the Princess Catherine's ball because of a saucy stolen kiss. Why was it that people in love thought everyone else should be in love too?

They were worse than reformed smokers.

'Come on, love,' Declan said, standing. 'I think it's time we go before you're whipping out the tape measure. And you've got a big day tomorrow.'

Olivia was relieved when Kara took the bait. With them gone she'd have the perfect excuse to be gone too.

'Well, let me know if you change your mind about the ball,' Kara said as she shrugged into the jacket that had been slung around the back of her chair. 'Or the dress shopping.'

Olivia nodded, relieved that talk of the ball would soon be over. 'I will,' she said with absolutely no intention of following through.

The couple turned to leave, but at the last moment Kara stopped and turned back mid-collar-straightening.

'Oh, God,' she said, looking at Olivia. 'I just realised… *Olivia Fairchild*… Your parents were the flying doctors that were killed a few years back in that terrible bushfire, right? I'm so, *so* sorry…that was such a tragedy.'

Olivia blinked as a hot spike of pain cleaved her right through the middle. So far away from home and five years down the track she hadn't expected anyone to get the association, and even though Kara was an Australian it was completely unexpected.

'Oh…yes,' she said, forcing the words out around a throat that felt as if it was collapsing in on itself. 'Thank you,' she stammered. 'It was a…shock.'

'It was awful,' Kara agreed. 'Just awful.'

'Yes,' Olivia said, nodding automatically, her head roaring with a tsunami of suppressed emotions.

Ethan looked from Olivia to Kara and then back to Olivia again. Olivia looked like she'd been struck, her peaches and cream complexion almost waxy now it was so pale. He frowned. *What the hell…?*

Olivia's parents were dead?

Ethan glanced at Kara, who clearly realised she'd spoken without thinking and didn't know what to say next. She looked at him, lost, and then shrugged, a panicked *help me* look on her face.

He nodded his head at her. 'It's okay,' he murmured. 'Go home and get some sleep. We need your A Game tomorrow.'

Declan nodded at Ethan over Kara's head. 'C'mon, darlin',' he said, and Ethan was relieved when the couple quietly withdrew.

Olivia sat staring at the glass of wine she'd barely touched and Ethan wished he knew where—*how*—to start. Olivia had been so close to her parents. He remembered what a foreign concept that had been for him and how they'd both struggled to understand the dynamics of each other's families when they were used to different upbringings.

'I'm sorry,' he said.

Olivia shut her eyes. She didn't want to hear his

condolences. She didn't want to share such a terrible gut-wrenching part of her life with him. It was too… *significant*—something lovers shared—and at the moment she could barely breathe from the sense of loss weighing down her lungs and settling in her bones.

She'd forgotten how much it hurt. How much she missed them. Being overseas, being away from it all, it was easy to forget it had happened. Easy to pretend she'd go home and they'd be waiting for her.

Sometimes the stark reality that she'd *never* see them again—which played like a soft chant in the back of her head anyway—roared out at her and hit her like a blast wave to the chest.

'It's fine,' she said, her thumb rubbing absently over the cool fiery opal in her ring, remembering the day her parents had given it to her.

'It's *not* fine, Olivia,' he dismissed tersely, then frowned at her, trying to understand. 'Why didn't you tell me?'

Olivia glared at him. 'Oh, you're annoyed because I didn't *tell* you?'

Ethan sighed. 'No, Olivia. No. I just…I wish I'd known.'

Olivia clung to the slow burn of anger in her chest. It was easier to be mad at him than at two dead people, than at an act of nature that had killed fifteen others that day.

She sucked in a breath as a wave of pain crested in her throat. 'You could have *asked*.'

Ethan blinked at the low accusation in her voice, trying to think back to the conversations they'd had since she'd returned. It was true they hadn't really talked about anything personal—hadn't he only just thought that tonight?—but…

'You said your parents had given you the money for your charity.'

Olivia snorted. 'They did,' she said bitterly. 'In their will.'

Ethan was silenced by the depth of her grief. He'd lost his father a decade ago, his mother ten years before that. And despite finding out about his mother's infidelities after her death, and his contentious relationship with his father—or maybe because of them—his loss and grief had been compounded.

But that had been a long time ago.

Aaliyah's death, on the other hand, had not. And, whether Olivia knew it or not, he understood the rawness of grief. He also understood now that *this* was what her reserve was about.

She was hurting.

She was grieving.

'What happened?'

Olivia felt a hot tear well in her eye and fall down her cheek and she brushed it savagely away. She knew he wasn't going to let it go—best to just get it out there as quickly and painlessly as possible.

'Five years ago…a massive bushfire…it swept through Outback Queensland. We were all there. Mum and Dad were pitching in with the authorities, out driving a rusty old four-wheel drive somebody had commandeered for them, helping to evacuate all the outlying properties, giving first aid, et cetera.'

Olivia could still smell the thick smoke blanketing the air, feel the sting of her eyes and the irritation of her airways, hear the almighty roar of the fire as the wind swept it along at a horrifying pace.

She picked up her glass of wine and stared at the fluid level as she absently swirled it. 'I was in the rural hospital, dealing with the casualties as they came in. I'd wanted to go with them but they said I was needed at the hospital. And I was, of course.'

Another tear fell and she dashed it away too.

'I'd just finished organising an evac for my third escharotomy of the day when the police came. The wind had changed...they'd been cut off...surrounded...'

Olivia shut her eyes, trying to block out the demons that had dogged her for so long.

'I dreamt about how they must have died for months afterwards. How *terrifying* it must have been. How terrified *they* must have been... I know they would have been thinking about me...worried about me...'

Ethan sucked in a slow ragged breath. He could tell her the smoke would have rendered them unconscious first. He could say it would have been quick—so quick. Those fires moved at a horrendous pace.

But she knew all that. She was a doctor. Except when she shut her eyes.

Then she was a daughter.

'I'm sorry,' he said again.

Olivia opened her eyes. She didn't want him to be sorry. She wanted them back. But Ethan couldn't do that. Nobody could. And she was damned if she was going to vent her spleen to a guy with shadows in his eyes who had rebutted every effort she'd ever made to get him to open up to her.

She shrugged, clawing back her composure. Reaching for the reserve she wore now like an armour against the things that threatened to cut her off at the knees.

'I guess that goes in the *bad luck* basket, huh?' she said, her voice still husky with emotion as she raised her glass in his direction.

Ethan's gut clenched at her faux flippancy. 'Olivia... Don't... You can talk to me...'

'No, Ethan. You and I...we *don't* talk.'

'Maybe we should.'

Olivia snorted. *Like that's going to be a two-way street.* 'Okay, then,' she said, her voice heavy with sarcasm. 'You go first. Tell me, Ethan...' she leaned in closer to him '...what happened to you while you were in the military that made you even more screwed up than before you left?'

Ethan shook his head. 'Olivia—'

'Bum-*bah*!' Olivia hoped that sounded like a game show buzzer. 'Wrong answer.'

'Olivia.'

She ignored the note of warning in his voice. She was riding a surge of anger that she thought had been resolved a long time ago.

Obviously not.

'Oh, no, Ethan. *No, no, no.* You don't get to hear *my* sob story and then just stay all stoic and clammed up. You don't get to have all of *me* and keep all of *you* to yourself like last time. That got me burned bad.' Olivia gave an hysterical little laugh at the irony of her word-choice.

Burned.

'You want me to talk to you? Well, that's a two-way street and we both know...' she paused and threw back her wine in three long swallows '...that's not the way you play the game.'

Then she placed the glass on the table and stood. 'I'm going to check in on Ama before I go home. I'll see you tomorrow.'

Ethan stood too. 'I'll come with you.'

Olivia glared at him. 'No,' she said. 'You will *not*.'

CHAPTER SEVEN

ETHAN STOOD IN the corridor just outside Theatre Nine the next morning, watching Kara and Olivia scrubbing up through the glass window in the swing door that led into the scrub room from outside.

They were chatting—not that he could hear what they were talking about. He wondered if it was about Kara's revelation last night. About Olivia's parents. Or maybe about the ball again.

Although he doubted it. If he knew Olivia it would be about Ama, about the surgery. She liked to go over the game plan as she scrubbed. He'd forgotten that about her, but working with her on his recent surgeries had brought it all back. She'd want to be focused on today, on the surgery. She'd be going over and over the plan in her head.

The last thing she'd want was to be in a bad emotional place. She was going to need all her concentration for today and she wouldn't want to have any distractions.

He admired that about her, and working side by side with her these past few days he'd been impressed by what a first-class surgeon Olivia had become. He'd always known she would be—she'd been impressive a decade ago, when her surgical skills were in their infancy—but he was pleased to see that his predictions had come to fruition.

Pleased that he'd had the opportunity to see her in action again.

Pleased that nothing seemed to faze her.

Her front line experience had shaped her into a mighty fine surgical all-rounder, as it had him, and no matter what surgery he was doing she'd scrubbed up and joined the fray, Ama's schedule permitting.

'Excuse me,' someone said from behind him.

'Sorry,' Ethan said, stepping aside as one of the scout nurses carrying a sterile tray of instruments pushed open the swing door and entered.

Ethan felt his muscles ache slightly at the sudden movement. After Olivia's news he hadn't got much sleep last night, and he'd hit his home gym around midnight, hoping to cause enough exhaustion to cure his insomnia.

It had been that or the bottle.

He'd been working on his physio every night since he'd begun spending his days working side by side with Olivia. He'd been suffering from a restless energy when he got home each night and it helped.

He'd always welcomed the quiet of his apartment, but it seemed oppressively so after a day with chatty Olivia. She seemed always to be in his head, and alone with his own thoughts—thoughts that usually involved Aaliyah—he'd been desperate for something to drive her out.

So he'd been exercising. Hard to think of anything other than pain when he had to push himself through. Still, he was already feeling the benefits in the strength and stamina of his quads.

And it was a much better option than what he would have chosen not that long ago—liquid denial.

Kara and Olivia finished up their scrub and headed for the Theatre, arms out in front of them. Ethan quickly pushed open the door and stepped into the scrub room.

'Olivia,' he said, and both women stopped and turned around to look at him. 'Can I have a moment, please?'

Olivia stifled a sigh. She'd thought it would be too much to ask to just get through this day without some kind of post-mortem over last night. Kara had already apologised three times during their scrub.

Olivia turned her head and smiled at Kara. 'Go on ahead,' she assured the junior surgeon. 'I won't be a moment.' When Kara was gone she turned back to Ethan. 'I don't want to do this now, okay?'

Ethan nodded. He'd suspected as much, but he didn't want her going in there with any kind of unspoken stuff between them—they needed to be a team. Best to clear the air now. 'I just wanted to—'

'I know what you "just wanted to," Ethan,' Olivia interrupted impatiently. 'But not now, okay? Can we just get through Ama's surgery? Can today please just be about Ama?'

Ethan shoved his hands on his hips. Clearly she was in the zone and *did not* want to be yanked out of it. 'Okay.'

Olivia nodded. 'Good. See you in there.'

The surgery was involved. They began with removing the protruding teeth that had been warped and buckled by disease, then they cut away all the old scar tissue. Bone was harvested from Ama's hip to replace the missing section of maxilla and plated and screwed into place. Then a thick piece of skin was removed from her arm and used as a graft to cover the gaping hole in Ama's face.

Such a large piece of grafted skin required a blood

supply, so they used a small artery and vein from the neck to provide this. Lastly they were able to rebuild the mouth, using what Ama already had and reshaping it to the way it had been before she'd fallen victim to NOMA.

Five hours later Ama's face was finally whole again. The surgery was done and she was on her way to the High Dependency ward, where she would be closely monitored for the first twenty-four to forty-eight hours.

'That was incredible,' Kara said, her eyes sparkling as she degowned and tossed it in the bin.

Olivia nodded, relieved and very happy with the result. 'Yes.' She grinned. 'It was.'

Ama's face would always be different from everyone else's. Her cheek would look a different colour and consistency to the rest of her face, with an obvious demarcation around the graft, and her lip line would always be just a little bit deviated.

But she'd be able to swallow, eat, chew and talk properly. And, more important, she'd have a more socially acceptable face. She could go to school. She could make friends and play with the other children.

She could be a *child*.

'You guys were awesome,' Kara continued as she and Olivia headed to the change-room.

Olivia wanted to get up to the HDU as soon as possible—Ethan had gone with Ama.

'You didn't even really talk to each other but you both seemed to know what each other needed. It was like you'd been operating together for years!'

Olivia had been so engrossed, so in the zone, she hadn't really noticed. But, looking back, she realised Kara was right. She and Ethan had worked together like a well-oiled machine. But then they'd always been very compatible—in *every* way.

'It's just practice,' Olivia dismissed. 'You do this for long enough and it becomes second nature.'

'Well, you call it what you want,' Kara said as she pushed open the change-room doors. 'I call it synchronicity. And it was pure magic to be a part of it, so thank you.'

Olivia didn't know what to say to that. Everything had gone very smoothly—no rabbits out of hats required. 'You weren't so shabby yourself,' she said.

Kara blushed and looked at Olivia, her face glowing from the compliment. 'Really?'

Olivia laughed. 'Yes, really. Now, stop fishing for compliments and let me get dressed so I can go see our patient.'

Kara gave a cheeky salute. 'Yes, ma'am.'

But she left Olivia in peace and Olivia was dressed and heading to the HDU in ten minutes.

The first couple of hours post-op Ama was pretty out of it. Olivia, Ril and Dali sat quietly by her side, talking occasionally but essentially maintaining a silent vigil. Ethan checked on her a couple of times, with Olivia assuring him that she'd page him when Ama woke or if any complications occurred.

It was in the third hour that things started to go wrong. Ama awoke in a great deal of distress and pain. She was clearly frightened and thrashing around the bed, pulling off her oxygen mask, calling for her mother.

She was given a bolus of painkiller intravenously and her morphine infusion rate was increased. It worked temporarily, but she became more agitated and distressed again over the next hour—crying and at one stage, before

Olivia leapt up to stop her, clawing at her face, blindly beating at it.

Ril was becoming distressed by her daughter's condition as more pain relief was given, the infusion increased further and some sedation added in on top. And both Ethan and Olivia were worried she would damage some of the reconstructive work they'd done with all her thrashing around. They were particularly worried about the viability of the graft. They checked beneath the dressings, but whilst it was oozing there didn't seem to be any excessive blood and the graft still appeared intact.

Nonetheless neither of them wanted to take a chance, and Ethan ordered arm restraints which wouldn't allow Ama to bend her elbows. A nurse wrapped them around her arms and Olivia felt better knowing that Ama wouldn't be able to reach her face any more if she remained unsettled.

When next Ama woke she was talking gibberish.

'I don't know what she's saying,' Dali said to Olivia, and there was fear in her eyes for her young charge. 'They're just words that don't make sense and then she talks crazy stuff about spiders on the ceiling.'

Both Ethan and Olivia looked at each other. 'It's the morphine,' she said.

Ethan nodded. Of course he should have thought about the possibility of Ama reacting badly to the morphine— the spider hallucinations were a clear sign of that—but the language barrier made everything so much harder.

'We'll change it to another opioid.'

A different infusion was started, and a bolus of it given, but Ama was in a significant state so was started on an infusion of a drug to keep her sedated, which finally managed to settle her completely after another half an hour.

By early evening she was sleeping heavily, although responding briskly to stimuli, and everyone was exhausted. Ril had fallen asleep in a hard plastic chair beside the bed, holding her daughter's hand, her head on the mattress at an awkward angle. Dali was also dozing.

Olivia looked at the monitor. All Ama's vitals looked in good shape and the oxygen mask was firmly in situ. The figures blurred before her eyes as she felt her eyelids drooping. It had been a long and exhausting day. After the smoothness and success of the surgery none of them had planned for this kind of stormy post-op course, although things like reactions to opioids weren't uncommon.

It had been draining. And awful to see such genuine distress and terror in Ama, who was usually so bright and sunny despite all the reasons for her not to be.

Add to that the tumultuous events of last night that had led to very little sleep, and Olivia was finding it hard to keep her eyes open. The room was so quiet and the steady *beep, beep, beep* of Ama's monitor was strangely hypnotic. Despite the hard plastic of the chair she was sitting in, it was bliss to shut her eyes. Just for a moment.

Olivia wasn't sure how long had elapsed when the trilling of Ama's monitor woke her. She was disorientated at first as she looked at her watch—almost 10:00 p.m. Her back and neck protested as she squinted to focus on the monitor and identify the alarm in the darkened cubicle.

The oxygen saturations had fallen into the eighties. She also noted there was some tachycardia, and Ama's blood pressure was a little on the lower end—but it had been anyway, since the sedation had begun.

Olivia stood up and went over to Ama's bedside. The oxygen mask had slipped off. She went to place it back on but her hand stilled when she noticed the pallor of Ama's lips and the gurgly sound of her breathing.

'Ama?' Olivia said, reaching for the girl's hand to give it a squeeze. The hand was cold and clammy. Olivia frowned as she placed the mask and called, 'Ama!' again, giving her the firm shake of the shoulder to which she'd responded briskly just over an hour ago—nothing.

Ama's nurse arrived. 'The ICU registrar is a couple of minutes away,' she said. 'Ama's been getting increasingly tachycardic the past fifteen minutes, and her sats are starting to drift, so I want him to check her out.'

Olivia nodded, pleased the nurse was on the ball. 'Can you page Ethan too, please?' she asked.

The nurse went off to do Olivia's bidding. Ama's saturations had barely improved, so Olivia turned the oxygen up.

'Ama?' Olivia said, applying a painful stimulus to the girl's sternum, using the knuckle of her index finger and rubbing hard. Still nothing. Olivia reached over and paused the infusion of sedation, which she noticed had been decreased significantly since she'd drifted off to sleep.

Ama should be responding.

The tone of the saturation trace dropped and Olivia glanced up to see they were only eighty per cent now, despite the extra oxygen.

She also noticed the respiratory trace was slowing right down. A very bad feeling welled in the pit of Olivia's stomach as she flicked on the light and assessed the movement of Ama's chest. It seemed to be barely moving at all.

Ril woke up, blinking as bright light flooded the cubicle. So did Dali. They were speaking to each other in their language, and Dali was asking Olivia questions, but Olivia was back at the ABCs of medicine.

Airway.

That was always priority number one in medicine, and Olivia was beginning to think Ama's was compromised. The gurgling she could hear was a concern, and Olivia leaned down, her ear to Ama's mouth, as she used her index finger to give Ama some jaw-thrust. Blood welled out of Ama's mouth and Ril looked horrified, pointing and crying and talking rapidly to Dali.

'What is wrong, Olivia?' Dali asked. 'What is wrong?'

Now Olivia was certain Ama was bleeding, but had no idea to what extent.

The feeling of foreboding increased.

'I'm not sure,' she said, reaching for the Yankaeur sucker jammed under the pillow, 'but Ethan's coming and we're going to take good care of her—do you hear? Please take Ril along to the parents' lounge and I'll come and explain everything as soon as I can.'

Olivia had a feeling this was going to get messy. And the thick blood slurping noisily into the tubing from Ama's mouth confirmed it.

Olivia was aware on a peripheral level that Dali and Ril were having a heated exchange but she shut it out. Ama was her concern.

Come on, little girl. Don't do this.

Do not do this.

'Dali,' Olivia said as the blood kept coming and Ama remained unresponsive, despite the very potent stimulus of a large plastic sucker hitting the back of her throat, 'get her out of here *now*!'

The nurse returned as Dali led a wailing Ril away. 'She needs a twenty mil per kilo bolus of whatever you have running,' Olivia said. 'And get some of her blood from the fridge.'

They'd cross-matched six units for surgery but had only used one during the operation because the blood loss had been so minimal.

Ama was making up for it now.

Two more nurses entered the cubicle area as the registrar arrived. And Ethan about thirty seconds later. She'd never been more pleased to see him. She was aware that she was quaking on the inside but her training was taking over. Later she'd probably throw up, but right now she was in the zone.

'She's bleeding,' Olivia said, not looking up from Ama.

Ethan felt the same surge of adrenaline he always felt when an emergency evolved. He used it to his advantage to focus himself, to hone his intuition.

'Let me look,' he said, striding over to where Olivia stood. 'Pull the bed out.'

One of the nurses released the brakes on the bed and moved the bed down so Ethan could slip in at the head of the bed. He angled an unresponsive Ama's jaw open and could see nothing for the blood.

The alarm behind him trilled again as Ama's heart-rate started to fall.

'Get the resus trolley,' Olivia told one of the nurses as she watched the alarming drop of Ama's heart-rate on the monitor.

'I need a laryngoscope,' Ethan said.

Within seconds they had both. Ethan tried to look

down her throat using the laryngoscope but his view was totally obscured by congealed blood. He pulled out.

'Get me a trache kit,' he said.

One of the nurses scurried off to get one as the other two busied themselves drawing up resus drugs. When Ama's heart-rate hit fifty Olivia started external compressions and asked for atropine to be administered.

The nurse who had fetched the sterile trache pack opened it for Ethan and opened a sterile pair of gloves for him.

'Page Jock,' Ethan said as he plunged his left hand into the left glove, preparing to do a down-and-dirty emergency tracheostomy. Securing Ama's airway was vital. 'Tell him to get his butt back in here. As soon as this trache is done we're going back to Theatre to get the bleeder.'

The nurse squirted Betadine over Ama's throat as someone else laid the back of the bed flat, then raised the bed higher to accommodate Ethan's six-foot-two frame. The atropine had done the trick and Olivia had stopped compressions for the moment. She also asked for a pair of gloves, knowing that Ethan might need a hand, leaving the registrar to monitor everything else.

Ethan made a quick incision into Ama's throat, his plan being to secure the airway by the insertion of a tracheostomy tube and get to Theatre ASAP. But when he opened the neck there was so much blood it took him longer than he'd hoped, and he and Olivia literally had to scoop out the congealed blood to identify where he was going to stick the tube, all the while conscious of the screaming alarms and the ticking of the clock.

He finally placed it after two fraught minutes, and it was a relief when Olivia squeezed in the first breath via the bloodied Laerdel bag and there was immediate chest movement and improvement of the oxygen saturations.

Ethan glanced at Olivia. She had blood on her clothes but her look of sheer relief was exactly the way he felt—as if they were back in the field and they'd executed a major save together. For a moment he'd never felt closer to her.

'Let's get her to Theatre,' Ethan said.

Olivia nodded. 'I'll have a quick chat to Ril and join you.'

By midnight Ama was out of Theatre and had been taken to ICU this time. They'd identified the bleeding—most probably caused by Ama's initial thrashing around—and she was going to be kept ventilated and sedated overnight and hopefully have the tracheostomy removed in the next few days.

By the time they'd seen her settled in the unit and spoken to Ril and Dali it was close to one in the morning and Olivia was dead on her feet.

'C'mon,' Ethan said to her as she hovered around Ama's bedside. 'Home for you.'

Olivia shook her head. 'I want to stay.'

'You're exhausted,' Ethan said, pulling her to one side. 'You need a break.'

'I'll catch some sleep in a spare office somewhere later,' she dismissed.

'Olivia.'

'I'm fine,' she reiterated, looking over his shoulder at the monitor.

'Olivia…' Ethan said again.

Olivia dragged her gaze off the monitor to look at him—his tone had brooked no argument. *I'm fine.'*

'You are not fine,' he said. 'You are running on empty. You need to get out of those clothes, which have blood on them. You need a shower. When did you last eat? You need food. And you need to sleep—a *decent* sleep on a decent bed, not some awful office examination couch.'

Olivia looked down at her clothes, realising for the first time that they had a patch of dried blood which looked as if someone had dabbed her with a large paint-brush dipped in red paint. Ethan was still in his Theatre garb.

'I'll get some scrubs,' she murmured.

'Liv...' Ethan shut his eyes, cursing to himself as the word he shouldn't use slipped out. *Damn it.* He was too tired to care. 'She's stable now, and sedated. At least go home, have a shower, change your clothes, have something to eat.'

Olivia didn't even register that he'd called her Liv. At least not on a conscious level. Having a shower and something to eat sounded like bliss—she was starving. All she'd had to eat since breakfast was a packet of crisps from the vending machine. But she was staying a twenty-minute cab-ride away from the hospital and she wanted to be close while Ama was still in ICU.

Olivia shook her head. 'I can't,' she said.

Now the drama was over she was starting to feel a little shaky. She'd been so terrified they were going to lose Ama at one stage.

'I talked them into this. I told them we could fix her. I promised Ril she would be okay...'

'Olivia, she *is* okay.' Ethan put his hands on her shoulders and waited until she was looking at him. 'Listen to me,' he said. 'This isn't your fault. This isn't my fault. Bad things happen sometimes and post-op haemorrhage is always a risk—you know that. And there was a combination of factors here. But she's fine. You did good.'

Olivia saw the flecks in his eyes flare to life with the conviction of his words. She knew he was right, but a combination of adrenaline overload and low blood sugar were clouding her judgement. '*We* did good,' she said.

Ethan smiled. 'Yes. We did. Now…' He squeezed her shoulders gently before dropping his hands. 'Go home.'

Olivia shook her head. 'I'll just go to the Theatre change-rooms and have a shower. I'll get something from a vending machine.'

'No, Olivia. You need to get out of here for a while. Clear your head. Get some distance. This case has taken up your whole life for weeks and weeks now.'

'I'll be too far away,' Olivia said, starting to get a little fed up with his persistence now. 'I don't want to go too far.'

Ethan stared in exasperation at her. 'Fine—come to my place, then. I'm heading there and it's only a five-minute walk. You can shower, change, eat and then if you really insist on coming back I'll walk you.'

Olivia chewed her lip, undecided. She desperately wanted a shower and something to eat. Sleep she could live without. It was tempting. 'You're still in the same place?'

Ethan nodded. 'Yep. And Il Conte is still just down the road, and I have a takeaway container of their best spaghetti in my fridge.'

Olivia felt the flutter of her belly as a hundred great memories rushed out at her. How many more would be waiting for her at Ethan's place? She doubted there was a square inch, certainly not a single horizontal surface, they hadn't made love on.

But it *was* the perfect solution—a place close by for a quick pit stop and then off again.

In and out—no time for the memories to cling and hold.

And there was a time she would have killed for Il Conte's spaghetti.

'Okay,' she conceded. 'But I'm coming straight back.'

'Of course.'

'Let me just check on her one last time.'

'Okay. I'll get out of these and grab some fresh scrubs for you and meet you at the entrance in ten?'

Olivia nodded. And hoped to God she hadn't just made the biggest mistake of her life.

CHAPTER EIGHT

It took Olivia ten seconds to realise she *had* just made the biggest mistake of her life. Stepping into Ethan's apartment was like entering a time warp where nothing had changed. The upstairs apartment of the old Victorian terrace was exactly the same and it was as if they were coming home from work together as they so often had, chatting about their day, anticipating a long session of lovemaking.

Even just standing inside the entranceway old memories floated around her, dizzying her with their potency.

She really needed to eat something.

Hell, she could recall a time when they'd fallen to the floor right where she was standing, so eager to get their hands on each other they hadn't been able to wait. The door had barely clicked shut, for crying out loud.

And…oh, God…the door—Ethan had pressed her against that once and brought her to a screaming orgasm in under a minute.

'Go have a shower,' Ethan said, brushing past her. 'I'll heat up the spaghetti.'

Olivia doubted her legs would carry her that far, afflicted as they were suddenly by a bad case of the shakes. Her head spun a little. 'Actually, do you mind if I eat first?' she asked. 'I think my blood sugar is bottoming out.'

Ethan turned. She looked pale and washed out. She swayed a little as he watched and he took a step towards her.

'Don't,' Olivia said as she reached for the nearby wall for stability.

If he touched her she'd melt right into him, and God alone knew where *that* would lead in this place where she'd spent about seventy-five per cent of her time in his bed. Or on his couch, or his table, or against his walls or his door...

'You look like you're about to fall over.'

'I won't,' she assured him, waving him back. 'As long as you feed me pronto.'

Ethan nodded. 'On it.'

Olivia followed him into the gleaming steel and granite kitchen at a slower pace and sat down at the big central black marble counter that hosted four bar stools. Her stomach grumbled and her hands shook as she placed them against the cool surface.

Somewhere else they'd made love.

Her brain shut down that memory before it even got out of the starting gate and she concentrated instead on Ethan, clattering around, putting a bowl in the microwave, piling another one with spaghetti, waiting to put it in. She noted the familiar Il Conte container, and how amazing the food smelled even cold, and she almost told him not to bother to heat it up she was *that* hungry.

'You want a coffee?' he asked. 'Probably be handy if you're going back.'

Olivia nodded. It was going to be a long night, and she was going to need all the help she could get. He turned to a fancy coffee machine that *was* new, placed a pod in the top and a cup under the spout and pressed a button. The microwave beeped and he pulled the bowl out, giving the spaghetti a stir with a fork. She watched steam rise off it and her mouth watered.

He went to return it to the microwave. 'It'll be fine like that,' she assured him.

Ethan frowned. 'It's not heated all the way through. It's only just warm, really.'

Olivia shook her head. 'Don't care,' she dismissed, holding her hand out for the bowl. 'Near enough is good enough.'

He chuckled as he passed it over. Her belly growled again and she wasn't entirely sure it was anything to do with food. His sexy stubble was even more so as he stood in his kitchen, serving her spaghetti and coffee as he'd done a hundred times before.

Olivia demolished the bowl in two minutes flat. She didn't lift her head, she didn't converse, she didn't notice when Ethan placed her coffee on the bench. She just ate, barely registering the aroma of basil and the sweet taste of fresh tomatoes.

When she was done she looked up, finding Ethan's amused gaze. 'Sorry.' She grimaced.

Ethan laughed as he cradled his coffee cup in his hand. 'I always did enjoy watching you eat,' he murmured.

Olivia remembered all the other things he'd enjoyed watching her do. Laughing at a joke, slipping on a pair of high heels, shaving her legs.

Getting undressed.

Coming as if the world was going to end.

Her stomach growled again, and for damn sure this time it was *nothing* to do with food. He was watching her mouth and, nervous, she licked her lips, finding some stray sauce and removing it with her tongue.

Ethan almost groaned out loud as her nervous licking still managed to miss a bit of sauce. Once upon a time, standing here in his kitchen, with her sitting opposite in that chair, he'd have just leaned across the bench and licked it off. And the desire to do so now thrummed through his veins like a siren call.

He'd *never* wanted to taste her this badly.

Instead, exercising the control he'd perfected in the military, he ground his feet into the marble tiles, reached for a serviette from the counter behind him and passed it to her. 'You missed some.'

Olivia took it and dabbed at her mouth, excruciatingly aware of his intent stare. Of the way he'd paused, coffee cup halfway to his mouth, and just looked at her, taking in every movement. She knew that stare. It was stirring memories and stroking along her pelvic floor, causing the muscles there to preen in an utterly Pavlovian response.

Shower.

Shower, shower, shower.

Her brain was doing its best to drag her back from the edge. To remember how he'd used her, hurt her. She'd *made love* to him a hundred times in this apartment, fallen *in love* with him, and all the while he'd just been *having sex* with the woman his brother had wanted.

'I think you're done,' he murmured.

His voice blew over her, soft as feathers. Caressing her skin and tickling a memory of the past out of hiding.

The time he'd tied her wrists and ankles to his bed and spent hours taunting her, touching her spread-eagled body, tracing his tongue all over her. Backing off every time she built, refusing to let her come, gorging himself instead on his tactile feast and driving her mad with lust until finally he'd relented.

'I think you're done,' he'd said.

And when he'd put his mouth to her she'd had an orgasm that had gone on for an eternity.

Her blood flowed slow and thick through her veins as the memory played out. It pounded through her head and washed through her ears. Her breath felt like syrup in her lungs. Her abdominals had turned to goo, like flaming marshmallow, melting her to the chair.

Olivia saw Ethan's knuckles whiten as his grip on the cup increased. Was he thinking about it too?

Ethan wasn't sure which memory Olivia was caught up in, but she needed to stop now if she wanted to leave here unmolested. Today had been intense—very intense. It would be bad to do something neither of them should just because they were reacting to the pressure of the day and a bunch of memories.

Even if they *were* really great memories.

She was looking at him as if she wanted to hurdle the bench and drag him to the ground. But she wouldn't thank him for it in the morning. He knew her too well.

'Olivia.'

Olivia blinked at the warning in his voice, the memory receding as awareness of the present filtered back in. A well of loathing rose in her chest and burned hard and high in her throat.

Ama.

She had to get back to Ama.

Olivia reached for her coffee cup and took a fortifying sip, too embarrassed even to look at Ethan. She took another and, as it wasn't too hot, blew on it and took a bigger swig. Then she placed it on the bench and stood.

'I'll have a shower and get out of your hair,' she said, still not looking at him.

Ethan didn't want her to go. Actually…he did. He wasn't sure he could last a night with her here in his apartment again and not just give in to what his body wanted. He'd felt dead inside for a year, but ten days back in her company and certain parts of him were very definitely coming back to life.

But she needed to sleep and that was more important. Maybe he could convince her after her shower?

'Scrubs on the back of the couch,' he said.

She didn't answer, didn't even acknowledge his words, just grabbed the scrubs on her way past and disappeared from his sight.

It was bliss under the hard, hot spray and Olivia wanted nothing more than to slide down the wall, hug her legs to her chest and nod off under the steady cleansing heat, until the tension in her muscles had eased and the squall inside her stomach had settled.

But she was afraid to shut her eyes. The whole shower smelled like him, smelled so male—soap and shampoo and aftershave—and she was reminded of how often they'd made love in here too.

A lot.

And Olivia knew the second she allowed her eyelids to shut she'd be there again, her back to the tiles, Ethan buried inside her, groaning *'Liv…'* into her ear as he came.

Or going down on her, looking totally in control despite his position of supplication on his knees in front of her, his hands holding onto the backs of her thighs, holding her up, as her world splintered around her.

Olivia ruthlessly shut off the taps as steam built in the

cubicle, heating the mix of male aromas to a wild liquid cloud, painting her body, marinating her in memories. Drifting her into dangerous territory.

Ama.

She had to get back to Ama.

She towelled off quickly, throwing on her scrubs *sans* underwear—she'd sling her duffle coat on over the top and no one would ever know she was going commando. The aroma of fresh laundry and Ethan's spicy soap surrounded her, reminding her of clean sheets and him, and she yawned, her eyes gritty despite the shower.

She turned off the heating lamps and stepped out of the en-suite bathroom into Ethan's darkened bedroom. A shaft of light from the hallway penetrated into the gloom, lifting the visibility level a little. Enough to make out objects like his big soft bed—still in the same spot—beckoning her like a fluffy freaking cloud, with its blizzard-white duvet and matching pillows—something that had always seemed so out of place in this overwhelmingly male bachelor pad.

It whispered to her. *Rest. Sleep. Dream.*

And the thought of getting just a couple of hours' shut-eye was utterly, utterly seductive. But she dragged herself back from it, padding through his bedroom in her bare feet, the thick rug luxurious on her soles as she headed for her bag and coat and a brisk walk in the cold London night.

Then an object sitting on a shelf near the door caught her eye and she stopped. It looked eerily familiar, and despite her brain telling her she needed to get the hell out of his room she was drawn to it by the insistent tug of ancient strings.

Its shape became more distinct as she neared and Olivia's heart beat a solid tattoo in her chest as she reached for it. The bronze was cool as she wrapped her fingers around the miniature figurine, but the spark of memory soon heated the object, sending warm tingles up her arm.

He'd kept it.

Stupid tears needled at her eyeballs as she looked down at the nude young woman reclined in a pensive pose and she blinked them back. He probably didn't realise he still had it. Which fitted right in with the rest of the decade-old stuff in this apartment that time forgot.

He'd bought it at Portobello Road market because he'd said the woman's secretive smile reminded him of her just after she came. As if she'd touched the stars and knew all their secrets. That had been two days before she'd found out about his dastardly behaviour. Two blissful days when she'd floated on cloud nine because this exquisite, dainty, perfectly detailed piece of eighteenth-century sculpture had reminded him of her and the magic they made together.

Olivia ran her thumb over that Mona Lisa smile, remembering that day. It was probably the last time she'd ever been deep-down-in-her-bones happy.

'She's still beautiful, isn't she?'

Olivia's thumb stilled. She was aware suddenly of the heat of him at her back. Of his overwhelming presence enveloping her in a cloud of old memories and new desires. It fluttered in her pulse and prickled along her nerve-endings, peaking her nipples and fanning along the bare skin of her nape—her hair was up to avoid getting wet.

'Yes,' Olivia said, placing her gently back.

Ethan wanted to bury his nose in the exposed stretch of skin in front of him, right where her nape joined her shoulder, which the square neckline of the scrub shirt left beautifully exposed. He wanted to sniff her there. Inhale deeply. Smell his soap on her.

Remember back to the days when his smell used to be stamped all over her.

He itched to pull her hair out of its rough and ready up-do. The wet ends of the tendrils that had half fallen down taunted him more.

'I *am* sorry about what I did, Olivia.'

Olivia shut her eyes briefly. 'I know,' she said.

'It wasn't all mercenary. I did care for you too.'

'I know,' she repeated, then she took a deep steady breath and opened her eyes as she turned to face him.

But he was close, so much closer than she'd realised, and his scent was intoxicating, and his neck was just there, its fat pulse bordering the hard ridge of his trachea, pounding right in front of her even through the thick growth of stubble.

She shut her eyes again as a wave of longing rolled through her, sweet and hot, like sherbet and crack cocaine.

She remembered how hard he'd fought for Ama tonight. How he'd taken over, securing her airway, fighting for the little girl's life. Scooping out blood, never giving up as he'd raced against the clock and the hazards of prolonged hypoxia.

'Thank you,' she said, her voice husky even to her own ears, thick and lumpy in her throat. 'For Ama.'

Ethan shook his head. She was looking at him with *those* eyes. Eyes frank with professional admiration and personal gratitude. A truly deadly combination. *Oh, crap.*

'Liv...'

And that was it for Olivia. A husky entreaty so masculine but so needy. She couldn't fight it any more. She couldn't deny it any more. She and Ethan had been on a slow trajectory towards each other since coming back in contact again and tonight he had sling-shotted into her orbit in a most spectacular fashion.

She was lost. Heat and lust clouded her senses until her head was full of him. Every breath filled her up a little bit more until she was drowning in the essence of him. The intelligence of what she was about to do was so far out of her reach her brain might as well have been residing in Australia.

'Oh, God...Ethan,' she muttered as she slid her arm up to his neck and yanked him closer until her body was flush with his, going up on tippy-toe, shoulder to shoulder, hip to hip, feeling the hard press of him against her belly.

The golden flecks in his eyes were glowing the way they used to, with passion and life, and she had no hope now of resisting him now the shadows that had warned her to keep away were gone.

'I can't not do this.'

And then she pressed her mouth to his and she was lost in a vortex of arousal so strong there was no room for thought or for second-guessing. It was just him and his lips and his coffee taste and the rapid dissolution of all those years pretending she was over him.

Ethan devoured her mouth on a surge of longing so all-consuming his knees almost buckled. But he felt her give against him and he held on to her tight, holding them both up in the maelstrom that descended.

He was lost in a heady cloud of want that he hadn't experienced in a long time. Ama and the near disaster they'd avoided was forgotten, the Hunter Clinic was forgotten, Fair Go was forgotten, even Aaliyah was forgotten as an all-consuming surrender stormed his body.

Olivia had got under his skin and ploughed through his defences. Her mouth was as sweet as he remembered—sweeter—like a revelation, like a homecoming. Her breathing was heavy—like a rough panting in his head. And when his tongue entered her mouth she made a soft whimpering noise at the back of her throat that took him way back to the beginning, to when she hadn't been able to keep her hands off him.

Back to when he could have had her any time, anywhere, anyhow.

And nothing else had mattered.

He didn't stop to think about consequences or regrets or common sense. The need to have her, to reacquaint himself with *every* delectable inch of her, swamped *every* cell in a dire imperative to mate and he followed where it led, hopeless to resist.

He moved according to the dictates of his body. He kissed and he touched and he felt, his senses filling with her, intoxicating him with desire, his head humming with the need to be skin on skin, to feel her under him, to move deep inside her.

Before he knew it her scrub top was up and off and his hands were full of the soft mounds of her breasts, her nipples hard and ready in his palms. Then he was moving his hands down, pushing under the waistband of her scrubs, cupping her naked bottom, pushing them down her hips and off, conscious on some level that she was kicking out of them.

And then she was naked and he needed just to look at her, to remember every naked inch of her. To take her in and familiarise himself with the pure visual delight of her.

She didn't protest as he picked her up, his mouth still joined to hers, their tongues duelling and clashing, their mouths trying to suck up as much of the other as they could.

He laid her on the bed and she looked just as he remembered: long and lean and utterly lovely. Lust had honed his night vision and he could see her nipples were pale and puckered tight. Her hair had escaped its messy up-do and was now spread out around her head like a cloud. Her half-closed eyes and pouty full lips were so damn sexy he almost lost it right then and there.

Olivia's head spun. She was so alive with the touch and taste of him she was practically levitating off the bed.

'Ethan…' she half sighed, half moaned, and held her arms out to him.

Ethan didn't need any further encouragement. He was suddenly awake, bursting with life and passion, and Olivia was his Princess Charming. She'd kissed him and woken him from a long sleep. A wellspring of desire he'd thought long dead was grabbing fiery possession of his groin and tugging hard.

He was out of his clothes in seconds, his erection, hard and urgent, springing gratefully free of the confines of his trousers, and as he joined her on the bed, his mouth lowering to rejoin hers again, her hand slipped along the length of him.

'Oh…' He groaned into her mouth as she gripped his girth just the way he liked it—good and firm.

Olivia revelled in the harsh scratch of his whiskers and in his guttural groan. And the way he filled her palm… *Dear Lord.* He'd always been big and solid, but feeling him again was like coming home, and when she stroked him she remembered just the way he liked it—as if it had been imprinted into her memory banks forever.

But he remembered about her as well, and she arched her back, gasping into his mouth as one hand slid to a breast and the other found its way to the slick folds at the juncture of her legs, stroking her just right too. Just the way she liked it—good and firm.

Olivia's head buzzed with the overload of sensations. But it wasn't enough. She wanted him inside her. Pounding hard and deep. Panting in her ear. Wanted to listen to him coming undone.

To come undone with him.

'Now, Ethan,' she said. *'Now.'*

Ethan heard and understood her demand for what it was—a call of the wild. The irrevocable need to mate, to be one. And maybe he should have been strong enough to resist it, to make this long and slow, to tease and taunt, to bring her to orgasm first before succumbing to his own overriding desire to be part of her.

But all the wasted years battered against him and he didn't want to waste another second.

'Ethan!' she called again.

He knew a sexual demand when he heard it, and he knew she needed him to be inside her as much as he needed to be there too.

He didn't think about anything other than her as she wrapped her legs around his waist, inhaling the smell of his soap on the skin of her neck as he buried his face there and thrust into her, sliding home, deep and sure, on a groan that seemed to echo up from the mists of time.

He didn't think about their history. He didn't think about Ama or the emergency trache he'd had to perform. He didn't think about his injuries.

He didn't think about Aaliyah.

He didn't even think about a condom.

He just let the sound of her gasp fill his head and the dig of her nails ground him to the bed and the frantic rhythm of their bodies take him away.

This was Olivia, and it was as if they'd never been apart.

'Yes,' she said. 'Oh, God…please, yes…don't stop…'

Ethan had no intention of stopping. He just held her tight and thrust over and over, her gasps pushing him higher and higher, urging him on, his heart-rate ratcheting up with each erotic slide of flesh into flesh.

Hard, hot, delicious tension coiled in his shoulders, buttocks and the backs of his thighs. Fire raged out of control in his loins and spread to his belly. It built to an inferno until every muscle burned and shook from the unbearable tautness.

'Let go, Ethan,' she whispered. 'Let go.'

And he did. In a shocking jolt everything snapped and he fell headlong into ecstasy, slipping his hand between them into all her slick heat, finding just the right spot and stroking her there as his world came apart, aware of her muscles clamping down tight around him and the sharp keening of her cry as she joined him.

And he kept rocking and thrusting, riding it out, keeping it going, until the last shudder had undulated through him and the last cry had been wrung from her mouth.

Until they were both spent and lying on their backs, gasping for breath and reaching for sanity, fighting and losing the battle to keep heavy lids open.

CHAPTER NINE

OLIVIA DIDN'T KNOW where she was when she first woke. It was dark and everything was unfamiliar. She was used to that, travelling so much, but this felt different.

It took several more seconds for the warm pillow beneath her head to register as human. Warm, male, human.

Holy crap!

She sat up as everything came crashing back. Ethan's apartment. Il Conte's spaghetti. A warm shower. A bronze figurine. Urgent, need-you-now sex.

Really great, need-you-now sex.

Ethan stirred, shifted, mumbled something and rolled on his side but didn't wake. He'd always been a heavy sleeper—something that apparently the military hadn't cured him of. But given how exhausted they'd both been it wasn't surprising.

But *she* was wide-awake. Panic skittered along her veins and edged up her heart-rate.

Crap! She'd slept with Ethan-freaking-Hunter. The one man on this earth she'd vowed she'd never, ever sleep with again! *Good going, Olivia. Really smart move. Nothing like taking a giant leap backwards in your evolution as a human being. Why not just give the man your heart on a platter and a great big knife to stab right through the centre of it?*

Did you learn nothing?

But then another thought came crashing through her self-loathing. *Ama.*

Oh, hell! She leapt from the bed, her heart-rate ratcheting up another notch—what was the time? She had to get back to the hospital.

Olivia could barely think straight as she dashed around, trying to find her scrubs and get dressed in the dark, trying and failing to leave the bedroom without a backward glance and annoyed at herself when the broad sweep of a naked shoulder made the muscles deep inside her belly twist—in a good way.

A really good way.

Damn it!

She forced herself out into the still lit hallway and the even brighter open-plan lounge/kitchen. She found her shoes near the lounge and shoved her feet in. Grabbed her coat discarded on a kitchen stool and shoved her arms in. Then she shoved fingers through her hair and hoped to hell it didn't look as if she'd just rolled out of bed with a man who was a very bad bet.

She snagged her bag as she hurried past the counter heading for the door, digging around in it for her phone, finding it as she reached the knob, and yanked the door open, clicking it shut behind her as she scrolled through, looking for any missed calls or messages.

None.

Her shoulders sagged in relief as she hit the stairs. But it wasn't enough—she needed to know more. Olivia speed-dialled the ICU as she scurried down the stairs. A nurse answered as her foot hit the bottom step and by the time she was out of the apartment and striding towards the hospital she'd ascertained that Ama was stable, sedated and doing well.

'I'll be there in five minutes,' Olivia informed the nurse, then hit the end button.

Only then did she notice other things. Like her frantic breath misting into the air, the cold slapping into her face as she all but burst into a jog on the footpath, the sting in her thighs as needles of frosty air penetrated the cotton of her scrubs.

Olivia pulled the collar up on her duffle coat and tightened the belt, hunching into its thick layers for added warmth. *It was freezing.* She'd forgotten how cold London was in November.

It had been warm in Africa.

It had been even warmer in Ethan's bed.

What *had* she been thinking? *The man feeds her spaghetti and keeps a dumb memento from their time together and she just opens her legs for him?*

The slight ache there mocked her for her stupidity, as did the dampness slicking her inner thighs. They hadn't even used a damn condom. Two *doctors* who should *know* better and they hadn't even stopped to be responsible!

She hadn't thought. Or cared. She'd just needed him inside her.

Her brisk footfalls were loud on the deserted pavement and each one formed the rhythm to her self-loathing.

Stupid. Stupid. Stupid.

Idiot. Idiot. Idiot.

Fool. Fool. Fool.

Olivia was grateful when she rounded the corner and the lights of the hospital were just there—close enough to reach out and touch. Like a beacon of hope, saving her from a bitchy internal dialogue and a series of thoughts that could only get more ugly.

She couldn't worry about any of the Ethan stuff right now.

They *were* going to need to talk, but for tonight—until Ama was out of the woods—she didn't want to think about anything else. She certainly didn't want to have a *conversation* with him when their sex was still on her skin and his kisses still imprinted on her mouth.

And, if she knew Ethan at all, he wouldn't be cherishing the idea of talking either. Hell, they'd spent months together a decade ago and he clearly hadn't spoken to her at all—not about anything of import. About what was going on with him, about his pain and anger. Clamming up and being all brooding and silent seemed to be his speciality.

And, for once, Olivia was glad of it.

Ethan woke with a start. Aaliyah's laughter was a faint echo in his head, teasing him somewhere in the distance, fluttering elusively just out of his reach, like a ribbon in the breeze.

But in his mind's eyes he tried anyway, his hand extending, grabbing nothing but air.

Same as always.

Aaliyah. I'm so sorry, Aaliyah.

Gloomy daylight bled in around the heavy curtains at his window, matching his mood to perfection. The low hum of London traffic was a fitting background to the mumbled recriminations of his thoughts.

He rolled his head to the side, where his arm was flung out on the mattress. The empty space was cold: no hint of bodily warmth, no dent in the pillow beside him to indicate anyone had been there.

Same as always. *But not.*

Olivia was long gone and he was…*relieved.*

He sat up in bed on a groan, his nudity mocking him. The smell of Olivia, of their joining, infused his senses, refusing to let it be just another bad dream. He ploughed his fingers into the cropped hair covering his bowed head.

'Aaliyah,' he whispered.

Hell. He'd promised her he'd love her only. *I'm so sorry, my love.*

And now he'd betrayed two women. Aaliyah *and* Olivia.

Olivia, who deserved better than some half-man, physically *and* emotionally crippled.

But, damn it! She'd got under his skin. Like she had last time. Sneaked in under his defences. And for a little while last night he'd felt alive again. He'd been relying on his work to do that for him this past six months. And it had been working.

But last night…

'Damn it!'

Ethan swung his legs over the bed. Work had been *more* than fulfilling for him. He'd felt accomplished. He'd felt as if he was making a difference—especially when he'd thought his days of making a difference were over.

When he'd been medically discharged from the military he'd doubted he would ever be fulfilled again. But Leo had given him a way and Ethan had been proud of the Hunter Clinic's humanitarian programme, developed and nurtured under his leadership.

And after Aaliyah that was all he'd needed. He was

done with everything else. Emotions, relationships. And resigned to it.

And then along came Olivia.

And he'd screwed it up a second time. Done something completely unforgivable. Not only betraying the memory of the woman he'd been going to marry but by reaching for Olivia again, whom he'd promised to leave alone.

Goddamn it!

Ethan rose from the bed, a slow burn of anger replacing his gloom and disappointment. How could he have done it? Where was his iron-clad self-control? Where was his single-minded focus? Where was *his word*, damn it?

He'd promised Aaliyah he'd love her only. Then he'd promised her he'd come back for her. And just last week he'd promised Olivia he'd keep his hands off.

All broken.

It seemed he was destined in this life to let everyone down, to destroy all that he held dear. People he loved got hurt, went away. His mother had died and he'd never stopped missing her, even when the truth about her had come to light. And Aaliyah. So passionate and dedicated. Gone too.

But Olivia, who'd had enough heartache of her own, was still alive, and after nearly destroying her once he *wouldn't* do that again. He operated best alone, where he couldn't hurt anyone.

He stalked into the bathroom, with a slow simmer of anger in his belly and a skinful of self-loathing for company. He flicked the cold tap on and stepped straight under the spray, hoping to hose them off enough to be able to function today.

Hoping he could hose Olivia away as easily.

* * *

Olivia was at Ama's bedside when Ethan arrived half an hour later. Ril and Dali had ducked out to get some breakfast. She looked up as he swept into the isolation room. He was in a dark suit with a russet tie and if anything he looked more haggard than ever. The lines she'd first noted around his eyes at their reunion were back with a vengeance and his stubble was now almost a soft beard.

But the flecks in his eyes flared briefly as his gaze roved over her—checking her for signs of damage, she assumed—and her heart gave a funny lurch in her chest.

And then she remembered how stupid she'd been. How those golden flecks had made her lose her head. *And her clothes.*

And how her focus had to be Ama.

Ethan watched her expression cool and followed her lead. 'Olivia.' He nodded.

Olivia felt absurdly close to tears at the formality in his voice and the stiffness of his expression. *What the...?* Clearly some recalcitrant part of her had been hoping that he'd tear down all her well-reasoned objections and whisk her up in his arms. But, like her, he'd obviously decided to focus on Ama and keep things strictly professional between them.

And that was a *good* thing.

'Ethan.' She nodded too, then turned back to Ama.

Ethan hadn't been sure what he was going to say or how he was going to act this morning but her coolness helped him decide. Mutual professional respect was the only way forward. They had to see each other and they had to work together, both now and in the future. And to do that they had to forget what had come before. Forget their baggage. Maintain a strictly collegial relationship.

And keep the hell away from each other in between times.

Hadn't they already agreed to that anyway?

And failed.

Ethan pushed it all away, slipping into a skin he knew well—*Mr Hunter.* 'How is she this morning?' he asked.

They had a ten-minute conversation about Ama's progress and the plan for the next few days, which involved removing the tracheostomy and getting her out of ICU. Ril and Dali returned then, and Ethan and Olivia had a long talk with them about the previous night and what the next days and the next steps were for Ama.

Ril was worried about her daughter still, but encouraged by her progress, and Olivia assured her again that she would be with them all until Ama was well enough to go home and she would be the one taking them back to Africa.

Ril smiled as Dali translated, patting and rubbing Olivia's arm, nodding and speaking words of gratitude in her own tongue as tears shone in her eyes. Olivia was extraordinarily moved by Ril's faith.

When Ril was satisfied she returned to the chair by her daughter's bed and Ethan turned to Olivia and said, 'They want us to sit in on the ICU round—you want to join me?'

Olivia nodded. She did want to be able to co-ordinate Ama's care with the ICU doctors.

'It's starting now. Shall we?' he said, and indicated for her to precede him out of the room.

Olivia told Dali where they were going and then walked ahead of Ethan, conscious of his gaze on her back. Conscious that only a handful of hours ago she'd been in his bed. Conscious that, under her coat, she was wearing the same clothes he'd stripped her out off. That his smell clung to her skin. That the evidence of her arousal and their unprotected sex had mingled to feel all hot and slick between her legs.

'Whereabouts?' she asked, her head slightly turned.

Ethan fell into step beside her. 'End of the corridor, turn right, third door on the left.'

She didn't acknowledge him, just followed along silently beside him, and he took a breath and broached the subject of the elephant stomping along beside them.

'About last night...' he said.

'No.' Olivia shook her head vigorously, not breaking stride as her heart did a crazy leap in her chest. She'd been sure he'd be in ostrich mode. 'Let's not do this, okay?'

Ethan tried to keep it casual as they walked down the very public corridor. He wanted to get this thing between them on to an even keel as fast as possible, and the only way to do that was to clear the air about what had happened at his place last night.

They couldn't just pretend it hadn't happened. That was a sure-fire way to breed resentment.

'We *do* need to talk about it, Olivia. Hell,' he said lowering his voice, 'I didn't even use a condom.'

That particular little gem had come to him in the shower.

The fact that it hadn't even crossed his mind at the appropriate time had been shocking. He wished it had—not least of all because he didn't have a condom anywhere in his apartment and that would definitely have brought them both to their senses. There'd certainly be no need for this awkward morning-after conversation, walking down a busy corridor in a *children's hospital*, whispering about unprotected sex as if they were teenagers!

'You think I don't know that?' Olivia demanded. 'I'm not wearing any underwear. Trust me, I know. And I know we need to talk about this, and we will,' she said. 'Just *not now*. Not while Ama's still in ICU, okay?'

Ethan nodded, clamping down hard on the leap in his pulse and the hitch in his breath at the thought of her going commando. Things stirred and he battered them down with all the authority of a dictator crushing a revolt.

He cleared his throat. 'Okay, sure,' he agreed.

'Thank you,' she said.

And they both continued in silence.

That was pretty much the pattern for the next few days. Quick, professional meetings involving stilted conversations about Ama and her progress. Nothing personal, just medical.

Day two post-op Ama's tracheostomy was removed and she was moved to HDU. They had none of the opiate problems that had been the catalyst for her post-op bleed and Ama, although quiet and exhausted from her unexpected complications, improved every day.

Two days later she was back on the ward and Olivia was finally starting to feel that they had turned a corner. Ama wasn't back to her full cheeky, happy self, but she was showing interest in the world around her again and even asked for the television to be put on.

Olivia thought that was real progress, and for the first time since the operation actually allowed herself to think about other things.

Naturally her thoughts turned to Ethan.

* * *

Ethan, on the other hand, whilst exceedingly pleased with Ama's progress too, was increasingly crotchety and frustrated.

He hadn't been able to sleep since Olivia had slept in his bed. At first he'd thought it was just her scent keeping him up, but he'd changed the sheets to no avail.

He lay awake for hours, his brain circling around what he'd done, his gut heavy, and when he slept it was with strange dreams of Aaliyah and Olivia. He was chasing them both as they ran from him, teasing him with their laughter, only to catch one and watch as her face blended into the other. Changing back and forth until he didn't know whether he was holding Aaliyah or Olivia.

It took him two sleepless nights to realise that the feeling of a lead weight in his belly was his guilt flaring to life again. This bed had belonged to Aaliyah, even though she'd never slept in it. She'd come to him in his dreams here, and as much as they'd tortured him with their heartbreaking clarity they'd also kept him close to her.

He'd used to welcome the night and sleep, when he could be with her again.

But now Olivia was in the bed too. In his head. And the guilt was eating him up.

After that realisation the dreams changed. They became bloody and disturbing. They became nightmares. Slices of that awful day when all hell had broken loose magnified tenfold in his head.

The heat and the smoke. The noise of bombs and gunfire. The blood. The carnage.

Aaliyah's, *'Go, Ethan, I'll be fine,'* played like a broken record, waking him in a cold sweat.

Driving him out of the bed. *Their* bed. But not any more. Because Olivia was in it too. In his head again.

The empty bed mocked him. He was alive and getting naked with Olivia when Aaliyah was dead. Dead because he hadn't got back to her in time.

A few weeks ago he would have poured himself a drink or twelve. But something had changed—he didn't seem to crave it as he had. As his father had.

Ethan had worried that there was some genetic component and he would turn out like his old man, become the type of person he'd despised in his father.

It was a relief to realise he didn't *need* it.

He headed for his home gym instead and pounded it out on the leg press and treadmill. Filling his head with Aaliyah, trying not to think about Olivia. Trying to exercise—exorcise—his guilt into oblivion. Trying to exhaust himself.

He needed to sleep.

A tired surgeon made mistakes!

On the morning of day five Olivia was going slightly stir-crazy from spending all day cooped up in the hospital. She hadn't had any form of exercise in weeks now and she was beginning to feel it. As a jogger, she usually pounded the pavements wherever she was, but going out in a freezing London morning was not something she welcomed.

Instead she decided to take up Leo on his offer of using the Hunter Clinic pool in the basement next to the gym. It was heated, and she could slip in there early, while no one was around, do some laps and be dressed and at the hospital by eight.

She needed to do *something*. Dali had texted her to say

that Ama wanted to see her new face. They'd all seen it
and were very happy with how it looked—Ril had even
cried—but Ama hadn't been interested. Olivia had been
concerned about her reaction but Ethan had put it down
to her extended recovery time and assured her it was
fine, that Ama would get to it in her own time. That she
needed to be ready.

And she was ready today.

Olivia was both nervous and excited, with butterflies
dancing in her stomach whenever she thought about how
Ama might react. She hoped she would be pleased. She
hoped the old cheeky Ama would be back.

But in the interim she had to do something to rid herself of her nervous energy and, lucky for her, she always
packed a swimsuit wherever she went!

Ethan increased the speed on the treadmill, trying to
outrun the thoughts pounding through his head. He was
using the clinic gym because his whole apartment, not
just his bed, seemed to remind him of Olivia now. After
being away from it for a decade and coming back to it
again with Aaliyah's death still so fresh, it, along with
his head space, had felt exclusively hers.

The place they would have lived. The kitchen they
would have cooked in. The couch they would have snug-
gled on.

The bed they would have slept in.

But now Olivia was there too.

Sure, she'd been there before. Had spent a lot of time
at his place. But that had been a long time ago—in a different lifetime practically. When he'd been spoiled and
angry and unworthy of her love. Of anyone's love.

When he'd thought he'd been as injured as he could possibly be. *Man—had he been mistaken!*

Because a lot had happened since then. Aaliyah. His injuries. And now Olivia.

Who was everywhere in his apartment.

He'd had to get out.

Olivia heard a machine's noise and some grunting as she headed to the pool/gym area and hesitated for a second. She'd thought this early she'd be here by herself. But all she wanted to do was swim. A little bit of splashing surely wouldn't disturb anyone doing a workout. Especially not if they were making that much noise.

And maybe it was Leo. She needed to give him an Ama update anyway.

But as she walked closer she realised it wasn't Leo. It was Ethan. He wasn't wearing a shirt, exposing his broad back and shoulders completely to her view. A back and shoulders she'd know anywhere. The same back and shoulders she'd clung to the other night as he'd pounded into her like a man possessed.

Sweat beaded on his nape and in the furrow of his spine as his traps, rhomboids and lats bunched and re-laxed with each yank on the rowing machine handle. He was gliding frantically back and forth on the seat as if he was rowing for gold—or trying to outrun his demons.

Olivia almost turned and walked away and left him to his punishing exercise. There was no way he could have heard her above the noise of the machine and his own significant exertion. But they still hadn't talked, and she figured now Ama was better and they were alone it was as good a time as any.

She took a breath and continued towards him, leaning her butt against a nearby bench press apparatus.

Ethan started as the woman he'd been trying to row out of his head appeared beside him in a white fluffy robe tied loosely at the waist.

He almost groaned out loud. Did she *have* to be everywhere?

He turned back to concentrate on his workout, zoning her out of his peripheral vision as he regained his rhythm and rowed harder.

Olivia watched him ignoring her for a few moments, his eyes locked on the screen in front of him, where his programmed workout was ticking down. Her gaze dropped to his chest. She hadn't meant it to—it just did. The light smattering of hair across his pecs and bisecting his belly was so familiar to her, yet she didn't recall being conscious of it the other night.

Nothing but his mouth on hers and his hardness inside her had registered.

Annoyed at the direction of her thoughts, she folded her arms and asked in a raised voice, 'So, are there any sexually transmitted diseases I should know about?'

CHAPTER TEN

OLIVIA WAS SORRY that she got no discernible reaction from Ethan save for a tightening of his jaw. He just continued to pull on the handle of the rower and glide back and forth with powerful precision.

She wasn't actually worried about it. She was on the pill and Ethan, for all he could have been with his looks and his money, had never been a man whore. Or casual with contraception. They'd had a *lot* of sex and never *not* used a condom, despite her already being protected against pregnancy.

But it *had* been ten years, and in lots of ways the man before her was more of a stranger now than he'd ever been.

And weren't men in uniform supposed to have women throwing themselves in their paths?

Her gaze dropped to the bunching of muscles in his arms as they bent and straightened, bent and straightened. Ethan must have been a sight to behold in combat gear. All tall and broad, his tight butt emphasised by his long-legged stride. What girl could have resisted that when combined with his charming smile and his penchant for going all shaggy with his stubble?

She could imagine him right at home in some rocky

barren landscape in the middle of nowhere, doing what he did best—saving lives.

A minute later the machine beeped and Ethan, his thighs screaming, eased back on the pace, gliding up and down the rower more sedately now as he allowed his muscles and his temper time to cool down.

Olivia had been in his head and his dreams for the past five nights and now she was here, busting his balls. He refused to look at her, to answer her, until he was totally chilled.

When the cool-down period ended he finally pushed the seat back into the starting position, took his feet out of the foot plates and grounded them on the floor. He picked up his towel from beside the machine and dried off his head, nape and chest, then looped it around his neck and hung onto the tails.

'You're joking, right?' he said as he finally turned his head to look at her.

His eyes had gone from dull to downright chilly and Olivia suppressed a shiver. He seemed even further away than ever. 'I don't know you any more, Ethan.'

Ethan returned her gaze unflinchingly. 'You know me.'

God, if anyone knew him it was her. Not even Aaliyah had known him so warts and all. She'd only seen the good side of him, working side by side with him in a remote civilian hospital, swept up in the life and death of it all.

Easy to be heroic.

It was Olivia who had seen all the ugly stuff too.

Olivia looked away from the intensity of his eyes, her gaze dropping to the floor. She didn't want to think about the truth of his words. She shrugged. 'Maybe you had a girl in every port?'

Ethan's hands gripped the towel harder. There'd been very few women since Olivia and no one serious. Not until he'd totally lost his heart to Aaliyah anyway. 'I wasn't in the freaking navy, Olivia.'

Olivia toed the thin floor-covering. 'So you're clean?'

Ethan nodded. 'Yes. And I take it you are also—and still on the pill?'

It was Olivia's turn to nod. 'Good,' she said, prising her eyes off the ground. 'I guess we've had our talk, then.'

But they didn't get all the way to his face. Her gaze snagged on the bulk of an exposed quad. A quad deeply furrowed by the criss-cross of pink scar tissue, each deep fissure naked of the dark blond hair covering the rest of his thigh.

'Oh, God, Ethan...' she gasped, looking up at him and then back down at his legs, seeking the other exposed quad too, shocked at the state of them. 'Bloody hell...'

Ethan quickly whipped the towel off his neck and threw it across his lap. 'It's nothing,' he dismissed, cursing himself for not thinking. His gym shorts came to just below his knee—more than adequate cover—but he hadn't counted on the hem riding up to expose his injuries.

Or for her to be here.

The only person who had ever seen his scars apart from the myriad doctors and nurses who had treated him in hospital was Lizzie, who'd had the unenviable job of dressing his stubborn wounds as his home care nurse.

Olivia felt hot tears spike at her eyes. This was not *nothing*! No wonder his legs had almost given out on him that first time they'd seen each other again. She felt awful. They'd both been naked together the other night and she'd been more interested in having him inside her than worrying about his wounds or checking out his body.

Before she knew what she was doing she'd dropped to her knees beside him, pushing the towel aside. 'Ethan,' she whispered, looking up at him and then looking back down, one tentative finger following a deep ridge from one side of his thigh to the other.

She remembered that he'd said gunfire had caused his injuries and looking at them objectively, as a doctor, she knew it to be true. She'd seen too many bullet wounds in Africa.

Dear God, the pain he must have gone through.

And then without conscious thought she was lowering her mouth to where her finger had been. Kissing him better. Knowing that it was too little too late. Hating that he'd been so terribly wounded. That she'd judged him so harshly.

Ethan looked at her downcast head. The brush of her lips against the numb edges of his wounds and the caress of her honey-brown hair was strangely erotic.

He wasn't strong enough for this.

He'd just spent an hour trying to exorcise the memory of her. Trying to recapture the essence of Aaliyah. Her stoic, haunted beauty. Her steady, calming presence.

'Olivia...' he murmured, shutting his eyes, touched by her empathy, aroused by the visual of her bent head over his legs, the feel of her mouth hot against his thigh. Hating that something so obviously emotional, that gouged at his gut, also yanked at his groin. How could something so innocent be so sexual?

She had to stop. Or he was going to do something he regretted. The loathing he felt for himself cranked up another notch.

'Olivia!'

Olivia raised her head and looked at him as she sat back on her haunches. He looked torn, and the flecks in his eyes were glowing again, like the flash of fire in her opal ring. 'I hate that this happened to you,' she said. 'I just want to be able to…take it all away. To go back…'

Go back to the beginning. To stay and fight for him rather than storming out in a fit of pique. Even if he had deserved it. Maybe he wouldn't have joined up. Maybe she could have helped mend the rift between him and Leo.

Ethan shook his head. 'You can't,' he said, fighting against the compassion he saw in her eyes.

'How did this happen?' she whispered.

Ethan shook his head. His heart was clinging desperately to Aaliyah, to the promises he'd made her, but other parts of him wanted to scoop Olivia up, press her into the hard floor of the gym and fill the entire cavernous room with her cries.

To forget about how it had happened.

But he'd hurt her once before and he wasn't going to screw up his life—or her life—again with the mess that was in his head. There'd been enough loss in his life and he wasn't going to spread any collateral damage.

He wasn't a good bet. He knew that.

But she needed to know that.

He didn't want her to see him like this—as some man crippled by what had happened to him. As an object of sympathy. He didn't want her sympathy. She needed to stop thinking of him as some wounded man and remember how he'd crushed her heart into the dust.

Pulling himself together, looking down at the ugly

ridges that marred his skin, he was glad now though that she *had* seen them.

They were his constant reminder that he'd let Aaliyah down. That he didn't deserve a woman's love.

A tsunami of anger rolled inside him. She wanted to know how it had happened? *Fine.*

'There was this woman,' he said, glancing at her. 'Another doctor. Aaliyah. Aaliyah Hassan.'

Olivia swallowed at the way he said her name. There was a softness there—an affection. He'd sure as hell never said *her* name that way.

'I was working with her in a remote hospital in the south,' Ethan said. He paused and took a swig of water from the bottle on the ground beside the rower. 'They got a lot of civilian and military wounded through there,' he said, staring into the bottle. 'I was kind of...seconded there with some other medical personnel for quite some time. She was...amazing.'

Olivia didn't need him to say it. The truth of it was in the melting of his eyes and the way her stomach fell. 'You loved her.'

Ethan looked at Olivia. 'Yes. We were engaged to be married.'

Olivia was surprised how much it hurt and immediately castigated herself. Had she thought a decade later he'd be pining away for *her* somewhere, regretting his actions?

They'd both got on with their lives.

'What happened?'

'The area where the hospital was situated came under attack one day. We had to evacuate. It was...carnage.' Ethan shuddered at the memory. 'Aaliyah and I and a team from the base worked for hours on the evac, with shells landing all round us. It was almost done—we just had two criticals and another six patients to get to safety—and I told Aaliyah to go with them, that I'd wait behind. But they'd been her patients and she didn't want to leave them. She told me to go. There were some of my guys there for her protection, so I left.'

Olivia shut her eyes. She knew how this was going to end even before he finished—even before she looked down to see him kneading the scarred flesh of his thighs as if he was trying to pull it off his bones.

'I told her I'd be back for her in thirty minutes.' He looked up from his legs at her. 'They only had to wait another thirty minutes.'

Olivia nodded as she opened her eyes. 'You didn't get back in time?'

Ethan raked a hand through his sweaty hair. 'I did. We did. Two ambulances got back within thirty minutes. I was pushing one of the gurneys across to the entrance. Then this gunfire came out of nowhere, slamming into my legs, and I was falling to the ground. And then a shell slammed into the building and it just blew…it was… *flattened*. And I don't remember anything after that… not until I woke up in a field hospital.'

Olivia didn't need him to say the words. It was obvious that his fiancée had died in the building. 'And you feel guilty?'

He glared at her. 'You think I shouldn't?' He snorted.

Olivia knew a lot about this kind of guilt. *Survivor guilt.* 'You think you should have been in that building instead of her?'

'Yes. I wanted her out. I'd been trying to get her to evac with the others all day.'

'So…you'd be dead instead of her?'

'Yes,' he snapped.

Olivia tried not to flinch at his answer. She for one was pleased he hadn't been in the hospital when it had been flattened.

Ethan sighed. 'I don't know,' he said. 'Maybe things would have been different, would have gone down differently.'

Olivia nodded, knowing intimately how that question had haunted her. 'Do you think me being with my parents that day would have made a difference?'

Ethan felt the question slice like a stiletto between his ribs. The thought of Olivia burning to death with her parents was too horrific to contemplate. 'That's not the same thing, Olivia.'

Olivia cocked an eyebrow at him. They both knew it was *exactly* the same thing. 'Do you think I should feel guilty about that?'

Ethan looked at the floor. 'Of course not.' He looked up at her. 'Do you?'

She shrugged. 'I did. For a long time.'

'And how did you get past it?' In the beginning his guilt had been paralysing. And even now, particularly since Olivia, it was too much for Ethan to bear.

'I realised I wasn't living.' Olivia drew in a shaky breath. It had taken her a long time to come to terms with that. 'And my parents wouldn't have wanted that any more than they'd have wanted me there with them in the vehicle that day.'

Ethan stared at the woman in front of him. She'd been through a harrowing time a few years back. Had made the same kind of choice that he'd had to make. But she'd grown up in a stable, warm, loving environment and had always been well-adjusted.

He hadn't. He didn't have those kind of emotional

building blocks. For all that he'd loved his mother, the truth was that she'd been a vain socialite who had rarely been at home and his father had been first a bombastic, domineering taskmaster who'd thrived on the rivalry he'd whipped up between his sons, then later a morose drunk.

Olivia waited for him to say something but his dull brown eyes seemed lost somewhere in the past. 'Do you think Aaliyah would blame you?' she pushed. 'Would want you to be blaming yourself?'

Ethan looked down at his legs, at the scars that reminded him every day of Aaliyah. Of how he'd let her down. *Of how he'd failed.*

He stood abruptly, the towel slipping off his shoulders. 'Don't say her name,' he said.

He couldn't bear to hear Aaliyah's name coming from Olivia's mouth. They were so mixed up in his head he couldn't deal with another variation.

Olivia blinked at the vehemence in his voice, striking right into her heart. She pushed out of her leaning position, standing up straight. 'Ethan?'

'What do you want?' he demanded, glaring down at her.

'To help you. I understand what you're going through.'

Yes, keeping out of his way would be wiser, but she couldn't walk away from him right now.

Not when he looked so gutted.

Ethan's lips curled. 'You don't understand,' he said contemptuously, aware he wasn't acting or sounding rational but unable to stop himself. She was looking at him with those eyes, all warm, gooey and compassionate, as if he deserved her empathy, and it made him even more incensed.

Because he didn't.

'Whatever it is you think I deserve, I don't,' he said.

'I loved her and I left her to *die*. Hell, Olivia, I *used* you to make my brother jealous. You once said that my relationship with Leo was toxic, but you know what? I think maybe it's just me that's toxic. Me that destroys everything good in my life. Maybe I'm just my father's son? On the path to self-destruction. I'm damaged goods, sweetheart.'

Olivia couldn't bear the raw pain in his voice but she knew Ethan needed to get this stuff off his chest. 'Were,' she said.

'No, don't do that, Olivia.' He shook his head vehemently. 'I know that look. Even when I was destroying you ten years ago, when you realised what I'd done, you looked at me with those disbelieving eyes. Like I *really* wasn't a bad person. Next you'll be dropping by to check on me and cooking me dinner. Don't build castles in the air over me. *I don't deserve it.* What I did to you, what I did to Aaliyah, they're imprinted in my brain. I can't just forget.'

Olivia blinked. Was that what she was doing? Was she building castles? Was she falling in love with him again? A man whose heart was buried in a foreign land with the woman he loved? A woman he couldn't forget?

She shut her eyes against the truth of it. *No. Please, no.*

It had been bad enough the first time around. Loving a man who hadn't loved her in return. Only this time she'd be competing with a ghost.

She was a fool of the highest order.

'What if I can make you forget?'

Olivia blinked as the words spilled into the tense space between them. She had no idea where they'd come from or even what she was offering. A relationship where he used her again? Or something more platonic, where she helped him work through his guilt?

And lost a bit of herself every day? Loving him with nothing in return?

Oh, hell, she was a first class idiot.

Ethan looked down at her, at the slice of cleavage he could see where the robe gaped. He had no doubt she could make him forget everything in a hundred different ways—she already had.

But it always came back.

And he'd just hate himself a little bit more. And so would she—eventually.

He lifted his left leg and placed his foot on the apparatus beside her, the pink scars stretching as he leaned forward onto the leg. She looked down at them and then looked back up at him, her gaze killing him with her empathy.

'I have these to remind me,' he said bitterly.

Then he pushed off the machine, picked up his towel and water bottle from the floor and limped away without looking back.

Olivia swam up and down the twenty-five-metre pool non-stop for half an hour after that, her brain churning as she followed the black line.

I love him. I love him. I love him.

She was in love with Ethan Hunter. Again.

Still.

Had she ever really stopped? Sure, she'd despised him for a long time, and she'd buried herself in her work until it didn't hurt any more. But that wasn't the same as not *loving* him any more.

She hauled herself out of the pool, water sluicing off her, sitting on the edge in a puddle.

Stupid.

Stupid, crazy idiot.

Even more stupid now, given that Ethan was in love with someone else. *A dead woman.* A woman whose death had trapped him in a cast-iron cage of guilt and penance where he didn't think he was deserving of love.

The mere thought both broke her heart and expanded the love in her chest even more.

Prime, numero uno *idiot*!

He'd made it clear that he wasn't going to let her in, that his heart belonged elsewhere, and she knew she couldn't go down that track with him again. She wasn't going to beat her head against the same brick wall she hadn't even realised she'd been beating her head against last time.

She had to have more self-respect than that, no matter how much Ethan's story tugged at her excessively sappy heartstrings!

He was right. No castles in the air for Ethan Hunter. Not this time.

Olivia's heavy thoughts dogged her all the way up to the clinic after she'd showered and changed. And she was still mired deep in the question of her sanity when she almost ran smack-bang into Lizzie, Leo's wife and the nurse in charge at the Hunter Clinic, as she stepped into the main section of the building from the basement stairs.

'Oh, sorry,' Olivia apologised, taking a moment or two to gather her thoughts.

Lizzie was in early. It was still barely seven-thirty. She'd crossed paths with the impressive head nurse a couple of times over the past few weeks and had been invited to their place next week for dinner.

'It's fine,' Lizzie dismissed with a quick smile. 'You look a little distracted.'

'What?' Olivia asked. 'Oh…no, sorry, just…' She

shook her head. *Just what?* Inventing new and imaginative ways to murder your brother-in-law?

'Ah,' Lizzie said. 'I know that look. It's a man, yes?'

Olivia blinked. She was so stunned by the question she heard herself saying, 'Yes.'

'Come on,' Lizzie said. 'I have just the thing for that.'

Olivia glanced at her watch. She still had time, so she followed Lizzie to Leo's office. Lizzie headed for Leo's desk and Olivia hoped Lizzie wasn't going to offer her some medicinal whisky at seven-thirty in the morning.

Lizzie sat in Leo's chair, then reached down and to the side. Olivia heard a drawer opening and some riffling before Lizzie produced an intriguing flat box with beautifully embossed gold letters she couldn't quite make out.

Not that she needed to. Chocolate boxes looked pretty much the same the world over.

Lizzie opened the lid and inhaled appreciatively. She offered the box to Olivia who, despite not being a huge chocoholic, took one anyway.

'Leo always keeps a stash here for me. The baby has made this old sweet tooth even sweeter, and God alone knows I ate truckloads of the stuff when Leo and I were dancing around each other.'

Olivia unwrapped the golden foil and bit into the sweet treat. It melted on her tongue and fizzed seductively against her tastebuds. She shut her eyes as it rushed through her system. 'Mmm,' she said, opening her eyes. '*This* is good chocolate.'

Lizzie nodded enthusiastically as she picked a second out of the box. 'They're from the kingdom of Sirmontane. Marco—or I should say *Prince* Marco of Sirmontane, who Ethan patched up after being wounded in battle and who is engaged to Becca, our hand therapist—keeps me in constant supply. I've never been to a royal wedding before—I'm very excited.'

Olivia had tried not to flinch when Ethan's name was mentioned but it had been unexpected. She was pleased that Lizzie seemed too engrossed in reaching for a third chocolate to notice.

'Sirmontane is known for its excellence in chocolate,' Lizzie said, offering Olivia another, which she took without hesitation. 'Better than anything you'll get from Switzerland.'

Olivia nodded. It *was* exceptional chocolate. She'd heard about Prince Marco, and had met the lucky Becca once, but she hadn't known that Ethan had been his surgeon. Just the mention of his name took some of the sweetness out of the experience.

Lizzie nodded. 'The perfect antidote for what ails you, don't you think?'

Olivia nodded non-committally as she savoured the smooth rich flavour on her tongue. It really was quite spectacular, and had made her temporarily forget her man problems, but ever since Lizzie had said his name Ethan had become front and centre again.

Why did she have to love *him*?

Lizzie narrowed her gaze. 'I'm going to take a punt and guess that you're not thinking about the marvels of European chocolate?' she asked.

The sweetness coating her tongue turned to dust in her mouth and Olivia shrugged. 'No.'

'Are you thinking about Ethan?'

Olivia blinked. She liked Lizzie from what little she knew about her, but Olivia wasn't sure if she wanted to get into *this* with Lizzie, given the whole love triangle history she'd shared with Leo and Ethan.

'I do know, you know…about what happened ten years ago. Between you and Leo and Ethan.'

Olivia wasn't sure what she should say to that. Was Lizzie angry? Was she going to call her names or want pistols at dawn? 'Oh.'

'Leo thinks there might be a chance for you and Ethan this time around. A real chance. Do you love him?'

Okay. Now Olivia really didn't know what to say. Lizzie sure didn't beat around the bush. 'I… I…' What was the point in admitting it when it was a futile thing to feel anyway?

'Do you know what happened to him on his last tour?'

'Yes.' Olivia nodded, pleased to be able to answer one question at least. 'I read it in the paper and he and I… we've talked about it since.'

Lizzie sat back in Leo's chair. 'He's been through a lot. His injuries were horrific.'

'I know,' Olivia agreed. 'Not to mention Aaliyah.'

Lizzie frowned. 'Aaliyah? Oh, you mean Dr Hassan? The doctor that was killed when the hospital was bombed? Yes. He hasn't really said much about her, but I think he feels a degree of guilt over that too. I think everything about that day feeds into a significant case of PTSD.'

It was then Olivia realised that Lizzie didn't know about Aaliyah. Didn't know that Ethan had lost the woman he loved that day. Which probably meant that Leo didn't know either.

He hadn't told anybody.

Except her.

What the hell did that mean?

'Look,' Lizzie said, leaning a little closer and offering Olivia another chocolate. 'I know this is none of my

business, but Ethan is kind of lost, and he needs someone
to stick with him, and I think, by the way you flinched
when I mentioned his name before, that you're probably
the one to do it.'

Olivia shook her head. Lizzie might be well inten-
tioned but there was a lot she clearly didn't know.

Lizzie raised her hand at Olivia's objection. 'I know
these Hunter men. I know how they push you away. But
I also know that they didn't exactly have warm and fuzzy
upbringings and that they're hurting deep down inside—
Ethan probably more so than Leo.'

Olivia admired how Lizzie was on Team Hunter. A
wife should be. But… 'I don't think you know the full
story,' she said tentatively.

'I know Ethan behaved reprehensibly,' Lizzie said.
'But if you love him, please, *please* don't give up on him.'

Olivia watched as Lizzie's hand fell to her belly, to a
baby that wasn't even on show yet. 'The Hunter men are
worth the fight.'

Olivia felt absurdly like crying. If only it were that
simple.

She knew how great it felt to be Ethan's woman. Even
if he had been with her for all the wrong reasons he'd
always been very attentive. Made her feel as if she *was*
special. And she believed a lot of that had been genuine for him.

But there was another person now in their already
complicated relationship. A woman he'd made it clear
was his one and only love. How was she supposed to
compete with Aaliyah?

Was she destined always to love a man who didn't
love her back?

'Another?' Lizzie asked.

Olivia nodded. Why not? Chocolate was simpler than the problems that whizzed and clashed in her brain.

And it might be the closest she'd ever come to gratification again.

She found the biggest one and sank her teeth into it.

CHAPTER ELEVEN

THREE DAYS LATER Ethan stood in the doorway of Ama's hospital room and watched as Ama admired herself—actually, *preened* was probably a better word—in front of a small hand-held mirror. She angled her head from side to side and brought the mirror closer for a moment or two, before taking it back to appreciate a wider frame.

She'd been looking at herself in the mirror practically non-stop since she'd first seen her new face a few days ago, and he never got tired of seeing her reaction. She still had the staples in her graft, and there was residual swelling around the operative area, but her face was now 'whole' and it was obvious Ama was thrilled with the result.

Yes, they had more work to do in the next couple of months, and the dressing over Ama's trachea from her healing stoma was a constant reminder that not everything had gone smoothly. But the aesthetic part of the reconstructive surgery had been an outstanding success.

Olivia was clearly ecstatic with the result. He watched her as she sat on the bed in front of Ama, and even though Ethan could only see her in profile he knew she was grinning broadly at Ama's mirror antics. He enjoyed the sight for long moments, because the minute she saw him it would all change.

She'd been cool towards him the past few days. Not that he could blame her. He'd pushed her away in his need to cling to Aaliyah and this was the result. But still, he hated to see the distance in her gaze, hated the walls between them even though he was responsible for them.

Even though he knew it was the best way forward.

As he watched, Olivia gave Ama the pen torch and he could see the girl's eyes shining from way across the other side of the room. Ethan remembered how Olivia had talked about having children one day. He thought about all the kids at the Lighthouse he'd seen her with too. She was a natural and, watching her with Ama, he knew she'd make a great mother.

Something stirred in his chest at the thought of what her babies might look like—stirred, tugged, kicked—but he quashed it. Whatever mini-Olivias looked like it was none of his damn concern.

Ama giggled and dragged his attention back to the room. She popped the pen torch into the side of her mouth that hadn't been operated on and, with her mouth closed, flicked it on. Ama watched as her cheek glowed red in the mirror and she laughed so hard Ethan thought she was going to fall off the bed. It was so infectious, so joyous, so innocent—as it should be—he couldn't help joining in.

He saw Olivia's back stiffen slightly as he entered the room but she turned and gave him a small smile, and even if her eyes were cool her demeanour was one hundred per cent professional as she stood politely.

Ethan sat on the bed where Olivia had been and there was some more playing with the torch, and Ama, who'd really come out of the shell she'd been in post-op, chatted as if she'd been mute all her life and had just found her voice. Dali was scrambling to keep up with her and Ethan laughed at her enthusiasm.

He glanced at Olivia, who was looking down at Ama with affection in her gaze. Was she thinking the same as he was? Would Ama have been this carefree—this animated, this happy—if she'd been married off at such a young age?

Was she thinking about the potential Ama had now?

Olivia had literally given this lucky little girl her life back.

'Well, I think you are way too well to be in hospital, Little Miss,' Ethan said, looking back at Ama. 'I think it's time you went and stayed with your host family until your next operation.'

Olivia watched Ril and Ama's face as Dali translated. They were so rapturously happy she could feel tears scalding the backs of her eyes. Fair Go had sourced an African family to host Ril and Ama in between surgeries, and she knew how much they were both looking forward to some familiarity.

There was a flurry of excitement in the room and it was hard for Olivia not to get caught up in it. She'd been keeping herself in check around Ethan, but when he smiled at her with a *how-great-is-this?* look in his eyes she found herself smiling back.

It *was* great. Apart from a hiccup or two, Ama's surgery had been successful and that was something to celebrate. There was no reason to be churlish because their personal baggage sat like a loaded luggage carousel between them.

But when he cocked his head to indicate he wanted to talk to her outside she felt the barriers going up. The man was rocking a pair of scrubs again and she really wasn't strong enough for this.

Now Ama was being discharged there was no need to see Ethan on a regular basis until Ama came back in for her next scheduled op. And once Ama was back in Africa Olivia would be gone also. Sure, she'd be coming back and forth to London on charity business, and she'd also be in phone and email contact with him, but that would be so much easier than this.

Having to face him so soon after their talk in the gym, after realising she still loved him, was too hard. She could accept that she loved him, and that he'd never return that love, but not if he was parading around in her deepest secret fantasy garb, taunting her with what would never be hers.

Olivia took steadying breaths as she stepped into the corridor with him, hoping this wasn't anything personal. He'd made his position clear and she was fine to walk the line he'd drawn.

'Tell me again where Ama's staying?' he asked, folding his arms across his chest.

Olivia tried not to notice the way the scrubs pulled tight against his biceps and to concentrate on what he'd asked, relieved it was all business. They had a brief conversation revolving around Ama's discharge planning and her living arrangements in between ops.

'I'll get Helen to make an appointment for Ama in my rooms on day ten,' he said, making a mental note to tell the very efficient Hunter Clinic senior receptionist when he got back there this afternoon. 'The staples have to come out then, so it might as well be the first follow-up.'

Olivia nodded. 'I'll see that she gets there.'

Ethan studied Olivia for a moment. It sounded as if

she wasn't going to be attending herself and he wondered just how much he was going to be seeing of her now. He knew it was a good thing, to get some distance from each other, but perversely he didn't want *not* to see her either.

Talking to her the other day had been harrowing, and he'd been harsh and awful, but he'd felt as if a weight had been lifted from his shoulders.

Hell, he'd slept through three nights in a row.

Olivia turned to go—clearly they were done here. But his 'I need to thank you for the other day,' pulled her up.

She turned and arched an eyebrow.

'I know I was…harsh, and I pushed you away, but… it really helped being able to talk to you…about what happened. About…' he dropped his voice '…Aaliyah. I feel…better. I'm sleeping better.'

Olivia couldn't believe what she was hearing. She shut her eyes against it, wishing it was as easy to shut her ears. She didn't want to know how much *better* Ethan felt. Did he have any clue how much *worse* she felt?

A wave of anger and frustration welled in her at his obliviousness. 'I shouldn't be the only one who knows this, Ethan,' she said, lowering her voice to a scathing whisper as she folded her arms. 'Hell, I can't believe you've never *told* anyone. Don't you think that Leo should at least know?'

Ethan was taken aback by her contemptuous disbelief. He'd never thought to tell Leo. It had all been too big, too horrible even to contemplate. He'd just been hanging on, getting through each day and then Olivia had come back. He and Leo might be closer now, but he doubted they'd ever be *that* close. 'Why?'

Olivia shook her head. 'Dear Lord…why do you *think*, Ethan? Because he's your brother, you idiot. He *loves* you. You've taken all this time to mend your fences and work on your relationship and yet you keep this big... *huge* thing that's been weighing you down and screwing you up for over a year all to yourself? *He's your family*, Ethan, and I know you don't really know how that works, but trust me on this—you share this kind of stuff with each other.'

Ethan frowned. She was really ticked. 'Okay...maybe you're right...maybe it *is* time I told Leo. But I don't understand why you're so angry about it.'

Olivia all but rolled her eyes. *Because I love you too, you idiot.*

'Hey, Olivia, just checking you're—' Kara stopped when she realised that Olivia wasn't alone in the corridor and that things were a little intense between her and Ethan. 'Oh, sorry,' she apologised.

'Don't be,' Olivia said stiffly, glaring at Ethan. 'Perfect timing.'

She turned and gave Kara a strained smile. Kara looked from Olivia to Ethan and then back to Olivia. The look on her face said she wasn't sure at all about the timing.

'You wanted something?' Olivia prompted tersely.

Kara put up her hands in a placatory manner. 'I was just seeing if we were still on to go dress shopping this arvo.'

Olivia groaned inwardly. Damn it. The hospital ball. She'd forgotten that Kara had finally harangued her into going. But with Ama being discharged and spare time on her hands she was going to need something to fill it.

'Sure,' she said, softening her smile and nodding reassuringly at Kara. 'Looking forward to it.' *Like a scalpel to the jugular.*

Kara nodded and scooted away with what Ethan could only describe as indecent haste. 'So…you're going to the ball, then?' he asked.

Ethan had thought she'd resisted all Kara's entreaties to let her hair down and have a night of fun.

Olivia felt tension lock her jaw at the surprise in his voice. Right at this moment she resented the hell out of how well he *thought* he knew her. 'Yes, I am,' she said, her voice not so much of a whisper any more. 'And I'm going to dance with *every* available man there. *And* I will be making it my mission to not go home alone,' she lied. 'You got a problem with that?'

Ethan felt her angry challenge kick him right between the eyes. As it happened, he had *big* problems with it. He knew he had no say over who she did or didn't sleep with, and that she was a free agent, but the thought grabbed at his gut and squeezed hard.

He was aware of the curious gazes of the staff passing by them in the corridor. 'Why don't you say it a little louder?' he said, keeping his tone low.

Olivia saw red. *Patronising bastard.* She opened her mouth to refute his statement about the volume of her voice when a male nurse winked at her as he passed by. 'Put *me* on your dance card, darlin',' he said in a thick Irish accent.

Olivia blinked, startled by the offer, heat flushing her cheeks. 'You got it,' she said, and then smiled as the Irish charmer grinned and clutched his heart, all without missing a step.

Ethan clenched his fists by his sides and made a mental note to talk to the guy about *boundaries.* 'Olivia…' He shook his head. 'This isn't you.'

Olivia returned her gaze to Ethan's face. He did look

less tired than she'd seen him. 'Oh, yes it is,' she said testily, lowering her voice again. 'This is who I am now.'

Now he'd made it clear his heart was taken.

Ethan took a step towards her. 'Olivia.'

It was like a punch to his solar plexus when she took a step back, her eyes frosty. It had never been his intention to hurt her. *Again*. He'd laid his cards on the table to *avoid* hurting her. But right now she looked as if she'd never hated him more. Not even that day she'd overheard the argument between him and Leo and called them toxic.

Olivia wanted to step closer so badly she had to grind her feet into the floor to stop herself. Ethan was right—it wasn't her. But she had to break his hold over her.

He was damaged and, damn it, she deserved someone whole.

Someone who had their whole heart to give.

He was waiting for her to say something; she could tell. But there were no words, just a heart that was crumbling in her chest. So she turned and walked away.

There was a knock at Ethan's door at six o'clock the next night. He'd been prowling around his living area nonstop since he'd walked in half an hour ago, and a bottle of whisky was sitting on the kitchen bench.

He felt restless and edgy, but every time he stopped to pour himself a drink he realised he didn't want it. He wished he did—he wished he could drink the whole damn thing and forget about Olivia dancing with every man at the ball.

He didn't know why this was making him so crazy, but he knew whisky wasn't going to make it better.

Right now all he wanted to do was go to Olivia's place,

drag her into his arms and kiss her senseless. That was what he craved more than whisky.

But he didn't have the right. He couldn't offer her what she needed. What she deserved.

Leo was standing on his doorstep in a tux when Ethan opened to the second knock. As if he needed another reminder of the ball. 'You really didn't have to dress to come see me,' Ethan said derisively.

'I didn't wear this for *you*, brother dear. My wife usually lasts an hour with me in a tux before she wants me out of it. My motives are purely ulterior.'

Ethan screwed up his face. 'Too much information,' he said, standing aside, indicating for his brother to come in and following Leo's broad shoulders down the short hallway into the living area. 'Did Lizzie send you?'

It had been a clinic day for him today, and Lizzie had been relentless in her campaign to have both Hunter men in tuxes representing the Hunter Clinic at the ball.

'Yes.'

Ethan gave a half laugh, half snort at the bald admission. 'I'm not going to the damn ball.'

Leo folded his arms and didn't look as if he was going to be moving any time soon. Not without Ethan anyway. 'She's going to be annoyed with me if I don't show up with you.'

'Well, only for an hour, by the sounds of it. I'm sure you can tough it out. Flirt with her a little. You might be able to get her out of there in under an hour.'

Leo chuckled and Ethan felt a pang at how obviously happy his brother was to be under the thumb. Ethan watched him stroll towards the kitchen bench, hands in his pockets.

'Good to see you actually have your own whisky instead of always relying on my stash,' he said as he took his hands out and lifted the bottle, inspecting the label. 'You planning on drinking all of this tonight?'

Ethan looked at Leo. He read the unspoken thoughts in his brother's eyes as the spectre of their father rose between them. 'No.' Although a few weeks back he would have given it a good shake.

Leo nodded. He put the bottle down, then perched himself on one of the bar stools. 'Okay. So what's going on with you?' He held up a hand as Ethan started to interrupt. 'I know you and I don't really do this...*talking* stuff...but I do hope you know you *can* talk to me?'

Ethan regarded his brother steadily. He looked uncomfortable, and Ethan knew it couldn't have been easy for Leo to initiate this. They'd had some frank discussions in the last six months. Got a lot of things out in the open. Told some home truths. But those had eventuated from tense, heated conversations. None of them had started out as a simple, *'What's going on with you?'*

And then a thought struck him and he narrowed his eyes. 'Has Olivia been talking to you?' *She wouldn't say anything, surely?*

Leo frowned. 'No.' He looked at his brother speculatively. 'What about?' He sat up straighter. 'Is everything okay?'

Olivia's voice played through Ethan's head.

'Don't you think that Leo should at least know?'

'He's your family, Ethan.'

'You share this kind of stuff with each other.'

'No...she's fine... We had a talk yesterday, that's all. She kind of told me off.'

Leo chuckled. 'She's pretty good at that from what I

remember. I don't think anyone can say the word *toxic* with quite as much disgust dripping from it as Olivia.'

Ethan gave a half-smile. She had given them both a right dressing-down that day. 'She reckons I should tell you about what happened to me on tour.'

Leo shook his head. 'I know what happened, Ethan. The papers gave a pretty good rundown of it and your injuries speak for themselves. I think I can fill in the gaps. I don't want you to rehash it if you don't want to.'

'Not about that,' Ethan said. He headed to the kitchen and grabbed two crystal tumblers from one of the overhead cupboards—this *was* going to require some alcoholic fortification.

He cracked the lid on the bottle of whisky and splashed a couple of fingers in each glass. His hand shook. He couldn't believe he was about to open up to Leo. Prior to three days ago no one had known about Aaliyah, and now not only did Olivia know, he was about to tell Leo also.

But Olivia was right—they were brothers, and if he wanted their relationship to continue, to thrive and grow instead of always being stilted...

And he did want that, he realised.

He pushed a glass towards Leo before swallowing half of his down. 'There was a woman...' he said.

Leo looked at Ethan. 'Oh,' he said, and swallowed half of his whisky down too.

CHAPTER TWELVE

FOR THE NEXT fifteen minutes Ethan talked and Leo listened. Ethan was grateful for his silence. It enabled him to tell the story of him and Aaliyah in his own words and it all just tumbled out.

'I'm sorry,' Leo said, when Ethan seemed to have talked himself dry.

'Thank you.'

'I wish you'd told me earlier.'

'Yeah,' Ethan acknowledged as he stared into the depths of the whisky he was swirling in his glass. 'Sorry...'

Leo shrugged it off. 'And Olivia knows?'

Ethan nodded grimly. 'She does now.'

'She loves you, you know?'

Ethan glanced up sharply at his brother, pleased he didn't have a mouthful of drink. His heart leapt painfully in his chest at the possibilities. *At the impossibilities.*

'She *told* you that?'

Leo shook his head. 'No. Of course not. But I've seen Olivia in love with you once before, remember? I know what that looks like.'

Ethan shut his eyes. If anybody knew after their love triangle debacle, it was Leo. *This was bad.* He'd seen the other day how her compassion for what he'd been through had melted her heart. Hardly surprising—Olivia always had been one of the most empathetic people he'd ever known. She'd told him ten years ago that his big wounded eyes were what had attracted him to her.

And he'd been aware of the slippery slope. That was why he'd warned her about building castles in the sky.

But if he'd known…if he'd suspected…

What? He'd have been more direct? More direct than *I'm damaged goods* and *Steer clear*? The truth was his biggest fear was that he wouldn't have. That he would have ruthlessly taken advantage of her like he had a decade ago. For some reason she'd got back under his skin and he was beginning to crave her more than he'd ever craved whisky.

Ethan shook his head, pushing away the thought, clinging to the memory of the woman he loved. 'I love Aaliyah.'

Leo quirked an eyebrow. 'Are you telling me or yourself?'

Ethan glared at his brother as thunderclouds gathered in his gut. 'I would be very careful what you say next.'

Leo didn't look remotely concerned. 'You think you can only ever love one person, Ethan? Just stop for a moment and think about how *crazy* that is. That means I'd still be hung up on Olivia and have no room for Lizzie.'

Ethan's hand tightened around his glass. The idea of Leo and Olivia clawed at his gut with about the same ferocity as the shame he felt at his actions a decade ago. 'You didn't love Olivia.'

'No. But I could have. If she hadn't been so gung-ho about you.'

Ethan looked down into his drink. 'I'm sorry about that. She really deserved you more than me.'

Leo nodded. 'That's very true.'

Ethan glanced up, startled, then saw the smile on his brother's face and returned it with a grudging one of his own.

'Look, Ethan, if this Aaliyah was as amazing and compassionate as she sounds do you think she would have wanted you to *never* love again? To never *be* loved? Would you have wanted that for her if, God forbid, it had been you that had stayed behind in the hospital that day?'

Ethan held his brother's gaze, the truth of what he was saying looming large in his brain. Of course Aaliyah wouldn't have wanted that. And nor would he. She'd been a wonderful, passionate, beautiful woman. For her never to have found someone else to share that with would have been a travesty.

'No,' he conceded.

'I think she'd be pretty annoyed about it, don't you?'

Ethan looked into his heart. Aaliyah had been very passionate and opinionated—*annoyed* was probably a mild descriptor.

But still he couldn't let go. 'I can't... I feel like I'm betraying her.'

'Why is it a betrayal?' Leo demanded. 'Loving again after death and heartache and your whole world going to hell? That's resurrection, Ethan. That's affirmation that the love you felt for Aaliyah wasn't something wasted and lost forever. It honours her memory. It says that loving Aaliyah was so amazing it was worth all the heartache. That love is worth it.'

Ethan's head buzzed at his brother's reasoning.

'And can you look at me—*really* look at me,' Leo said, 'and tell me you don't feel *anything* for Olivia.'

Ethan knew he couldn't do that. His feelings for Olivia had been churning inside him for weeks now, and were becoming more and more muddled since they'd ended up all over each other in his bed. He'd been pushing them away, holding them back, because of the guilt he felt about Aaliyah.

But what if Leo was right? What if there was more than one person for everyone? What if loving again honoured his love for Aaliyah instead of betraying it.

What if he could love Olivia *without* betraying Aaliyah?

'Tell me what you've been feeling since you told Olivia about Aaliyah.'

Ethan dragged in a breath, still trying to wrap his head around the revelations of the night. 'I feel…lighter… better. Like a weight's been lifted. I've carried it around so long it felt like a block around my neck. I've been sleeping so much better. And I haven't had a drop to drink since I told her until now.'

'I think that's called catharsis. Interesting choice of who you chose to tell first, don't you think?'

Ethan shrugged. 'I guess.'

Leo looked at his brother and Ethan felt as if he was being weighed up. 'A little while back you pretty much told me I'd be a fool to let Lizzie out of my life, and so now I'm here, telling you the same thing. I think you love Olivia, but you're too screwed up by your past—not just what happened on tour, but before, way before that, with Mum and Dad—and too frightened of the future to admit it. But make no mistake: you are a fool if you let her get away a second time. Life's short, Ethan. *You* know that more intimately than anyone. Don't blow it by clinging to somebody who you know, deep down, wouldn't ask you for that sacrifice.'

Ethan felt a heat spreading in his chest as possibilities bloomed. Was Leo right? Did he love Olivia? He'd studiously avoided any deep emotional attachment to her last time because his agenda with her had had nothing to do with love.

But there'd been no agenda this time.

He tried to push the spreading heat, the possibilities back—he'd really screwed up with Olivia again. 'I think I may have blown any chance with her, Leo.'

'Yeah, knowing you, you've been a complete idiot,' Leo agreed. 'But love forgives, Ethan. Above all, love forgives.'

Leo was looking straight into his eyes and Ethan felt as if his brother wasn't just referring to the situation between him and Olivia. 'You should write for Hallmark,' he joked, because the enormity of what he was contemplating was too, too much.

Leo rolled his eyes. 'Yeah, yeah.'

But then suddenly it seemed right. As if something that had been holding impossibly tight in his gut had just twanged free.

'I love her,' Ethan said, and it came out on such a pent-up rush of emotion he felt as if he'd just breathed his heart up and it was lying on the marble benchtop between them.

He felt panicked and afraid, but also…hopeful.

It took a few moments but Leo smiled at him. Slowly at first, and then bigger, almost in time with the love blooming inside Ethan's chest.

'Well, let's go and get her, then.' Leo grinned, swallowing the dregs of his drink in one hit. 'Come on, Cinderella, you *shall* go to the ball. Where's your tuxedo?'

Olivia had never felt this alone in a room full of people in her life. She could see her reflection in the French doors of the opulent room, and even sipping champagne in a group of people she looked so damn forlorn not even she could bear to look at herself.

Kara had picked out the perfect frock for her—a purple frothy gown with shoestring straps that crisscrossed at her cleavage and spilled down into a full gauzy skirt with thousands of diamantés sewn into it. They shone like stars in the light from the expensive crystal chandeliers. It sat low on her back, making a bra impossible, and brushed against the floor.

She'd twisted her hair up into a hasty knot because she'd been too despondent to wash it, and the only accessories she'd indulged in were a touch of lip gloss and her opal ring.

Kara had exclaimed at how stunning she'd looked when Olivia had made her entrance, and every available man in the room, and a lot of the not so available ones, most certainly agreed. Her dance card was full. Olivia hoped that was just from opportunity rather than from word getting around that she was auditioning men to take home.

She wasn't going home with anyone.

In fact she was counting down the minutes until it might seem respectable enough for her to leave. Alone. When would it be okay to plead a headache and slip out through the door?

She hated that she felt so down. The ballroom was lit by thousands of tiny lights, like a fairy kingdom, and the band that was playing soft melodic jazz would at any other time have delighted her. Hell, the whole room was a visual feast, with the lights and the decorations from something out of *A Midsummer's Night Dream* not to mention the beautiful array of colourful fabrics swirling around.

Gorgeous women sparkled and dashing men dazzled in their elegant tuxedoes. Normally she would have been in her element.

But tonight, despite no shortage of men to dance with, she could barely raise a smile.

Her reflection mocked her. *What did you expect?* And it was right. She shouldn't have expected anything. But a part of her had, deep, *deep* down, hoped that Ethan would swing by and pick her up. That he would gallantly announce that he was her date and the only man she would be going home with.

God! She was such a sucker for a happy ending. And there was nothing like a grand ball to stir that old chestnut.

The man was damaged beyond repair, for crying out loud. And his heart was buried in an ancient arid landscape with a woman she could never compete with.

Stupid. Stupid. Stupid.

The lights blurred and formed stars before her eyes as she rapidly blinked back even more stupid tears. This had to stop. She was lucky—things were going well. Ama's surgery had been a success, she and Ril were settled with their host family and Fair Go was thriving.

So many more people in the world had it so much worse—Ama was a classic example of that. She should be deliriously happy.

And she was. But there was an emptiness inside her as well. And there was only one thing that could fill it.

Ethan.

Ethan *freaking* Hunter.

'I do believe you promised me a dance.'

Olivia was dragged from her introspection by a sexy Irish accent. She smiled at the familiar face—a nice-looking man, with kind, flirty eyes.

Far better than dull, lifeless eyes. This man looked as if he knew how to laugh and show a girl a good time.

'I do believe you're right,' she said.

He told her his name was Aidan as he led her to the floor, and when they found some available space he took her in his arms and held her at a comfortable distance. They made some polite chit-chat for a few moments.

'So,' Aidan said. 'You and Ethan, huh?'

Olivia almost tripped over his feet. It was on the tip of her tongue to deny it, but he was so open and honest-looking, so undemanding, she found herself smiling. 'Guilty.'

Aidan sighed dramatically. 'Surgeons get all the hot women. You know, you really should give a male nurse a go. We're *very* good with anatomy and we have a much better bedside manner. Plus—although I can't speak for anyone else—we're always exceedingly grateful.'

Olivia laughed, finally relaxing and enjoying the man's company. 'I'm afraid my heart was a done deal a long time ago.'

'Clearly the man's an A-grade fool.'

Olivia smiled. 'Yes. He's the top of his class.'

'Well, you know, having drunken sex with a lowly male nurse is a great revenge tactic.'

Olivia supposed she should have been shocked or affronted by Aidan's forthright conversation but she wasn't either. His tone was light and his gaze was flirty. She didn't feel threatened or unsafe. Just amused—and God knew she needed a laugh about now.

Aidan was good and kind—it shone from his soul. Not to mention smart—laughing a woman into bed was a very good ploy.

'Thanks. I'll keep it in mind.'

Aidan nodded and they danced for a few moments in silence. 'I'm just saying,' he said, pulling back to look into her face, 'I'd volunteer for the job 'cos that's just the kind of guy I am.'

Olivia laughed. 'You're a trooper. And I appreciate it.'

He sighed again. 'Not going to work, huh?'

Olivia shook her head. 'Sorry. If it's any consolation, I would if…'

Aidan nodded. 'If you weren't head over heels in love with the man who is now pushing his way through a crowded dance floor looking like he wants to make mincemeat of my face.'

Olivia frowned at him. 'What?'

But then an imperious voice, so English compared to the soft burr of Aidan's accent, said, 'May I cut in?'

Aidan looked at a tense-jawed Ethan, then at Olivia. 'It's up to you, darlin',' he said. 'You can dance with him or I can take him outside and beat him up.'

Olivia blinked at Aidan's joviality in the face of what was a fairly hostile situation. Ethan might be dressed in a tux but that was the only civilised thing about him right now as he glared down at the Irishman in stony silence.

'Just say the word,' Aidan chirped.

Olivia did a quick calculation of the body mass difference between the two men and her respect for Aidan trebled. He was going to make some girl an amazing partner one day.

'Thanks.' She smiled at him and squeezed his arm. 'You've been fabulous, but I think I can take it from here.'

Ethan relaxed slightly when the Irish nurse bowed gallantly and melted away. 'May I?' he asked.

Olivia's heart was thrumming against her ribs so loudly she could barely hear him. 'I didn't think you danced,' she said waspishly.

Ethan grabbed her by the waist and pulled her close. 'I do tonight.'

Olivia's arms went around his neck automatically, for stability, and then just because he looked so damn good and smelled a thousand per cent better. He swayed against her, and for someone who battled a limp and maintained he couldn't dance he managed to get to the end of the song without stepping on her feet or crashing into anyone.

They pulled apart as everyone else did, and clapped politely, but the whole time he was looking at her with lust and heat and sex in his eyes and Olivia's belly turned to mush and her legs to jelly. She felt as if they were the only two people in the room.

'Let's get out of here,' he said as the band started a new song, taking her hand and leading her to the French doors.

By the time they'd stepped out onto a terrace that was lit with enough tiny lights to power an entire fairytale castle Olivia was grateful for the cold air on her heated flesh. Her dress was not suitable for a November night in London, but she was so hot and bothered it was a blessing.

'Ethan, what do you—?'

It was as far as she got before he turned and cut her

off with a kiss that was so deep and hard and hungry all she could do was shut her eyes and hang on.

When he pulled away they were both panting, and Olivia was annoyed at herself for being swept away by the lights and the dancing and his dashing frame filling out a tuxedo as well as he did a pair of scrubs.

Hell, the man had even shaved.

'What do you think you're doing?' she demanded.

Ethan had been rehearsing his speech on the way over in a taxi with Leo, but then he'd seen her dancing with Irish and it had wiped everything other than the urge to break fingers from his brain. And then he'd been holding her, and she looked so damn good and so incredibly sexy there was no way he was ever going to remember the impassioned entreaty he'd worked on with Leo.

'I've been incredibly stupid,' he said.

Olivia blinked. 'You have?'

Ethan nodded. 'Yes. I have. I love you. I'm in love with you. But I couldn't admit it to myself. I felt bad even feeling it, and then Leo said—'

'Leo?' Olivia interrupted as her heart started to beat a little bit faster at the possibilities he was presenting.

'Yes, he came over and we talked, and I told him about Aaliyah, and he made me see that she would never have wanted me to bury my heart and my life with her.'

'Oh,' she said faintly, noting the bright glow in his eyes as the golden flecks outshone the fairy lights. Did this mean what she thought it meant? Dared she hope? Her pulse tripped at the thought.

Ethan pushed his fingers into her hair, cradling her cheeks, itching to pull it out of the knot and see it cascade down her shoulders, feel the heavy warmth of it sifting over his fingers.

'I've just been so…lost, Olivia. After Aaliyah I felt like I'd lost *everything*, and I was just existing in this dark, cold, barren place. And then you came back and brought the warmth and the light, and you got under my skin, just like you had the first time, and I tried to ignore that, tried to not want it, but I couldn't.'

Olivia fought against the urge to throw herself into his arms. She wanted him to be sure. 'Because you love me?'

Ethan nodded. 'Yes. You were right when you said Aaliyah wouldn't want me to blame myself for her death, and Leo was right about how Aaliyah would want me to love and *be loved* again. I guess I needed to open up to the people who love me and let them help me through, because when I did…it suddenly made sense. But you know us Hunters—not big on emotional declarations.'

Olivia could feel a block of emotion rising in her throat. Why hadn't the stubborn man had this kind of revelation a bit earlier? 'Oh, Ethan.'

Ethan was encouraged by the husky quality of her voice. 'I know I don't deserve a second chance. That all I ever seem to do is hurt you, Liv. But—'

Olivia cut him off with her mouth, raising herself up on her tippy-toes and throwing her arms around his neck. She didn't care about that. There'd been a decade of hurt between them, but he loved her and they had a lot of decades ahead.

'Yes, you do,' she said, pulling back after long breathless moments. 'We both do. So we screwed it up in the past? This is now, and we *both* deserve this. We're good people who have had crappy things happen to them— you bet your ass we deserve this. And you'd better be in this forever, Ethan Hunter, because I love you too, and *together forever* is the only second chance I'm interested in.'

Ethan smiled, and then he laughed, lifting her off her feet and swirling her around and around, her diamantés dazzling and sparkling. He felt as light as the air he was swirling her in, and more alive than he'd been in a very long time.

He eased her back to the floor and placed his forehead against hers. 'For ever and ever, Liv, I promise.'

And then he kissed her. He kissed her with everything he had, showing her all their tomorrows.

And it was good.

EPILOGUE

IT HAD BEEN a perfect day for a wedding. Not even a frosty October day had stopped the bride from wearing her mother's immaculately restored wedding dress. The vintage piece from 1950 fell only to the knee, and the cap sleeves bared her arms, but inside the opulent function room of one of London's swankiest hotels it was warm and cosy.

The tinkling of glasses caused a hush around the room and the occupants all turned to face the bridal table, draped in filmy white and decorated with sprigs of fluffy yellow wattle to match the touches of the Australian wild flower in the bride's hair and bouquet.

Leo Hunter stood up in his place and announced, 'It's been a hell of a year.'

A murmur of agreement ran around the wedding guests. Some laughed. Everyone smiled. Lizzie especially, who slipped her free hand into her husband's and squeezed. In her other she cradled their sleeping three-month-old baby girl. Little Francesca was the spitting image of her father and the light of their lives.

'It took a decade to get these two—' he turned to Ethan, sitting beside him, and Olivia, sitting on the other side of her new husband '—together, and another year for them to finally tie the knot amidst their busy schedules, but I think we can all agree it's been worth the wait.'

More general agreement and smiles.

'I'm not going to go on. I think everyone here knows that the Hunter men aren't big on all that mushy, emotional stuff.'

General laughter now at the understatement. Everyone present knew the Hunter siblings were great at terse exchanges and loaded silences and only reasonably new to the whole brotherly love thing.

'I just wish Ethan and Olivia all the love and happiness I know they both deserve. I also wish them luck in their new endeavour as they set off to Africa to train up local teams at the new facility the Hunter Clinic and Fair Go have jointly funded.' Leo raised his glass and turned slightly to face the bride and groom. 'To Ethan and Olivia. Good things always.'

Ethan and Olivia rose from their seats as people toasted them. Ethan held his hand out to Leo and they shook. 'Thank you,' he murmured as myriad glasses clinked together. 'It means a lot to me to have you by my side today.'

Olivia watched as Ethan and Leo embraced, tears pricking the backs of her eyes. She looked at Lizzie, who smiled and winked at her through suspiciously bright eyes.

Ethan waited for his brother to take his seat, clearing his throat from a rush of unexpected emotion, then turned to Olivia, who was glowing for more reasons than one. A surge of pure male pride flooded him at knowing that *he* was responsible for that look on her face, that *he* was the one going home with her tonight and every night.

He squeezed her hand as he turned to address the room and said, 'I think we can all agree that I'm the luckiest man in this room tonight.' Then he turned back to Olivia, dipped his head and kissed her very thoroughly to a resounding chorus of applause, cheers and hoots.

When he finally released her it was gratifying to see the way her dark brown eyes had melted into two thick, sludgy pools of sticky-sweet lust more desirous than any chocolate from Sirmontane.

Collecting himself from his own libido spike, he turned to speak again.

'As Leo said, we're not known for our emotional monologues, so I'm going to keep this brief too. I'd like to thank everyone for coming and helping us to celebrate our day. It *has* been a hell of a year, and it's great to look out at you all and see how many of us from the Hunter Clinic family have found happiness in that time. There must be something in the water.'

Everyone laughed and he waited for them to quiet down before he continued.

'For a long time I'd resigned myself to not ever being happy. Truly happy. And then along came Olivia… again…and she has made me happier than I ever knew I could be.'

He looked down at her and smiled as the room filled with coos and wolf-whistles.

Ethan faced their guests again. 'Up until last night I didn't think it could get any better than this—which just goes to prove you *can* get to thirty-six and know nothing, because now it appears I'm going to be a daddy and I'm no longer *just* happy, I'm whole.'

For a moment there was stunned silence, and then the room erupted in wild applause as the grinning parents-to-be were treated to a standing ovation.

'And now, if no one objects,' Ethan said as he hushed

their guests with a raising of his hands, 'I'm going to dance with my pregnant wife.'

Hoots and hollers met his proclamation as he took Olivia's hand and gestured for her to accompany him.

Olivia looked at her brand-new tuxedoed husband. 'We don't have to dance, Ethan,' she said over the din.

Ethan smiled. 'Yes, we do. I've been taking lessons.'

'Lessons?'

'Trust me,' he said, kissing her again. 'I'm a doctor.'

But their path to the dance floor was littered with well-wishers and it was a slow trip.

Lizzie and Leo were the first to embrace them.

'Welcome to the club, Ethan,' Leo said, and both Lizzie and Olivia were surprised when the brothers embraced again.

Iain and Lexi were next in line. Little Bonnie, recently adopted from China, was alert in her father's arms and smiled at the newlyweds in a way that melted Olivia's heart.

'She's such a cutie,' Olivia said.

Lexi smiled. 'Just like her father.'

Kara and Declan stopped them next, Kara giving Olivia a huge hug. They were both brown and relaxed, having not long returned from their honeymoon on the Great Barrier Reef.

'You know I'm taking total credit for this, right?' Kara said. 'If I hadn't badgered you to go to the ball...'

Ethan laughed. 'Okay, you can take the credit for the wedding, but *I'm* taking credit for the baby.'

Declan laughed. 'I'm sure Kara will give you that one.'

Marco and Becca were the last ones to catch them before they got to the dance floor.

'Zorro,' Ethan said, offering his hand to the other man, not remotely concerned to be addressing the second in line to the royal throne of Sirmontane so casually. 'So glad you could come and add a touch of royalty to our humble wedding. Not quite as spectacular as *your* marvellous celebration last year.'

Marco grinned at the familiar jovial banter. 'Nowhere near as many people to potentially offend either,' he said good-naturedly. 'Weddings, my friend, are just the icing. The cake,' he said, smiling down at Becca, 'is always the best bit.'

Becca rolled her eyes and clutched playfully at her heart. 'Such poetry, my darling.'

'Are you going to be okay, Clavo, with your limp and your two left feet?' Marco teased. 'If you need me to do the honours…?'

Marco, known for his ability to tango, had been Ethan's go-to man when he'd considered taking some dance lessons so he could wow Olivia in their first dance as husband and wife. The royal Prince and fellow war veteran had set him up with some exclusive lessons from a friend who ran a Latin dance club in Soho.

'You take care of your own wife.' Ethan winked. 'I'll take care of mine.'

And with that Olivia was finally alone with her husband on the dance floor. The strains of something soft and sweet filled the room as he swept her along in a dance that was slow and simple and sexy and all she had to do was follow his lead.

They didn't talk, because clearly the world's most competent surgeon was concentrating too hard on not screwing up, but Olivia's heart almost exploded in her chest at his willingness to go so far out of his comfort zone for her.

His limp was barely discernible these days, due to his strict adherence to regular physio—something which

he demonstrated ably as the song came to an end and he
dipped her dramatically, following through with a searing kiss to cat-calls, applause and wolf-whistles.

Another song struck up as Ethan righted Olivia and
other couples joined them on the dance floor. Ethan
moved into a slow shuffle. The scent of wattle and happiness suffused his senses as he pulled her closer.

'You look very sexy, Mrs Hunter,' Ethan murmured in
Olivia's ear, even though he knew his independent wife
was not changing her name.

'You're not bad yourself, Mr Hunter,' she murmured.
'Of course scrubs would have worked just as well for me.'

Ethan chuckled. 'I have some in the hotel suite.'

Olivia pulled her head off his shoulder swiftly, looking up at him. His cheeky grin let her know he was teasing. She shook her head at him.

'Oh, look, Ethan,' she murmured as the cutest sight
caught her attention over his shoulder.

She danced them around slightly so they could both
witness it. Their two flower girls were dancing with the
page boy, holding hands in a circle. Mia, the eldest, was
six and was Mitch Cooper's daughter. As they watched
Mitch and Grace cut in. Mitch picked up Mia and all
three of them danced together, their arms around each
other. Olivia even heard Mia call Grace *Mummy* and her
heart swelled in her chest. She knew how much Grace
had wanted to hear that word from the little girl she loved
like her own.

That just left Ella and Isaac dancing together. At two
and a half, Ella looked the picture of health after her risky
experimental cancer treatment in the US over a year ago
had been more than successful.

Olivia glanced over at Rafael and Abbie, whose marriage had almost disintegrated under the strain of their

daughter's illness. They were watching Ella like the two proudest people on earth, and their four-month-old son, Stefano, with dark curls just like his sister's, was proof that things were very good between them.

Isaac, who was five, was dancing with Ella a bit like the way Ethan had danced with her, his little tongue stuck out in concentration as if he was trying to be all grown up and not step on her toes. Olivia located Charlotte and Edward up amongst the band. She'd hired the band on Edward's recommendation and watching him now, seated at the baby grand piano, his fingers tinkling the ivories, she was glad she had. Edward was obviously familiar with the guys and they were happy to have him up with them, playing the piano like a professional musician instead of a microsurgeon.

Charlotte was sitting beside him, enjoying the show, but Olivia noticed her glancing frequently over at Isaac, keeping a watchful eye on him. As a single mum to Isaac for so long, Olivia knew that Charlotte found it hard not to hover, but Edward's love and commitment had made her more secure. Charlotte looked blissfully happy. They both did.

Seemed it was the night for it.

'How long do you think,' Ethan asked, nuzzling her neck, bringing her attention back to the tight circle between them and the heat that was building with every rock and sway, 'until we can leave?'

Olivia smiled into his shoulder. 'Well, I *am* pregnant. And pregnant women *do* get very tired.'

Ethan grinned, his lips just below her ear. 'I like the way you think.'

'Good,' she said. 'Give me your jacket and get me out of here.'

Ethan grabbed her hand and pushed her out into a twirl before pulling her back in and dipping her.

'Yes, ma'am,' he muttered against her mouth.

* * * * *

LET'S TALK
Romance

For exclusive extracts, competitions
and special offers, find us online:

Want even more
ROMANCE?

Join our bookclub today!

'Mills & Boon books, the perfect way to escape for an hour or so.'

Miss W. Dyer

'Excellent service, promptly delivered and very good subscription choices.'

Miss A. Pearson

'You get fantastic special offers and the chance to get books before they hit the shops'

Mrs V. Hall

Visit millsandbook.co.uk/Bookclub
and save on brand new books.